THE
GAUNTLET
AND THE
BURNING
BLADE

IAN GREEN is a writer from Northern
Scotland with a PhD in epigenetics. His
fiction has been widely broadcast and
performed, including winning the BBC
Radio 4 Opening Lines competition and
winning the Futurebook Future Fiction
prize. His short fiction has been published
by *Londnr*, Almond Press, *OpenPen*,
Meanjin, Transportation Press, The
Pigeonhole, No Alibis Press,
Minor Lits, and more.

ALSO BY IAN GREEN

The Gauntlet and the Fist Beneath

THE
GAUNTLET
AND THE
BURNING
BLADE

IAN GREEN

An Ad Astra Book

First published in the UK in 2022 by Head of Zeus
This paperback edition first published in 2023 by Head of Zeus,
part of Bloomsbury Publishing Plc

975312468

A catalogue record for this book is available from
the British Library.

Runes and border on maps © Shutterstock

ISBN (PB): 9781800244177
ISBN (E): 9781800244085

Typeset by Divaddict Publishing Solutions

Printed and bound in Great Britain by
CPI Group (UK) Ltd, Croydon CR0 4YY

Head of Zeus Ltd
5–8 Hardwick Street
London EC1R 4RG

WWW.HEADOFZEUS.COM

For Mum and Dad

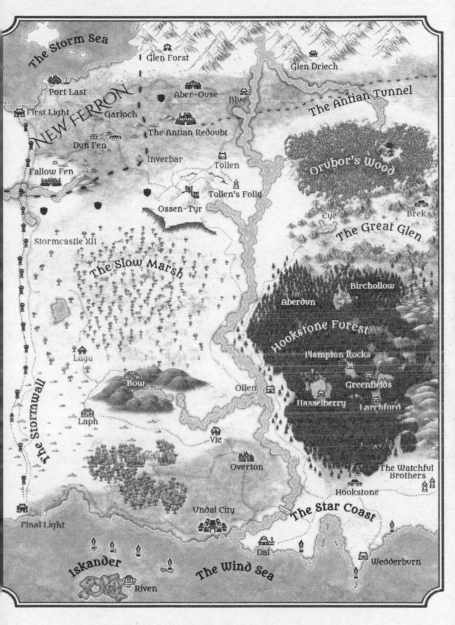

Map of the Undal Protectorate after Ferron invasion,
year 312 from Ferron's Fall (1123 Isken) – **Private
collection**, Knight-Commander Salem Starbeck

THE ROTSTORM

TALPID

FETTER-DUN

URFORREN

URARGENT

HOP VASSER

LOTHAL'S BONES

THE IRON DESERT

PERTCUPAR

NILLEN

HUNESH

BERREN'S VALLEY

JURRON

THE SHIELD ISLES

Map of the Rotstorm and Ferron ruin, year 307 from Ferron's Fall (1118 Isken) – **Stormcastle XII archive**, Commander Benazir Arfallow

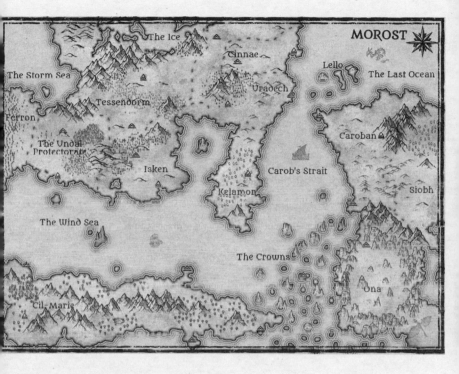

Reckoning of the lands of Morost, year 312 from Ferron's Fall
(1123 Isken) – **Castrum library,** Commissar Mage Inigo

ᛉ ᚷ ᛏ ᚠ

THE STORY OF THE ROTSTORM

The devils of Ferron planned to murder the god-bear Anshuka. They wanted to save their people from the cursed hell of the rotstorm in one fell swoop, fuelling their brutal plot with the lives of children sensitive to the pattern below the world, the skein. Reluctant warrior Floré stopped them, but the rust-folk still seek sanctuary from the unholy rotstorm and even older enemies linger in the shadows.

Floré's daughter Marta is dying from the terrible skein-magic she inherited from her father. The protectorate is weakened by the absence of the whitestaffs, the mystical order of healers and sages. They fled from the threat of Ferron's strange orbs of fire and light that cut through the night, retreating to their island citadel of Riven. Now Floré and her comrades must race to find a cure for Marta, to discover the truth of the whitestaffs' betrayal, and to fight back against the encroaching children of the storm. But the ancient dagger that could kill a god has been stolen by forces unknown...

Can Floré save her daughter from a foe that can't be seen? Can she push back the forces of the storm that are burning a bloody swathe across the protectorate? Can she discover the truth of the unseen foes before it is too late? Steel alone might not be enough.

PROLOGUE

THE SWAMP WITCH

Brude drank from a chalice of tarnished crystal, a remnant of the old empire. One of the eel wranglers had found it in the mire of the rotstorm. He had cleaned it with rag and tallow before presenting it to her earlier that day with murmured honours – thanks for vengeance against the Salt-Man and something about a brother or a son, or maybe both, lost at Urforren. She had been on her way back from the kitchens, hurrying through a slick of ice rain. High above the town, the rotstorm was wailing wind – a spiralling bruise of black and purple cloud cut through with the glow of lightning far beyond – and low thrums of thunder that stole the man's words even as he spoke. Brude did not want to speak to the eel wrangler, but she forced herself to stop and smile and to take the chalice with a solemn nod, looming over him. He did not meet her eye.

Back in her rooms she had gotten warm and dry and then she had used the storm within herself to press against the patterns of dirt until they rose from the surface of the cup, three centuries of peat water and probing root stains scoured clean in moments. It was so easy to sink into that storm of energy suffusing everything, to use it for the smallest of tasks. It was a seductive tempest, a churning power that could always be reached since the night the ghost-bear had cursed her – *changed her*. The old empire had called it the pattern; the Undal called it the skein; both studied and probed and made their notes. Brude knew it was a storm; it was instinct and feeling, not measurement, but to overindulge was to lose oneself. Brude cleaned the chalice and then held herself from the storm, stepped back from it. The storm was always there down to her very marrow, but she could always step away. *Not like Varratim.*

Thinking of her dead commander, his failed mission, his hubris, Brude poured thick mead from the Talpid hives, honey-gold and clouded. She drained the mead from the chalice, feeling the sweet liquid coat her teeth, and, blowing a sharp breath from her nose, she went to throw the delicate crystal against the wall. She stopped herself at the sound of footsteps in the corridor.

'*Ceann* Brude, are you home?' called a voice, and Brude twitched her head to one side. *Ceann? Surely not.* A smile tore across her face and she put down her goblet, snatched up the flickering candle and rushed up from her nest of blankets to pull aside the heavy cloth that was her door within the ruined fort of Fetter-Dun.

'Amon?' she called, turning up and down the dark corridor. The candle threw light along the damp stone of Fetter-Dun, catching on crags and imperfections and the trailing vines that had probed their way into the fortress. She saw him emerge from shadow. Amon was not touched as she was, the god-bear's ghost had not caught him as it had her and so many other children lost in the ceaseless storm. *Caught and changed*. To Brude, Amon looked perfect. She stooped over him, her elongated spine bent to keep her head safe from the low doorframes of the fort, and she hunched awkwardly to try and shrink herself lower as her thoughts of his perfection reflected into a visceral awareness of her own twisted form.

Fetter-Dun was empire built, back when nobody grew as odd and tall as she, before the ghost-bear took its toll. Brude ducked back inside her room, holding open the heavy cloth door and gesturing for Amon to join her. With a smile he edged past her, his head level to her chest as he turned sideways in the doorway. She could have enveloped him then, in her long arms, and she longed to pull him close. But Brude felt sick at the thought of touch, of the reality of her skin, her bones twisted to numinous relics of a foreign god even as she still lived and breathed. She inhaled sharply and caught the scent of his hair.

After Amon passed her she hurried back to her perch of blankets and waved for him to sit, but he was too excited, pacing nervously up and down across the broken rushes strewn on her floor.

'What is it, Amon?' she asked at last, her face flushing, and he stopped pacing and stared at her. In the dimness of the candlelight she took in his face: the heavy brow and strong jaw, skin pocked with stubble and endless tiny scars. His hair was long and dark, tied back behind his head, and he wore the stained leather and thick oiled cloak of someone accustomed to traversing the rotstorm and its acid mists. Thick leather gloves were tucked in his belt and his hands were bare, his hands with their perfect fingers that danced as he talked.

'I come from the reeve,' he said at last, with a half-bow, 'with news of your ascension, *Ceann* Brude. My congratulations.'

Brude huddled on her nest of blankets and pressed her back against the cold stone of the wall. *Ceann.* War-leader. Commander of the rust-folk. The last ceann had been Varratim, Varratim with his genius and his madness and his schemes, his wondrous machines of stone and iron and crystal unearthed from the empire's past. Varratim who was now dead and failed.

Brude slicked her hands over her hair, the shock of deep red still wet from the rain outside. Her fingers were so long that with her palm on her face she could feel the back of her skull – the twisted long fingers of a crow-man. *A demon,* she thought, remembering her fingers, her own normal fingers and hands and knees and body, not the twisted thing she had become. She remembered thunder, and the figure of the bear spirit hunting her as she fled through mire and mist. She remembered falling. *Ceann.*

'I had not hoped for this,' she managed to say at last, and Amon laughed at her sudden meekness, so out of character.

'And why not, Brude? You killed the Salt-Man. You flew the orbs as well as any. You helped us smash the wall north of Fallow Fen, and took the pains that came with it. The reeve knows your worth, Brude; you are a burning torch to take us to freedom. He wants to see you.'

Brude leaned forward and looked at Amon, his face and hands and arms and legs, his body so whole and normal, not twisted and wracked like hers. *The storm has ruined me; I will never be free,* she thought, and bit down into her tongue. She wanted him, or wanted to be him, or like him, and it was all too much to think about. Varratim had planned to undo the storm, to turn goblin and demon to human again by killing the god-bear Anshuka. When a Judge, a great spirit, was killed, all their work was undone. Every child of the rust-folk knew this, knew that the arid fields of Berren's Valley had once grown crops enough for all, knew that Jurron's great light sculptures had faded as Nessilitor fled, dying, to her watery grave in the Storm Sea. But Varratim was dead, and Brude knew it had only been a dream. She could never go back to what she was.

'Ceann Brude,' she said, savouring the words, 'Ceann Brude to take fire to the Undal, to take our people from the storm?'

Amon smiled at her and reached out his hand, and Brude stood and gripped it with her own, her oddly jointed fingers and knuckles enveloping his perfect hands – scarred and callused but perfect. In the candlelight she loomed over him and cricked her neck, sniffed.

'It is a hard thing, Brude,' Amon said. 'They have an army, troops trained. We have two orbs, the goblins, the rust-folk from the deep storm. The diggers have said they will come from the west, from the Talpid ruins. The reeve has word on the last of the wyrms. All are restaging to take the north, the port of First Light. The Undal will not let us leave the storm without a fight.'

Brude licked her lips and remembered the silence of the orb surrounding her as she killed the Salt-Man Janos, the scourge of Urforren. She remembered the righteous fire in her stomach, and felt the embers stir within her. She closed her eyes and felt for the storm. *There.* A roiling churn of chaos, always waiting. *Why did the bear gift me such a weapon?* She did not understand it. Brude opened her eyes and felt the ache in her shoulders, her spine, her hands, her feet. Always the ache of bones too long and sinews stretched.

'I think it is time to see the reeve,' she said, clasping Amon by the shoulder and pointing him towards the hallway. 'We have a war to win.'

~

Together they left the tunnels of Fetter-Dun, where once a great castle of Ferron had stood. The storm above churned, a dance of fractal lightning through roiling cloud, and Brude pulled her hood high.

'Please!' a voice called down, and she turned to the row of crow-cages. There were ten of them, twisted iron cages hanging from wooden gibbets fresh built but already pitted and rotted from the acid mists of the rotstorm. The metal of the cages was flaking rust and scabbed thick with blood from the prisoners within.

'These gibbets won't last the week,' Brude said, and Amon shrugged.

'They don't need to,' he said. 'The reeve has already questioned them. All that's left is letting the kelp grow high.' Brude sniffed and looked at the prisoners. There were seven left, Stormguard shivering in their red tabards. At the base of each gibbet, five feet below in the mulch and dark soil, tendrils of sinuous rotvine danced as they sought the hot flesh above. The vine was too short, but it grew fast. Brude reckoned it would reach the cages within a day, perhaps two. The commandos would claw at it, would bite it, would do all they could. The vine would not stop until it had fed.

'Please!' one called again. His Ferron was passable, even if his accent was ridiculous.

'This is pointless,' Brude said, and Amon shrugged again. She cast her eyes across the soldiers, some men and some women, all soaked and shivering and bloodied, scabrous sores growing wide around wounds as the acid mists of the rotstorm ate at their very flesh.

'It seemed to incentivise the answering of questions,' Amon said, gesturing at the weaving tendrils of rotvine, 'but there is no more to learn. Do they deserve more? Stormguard dogs. Let the vine have them.'

Brude stretched her neck and licked her lips, tasting the acrid mist of the rotstorm. Even behind the tumbled walls of Fetter-Dun the wind pulled at her, brought motes of acid rain and mist to settle on her skin. The air tasted sour, ferrous, like old meat.

'I am *Ceann* Brude,' she said, and flexed her fingers, felt the tendons straining in her palms and the ache in her knuckles. 'If we are to bring death, then let us bring death.'

With a sure movement Brude drew from her waist a wand of black iron, tipped in a red crystal, faceted and intricately runed. The Stormguard began to yell but she did not listen to them. With a moment of focus she found the storm within her soul and the pattern for flame in the ancient wand, and Brude burned the cages, one by one, stepping slowly down the line. The flame was a brilliant gold, tinged with red and orange at its ragged edge. Colours of the sun beyond the rotstorm. The light hurt her eyes and Brude remembered the first time she flew in Varratim's orbs above the clouds of the storm, how bright it had been, the sun a great eye that saw her completely. The Stormguard died screaming, and the rotvine below their cages strained upward towards the hot metal and charred flesh.

Brude sheathed her wand and stood with Amon in silence, watching the rocking crow-cages, the plumes of black smoke rising from the charred bodies within.

'Are you ready to see the reeve now?' Amon asked, and Brude did not look at him. She did not want to see the fear in his eyes. With a nod she turned, and together they stalked away from the flesh and bone and flame.

ACT 1

THE BROKEN BLADE

Throw them back into the storm our god has raised.
Draw a line and burn a ditch.
Never again will we be shackled.

Declaration of liberation of the Undal Protectorate,
Knight-Commander Jozenai

1

A KNOT OF RED SILK

'I have gone to war in the rotstorm. There are monsters in the storm, monsters beyond belief, but there are people as well. People the same as you or I, save the chance of birth. "Preserve the freedom of all people in the realm. Suffer no tyrant; forge no chain; lead in servitude." What are we if not tyrants? We send adult and child alike back to face a god's nightmare, and we offer no clemency. To turn away the refugees of the storm is to swing the sword ourselves. How many generations must they suffer in penance to their ancestors' crimes?' – **Break the Stormguard's chains!** Lillebet Arfallow, year 312 from Ferron's Fall (1123 Isken)

Flore ran sprints in the south courtyard until she could feel her heartbeat in her fingertips. She ran across the dust and weeds along the base of the five walls of the pentacle courtyard in Protector's Keep. At the end of each circuit she stretched her arms up the wall and drew in deep gouts of air, focusing on the sensation of her lungs filling with cold. Her right ankle ached deep in the bones, and the rune-scar on her right cheek stretched tight as she grimaced with exhaustion. Five long spans of healing and still she felt weak. The wounds were freshly healed, seams close to bursting, the muscles of her right thigh a knot of scar tissue where the runewand of Varratim had cut so deep.

Floré ran the circuit again, and the pain in her ankle and leg was joined by the aching twitch of pain in her right arm, old wounds reminding her always of the rotstorm and its lightning. There were trees in each corner of the courtyard and their leaves hung brown and gold as autumn bore down, early fallen leaves crunching beneath her boots as she ran. They had fallen and frozen where they lay, though it was only the first span of autumn. *Too cold for autumn.* Floré finished her circuit again and stopped to breathe, felt the chill on her skin of sweat going cold the instant she stopped moving. Even in this courtyard hidden deep in Protector's Keep, the cold from the Wind Sea seemed to permeate everything. An unseasonal cold. An unnatural cold. As Floré pressed her palms against the rough stone of the wall she stared up and saw the tendrils of branches above her. Dying leaves still clung to most, but others showed no leaf or bud or shoot. Cold and still.

'Again,' Benazir called, and Floré dropped her arms to her sides and started running, felt her lungs burn and her legs turn to lead weights even as she pushed. She ran the five walls, and at the end of that circuit Benazir raised an eyebrow and nodded at Floré, and patted the bare stone bench next to her. Benazir was bundled in thick travelling clothes, high boots lined with fur and a thick black cloak with a fur hood wrapped tight around her. Floré pulled a thick, worn shirt on over her training clothes before the cold could set in properly, then threw her own cloak around her shoulders and sat beside

Benazir. She coughed and spat and took a mouthful of water from the skin on the bench, grimacing. The water was cold enough to make her teeth ache. Floré leaned back against the stone wall and gazed up at the sky, the dim pink of sunset falling over high clouds that sped along.

Benazir awkwardly reached her left hand into her cloak and removed a small iron flask and tried to unscrew it with her thumb. The screw wouldn't budge. Floré turned to look at her friend and winced as Benazir fumbled with the flask. Benazir's hair was cropped as short as Floré had ever seen it, the straight black strands sticking up in tufts around the raised ridges of scars. Even her fringe was cut away. From her jaw to her cheekbone, the left side of her face was torn by four thick scars, reddish-purple welts, each an inch wide, stark against her smooth skin. The mark of the wyrm's teeth. Floré knew her friend's whole body was a map of scars now, her entire right hand lost in the wyrm's mouth.

Benazir had only been awake for a span, after more than forty days dead to the world. They had transported her from the wall to Undal. Floré had been there when she arrived. By then Floré was deep in her duties for the Grand Council as a newly promoted commander, helping to plan the defence of the protectorate against the ever-encroaching forces of the Ferron across the Northern Marches. She spent her days training and organising the Stormguard regiments of Undal City as they prepared to march north, conferring with Starbeck and the Grand Council as they tried to find pattern in the chaos and flurry of Ferron attacks. She spent her nights at Marta's bedside, pressing cold damp cloths to her daughter's head and joints as the girl shivered with fever, her muscles in spasms. *Skein-sick*. The arrival of Benazir gave Floré an anchor point, something to hold her steady in the chaos. The already slight Benazir was now a wraith, and if not roused would spend hours sat at high windows staring out at the sea. It didn't matter. Floré hadn't realised how adrift she had been without her.

'Bollocks to this!' Benazir said, and then started grappling with the metal cap on her flask with her teeth, holding the flask with her gloved left hand. The cap didn't move, and Floré prised it from her grip and opened it with a swift motion, taking a pull. Inside was Brek whisky, rough enough to scour blood from chain mail.

'That's mine,' Benazir said, and Floré waved her away and took a second swig. She grimaced and handed the open flask back to Benazir, resting her elbows on her knees. As Benazir drank, Floré ran her fingers over her own skull, her hair cropped back short enough it was barely curled. She had cut it to make Marta feel better about her own short hair, chopped roughly during her captivity with the rust-folk. Within a span half the cadets in Protector's Keep had shorn their own hair. Yselda had wept for three days after cutting her braid herself, unprompted. Floré smiled at that, and then sighed as her fingers caught the edge of her torn right ear – the top third of it lost to a wolf, the wound still fresh enough to feel sensitive to the touch. *So many wounds,* she thought, *so many tender fears.*

'We used to be pretty, I think,' Floré said at last, her fingers lingering on her torn ear. Benazir snorted.

'*I* used to be pretty, and *I* still am pretty, sister,' Benazir replied, handing back the flask. 'Your nose has been broken more times than you can remember, probably due to your memory being terrible from all the times people have hit you in the face.' Floré frowned at that. Benazir gestured with her gloved left hand, encompassing Floré entirely. 'You have a few thousand scars, some quite impressive muscles, and are devastatingly attractive, dear sis. But I don't think *pretty* is the word.'

Floré shrugged and smiled, and remembered Janos calling her pretty, utterly earnest. When her hair was ashen curls that tumbled to her collar, when she walked the forest paths of Hookstone in a dress, barefoot, collecting berries – fecund and black – which burst in her fingers. At the thought of him she felt a wave of nausea and bleakness crash over her mind, and suddenly it was cold, and she felt old and broken and scarred and useless. Janos, her husband, was dead, murdered by a crow-man as their home in Hasselberry burned behind him. She had left him in the shaman temple, left him to die, left him so she could save Marta. *I did save her, Janos,* she thought, and she shivered at the memory. A knife fight with a demon in the shadow of a sleeping god, her daughter kidnapped by orbs of light the size of wagons that flew through the air like ships in the sea. All to fuel some mad Ferron scheme, to kill a god.

She remembered the face of Varratim, the demon, his eyes broken by unknown magic, pupils gyrating and splitting and coruscating. *Children of the rust-folk,* he had said. *Every goblin, every rottroll, every wyrm even. A child. Anshuka will find you. Her dreaming form will hunt you down.*

In the courtyard Benazir leaned on Floré's shoulder, seeming to weigh nothing. Floré took another swig and they sat and stared up at the clouds.

'Starbeck wants us tonight,' Benazir said, her voice a small thing. 'Orders, at last: beyond the ditches and fortifications and wild schemes to capture orbs. Can we see Marta before then?'

Floré put her arm around Benazir and felt her wince. Her friend, the walking pile of scars with the distant look. Only Marta seemed able to lift the dark moods that took her – when Marta was well enough to smile. When she wasn't bedridden and fevered, or weeping and disconsolate as she yelled for a father who would never come to her call again. Floré could understand that only too well, Benazir's comfort and Marta's sorrow both.

'Course, mate,' she said, staring at the frozen leaves on the courtyard floor and frowning. *Every goblin, every rottroll, every wyrm even. A child,* she remembered, picturing Marta stacking blocks of coloured wood. The last spans had flown. Always there was something to be done: Marta to tend to, Starbeck to debrief, promotions and accolades and troops to deploy and garrisons to inspect, and she was so tired, and whenever she thought of Janos a weight fell on her shoulders, the weight of the dead, a burden she could not bear to name. Now she could run again. She could lift her borrowed sword.

'Marta, food, orders. What's not to love? I have an errand to run firstly. Will you join me, Bolt-Commander Arfallow?'

Benazir drew her cloak tight with her gloved hand, and rubbed absently at the still-healing scars across her face, gazing up at the clouds scudding above. She had killed a wyrm and saved Stormcastle XII, but Floré had not yet spoken to her of who she had lost, what had happened to make her stare so long at the churning sea from her high window, to stare at the clouds with such intensity. She did not ask about the people under Benazir's command who had fallen, never to rise. Benazir did not ask about Janos. They joked about scars, spoke about tactics to fight the orbs, and about Marta and food. Floré could not thank her enough for that, the unspoken millstone they each carried. It was enough to be with her friend again.

'Of course,' Benazir said at last, her remaining hand still rubbing at the scars on her cheek. 'Whatever you say, Bolt-Commander Artollen.'

~

Floré found Artus-mage deep below Protector's Keep. Winding passages of worked red and grey stone led ever downward, splitting into dozens of storerooms, classrooms, offices and miscellany. Floré had spent a year there with Janos before they moved out to Hasselberry. A year of him writing poetry in their garret flat high in the fortress above, a year of her teaching cadets within Protector's Keep the fundamentals of the Gauntlet – how to fight monsters. She knew the warren, knew where some skein-mages did their research in the echoing caverns dug out of the hard rock below, far from the eyes of their own masters up at the castrum across town.

After freeing Marta and arriving back in Undal City – cut and dazed and broken-hearted with Marta and Cuss and Yselda and an honour guard of Orubor scouts, the skein-mage Tomas burned and battered in the back of a borrowed wagon – Floré had slipped back into life at Protector's Keep like a piece of armour long forgotten. Her rank was different, her circumstance, her heart, but she knew which kitchen would have stew and bread, where to find a quiet space to practise her blade, where to stare out at the Wind Sea and the now half-abandoned docks of Undal City.

A servant made to stop and help them but Floré waved

him away and he flinched in recognition. *The two new bolt-commanders,* she thought with a sniff, her hand rising nervously to the rank badge affixed to the shoulder of her cloak – a lightning bolt cutting through a broken chain, embossed on a disc of steel. She let her hand linger on it as they marched deeper through the tunnels below the keep, felt the heavy weight of it. Her new sword of black steel was a familiar weight at her hip, the same simple design as almost all Undal blades, but she had lost the sword-knot that had been a comfort for a decade. She had lost her old sword with that knot of wet red silk striped in white amid the melee in Ossen-Tyr, before the rain of destruction on the town from the demon orbs of Varratim. Floré tried to draw strength from the new badge of rank, and pressed down into the gloom.

The lower levels of the tunnels were lit by sporadic candles, and through the darkness they finally came to Artus-mage's chambers. Benazir followed quietly, and Floré heard the limp in her friend's step even as she struggled to keep her own gait steady. The heavy oak door to the mage's chambers was open and from within she could hear a voice humming and breaking into moments of song. Floré knocked on the door and pushed it open, leaning her head in.

'Artus-mage?' she called, and then coughed as a wave of chemical fog swirled around her feet. It tasted acrid and rich with metals – *like the rotstorm mists,* she thought. Striding through the door, Floré and Benazir came into the room truly and Floré squinted. The room was lit by a dozen well-tended candelabra as well as the flicker from a roaring hearth, and it was far warmer than the cold of the subterranean corridors or the training courtyard. The room was long, and along each wall there were sturdy tables of metal and wood and marble laden with all kinds of materials and glassware, curved alembics and glass vials in neatly ordered racks. Racks of herbs and dark glass bottles, stoppered and sealed, climbed shelves up to the low ceiling.

In the centre of the room was the mage. He stood over a table of dark marble on which a complex diagram of interlocking runes and lettering was laid out in powder, geometric designs spiralling outward and then sealing into a circle. He was humming a song Floré did not recognise as he poured black powder from a tapered horn, tapping it ever so gently to place the powder into his pattern.

Artus-mage was an older man, skin pale and brown hair neatly cut back. He wore a set of simple black robes, and as Benazir cleared her throat he held up a single hand to the pair of them, not taking his eyes from his design. Floré shuffled her feet and looked at Benazir, who rolled her eyes. *Marta, food, orders.* Floré thought about waiting, and thought about grabbing the mage by his scraggly throat until he gave her the information she needed. She shivered at that last thought – a visceral desire for action, to be heard. She put both hands under her cloak and spun Janos's silver wedding band that now sat below her own and waited.

Benazir was peering around curiously at the contents of the mage's laboratory, chewing at her bottom lip as she presumably tried to discern their reason for visiting a research mage. Floré had not told her about Varratim's claim, that the god-bear Anshuka was turning children to horrors within the storm. That the Ferron were fleeing towards Undal for good reason. *That we have killed so many, and it is all our fault.*

Finally, the mage finished his patterns and set down his horn. He stopped humming and turned to them, dusting his hands free of powder. His eyes crinkled as he took in their casual clothing, and his tongue darted between his lips when he saw their matching badges of rank. Floré knew that, even if he had missed the ceremony, he would realise who they were. Two new bolt-commanders, one the saviour of Stormcastle XII, now the last northern point of contact at the wall; the other the saviour of the god-bear herself, who had returned from the forbidden wilds of Orubor's wood with a delegation of the near-mythical Orubor, the blue-skinned creatures bearing gifts of old magic the skein-mage council had been close to tears to even see. Artus-mage bowed his head.

'I apologise, dear comrades,' he said, his voice clipped. Floré could hear a hint of Brek in his accent, the softening of the vowels.

'To what do I owe the honour of your presence, Bolt-Commander Artollen, Bolt-Commander Arfallow?'

Floré nodded to him and made herself smile. 'We have questions, Artus-mage.' She paused. She had considered this moment for a long time. Considered the questions she had, the other skein-mages she knew and had known. Floré knew she must tread carefully. 'We seek knowledge of the goblin.' She focused on the skein-mage's watery brown eyes and not her memories of goblins cut, goblins crushed, goblins sliced, goblins burned. Not her memories of goblins trampled from horseback, skewered with arrows, impaled on long spears. She shivered. 'The goblin, the rottroll, the wyrm, the crow-man. The current understanding of their origin. Their anatomy. We are strategising the defence of the Northern Marches, and seek to understand where so many come from. How many could there be? We were told you are the man to ask.'

Benazir wandered to a table and reached her hand out, picking up a lump of quartz that had been shaped into a rough sphere and weighing it in her hand. Artus smiled slowly and nodded his head, then smiled again more broadly, a smile that didn't reach his eyes. The skein-mage council had been trying to get information from Floré for tens of days, politely requesting her presence so she could debrief them on the flying orbs of light, the runewands, the god-killing dagger of Varratim. She had attended them once, briefly: she was no mage, and her descriptions only left them arguing and baffled. Once Tomas had awoken from the ministrations of the lone whitestaff healer still in residence in Undal City, they had largely left her be. He had wands, and knowledge, and *ideas*. Still, whenever one of the keep's mages chanced across her they took the opportunity to question her until her patience broke. She could see Artus doing the calculation in his mind, knowledge for knowledge, indulgence for indulgence traded, and she sighed.

'Of course,' he said at last, 'anything for the protectorate's two latest heroes! And you were right to find me – my knowledge of the flora and fauna of the rotstorm is unparalleled, oh yes, but if you wish to learn, you must meet Olivar! Come, come along.'

With a quick turn and a wave he gestured for them to follow and shuffled to the back end of the research laboratory. Benazir set down the rough quartz sphere and let the mage lead them by a dozen steps before turning to Floré and tilting her head. 'What are you about?' she asked.

Floré just shook her head and followed the mage, clenching her right hand to stop the tremors and pain twitching along her old lightning scars. *Scars I got on a day I killed a dozen goblins and three crow-men.* She felt the aching up the nerves in her arm and bit down hard until the pain in her teeth distracted her from the pain in her arm. *I must know the truth.*

Artus led them through the lab and then surprisingly upwards through a narrow stairwell. As they climbed higher Floré saw a bedchamber and living quarters off to one side. Soon they reached a narrow side corridor and Artus produced a candle from the pocket of his robes. With a squint of his eyes he focused and the candle flared to life, casting pale yellow across his pallid face. He gestured to a wooden door banded in iron, and his tongue flitted between his lips.

'You have both been into the storm,' he said, 'and have seen the bite-kelp. The pepper-thorn. The goblins, the mooncalf white crocodiles, the crow-men, the stormblight, the rottrolls. You have even seen a wyrm, yes?'

This last point he made turning to Benazir, and in the darkness of the tunnel she scuffed her boot against the floor.

'We have both seen all of those things, and a dozen more,' she said tersely.

'Quite,' Artus replied, his voice suddenly low and thick with excitement. 'There are recurrences and differences in their *anatomy*, their *ecology*,' he explained, reaching to open the door. With a heavy latch lifted, it opened and Floré reeled back from the stink of urine and rotting meat. Artus stepped into the room and his candle cast across a wide and low dungeon of simple stone, chains and shackles hanging limply from the damp walls. The room had a single occupant who shrunk back from the light. Floré's hand went to her bare sword hilt and behind her she heard Benazir swear softly. 'Berren's black blood…'

Artus stepped forward.

'Olivar, my boy,' he called out in old Ferron. 'Come now, Olivar.'

Floré's grip tightened on her sword, and the chained goblin stepped from the shadows. It was naked, grey pebbled skin taut over thin bone. The beast was perhaps three foot tall, hands with overlong fingers ending in thick, ragged nails, eyes huge unblinking orbs of jet black. Its skin was speckled with scars and scuffs and dirt, and as it stepped into the light Floré could see the asymmetric lump of its head – no ears, no nose, just those huge eyes and a mouth that seemed too large for its frame. Its mouth was open and she could see rows of jagged teeth pointing back, half of them broken stubs of uneven yellow. Behind them a thick, wet, black rope of a tongue pushed and writhed. Floré felt sick.

'Come now, Olivar,' Artus called again in Ferron, and Floré felt blood rush in her ears. *A goblin in Protector's Keep.*

'What in the nameless fire is this, Artus?' she said, and he turned back to her with a quizzical expression.

'A goblin, Bolt-Commander Artollen,' he said, chuckling. 'You say you wish to learn of their anatomy, so I thought a live specimen might be helpful. Old Olivar is the only one the council allow me to keep. As you can see, he bears the same features as many of the other children of the storm – the teeth in rows that regenerate, the skin tough and resistant to piercing, to acid, to fire...'

As Artus spoke of piercing and acid and fire, Floré's eyes flitted across the scars on the goblin's body and she felt her breath catch. Benazir moved past her and stood closer to the goblin, kneeling on her haunches just past the reaches of its shackles. It shied from her, nervous. Artus droned on, waving his candle across the hunched creature, and it flinched back from the light, orb eyes reflecting the candle flame as if it were seen through dark water.

'... no visible ears, though they hear well enough, and if you dig down the substructures are all there. Lacking any reproductive anatomy. Overall, horrid little beasts. Some limited Ferron understanding and speech, normally limited to single words or phrases. Old Olivar here is not a smart one, but my predecessors tried to teach him Isken at one point – it didn't stick!'

Artus was smiling and Floré stepped close to him as Benazir peered around the dungeon.

'What of their origin?' Floré asked. 'The origin of them all. The goblins, the rottrolls, the wyrm. I heard a theory that they may have once... been human.'

The room grew still as Artus drew back from Floré and Benazir came to stand at her side.

'Human?' she asked.

Floré nodded, not meeting her eye. 'Human. Every goblin, rottroll, crow-man, wyrm even. Human, changed by the rotstorm. Children. An effect of the storm, some remnant of Anshuka's judgement.'

Artus licked his lips and then blew a snort from his nose. 'Nonsense. Utter nonsense. The anatomy is utterly distinct between each of those species, despite some features recurring. They are beasts from Ferron. There is no evidence to support the rotstorm *changing* people. If you study my anatomical charts and monographs, you can see that the goblins sprout fully grown from rotbuds, as they do during a surge, when the lightning and storm rolls out across new lands. The same for the others. Perhaps you could argue this for crow-men, perhaps, yes, though why it would matter is beyond me.'

The mage went closer to the crouching goblin and gave it a swift kick. Olivar tried to reel back but was too slow and limply it curled into a ball on the ground.

'This one we've had for over a hundred and fifty years,' the mage said, 'captured before the corvus epidemic, before the council reforms. Do you think a human could live that long? It explains their numbers, of course. Old Ferron stretched many leagues beyond our border, all the way to the Iron Desert. And perhaps all of that is storm now – and rotbuds hatching.'

Floré felt her jaw go slack. *A hundred and fifty years?* It wasn't possible. *Could a goblin live so long?* 'They do not age?'

Artus scratched at his nose and shrugged. 'This one does not. Normally they are dead long before we have a chance to find out. No, I do not think they age. You must understand, the evolution and ecology of these creatures is beyond our science. It follows no pattern or law. It is formed from chaos, a Ferron aberration.'

Before Floré could respond, Benazir was striding over to the goblin. Floré raised a hand, but too swiftly one of her friend's silver daggers was drawn from the folds of her cloak and, in a single movement, plunged deep into the goblin's back as it lay curled on the floor.

'No!' Floré yelled, echoed by Artus, but Benazir turned to them and Floré saw the rage in her eyes. No cloud of pain, no distant gaze. Benazir's eyes were clear, her stare a burning brand.

'*Forge no chain,*' she said, spitting the words and glaring at Artus, levelling her knife at him. '*Forge no chain,* you bastard. A hundred and fifty years? I don't care if it was Tullen One-Eye himself.'

Floré flinched at the statement. *Tullen One-Eye himself.* Benazir stood and flicked blood from her knife blade and wiped it on her trousers before sheathing the blade awkwardly.

'I had permission from the council, from Knight-Commander Starbeck himself!' Artus cried, but Floré silenced him with a raised hand and reached out towards Benazir.

'Consider your permission revoked,' she said and, supporting Benazir with a firm hand, she stalked from the dungeon in silence. Floré still had questions. *Were there goblins in Ferron before the rotstorm began? Wyrms?* She did not know. She remembered cold classrooms at the Stormwall, but recalled no mention of Ferron before the rotstorm other than tales of the great wolf Lothal, the cruel empress, and the wild skein-wreck Tullen One-Eye. Floré could hear Benazir's ragged breathing as they descended the stairs – *She is still so weak* – and with each step the unease in her heart blossomed.

As they emerged back into Artus's lab, Floré could see Benazir was grimacing, and the distant glassy look that had been dominating her friend so was replaced with something pulsing and raging that did not fade.

'Suffer no tyrant'—she gripped Benazir by the arm as they left the mage's laboratory—'forge no chain, lead in servitude. That was a good thing to do, Benny.'

Benazir pulled away from Floré, shook her head and limped down the dim corridor of Protector's Keep. Floré paused a moment before following a dozen steps behind. *Suffer no tyrant,* she thought, repeating over and over the precepts of the Undal Protectorate that had guided her for so long, but then she pictured the goblin Olivar, chained and scarred and slumped, and she pictured the hell of the rotstorm, the acid mist and the crocodiles, the bite-kelp and snaking vine and poison thorn. *The Stormguard suffer no Ferron to enter Undal,* she thought, *and the storm is one of our own gods' dreaming…*

Floré followed Benazir through the corridors of Protector's Keep in the heart of Undal City and shook her head. It was all too much. *Marta, food, orders,* she thought, and forced her expression into something that was almost a smile.

2

Three Daughters of the Mist, Unkind

*'Knight-Commander, we scouted the village at night
– no lamps or fires lit, window shutters ajar, doors left
open. No sign of life. The town had a population of three
dozen or more by the last census. At first light we entered:
evidence of looting and destruction, no blood. We found
the townsfolk in the new mineshaft, including the children
and aged. Massacred by spear. The eye rune of Lothal was
daubed on the shaft entrance in fresh paint: ↑. No evidence
of dead livestock as in the orb incidents – horses stolen,
and livestock left behind. Trail heads west towards the
village of Garioch. We found no sign of Captain Sorren. If
this was him as we fear, we will bring the council's justice.'*
– Report on the massacre at Crowpit, Agent Haysom,
Third Moon Trading House

Yselda sat uncomfortably as Tomas drank his warmed wine,
his eyes hidden behind close-fitting goggles of dark glass.
They sat in silence in Captain—*no*, she thought, *Commander*
Artollen's rooms, waiting for her return. The rooms were

28

high in the keep, with warm rugs on the floor patterned in orange and white, and a roaring hearth set back in the thick stone walls. Befitting her new promotion, the commander had an assistant to sort her meals, her clothes, her armour, or whatever else she needed. The assistant – Banner – was happily bustling in and out of the rooms, bringing fresh ewers of water and wine, a loaf of bread, and he had hung a pot of meat and potato stew over the hearth on a low hook. He was a portly figure with long locks of blonde hair and clean-shaven cheeks, always smiling to himself. He limped badly, favouring his right foot, but he used no cane, and when Yselda offered to help with the bowls and cups and glasses he waved her away. 'Entertain your guest, girl,' he said with a smile, and Yselda was forced to sit back down again.

She could hear the wind outside the high shuttered windows, a howling cold pushing in from the sea. Despite the warmth of the room, Yselda shivered. *It's going to be a Claw Winter. I know it.* She could picture Loch Hassel frozen, drifts of snow. *Mother.* She made herself blink and forced the image away, and cast around for something to talk about with the skein-mage Tomas.

Marta was in the next room playing with her blocks, and through the open doorways and the hallway Yselda could see the hunched figure of Cuss sat on the floor with Marta, quietly helping her build. Cuss, a head taller than Yselda and three times as wide, his arms and back and chest laced with scars from Varratim's goblin horde. He looked up and caught her eye and smiled, but she could see his brown eyes were so tired and sad. He always looked a moment from tears, and Yselda had found him weeping more than once in the quiet stairways between the cadet dormitories in the lower floors and the commander's new rooms. His brother Petron had been murdered by Varratim, and his mother and sister had been killed when the orbs of light attacked Hasselberry – those orbs floating through the sky, glowing serenely, shooting death and fire in great gouts. *He has nobody,* she thought. Yselda frowned and Cuss looked back to Marta and then the two of them were playing again, building, and chattering away quietly. Yselda was left sat silent opposite Tomas at the dining table.

Tomas followed her gaze through the corridor to the next room and his eyes seemed to linger on Marta for a long moment, the little girl with the same dun reddish-brown skin as her dead father, the mighty skein-wreck Janos. Janos, destroyer of Urforren, master of the pattern below the pattern. Janos the poet, who had lived in Hasselberry and told Yselda not to worry when Captain Artollen berated her for messing up her armour, or her sword, or some endless other thing. Marta had the same curled ashen hair and amber eyes as her mother, but Yselda thought she looked more like Janos than anyone else.

Marta waved through the door and Yselda waved back and smiled. The girl continued to play with Cuss. Looking at the little girl, Yselda felt a sickness in her heart. Lorrie and Nat, her adopted sisters, were six spans dead now – killed by the orbs of light, those strange machines that spat fire and force, flown by demons in the night. Lorrie and Nat and their parents Esme and Shand, and before them her own parents and brother so many years before, killed by more mundane cruelty. *Everyone I love is cursed to die,* she thought, with a stony stillness in her heart. *Better not to care at all.* Yselda stared at her hands for a long time but when she finally stirred, Tomas was still there, still sipping his wine in silence, still looking at her or at nothing from behind those opaque glasses.

Yselda smoothed her hands across the legs of her trousers and reached up to her shoulder to twist her hair in her fingertips before remembering how short she had chopped it back. Her dark hair now hung in a loose bob high above her shoulders. Her neck felt bare and cold. She looked down and then up from the stained wood of the table and cleared her throat. *Entertain your guest, girl.*

'Your glasses are new, Primus,' she said, and he smiled. Tomas was tall and gaunt, and while hunting Varratim and the orbs of light his right cheek and ear had been severely burned. A new growth of beard covered the unburned portions of his jaw, growing in to catch up with the small beard he had previously sported. His skin looked sickly pale beneath the dark leather and smoked glass of the goggles, except for the light pink of the burn scars, and above the goggles his hair was cut carefully and precisely short.

'They *are* new, Yselda. Very observant. You may call me Tomas, you know,' he said, smiling. Yselda found herself biting the inside of her cheek and averting her gaze. She didn't mind the burns on his face – surely the commander had worse scars by far. Scars were nothing to be ashamed of. *If it left a scar, it meant you survived.* She couldn't sit easily with Tomas, scarred or not – his soft words seemed to always hide a blade below. She remembered him teasing her about being too pretty for the Forest Watch in Hookstone Town, and he was always probing with his questions to Floré, always so careful as if waiting for a moment of advantage. He was still handsome but his arrogance and coldness left her uneasy. *Perhaps he is right to be arrogant,* she thought. He was a skein-mage, after all – he could pull fire from nothing, shoot lightning, perform incredible feats.

'What do they do, Tomas?' she forced herself to ask. He waved a hand dismissively and drank more wine. He was dressed in his full regalia as skein-mage primus of Stormcastle XII, soft doublet and trousers beneath a Stormguard commando tabard of red, trimmed in gold, with a bolt of lightning across the chest. He had a satchel slipped over his neck and shoulder and the bag rested lightly on his knee, worn brown leather clasped tight with three separate straps.

'My eyes were troubling me, after the fire, the orbs,' he said eventually, and Yselda nodded and blinked and tried to hold his gaze. Yselda had been knocked out in the final battle against Varratim by some demon skein-spell, and when she awoke in the meadow Commander Artollen had been there, and Marta, and Cuss was being tended to by the old Orubor woman with skin of blue and hair of silver-white. Tomas had been there too, dragged from the burning wreckage of a crashed orb by Orubor who moved like water through the long grass and wild flowers. She had never seen anyone look so close to death as he had in that moment. Somehow between the Orubor healing and then the ministrations of the last whitestaff left at Protector's Keep he was now up and about and seemed his old self again.

'You look much better than in the forest.' Tomas smiled at her comment and sighed deeply. 'Better than last span, even. I am glad you are healing well.'

'You saw me at perhaps my lowest, Yselda. You saw me when I thought I was utterly lost. But your captain saved the day, and now we are all here to deal with the question of *what next?*'

Commander, Yselda thought, *and you know it.* She had attended the ceremony along with what seemed like the entire Stormguard and the high council and every skein-mage in the city. She shrugged and tried to hold her composure. *What next?* A casual question for him, perhaps, but for her it threw open the dam in her mind, and the panic followed. *Can I stay with the commander? Would she even want me? Do I even want to be in the Stormguard? Are the rust-folk coming, in their orbs?*

Yselda let the panic wash over her. The orbs, those horrifying lights that came with their stillness and a silence that pressed at you, the silence of a noise too loud to ever be heard. *It could only be felt.* She remembered the light washing over her in Hookstone forest. The light that washed over her as if she were nothing and then moved to Hosselberry. The light that killed Shand and Esme and little Nat and Lorrie. She had faced down the demon Varratim with his orbs and his army and his magic, and he had waved her aside with barely a thought. *They took my home from me, and they didn't even care. They didn't even know who I was.*

Always there were questions, and always she did not know which to answer first, if there even were answers. And so they flooded over her and she let herself drown and be still in the current of life, meekly stepping forward wherever she was directed. Long spans at Protector's Keep, hidden away in the cadet garrison but given no true assignment. She had spent the spans as summer died practising with her sword and bow, joining every drill she could, but she and Cuss fell somewhere outside of the normal order of things. They were assigned to no squad. When she dreamt it was the old nightmares of wolves and snow, or new dreams of a field of goblins charging towards her and no arrows left at her side, that sickening silence pressing down on her chest. Screaming, soundless.

In Floré's room they sat in silence until Tomas reached for one of the cups in the centre of the table and poured Yselda a measure of wine. She nodded her thanks, sipped at the wine and gazed into the fire. *What next?*

'I went on a trip,' Tomas said, and Yselda cocked her head. Smiling at her interest, Tomas leaned forward onto his elbows and cradled his wine in both hands.

'A fact-finding mission, Yselda, for Knight-Commander Starbeck and the Grand Council. Since Artollen stopped the rust-folk from killing the great god Anshuka, we must consider their next move. The Orubor, undefeated and now on high alert, have the dagger that could have finished that task. Anshuka is safe, be praised.'

'All glory to the bear-god,' Yselda mumbled, and rubbed at the pale skin of her arm where goose pimples had risen despite the heat of the hearth fire. Shivering, she let her hand drop to the hilt of her own dagger, the silver dagger with its handle of worn antler and its blade so intricately incised with rune and pattern. The dagger the commander had given her. Not a dagger to kill a god, but a dagger that would kill a demon.

'I have been to the Stormwall, and I have been north as far as Laga and Bow to collect the reports, almost as far as the new garrisons being raised by Starbeck and the council,' Tomas continued, and Yselda had the impression that he was speaking to himself rather than to her. His gaze lingered on tapestries on the wall, tapestries depicting long-dead

Stormguard commanders, famed battles in the annals of Undal history. 'Refugees flood south, Yselda, soldier and farmer alike. The attacks south of Stormcastle XII seem to have been distractions, ploys to draw us away as Varratim went to kill our god. But to the north? The Stormwall is truly fallen north of Fallow Fen. Garioch, Dun Fen, Inverbar, Port Last, First Light: all overrun, or besieged, is the rumour. Why let them live, though? The rust-folk are setting themselves at Port Last. The first refugees from there have made it to Bow and Aber-Ouse. There are reports of stakes in the ground. Ditches. *Uniforms*, if you can imagine rust-folk in uniforms. Reports near Aber-Ouse of entire troops of the Stormguard massacring civilians they fear to be rust-folk. Reports of the orbs, always the orbs – now so fearful and so few – but still they are there, flying above and beyond it all, raining fire, watching our people as they flee or try to stand, depositing troops of rust-folk where they are least expected. And what are we doing? Gathering knowledge, gathering troops, gathering our strength. The realm stands on the precipice. Do you know where the whitestaffs are, Yselda?'

The abrupt change of topic caught Yselda with her mouth full of wine. *Did ho do that on purpose?* She shook her head. Her head had been full, imagining the war in the north, and she knew as little as everyone else about the whitestaffs. When the orbs struck, the whitestaffs fled to their island home of Iskander, to the monastery of Riven. *All* the cadets knew that. One of the older cadets stationed in the keep, Borvillain with the blonde curls and the big jaw, had told her no boat that had sailed to Riven since had returned, and the docks of Undal City were almost empty as the Grand Council sent increasingly desperate envoys to find out why their most esteemed teachers and healers and leaders had abandoned them.

Only a handful of whitestaffs had stayed behind, those attached to military hospitals or stationed at the Stormwall. They would only say that they had been summoned in the skein but could not abandon the sick. Yselda opened her mouth to respond to Tomas but then the door opened and Commander Artollen was there along with Commander Arfallow, the latter slight and withdrawn compared to the instant physical presence of Floré who stomped through the door, face flushed with exercise, clothes soiled with sweat and dirt. Her mouth twitched when she saw Tomas, and Benazir ignored them all to come and sit at the table near the hearth, next to Yselda. Benazir gave Yselda a brief nod and her eyes caught for a moment on the sheathed dagger Yselda still toyed with, and the ghost of a smile crossed her face.

'Tomas,' Floré said, 'we have to eat and then go and see Starbeck. Did you need something?'

Tomas smiled and leaned back in his chair, one hand adjusting the lay of his dark goggles over his eyes before trailing across his cheek and scratching idly at the scars there.

'Only you, dear Artollen. Only you. And don't worry – Starbeck is coming here.'

~

Banner was sweating profusely. Suddenly he had gone from preparing an informal dinner for the rustic Commander Artollen and her confidants to preparing dinner for the knight-commander of the Grand Council, head of the Stormguard, a man normally cloistered away behind a dozen attendants and assistants and guards as he guided the Stormguard, and thus the country, through every moment. Floré tried to calm Banner but he hurried in and out, calling for servants and help. The moment she had told him the knight-commander was joining them, Banner's face had fallen so utterly that Floré had wanted to laugh. *Starbeck has his fearsome reputation, but surely he hasn't become such an ogre the castle staff fear him so greatly!* Tomas sat quietly sipping his wine in his strange goggles, and Floré left him with Benazir and Yselda. Yselda was acting the steward, hanging up Benazir's cloak and pouring her a glass of wine.

Beneath the cloak Benazir's right arm was held tight in a sling, her wrist ending in a rough stump of thick bandages. Floré hung up her own cloak and headed back out to the nearest privy, washing her face and hands with the water ewer left there. The commander's corridor was well kept and warm, and the water was fresh and cool. She returned, then went to the bedchamber where Cuss was playing with Marta. The two of them were having a tea party, along with a stuffed bear Floré had found at a market stall when she and Marta had broken free of the keep for a morning, walking the wide avenues and twisting alleys of Undal City in the warmth of the dying summer. Before the first days of autumn, the season of Leaf. *Before the cold came.* Floré shivered.

'Mister Cuss is only allowed pepper tea,' Marta was saying, and Cuss was nodding along gamely and sipping from his empty cup. He screwed up his nose and spluttered. 'This tea tastes like... pepper!' Marta giggled, then dropped her cup and ran for a hug with her mother when Floré closed the door, her tea party unceremoniously abandoned. Sweeping up Marta always felt right, the size of her, the weight of her pressing down on Floré's chest, the way her hands wound around her neck. She gave Marta a squeeze and then smiled down at Cuss.

'My thanks, Cuss,' she said, and he shrugged and set down his cup with the others, slowly lumbering to his feet. The last six spans had eaten away at him, and though he was still burly he was certainly leaner than he had been back in Hasselberry. Six spans of injury and then the relentless training of the Stormguard cadets. Floré had thought his myriad wounds would kill him within the day, but the Orubor medicine of herbs and skein-magic seemed to have knitted the worst of his troubles. The Orubor, those blue-skinned elves with eyes like orbs, elongated ears; etiolated wraiths of the wood with serrated teeth. Rumoured to be mind-readers, rumoured to be cannibals.

Floré had met one, once, long before the nightmare of Varratim and the orbs: *Ashbringer*. An Orubor who came to Janos with questions on how to kill an unkillable man, obtuse and unclear but as polite as she was strange. For centuries nobody had entered their forest and lived to tell, but Floré, Cuss, Yselda, and Tomas had saved Anshuka from the demon and his orbs of light, and Anshuka was as much the Orubor's god as her own. They had joined in force, had healed the wounded, had then accompanied Floré swiftly to Undal City, and even now an embassy of three Orubor were somewhere in the keep, afforded every luxury, politely refusing Starbeck's requests for access to their forest, to Anshuka, and perhaps most fervently on his part to the remaining orbs of light that Floré and Varratim had flown from the Blue Wolf Mountains. *What do they mean to achieve here?*

Floré shook her head and squeezed Marta tight. She was only glad Cuss was okay, whatever strange magic had kept him from the next life. Cuss brushed the dust from the floor off his linen shirt and smiled a tight smile that didn't reach his eyes. Marta pulled at her mother's hair and began singing, off-key and loud in Floré's ear.

'I'll see you tomorrow for training, Commander?' Cuss said, and she shook her head.

'Stay, Cuss. Starbeck is joining us, and Tomas says he wants to speak to you and Yselda as well.'

Cuss's mouth parted at that, and then he filled his cheeks and blew out slowly. He rubbed the back of his tightly curled hair with one hand, and Marta started to pull faces at him, sticking out her tongue, her unknown song abandoned. Cuss pulled a face back and Marta giggled, and then with a wrench the stuffed bear began to float from the floor, rising with a stuttering sway until it floated by Cuss's arm. He stared at it and Floré held her breath. *Please, not again.* Marta began to cough, her thin body wracking as she screwed her eyes shut. Floré held her tight and leaned her head to her daughter's ear.

'Let it go, sweet pea,' she said. 'Let it be.'

Cuss grabbed the bear from the air. Marta grew still and stopped coughing after a long moment and then she screwed up her nose and clung to her mother, sniffling, eyes closed.

'Am I in trouble, Commander?' Cuss said, shifting awkwardly on his feet. Floré shook her head and smiled.

'Not while I'm around.' She lifted Marta higher and held her up so their faces were pressed together. 'Now, can I try some of this pepper tea?'

~

Floré washed the sweat from her exercise off in the copper tub. A girl she didn't recognise, dressed in the dour brown of the keep staff, brought ewers of hot water to her room. 'From Mister Banner,' she said, and then she was backing out of the room to the central chamber with its long table where Tomas sat in his ludicrous goggles and Benazir sat cleaning goblin blood from her dagger clumsily with a cloth napkin. Clad in a simple long dress of green over wool leggings Floré joined the table. Marta was eating a plate of cheese sandwiches, telling Yselda about a dragon who lived in the harbour.

'His name is Deviltooth,' she said, mouth full, 'and he eats nothing but fish.'

Yselda nodded along gamely. 'Is he a friendly dragon, or a nasty dragon?' she asked, and Marta rubbed breadcrumbs into her fingertips, her brow furrowed.

'He's a friendly dragon. He has blue skin. He roasts goblins, roasts and burns them with his fire. He won't let them hurt anybody.'

The girl's voice grew thicker as she came to the topic of goblins, and then tears were in her eyes. Yselda quickly distracted her with a question about bread, and Floré blew out a long breath and felt a cold anger filling her veins. Marta had been taken from her for only a few days, but the mark was indelible.

'Tomas, you know anything of a goblin being kept by Artus-mage in the keep? A prisoner. A test subject.' Benazir's question was pointed but Tomas simply shrugged.

'I don't know him,' he said, and then without pause moved on to a list of candidates for elevation in the ranks of the skein-mages of Stormcastle XII. Floré left them to it. Yselda was entertaining Marta gamely enough, and Cuss sat silent, staring off at a far wall. A loaf of black bread sat on the table before him untouched. Floré rubbed at the scar on her cheek and reached across, tearing the bread in two and offering him some.

'How goes the training, Cadet?' she asked. Cuss blinked slowly and looked down at the bread she offered, taking it in his hand but making no move to eat. He met her gaze then dropped his eyes.

'It's all right.' He shrugged. 'The Gauntlet is best, but all the lessons on the Balanced Blade are a bit beyond me. Ranged combat and strategy aren't really my thing. I don't think I'm who they have in mind for that. My sword-work is a lot better though!'

Floré smiled at him, and spoke quietly of the intricacies of the low guard, and tactics against the Tessendorm barbarians with their heavy clubs compared to the armoured knights of Isken.

When Starbeck finally entered the room, Banner began a formal announcement of his names and title but Starbeck halted him with a raised hand. Starbeck was as gaunt as ever, a wolf in a man's body – his eyes were never less than calculating, his face betraying no expression. As the door closed Floré saw two of Starbeck's personal guard waiting in the hallway, Stormguard City Watch in grey tabards with long knives at their belts.

'This is to be a private, informal chat, my man,' Starbeck said, and Floré swept up Marta from the table and put her into Banner's arms.

'Be with her, please, Banner,' she said. Banner's mouth opened and closed, and then he nodded and took Marta out of the dining chamber, his eyes glancing back at the knight-commander. Marta was still clutching a cheese sandwich in one hand, and lumps of cheddar trailed them as they left the room, Marta coughing into Banner's shoulder. Starbeck's gaze dispassionately followed the pair as they left, and Floré bowed her head incrementally to Starbeck.

'Wine, Knight-Commander?' she asked, and he acquiesced and took a chair at the head of the long table. As they settled, Cuss and Yselda were clearly nervous in their silence, Tomas was all smiles, and Benazir was staring into the fire. Drinking a swift mouthful of water, Floré gripped her right hand with her left under the table. Her right arm was twitching and aching, the old lightning scar of the rotstorm burning at her bones. It always came back when she least expected it, or when she needed to concentrate elsewhere. She sang in her mind the chorus to 'Three daughters of the mist, unkind', an old song and one of Janos's favourites.

Kiss your daughters, count their toes, hear the daughters, wail and woe.

Since his death she caught herself singing it over and over again in idle moments, imagining him in the pine of Hookstone forest, dappled in sunlight. By the time the last word passed through her mind the pain in her arm had eased from an acid etching to a dull diffuse ache in her marrow, but she felt tears prickling at her eyes. Always she had to trade one pain for another. *Hurt, not injured,* she thought. *I can do the work.* Flexing her fingers she returned her hands to the table and her focus to the room.

'Ghastly, I know, Commander,' Tomas was saying, 'but my eyes have grown rather sensitive since the crash of that orb – perhaps the flame, or a blow to the head. I can still operate at maximum efficacy, I assure you.'

Starbeck was nodding. He sat with a spine like a spear shaft, no deviations as it rose from chair to skull. Though

he held a glass of thin red wine from Cil-Marie, the kind
Floré's father had favoured, Starbeck drank no more than a
sip. Floré frowned at the ewer of wine. *Did Banner bring me
that because of my heritage, the traces of Cil-Marie in my
face? Or is it coincidence?* She made a mental note to keep
track – if the wine appeared more than random chance might
favour, she would have to speak to him. She was as Undal as
the next girl, and didn't need some token of a far-off land to
feel comfortable. A jug of cheap Isken duck-eye would do her
just as well. Regardless of his intentions, she would have to
speak to him.

'I won't be joining you for dinner,' Starbeck said, and Floré
spared Benazir a quick glance. Benazir had turned and was
watching Starbeck intensely, her eyes sharply focused and
steady, not the vague creature staring into flame or distance
she had been so often.

'Orders, sir?' Floré asked, and Starbeck's mouth twitched
upwards at the corners, the slightest inclination of a smile.

'I have a question and news, and orders, Bolt-Commander,'
he continued, his voice monotonous and thick. As ever, his
eyes were cold and still, and no trace of emotion crossed his
face. His jaw had the habitual few days' growth of stubble,
the mark of a man of the commandos – there was no shaving
past the wall, but a full beard might catch briar or soak with
acid rain. Starbeck was without his usual regalia, but even
his informal clothing was simply a Stormguard uniform
without the tabard or armoured elements. Floré had never
seen him in clothes other than those any Stormguard could
find simply from the quartermaster – Starbeck was not
a man to indulge in the louche trappings of Undal City
society.

'Firstly the question,' he said. 'Is your daughter Marta, the daughter of the skein-wreck Janos, still sick?'

Floré didn't answer immediately, her gaze falling to her glass as she composed herself. The Whitestaff Mallendroit had visited that morning, as he had each morning in the spans since she had come south from Orubor's forest. He had sat with Marta, spoken in low tones and spent long minutes in meditation, and afterward her coughing and fever had subsided. Ever they would return. She spared a glance to Marta's chamber door and stretched her neck before meeting Starbeck's gaze.

'She is.' Floré filled her glass of wine and drank a slug hurriedly, wiping a trail of thin red from the corner of her mouth. The wine was sour and sharp. She examined it in her cup, swirling it as she continued. She pictured Marta the night before and the night before that, shivering and wracked with fever, weeping in pain, crying for her father as the magic ate at her, magic she could not stop reaching for, even in her dreams. Floré had held her tight and whispered and sang to her but there was scant comfort she could give. *Keep her safe,* Janos had said.

How?

3

New Temples, Old Trees

'Wounded are more costly than dead. A torn artery will retract and perhaps heal; an artery cut clean through will bleed until the blood is gone. If you seek to kill, sharpen your blade. If you seek to burden your enemy with the care of his wounded, dull your blade. The barons of Tessendorm learned well that the dull blade cuts longest.'
– Commentary of the Ferron–Tessendorm campaign, Consul Semphor, year 627 Isken reckoning

Ashbringer craned her neck upward to look to the top of the Falls of Dust. In summer, the flow was not so bad, the river a thin creature, but this autumn the rains to the north were steady and the water tumbled down the two hundred feet of jagged rock. At the top, her home: *Orubor's wood*, the humans called it. Ashbringer smiled and leaned deeper into the shade of the rowan tree she had chosen as her vantage, her bare feet crushing ripe red berries that had tumbled from its branches. Her shaven head and long ears were hidden beneath a simple hood, and she wore long skirts that trailed the ground and thin gloves to hide the blue of her hands and feet. All Orubor had blue skin, the serrated teeth of a predator, the lean build of a hunting cat.

Running her hand across the antler hilt of the broken silver sword sheathed at her hip, Ashbringer sang low and slow a song of the forest as she gazed at the pilgrims in the valley below. She felt one of her rune-scars flare with heat, one of the intricate patterns that covered her skin, as she called to the pattern of it and the pattern below that, the idea of shadow. Beneath the boughs, the air dimmed and Ashbringer allowed herself a moment to sit and look on from the newly accreted darkness.

From where she perched beneath the rowan, she had a view down to the green valley where the Falls of Dust brought the river Boros from Orubor's wood into the Undal Protectorate. Up the jagged rocks of the falls there were dark trees, the ancient forest unharvested and untilled, the sanctum of the slumbering bear-god Anshuka. For centuries, her people had guarded the forest with no mercy and no quarter. Before that, their history was lost – she only knew they were the original, the people of the great bear. *Anshuka* was what the humans called her, the Undal and before them the Ferron who called her away. *Anshuka*, Ashbringer would call her if ever she spoke of the god aloud, but in her heart there was a secret name, a secret only to the Orubor and the people of the bear. The true name of the bear, never to be uttered. The pilgrims in the green valley sang to their god and rang their brass bells, and their sombre shamans clutched talismans and preached wherever they could find a stump to stand above the throng. Throughout the valley dozens of humans were gathered in little groups, a wagon here, a caravan there. Some of them sang as they reached the base of the falls and drank the water and laughed with joy.

Ashbringer blinked slowly and tracked her eyes from the joy of the pilgrims up to Orubor's silent wood and Anshuka sleeping within it, the rush of the river Boros through dappled glade and twisted briar. She had followed the river, followed the trail of whoever had killed her kin. At the top of the Falls of Dust, miles upriver, four of her kin had been cut down as they carried the skein-blade of Varratim from the Highmothers' conclave to the weaponsmiths of Elm. One had survived, and no trace of the killer or the blade was found.

'You will find who did this,' Highmother Beech had said to her, her long hair glinting in moonlight. The Highmothers had met with their assassin beneath a moon that hung low and sharp in the sky, a cloudless night. The lone survivor of the attack had brought the news and a hunt had spread, but the killer had fled the forest. *A skein-mage,* Ashbringer thought. *Only a skein-mage could kill an Orubor patrol alone, and even then only a strong one.* Aside from Ashbringer and the new embassy to the Undal, headed by Highmother Ash, none could leave Orubor's wood. Ashbringer did not disagree with this, though it made her burden greater. *Anshuka must always be guarded, above all else.*

'You will spill their heart's blood,' Highmother Elm had continued, her serrated teeth bared. Ashbringer had bowed her head in obeisance: she knew well Highmother Elm's pain. The Orubor slaughtered at the river had been of her community, her blood, her children. She wanted revenge as much as justice.

'You will retrieve the weapon,' Highmother Willow had said, her voice almost a whisper, her hands reaching out to warm on the fire that sat between them all, its furthest flickering light touching the shadow of the god-bear Anshuka as she slept in the wood, as much a mountain as a bear.

'You *must* retrieve the weapon,' Highmother Pine had said, her opaque golden eyes reflecting sparks of firelight. Highmother Pine had stared long at the sky above the forest, the stars, each one a soul. Ashbringer had bowed her head again, and then began to toy with the broken blade of her silver sword, pressing her palm into the break of it, feeling it cut into her flesh.

'I will find it and keep Anshuka safe,' she had said, and Highmother Oak had laughed. Highmother Ash was with the children of Baal, the *humans*, down in Undal City, and her normal calming tone was missing. The conclave felt taut. Ashbringer had frowned at that laugh. *I am so slow sometimes,* she thought, sat beneath her rowan tree in shadow, remembering the words of the conclave. *How am I to be what they need when I am so slow?*

'Not only that, my daughter, my assassin,' Highmother Oak had said, her voice a worn and ragged thing. 'Not only that. Deathless, you have hunted. You have sought. You have struck at him, as is your geas, your family's quest since Anshuka took to her sleep. *Think,* child. If this weapon could kill Anshuka, then it will kill the Deathless. Take your eye, take your heart, take your broken blade. Find this weapon, and do what you were born to do.'

Beneath the rowan bough in the valley of light and green, Ashbringer frowned at the memory of the Highmothers and plucked a berry to chew, feeling the sharp acidity of it rolling across her tongue and pressing one hand to the trunk of the tree in silent thanks. She watched the pilgrims, and focused on the new temple they were raising. Since Ferron fell, over three centuries before, the people of the Undal Protectorate had been coming here to pay tribute to the god-bear; Mother's Den, they called the valley. Orubor's wood above was ringed in stone and briar and dense forest, delineated by sharp protrusions of granite – surely the work of the great bear herself, a bulwark rampart of stone to keep the world from her den. The life of any child of Baal who entered the forest was forfeit, and Ashbringer had killed plenty of pilgrims and madmen and explorers with her own hand. She frowned at the temple.

There had been temples here before, one not a hundred yards from the new frame being lifted. Some were burned down by in-fighting amidst the shaman sects of Undal, little that she knew or cared of those. The Undal were a junta, a government controlled by the military, a council of whitestaffs and workers advising the Stormguard. The shamans fell outside that, a loose network of the fervently devout, spread across the country, independent and at times a strong voice in itself. They lived in their monasteries and dedicated their life to worship of the god-bear, venturing out only to support the whitestaffs with the sick and needy or to preach their interpretation of the god-bear's wishes. Ashbringer shook her head. She had stood in the shadow of the sleeping god, and knew in her heart that the shaman should be working, not praying, to improve their lot. *The mother does not give gifts idly.*

Temples rose and temples fell. The Undal had their civil wars and their bandits as well as incursions from neighbouring powers like the brutal barons of Tessendorm. One temple had lasted more than a century until one of the Claw Winters came unheralded, and all who would tend it froze in their sleep. It had been left empty many years past that, and as a child Ashbringer heard the tale of the spirits who haunted it from her kith and kin. That temple was gone except for the shell of a hearth, nothing left but fern and flower wending around fire-blackened stone.

This new frame a hundred yards along the valley edge was different, and it took her a moment to realise why. They were raising their frame of pine struts over a crúca stone, a jutting rock, black and slick compared to the surrounding granite. Ashbringer frowned and let the shadow around her fade. Stepping from the boughs of the rowan she started to walk down to the pilgrim caravan raising the temple, stalking her way through heather hillocks and wild bushes of gorse that were blooming a season early. The air was cold and the deep yellow flowers of the gorse caught the sun. *A Claw Winter is coming,* she thought, shivering, glancing up at the dark silence of her home forest high above. The Highmothers had told her it was true. *The mother is having nightmares.* A Claw Winter would bring untold cold and snow, failed crops, chaos. As she descended the last hundred feet the dozen pilgrims gathered around the crúca stone, fumbling with rope and scaffold, stopped in their work. Ashbringer made no attempt to hide.

'Good morning, though it be a cold one,' she said, and the scaffolding fell with a crash. Half of the people holding it up had fallen to their knees in supplication, and those remaining could not hold the weight of it.

'Praise be given, holy guardian!' a man said, his face pressed to the dirt, and Ashbringer held her hands out with her palms raised peacefully. His welcome was repeated by all present, some a quiet mutter and an averted gaze, others an unblinking stare and a barked response. *They have not seen my kin before,* she thought with a smile, *or they'd already be dead.*

'I am sorry to disturb you, but I have a question,' she continued, carefully working her thick tongue and thin jaw around the tricky sibilants of the Isken trade tongue. She longed for the sweetness of her own language, but no child of Baal spoke the forest tongue. A woman clad in the grey and black of a shaman let her hand rest heavy on the handle of a blunt mace looped in her belt and Ashbringer cocked her head at that and smiled.

'We are not in the forest,' the woman said, her voice close to breaking, and Ashbringer blinked and looked around.

'Yes,' she said, 'I can see that.'

The woman scrunched her nose and threw a glance at the other pilgrims, then over to where two horses were hitched to a covered wagon. This close, Ashbringer could see the wagon was full of building supplies and wooden boards.

Ashbringer walked between the pilgrims and stepped over the fallen wooden frame. A few recoiled as she drew close, but one young man met her gaze with an open smile and she bowed her head to him. He had dark hair and a soft chin, and he was still listlessly holding a rope that had been supporting the scaffold of the new temple.

'Why here, son of Baal?' she asked, and he glanced at the shaman for a moment before meeting her gaze and shifting his feet.

'To worship the great bear, holy guardian,' he said, 'to be close to her.'

Ashbringer moved forward into the fallen scaffold of the temple wall and lightly stepped up so she was standing on the crúca stone. She knelt low and placed her hands on it, felt the thrum of energy deep below. *All the world a pattern,* her mother had told her, *and in every pattern there are knots and tangles.*

'I am sorry,' she said, extending her senses to the skein and searching for the near imperceptible knot of the crúca stone. If she focused she should be able to feel it, the nexus of the world's pattern, the snag in the weave, the join in the web. The skein spread out before her, a morass of tangled light, pattern, life and chance and past and present and perhaps future, energy and thought and matter all visible at once.

'Not *why here* as in this valley, dear friend,' she said, her eyes focusing on the slick black rock, '*why here* as in this... stone.'

The man started to talk but the shaman had gone to his side and she gripped his arm tight.

'There is to be a rite, at the next full moon, at the request of the shramana – the high shaman,' she said, her voice fast. 'We chose this place to be close to Anshuka, and the shramana said to seek a stone like this for our ceremony. We can move if it displeases you, holy guardian.'

'My father called them luck stones,' the young man said, and the shaman shushed him with a sharp gesture.

Ashbringer frowned at the frantic energy of the woman, but then she shrugged. She had long-ago learned that the children of Baal would be panicked by her appearance. To them, the Orubor were cannibals and killers, the monsters of the wood. Focusing, under her hand she felt the little knot of energy, the nexus where the weave and pattern of the world had caught and made a crúca – a *hook*, the humans would call it, though none of their skein-mages had the sensitivity to find it, she was sure. *Luck stone,* she thought. *Ever I learn about them, ever there is more to learn.* Ashbringer patted the rock beneath her and stepped down, glancing back at the Falls of Dust behind.

'I wish you calm skies, and the mother's blessing on your rites,' she said, and to their echoed thanks she stepped from the temple scaffold and out to the path. There was no sign of the skein-mage who killed her people in the valley, no trace in the skein. *I must go south.* A hundred pilgrims a day would wander this route. She would find the culprit with no bushcraft or keen eye. She walked and walked, and as she walked she sang, and she plucked late berries from the bushes that lined the road and burst them with her jagged teeth as she thought. Not two spans back she had tried again to kill Deathless, Tullen One-Eye, the Ferron skein-wreck who had toppled nations and murdered a god. She had failed, as she always did, and she had left him to his wanderings in Hookstone forest. For the first time she frowned at the name of that place. *Is there a crúca in that place?* She shrugged. It didn't matter – crúca were curiosities, nothing more.

'I will find the dagger,' she said out loud, and her words were heard by nobody except a crow perched on a twisted bough. The scars on her chest itched and she rubbed at her collarbone as she walked on, remembering the burning cuts of Varratim's wand – the wand now concealed beneath her cloak. *I will find the dagger,* she thought, *and then I will find Deathless, and I will cut out his heart.*

The thought made her smile, and Ashbringer walked the valley path with a song on her lips. She wanted to run, but knew in her heart that the steady gait would cover more ground. So she walked and she sang, a hunting song she had learned as a child when she took her long bow to the deep forests of Orubor with her teacher. Together they had sung, voices quiet as whispers, as they had hunted a group of pilgrims who had broken into the sanctuary of the forest. Ashbringer could scarcely draw her bow back then, and until that day had killed only rabbits and deer.

'Run, run, towards the light; run towards the mother,' she sang, and remembered watching her teacher kill the first pilgrim. She had used her bow, waiting until the pilgrim went to piss on an oak older than time. The arrow struck him in the neck, and before he hit the ground they were both running for the other pilgrims, her teacher singing low, Ashbringer breathing fast, the words barely coming from her. The two pilgrims turned at the sound of their companion slumping against the tree and falling, and her teacher caught the second pilgrim, an older woman, and twisted her neck until it snapped before she even had time to scream.

'Run, run, hide from night, run and live to die,' Ashbringer sang. As she walked clear of the valley with long strides, she remembered loosing her arrow into the final pilgrim – a man clad in black, a man tall and strongly built. Her arms had ached from the strain of the bow, and her arrow had sunk deep into his chest. The pilgrim had fallen on his back, and her teacher had swiftly walked to the man and drawn her knife across his throat, batting away the man's feeble attempts to stop her. It was a knife with a blade of silver etched in runes that sparked with blue light as the blade drew blood.

'You did well,' Highmother Ash had said to her, 'but aim lower next time. A slower death, but the ribs might have stopped your arrow.'

Young Ashbringer had nodded, had watched the man lie so still, save for the blood pooling out over the earth and grass below.

Ashbringer left the valley of Mother's Den at a steady pace, ready to hunt the skein-mage who had stolen the dagger; ready to kill the deathless man. She sang as she walked, one hand on the hilt of her broken blade.

'Run, run, towards the light; run towards the mother, Fight, fight, fire so bright; fight for root and tree.'

~

Floré refilled Starbeck's cup and glanced around her room. Benazir and Tomas were watching her expectantly, but Cuss and Yselda had both glanced at the door to Marta's room when Starbeck asked his question. *Is Marta still sick?* Floré rubbed a finger across the wood of the table, pushing at the grain, and sighed, tension building in her shoulders. Outside the wind was rattling the window shutters on the high towers of Protector's Keep, and she could hear distant bells ringing from the shaman temple, deep reverberations cutting through the cold.

'Marta reaches for the skein like a mage fifteen years her elder,' Floré said, falling into the cadence of military briefing and forcing herself to keep her voice calm and dispassionate, 'but she is too young to control herself, or stop herself. It takes from her. Whitestaff Mallendroit says it is beyond his skill to stop her, though he eases the symptoms each day. Janos was teaching her, and able to mitigate the effect if she... got carried away. She is better today, but each day is another battle and she grows weaker. She dreams of it, and in her dreams she touches the pattern and it takes from her then. Even if she did nothing as she woke, every night it is worse. She can reach for the pattern and change it but there is no control. Mallendroit says there is no medicine here that will heal her. The commissar-mage and the castrum have found no record of a skein-wreck ever having a child, and the Stormguard mages they command are almost all combat-focused. A few academics researching rune-blades and industrial applications, as ever, but the healing arts were left to the whitestaffs.'

The castrum was the Stormguard skein-mage academy and research centre in Undal City, and Floré and Marta had spent ten days with the mages' probing and tests. *A full span wasted and nothing to show,* Floré thought. Though they hadn't wanted to say it, she could see the mages feared Marta. Commissar-Mage Inigo had made claims he could teach the girl control, but control was not enough. *One night she'll reach too far and I'll wake up to silence.*

Starbeck nodded and Cuss shook his head, swearing under his breath, 'Berren's black blood.' He picked up a piece of bread and started idly nibbling at it, his eyes focused on the table in front of him. Yselda and Tomas showed no reaction, each utterly still and focused on first Floré and then Starbeck, reading faces. Only Benazir met Floré's eyes a moment, a moment that Floré understood. *Benazir will help us,* Janos had said as he lay dying. It was a calm gaze, a gaze that said, whatever was necessary, Benazir would do. Floré felt a shiver in her chest in appreciation of her friend.

Starbeck primly took another sip of wine and then spread his hands on the table.

'News, then. It is threefold, some of it known to some of you, some to none. Firstly – as you know, the rust-folk have taken Port Last and the Northern Marches, and seem to be establishing fortifications and logistics in a way we've not seen before. They're sending refugees south, and the two remaining orbs of Ferron we know of patrol a line from Fallow Fen east to Inverbar, then north to the Storm Sea. They do this openly, and obviously. Any within the area the orbs circumscribe are told to flee on pain of death. Perhaps an eighth of our realm is now under *occupation*.'

Tomas and Benazir both made to speak but Starbeck motioned for silence, his brows furrowing. Floré pictured a map of the protectorate, the top left chunk of it now full of the worst the rotstorm could bring: goblins, rottrolls, bite-kelp, *crow-men*. She felt a hot wave of anger shiver up her body and she bit the inside of her lip. *Preserve the freedom of all people in the realm* were the first words of her oath to the Stormguard. She had spent her life fighting the monsters of the rotstorm that defined the protectorate's western border, that storm of magic and monster, acid mist and puissant lightning. Janos and Benazir had both lost their families, their homes, to the monsters that spawned in that endless storm, the storm of Anshuka's wrath incarnate against the crimes of the Ferron Empire.

Floré knew this news already, of course – as soon as she had arrived back in Undal City Starbeck had fast-tracked her promotion to bolt-commander, and she had been working on the defensive plans, shoring up the city garrison even as she waited for a true mission, as the Grand Council spoke long into each night and then sat back and bided their time. She knew there were garrison forts established near this new border, that the Lancers were massing there to prepare for some assault. *But what can we do against the orbs?* The only reason any of the strange flying machines had been destroyed was that Floré and Heasin and Tomas had brought them down in their own stolen orb. *And now the Orubor won't let us near that.* Floré bit her lip to quell her anger at the strange creatures.

'Our garrisons there have been driven back, but harried no further than this line,' Starbeck continued, his monotone growing steadily lower, 'and those fleeing south speak of a demon clad in black, with hair aflame. *Ceann Brude* they call her. A crow-man. The rumour is that a delegation will follow, to negotiate the terms of peace.'

Floré leaned back in her chair and flexed her knuckles and waited for the hammer to fall. She was the gauntlet; bolt-commander. The heavy hand. She had, with Benazir, spearheaded the retaking of Fallow Fen. The assault on Urforren, where now there was nothing but a mile of ever-burning salt. *I saw Lothal's bones. I'll go north and drive the beasts back into the storm.* Even as she thought it a note of dissonance spread across her from her gut, and the rage that warmed her face faltered. *Every goblin, every wyrm, every demon a child...*

'The second piece of news,' Starbeck said, 'which you all should know, is that the Orubor will allow us no access to their wood, nor to Anshuka herself, nor to the orbs you captured during the events of this summer. All we have to show for that escapade is the runewands that Tomas retrieved, though it will take our mages many moons to reverse-engineer and mass-produce them, if it is even possible.'

Tomas leaned forward and smiled at that, raising a finger in triumph. Next to him Cuss was huffing through his nose and blinking rapidly.

'All is possible with the skein, Knight-Commander! We will have their secrets soon enough. The coterie stationed at the castrum are sparing no moment, and my own investigations are yielding great strides daily,' Tomas said, and then leaned back looking utterly contented.

'We have Anshuka,' Cuss said quickly, his fists full of bread suddenly clenched, his eyes glaring at Starbeck. 'We have *Anshuka* to show for it, for everything we lost, we have her and a hundred dead goblins, and fewer handfuls of magic nightmare orbs that spit fire, *and a score fewer crow-men*. It *was* worth something.'

The boy's gaze dropped from Starbeck's placid face and utterly still eyes, and Floré raised her hand a fraction to him and motioned him to calm.

'He is right,' she said, and when Cuss raised his eyes she nodded to him. 'If we hadn't captured that orb, Anshuka herself would be destroyed, and who knows what chaos that would bring? Knight-Commander, you speak now of two orbs holding back our armies from the Northern Marches, burning patrols, driving refugees south. What of Ossen-Tyr? When the orbs attacked there in a co-ordinated manner they burned the town half to cinders in twenty minutes – *and that was not even their aim*.'

Floré rubbed at her nose and scratched at the rune-scar on her cheek, the legacy of Varratim's torture. 'Cuss's brother Petron kept Marta safe in those caverns, and he died. Countless other stolen children were killed by Varratim for his rituals. Heasin of the Tullioch died fighting those orbs, to protect *our* god. Tomas and Cuss and I will be scarred forevermore. The situation is bleak, Knight-Commander, but those sacrifices were not in vain. We killed more crow-men than in a season of campaigning beyond the wall, and we took those orbs before they could be brought against us in battle – *a battle we would not win.*'

Floré sat back, cheeks flushed, and Starbeck nodded in deference. Cuss held his bread and gave Floré a quick glance of thanks as the knight-commander rubbed at his chin and snorted.

'Not many chastise me as often as you, Commander,' he said. 'My apologies, young man. I know what has been lost. I am merely frustrated by the Orubor. Why send an embassy to us now, if not to aid us?'

They sat in silence around the table for a long moment.

'What is the final news, sir?' Yselda asked quietly, but Benazir cut in before the knight-commander could respond.

'Whitestaffs still missing,' she said, and she was nodding to herself, rubbing her fingers over the grain of the wooden table. 'That'll be orders too, aye?'

Starbeck sipped his wine and leaned back in his chair. He smiled at Benazir, a rare flit of emotion, and Floré felt her pulse quicken. *He has never smiled for me truly, not once.*

'Always a step ahead, dear Benazir, but that is not my news, though you guess rightly at your orders. You all know,' Starbeck said, 'that our mystical comrades have deemed fit to withdraw at this, our direst hour. The brutality of Ferron has never been a rational thing. From colonial times to the ragged remnants we face, ever it has been violence, and the oppressor's violence only retreats in the face of greater violence. That is the role of the Stormguard. The whitestaffs are meant to be our support, our healers, our sages: geographers, logisticians, hydrologists, intelligence, storm-tracking. They are intrinsic to the state, and the sharpened blade that must fall. Intelligence gives strength to the arm. Without them we are weakened, and the night grows dark.'

Starbeck ran a hand over his face and seemed to sag a little, and Floré for an instant saw a tired man rather than the poised wolf. Thick streaks of grey had grown into his hair since she had seen him first at Stormcastle XII all those years ago, bolts of lightning and roiling storm behind him as he addressed her and the other fresh cadets. His expression was no softer but lined and slackened with age and worry. They all sat in silence in the light of the hearth and the glow of the candelabra until Yselda coughed and Starbeck seemed to come to his senses.

'I have sent a ship a day,' he said, 'since they left us. It is a two-day journey south to Riven, three if the wind is against you. Two days through the reefs, but it is our best charted path for all the waters of the Wind Sea. Ships left to make the crossing daily, before, and returned as swiftly. Now, none have returned. Spans pass and *none* have returned. Ships we send east fare no better. Ships sent in convoy fare no better. No ship has come to us in spans and spans. No trade, no news of the world beyond except by rider to Isken. From there, the word is that any ship that crosses into Undal waters is not heard from again.'

Floré pictured the iron sea to the south, white-capped waves and a sky of sword-metal, a cold wind tugging at you, so different to the fetid, hot acid gusts and gales of the rotstorm. Reefs that would rip the hull from a boat, and beasts below that would eat any who survived the cold long enough to swim. Natural, but no less deadly than the rotstorm. She shivered.

'Your orders are to go south,' he said, 'to retrieve the

allyship of our comrades, and remove whatever stands in the way of their return. Seek their counsel on the orbs; bring them back into the fold. Our navy is almost gone, and I can spare no more from Undal City's defence. Your ship is the trader *Basira's Dance*, under Captain Muirgainas. A smuggler. He will take you a route none yet have tried. Commander Benazir has the charge of this mission.'

Benazir sat back in her chair and scratched her nose.

'What of Stormcastle XII?' Tomas asked. 'I *am* primus there, Benazir is commander, and it is the last outpost of sanity before whatever madness holds the north. We should be there with Voltos, surely?'

Starbeck nodded to Tomas. 'You are primus, Tomas, and Benazir is commander. But Commissar-Mage Inigo has agreed to allow you leave to join my expedition. Thum-Pho will return to XII as primus, temporarily of course. As for Benazir, we are moving the lancer legions north. Stormcastle XII will be one of their forward staging points, under Knight-Commander Dour. She will have temporary command there. She has her own Antian adviser, as well. Voltos should reach us by tomorrow's departure. He will join you.'

Floré smiled at that. Voltos was an Antian, one of the curious mole-dog people who lived under and amongst most of the strait kingdoms. One redoubt of theirs remained in the Undal Protectorate, a towering keep to the north of Ossen-Tyr. From there the Antian tunnels extended east to Tessendorm, to Isken, and all up to Carob's Strait through the other kingdoms that patchworked the northern continent of Morost. After the last Antian war thirty years before and the armistice that followed, Voltos and his kin had acted as advisers and attachés to the Stormguard. *An old enemy will always spot your weakness before you do,* Floré thought with a smile. The idea of having Voltos with her, his worry and sage advice, calmed her heart.

'You think I'm up to this, sir?' Benazir asked Starbeck. Floré shifted in her seat and set her jaw.

'She's up to it,' she heard herself say, and then Tomas was leaning forward again, blocking Cuss from view. He smiled a tight grin with no teeth showing, the flesh of his cheeks crinkling as it pressed the dark metal frames of his goggles.

'Given the nature of the mission and the challenges we may face,' he said, 'and given Bolt-Commander Arfallow's recent injurious adventures, might I suggest I take point on this, sir?'

Floré felt her mouth twitch in a snarl and her hand rise, but Starbeck shook his head quickly at the idea.

'No, Tomas, Tomas-Primus,' he said. 'You will accompany, but you have another mission.'

Tomas sat back and licked his teeth and smiled again. 'Of course, sir.'

Starbeck waited a beat and met eyes with Floré, even as he spoke to Tomas.

'The Orubor embassy here in Protector's Keep summoned me today. Anshuka is safe, encircled by every force they can muster. Yet they inform me the dagger of Varratim has been... *stolen.*'

4

THE CURSE OF THE BEAR

'What is the Claw Winter? It is when Anshuka's nightmare turns from the rotstorm of Ferron to her own children. When we have displeased her, and she has the bitterness of a mother betrayed. The winter comes early and strong, and the darkness and cold bite at the heart of us. The snow and ice and storm she sends are a reminder that all we have is at her blessing. We must endure, and in spring we must mourn the dead and thank her for her mercy that any should live. In Ferron, they live under storm forever in their penance. We are chosen and we are saved, and the Claw Winter is a reminder that a debt is owed.' – **The Book Of Judges**, Shaman Gait

Floré stood from the table and began to pace.

'What do you mean, *stolen*?' Tomas said carefully, and Yselda let out a soft moan and buried her face in her hands. She had seen the dagger, Floré knew. She understood its potential. It wasn't just a dagger. It was a skein-blade honed on the pattern of an unknown number of skein-sensitive children,

64

the pattern of their innocent connection to that larger web of magic that underlaid the world. It was a nexus of power, a blade that could kill a god. Floré had held it in her hand, blade of obsidian and hilt of twisted bone, a green gem at its pommel. She had felt a strange weight to it – not physical, but a weight of *potential*.

Starbeck refilled his wineglass and took a sip before continuing. 'They were moving it to be researched by one of their occultists or wizards or whatever they call them. Their patrol was wiped out by a skein-user. This is what I know. They informed us to ensure we take appropriate action, should it fall into our hands.'

'What is appropriate action, with a knife that kills gods?' Floré said quietly, and Starbeck shrugged.

'In the same breath almost,' he went on, 'they confirmed the rumour that has been spreading as folk tale since before I was a boy. A rumour some of you repeated to me when we debriefed. That Tullen One-Eye, scourge of Undal, killer of Nessilitor the Lover, breaker of the Tullioch Shard, is in fact alive.'

Cuss poured himself a glass of water from the clay ewer, then spilled it on the table and began to mop furiously with a cloth napkin Banner had laid out. Tomas was clutching his satchel with one hand and with the other tracing slow runes and shapes and curving patterns on the tabletop with his finger, murmuring to himself.

'Orders, sir?' Benazir said again, and Floré gripped at the sill of the window and stared out into the night. The peaceful night, no storm, only dark cloud above and the whipping winds from the sea. *No storm, not yet. Not here.* Starbeck wanted her to take to the seas that had swallowed however many hundreds of sailors in the last seven spans since the whitestaffs had retreated. *He wants me to leave Marta.* Floré felt acid in her throat and let out a sharp breath.

'For you, Benazir: retrieve me the aid of our whitestaffs. Whatever the problem is, fix it. The Ferron have taken our land, and make no mistake, they will seek to grow whatever gains they find. We will drive them back into the storm and water our last crop of the year with their blood. Bring me the whitestaffs. Commander Artollen, aid and support Benazir. Keep her safe, and bring the heavy hand to any who oppose her will. When you are there, there are answers you might seek, Primus. How might we find a dagger that is so singular in power? How might we find and kill a man who has lived three hundred years, who has broken nations? You may also'—turning to Floré—'perhaps find aid for Marta there. With her father gone, she may be the next great hope we have for a skein-wreck to keep our people safe. She is a child now, but wherever humanity tries to build and prosper in peace, there will be a wolf at the door with a hunger in its heart. We must ensure she is there to keep Undal safe when we cannot.'

Floré felt her mouth open and she was breathing deeply and the scars in her arm were tingling and burning and in her mind she saw Marta calling on the skein to turn a goblin, a living creature – perhaps even a child not so different from herself once – into a pillar of so much salt to be strewn by the wind. When he lay dying, Janos had said to her, *Find Marta; Benazir will help you.* She had found Marta without Benazir's help, but perhaps Benny could help her find a cure to the skein-sickness eating away at the girl. *Perhaps she can help me save her from what the protectorate would do with her.* She shuddered at the thought, of Marta as a weapon, sweet Marta facing a lifetime of violence. *Why must it always be war?*

'I will send you a squad of Stormguard,' Starbeck said, 'and I thought it best if young Cadet Grantimber and Cadet Hollow here act as stewards to you two bolt-commanders. They have proven their salt, and trust is in short supply. Private Grantimber and Private Hollow – I should say – if they agree?'

'Thank you, Knight-Commander,' Yselda said, her eyes downcast and voice quiet. Cuss sat next to her, his eyes fixed on Starbeck, his face slack. For a long moment he was still and then he glanced to Floré, his gaze questioning. Floré simply smiled back at him, a sad smile. *He wants me to decide for him.* The sweet village boy had lost his brother, his sister, his mother, all to the rust-folk. She had seen the pain in him these last spans. She had seen him in the practice yard at all hours, a furious anger driving him until he was spent, returning each day. *He wants revenge,* she thought, *but does he need it?* Regardless of how he felt, she knew the Stormguard would provide for him, would give him a home. Floré shrugged at Cuss.

'It's your decision, son,' she said, 'and there is no right or wrong answer.'

Cuss stared at her a long moment and then turned back to the knight-commander and bowed his head.

'Thank you, sir,' he said. 'I won't let you down. I promise you that, sir.'

Starbeck nodded and from his pocket retrieved four thin strips of cloth, vibrant green silk with a strip of white at their core.

'These are for you,' he said, and passed them along to the

two cadets, and to Tomas and Floré. 'Sword-knots, to mark your victory in Orubor's wood, to remind you of your deeds and your courage. A new pattern for a... unique victory. The Orubor embassy and your commander told me of all you have done, this summer. The heat may have left us, and a Claw Winter seems inevitable. It will be long months of darkness and bitter cold ahead, and we are beset by enemies. Tie these to your blades and take heart.'

The two cadets were speechless, and Floré beamed with pride. *Her* cadets. Her old sword-knot was lost somewhere in Ossen-Tyr when she was taken by the orbs of light, thrown down in a brawl against criminals before the orbs destroyed half the town. Her old knot had been red silk with a white core, cut from the robes of Mistress Water herself, a silk that was ever damp. Mistress Water had spent a lifetime in a Ferron salt mine, a desiccated hell, and it was said that after she found the skein and its powers she was never dry again, always comforted by the balm of cool water. Mistress Water who had woken Anshuka, Mistress Water who had founded the whitestaffs and ended the reign of the Ferron Empire... *and I lost it in a midden.* Floré clutched the new sword-knot and felt it, soft silk against the rough skin of her hands.

'I have some equipment and items for the rest of you as well, with the quartermaster,' Starbeck said, 'but for these I wanted to make a personal delivery.'

Benazir raised a glass in toast to the two cadets and the others at the table joined, Yselda and Cuss still wide-eyed, but then the door opened from the hallway and Banner was there, long blonde hair slick with sweat, unsmiling. *Running to prepare an unneeded feast,* Floré thought. She could smell the rich gravy from the pot swung over the corner of the hearth, but knew Banner would have been rushing to prepare fare more befitting the knight-commander of the Grand Council, even though Starbeck had waved aside the offer of food. Floré held a hand up for a moment of pause to the table. Banner pushed the door firmly closed behind him.

'Banner,' she said, but he ignored her, his eyes locked on Knight-Commander Starbeck.

'*Suffer no tyrant!*' Banner cried, his voice a strangled croak, and for Floré time slowed. In a heartbeat she saw the glint of steel in her aide's hand, half covered by a dishcloth, and then he was lunging forward at Starbeck and swinging wildly. Floré leapt to her feet but Banner's momentum died and he flew back across the room impossibly fast, crashing into the heavy oak door he had entered from with a sickening crack and then a heaving retch, his limbs flailing as he crumpled over on himself on the flagstone floor. Tomas had one hand raised and thrown before him, the other still clasping his glass raised in toast, his face a picture of utter concentration as he ground his teeth and focused on the skein. Through his shirtsleeves red light poured as the tattooed sigils and runes covering his arms glowed, as he accessed the pattern etched on his skin and the pattern below that, the pattern of skein he had memorised to give him this power, the power to throw a man as if he weighed no more than a goblet.

Banner sobbed on the ground and tried to pull himself up but the force of the blow had broken him. Floré went to him and with a twist of her wrist his knife was taken, a long dirty kitchen knife with a blade worn down from years of use. With the knife gone, Banner seemed to lose all sense of struggle and slumped down, eyes turning glassy. Thick black blood was pooling in his hair where his head had struck the door or wall when Tomas had flung him. His breath stuttered and Floré turned back to the table, her face scrunched in confusion. *He watches Marta,* she thought; *he watches Marta and makes sure my armour is clean and we always have fresh bread.*

At the table, Cuss and Yselda were standing, Cuss fumbling to slip dull steel knuckledusters over his fingers, Yselda with a glass of wine spilled across her shirt and Benazir's old dagger clutched in both hands close to her chest. Her new sword-knot had fallen to the table, crumpled. Benazir, Starbeck, and Tomas were still sat, all of them still holding their glasses.

'These reformists always have such a flair for drama and such a deficit for delivery,' Starbeck said, and he refilled his glass. Despite his steady tone Floré saw the table at his right hand was staining red in a pool of wine, sickly red and sweet. His guards swept into the room, blades bared, and Floré left them all, pushed through the two doors to find Marta asleep in her room, curled in bed, silent and still. Hands shaking, she smoothed hair from Marta's face and stole backward, closing the door and holding the handle fast, turning back to the dining chamber and chewing her lip.

'What do they want?' Tomas was asking, and Floré saw Starbeck's guards were barricading the door from the inside.

'They want me to step down. They call for *elections,*' Starbeck said, 'as if a popularity contest will bring the right mind to the council's helm. They say I clutch at power, and so on, and so on. As if I am enjoying myself, spending my life fighting nightmares and barbarians and whatever else, in endless meetings for their benefit.'

Floré could think of nothing to say. She knew the reformists were a growing voice of dissent against the totality of the

Stormguard's control over the protectorate, but had not realised things were so bad. *Banner*.

'Basira's Dance,' Benazir said with a sigh, and raised her glass and drained it. Starbeck and Tomas followed her lead, but Floré could only stare down at the shivering and twitching body of Banner, her tongue between her teeth as she thought of his final words. *Suffer no tyrant*.

~

The reeve held his chambers in the tallest tower of Fetter-Dun, three storeys above the sodden earth, a mote of solidity against the wild rotstorm raging above. Brude climbed the stairs quickly, clenching and unclenching her fists. She wore the uniform of black given to her by Varratim, sewn in the Blue Wolf Mountains from the remnants of the strange materials they had found there. At her hip, a simple dagger of black iron with no cross guard was sheathed next to her two runewands. Each was ten inches of starmetal, black iron from a fallen star. One ended in a faceted blue gem of tourmaline incised with elaborate runes, the other an intricately shaped ruby with its own arcane inscriptions etched on every face. Her runewands. Her trophies – *the dagger that killed the Salt-Man, the wands of Old Ferron*.

Amon trailed behind her, both of them brushing rain from their faces. The brief foray across the courtyard to reach the reeve's chambers had left them drenched, even with the flames of Brude's wand bringing death to the Stormguard prisoners. Brude hesitated at the doorway, a door of thick wood banded in iron, and Amon laughed and stepped around her, reaching for it. He paused.

'Don't become hesitant now, my friend,' he said quietly,

smiling. 'The reeve knows your temper and your style, and has made his choice. All will follow it. Trust in your heart.'

Brude smiled gratefully and nodded to him, and Amon opened the door. The chamber inside was lit by firelight and at least a dozen wax candles piled haphazardly around the room on stacks of paper, vellum, books. The reeve stood over a table covered in a map of the old Ferron Empire, and Brude squinted at it, then at him. The reeve was not a crow-man. He was of average height and build, his dark hair thinning and trimmed short, a tight beard wrapping his jaw. He was dressed in a simple dark shirt and trousers, and he smiled genially up at her. The reeve did not lead through strength or magic. The reeve led because he could take two men fighting over a scrap of food and make them brothers.

'Welcome, Ceann Brude. My congratulations. You are to be our burning brand. What say you?'

Brude stepped into the room and unfolded her spine, stretching up to her full height. She bowed her head in acknowledgement and pointed to his map.

'I say we bring fire and blood. The storm comes to them.'

The reeve smiled up at her and gestured to the map. It showed Ferron before the storm, but was covered in annotations: settlements lost, ancient cities now dust, new towns risen. The reeve traced his finger along the eastern border where Ferron met Undal, then spread his hand west.

'We once had space, and land, and resources. The Iron Desert to the far west; the tree city of Hunesh; Berren's valleys. We were scattered in the storm, but Varratim's discovery in the west of Ferron's trove united us with hope.'

The reeve let his finger linger over the city of Urargent, the once mighty capital of Ferron. On the map it was ringed in red, and a dozen notes besides. Urargent was deep enough in the storm that even crow-men feared to go there. The ruination had been complete, in Anshuka's wrath. The storm there was brutality incarnate, and survival was never certain. Varratim had delved into the ruins and brought forth his prizes, the first orb of light, and the location of the others.

'Did Varratim tell you all he found?' Brude asked, and the reeve tilted his head to one side. Across the room, Amon poured them each a cup of wine and joined them at the table. The reeve toasted them both and drank deep before responding.

'Varratim told me much of what he found. He was perhaps too caught in magic and gods and not the *practicality* of our fight. Fools talk of tactics, Ceann Brude. Amateurs talk of tactics. For too long we have been amateurs, untrained and fighting only for survival. Amateurs talk of tactics; soldiers talk of *logistics*. How do we feed our troops, shelter them, keep them warm and fed in the winter to come? How will we communicate? What is our goal? Beans and bandages and blades. Varratim wanted to win the war with a single blow to the god-bear, as we distracted our enemy with our assault on the Stormwall. The folly of heroism, the naïveté of a romantic.'

The reeve drained his cup and smiled at Brude. She shifted on her feet, a grimace flitting across her face.

'I am a crow-man, Reeve,' she said, flexing her overlong fingers and wincing at the pain. 'I am not a... *logistics* person. I am a storm incarnate. I am the curse of the bear, but her fire has forged me into a blade that might cut her own people. You want me to tally bandages?'

Brude could not keep her face calm, could feel the anger curling her lip. Amon smiled up at her, and so did the reeve. Brude furrowed her brow.

'Is this some joke? I do not understand.'

'No joke, Brude,' Amon said quickly, and the reeve nodded along with him. 'We have an ally. Someone who knows war. Someone who can help us *keep* what we take. Not like Fallow Fen, last time, chaos and blood and after a decade they threw us back to the storm. They can help us. They *will* help us.'

Brude rocked back on her heels and ran her hand across the handle of her knife. Amon came to her and put his hand on her arm.

'While you and Varratim chased the god-bear, the reeve sent me. I have gone far, Brude, this year. Further than I thought possible. Our cause is not without allies, and the Undal not without enemies. I have brought back a soldier. She will help us, with knowledge and tactics and logistics. You will be the storm; she will be the silent guiding hand.'

Brude leaned forward to look at the map and felt a sourness in her gut. She frowned again. 'Why would she help us, your soldier?'

The reeve laughed and used a taper to light another candle, carrying it over to a banded chest at the back of his room. Opening it up, Brude saw a pile of gold coin, bracelets, chains, goblets. Gemstones worked into ornate necklaces, a dagger with a handle of coral and pearl and a blade of black stone.

'We are not without treasure, Brude,' he said. 'We sit on the remnant of the mightiest empire ever to grace Morost.'

The reeve let his fingers trail through the coins and smiled back at Brude.

'And as Amon says,' he continued, 'the Stormguard and the Undal are not without enemies. You will like the soldier, Brude. You are our ceann. She is another blade at your hip.'

Brude found herself nodding, found herself smiling and then laughing. Amon and the reeve joined her, and she took a long drink from her cup.

'This is a good day, Reeve,' she said.

He nodded. 'It is not over yet.' Then the honour came.

Brude, who killed the Salt-Man, the Undal mage who turned Urforren to ash and burning salt, who killed a hundred crow-men, a thousand rust-folk, more goblins than could be counted. Brude had stuck her knife in the Salt-Man's gut and wrenched, and so she was to be honoured. Amon fetched the inker, an old woman with hands gnarled like bite-kelp roots who came with her mallet and her needles and her vials of ink packed tight in a satchel of worn and weathered leather. The reeve spoke to her as the inker tapped needles into Brude's skin, over and over. The pain was real and strong and sharp but Brude was an old friend of pain – each night she dreamt of the god-bear's ghost hunting her through the storm, and each morning her bones woke her, aching in their very marrow, unnaturally extended, their pattern inexorably changed. *I know pain.* She felt a sickness deep in her core as her face was changed. Her face, the only part of her no different to any human, would forever be marked. *A pretty face doesn't matter if it sits atop a monster.*

'You have avenged us, Ceann Brude,' the reeve said, 'but we are not yet free.'

The needles burned. A circle around her eye, a great circle of black arcing over her eyebrow before cutting down and under her eye socket. The blood began to flow and fill her vision and Brude asked for a mirror. Amon found a plate of polished tin in the reeve's apartment and held it up to her. Her red hair slicked back by the rain, the freckles on her face stark against pale skin. A circle of black around her eye, diagonally bisected by a line that cut across her eye itself. When the inker tapped her needles onto her eyelid, Brude felt bile rising and had to grip the arm of her chair, heard herself hiss.

'The Salt-Man has been killed but the protectorate yet stands,' the reeve said, and Brude could taste acrid spit in her mouth and feel hot blood in her eye. 'They will not suffer us to live, even as their god makes us into monsters. We must be free, Brude. You will take us there.'

Brude gnashed her teeth and finally the inker wiped her face, the cloth coming away black with crow-man blood. She could already feel herself healing, the storm within her surging to build her back together. When she shut her eye the symbol was complete: Ø. The Ferron rune for salt.

'There are those amongst us who call for peace, Brude,' Amon said quietly as she examined the tattoo. His usual smile was gone, his face pinched. 'Those who say we should try to pass the Iron Desert to the west as our ancestors attempted. Those who say we should go to the Undal Protectorate and beg for their mercy, for passage through to the strait kingdoms, where we might try our luck. That I should send my soldier away, and you should lay down your knife. What will you say to them?'

Brude looked at her reflection. Her face was still her face, not the oddly jointed hands, the overlong limbs, the ache in her bones, the certainty that her organs were all maligned and queered. Her face was still her own face – freckled and pale, the scar on her left cheek, the holes where she had pierced her ears for plugs of bone, the thin lips, the eyes blue and dark. *I am still me,* she thought.

'I come from Pertcupar,' she said at last, lowering the tin plate and meeting the eyes of Amon and the reeve. The inker left the room with a muttered blessing.

'Pertcupar where two forests once met. West of here, past the ruins of Nillen, far south of the diggers at Talpid and their works. It is too deep in the storm for the Stormguard to ever reach. Why not stay there, Amon; stay and work the land?'

Amon laughed, but did not smile. They all knew the answer: the rotstorm, acrid and surging with brutal lightning, mists of acid, winds and rains that would turn most crops to mulch long before harvest; and within the rotstorm, plants turned violent by Anshuka's wrath, creeping vine and pepper thorn; and within the mists at night, the mists that burned your face as you walked, the ghost of the bear Anshuka prowling in the darkness, seeking children to turn to crow-man, goblin, stormblight, rottroll, wyrm, or worse.

'If we go west it is storm until the ruins of Urargent. It is storm beyond that. The rumour is it stops halfway through the Iron Desert. I know no one who has made it even past Urargent. Even if it stops, it ends in the Iron Desert itself – not good for farming, Amon. It is death to the west. Beyond the desert who knows what fresh hell awaits.'

'We could scout,' Amon said, 'with the orbs. We could find out for sure what lies west.'

The reeve tapped at the tabletop impatiently, and Brude could see this had been discussed before. She stood and loomed over the map, staring down at the Undal Protectorate, once mines and plantations for the Ferron Empire, now its own fiefdom, with its precious Stormwall and its blessed freedoms.

'I'll not risk the orbs on the desert when we have but two remaining,' she said, her crooked finger landing on the northern end of the Stormwall: the Northern Marches, where fresh ink marked the initial forays of the rust-folk raiding parties.

'There is land, good land, here for the taking. They offer us no succour, so we will take what we must. The reeve's plan is righteous. We take a slice of the north, and we burn a line across their map. We dig our ditch. We send them their people. We distract them with hell itself, and we spend the winter building. When spring comes, we will be ready.'

'As you say, Ceann Brude,' Amon said, and nodded his head deferentially.

'As you say, Ceann Brude,' the reeve said, and bowed his head low.

'Bring me the soldier,' Brude said, 'and let us go to war.'

5

BLADE OF THE MATRIARCH

'The idea that there is no solution is a fallacy the Grand Council perpetuate. There is land to be farmed, in the Slow Marsh or the Northern Marches. Isken welcomes immigrants of all creeds and origins for the price of a few years' labour. Who does the endless war truly support? It supports the Stormguard. A common enemy unites us, and for three centuries they have gained in power until the Grand Council is nought but a farce. Who speaks for the people of the Undal Protectorate? The Stormguard are sworn to lead in servitude, but whom do they serve but themselves?' – **Break the Stormguard's chains!** Lillebet Arfallow, year 312 from Ferron's Fall (1123 Isken)

Undal City had long ago sprawled beyond its defences, but the keep and central city were still encircled by the stout Undal walls of worked stone. Protector's Keep was a mix of Undal stonework over the top of Ferron ruin. What had once been the Ferron overseer fort for the coastal plantations had been used as foundation for the sprawling ramparts and towers of the keep, a warren laid down over three centuries of war and peace. The black seamless skein-wrought stone of the overseer fort was mostly hidden, but as Tomas left the keep through the eastern servants' entrance and headed to the dock, he passed patches of that ancient stone and let his fingers linger.

He realised he had been standing still for a long moment when a kitchen porter quietly coughed and squeezed past him in the dark stone passageway. His hand was extended, almost touching the wall but held back a fraction. Through the smoky glass of his goggles Tomas could scarcely see it as one normally would, but since attuning his senses to Varratim's dagger he felt he could ever see the skein and its pattern, a layer atop his own sight that did not leave him when he stopped his conscious connection to that web of sprawling and convoluted pattern. Tomas smirked in the darkness of the hallway. *I see so much better now.* He wasn't sure how long he'd been standing in the hallway; his thoughts felt fuzzy. *I need to concentrate.* Too many long days and nights, nights studying the runewands with the skein-mages, too many secret sessions studying Varratim's dagger, that nexus of skein that entranced him so.

He could sense the pattern within the old black skein-wrought stone, a pattern he had never felt before. *Did I simply never seek it? Or are my senses so much greater?* It was the pattern of shaping, the pattern of rock and carbon shaped at its most intricate level to be strong, to hold the will of the one who forged it. With a shiver he pulled his hand back and let it rest at the satchel that hung at his hip. *Interesting.* One of the greatest limitations of the skein was the inability to make any effect *hold*. If the mage died, so did his magic, and keeping a spell in place was a constant drain of energy, no matter how slight. Staring at the stone that still held its shape three centuries after Ferron fell, Tomas was unsure if it held the shape because the spell lingered, or because it lay in its final form. *Another effect to study.*

Shaking his head, Tomas pulled back and tried to focus. Striding from the dark tunnels below the keep and out past the guard post with a wave, he headed down towards the docks. It was a bitterly cold morning, and the road was quiet and grey. A few streets before the quayside Tomas turned off, and after three side streets he reached his destination. This close to the centre of Undal City even the side streets were wide and clear, the windows glass-filled and their frames painted in jaunty colours.

Tomas preferred the east ward and the Star Market to the rest of the city, the western end of town with the stink of the fishing harbour or the northern forest gate full of traders and caravans and the oppressive weight of the castrum sat on its hill, the Commissar-Mage Inigo and his flunkies always ready to comment and offer direction. The forest gate was now flooded with refugees as well, all those driven south by the Ferron, who didn't dare stop at the smaller towns of the Slow Marshes, who kept coming south until the walls of Undal City embraced them. In the east, in the shadow of the keep, Tomas could move unfettered by prying eyes, and the stores took the choicest pieces from the trading ships that moved up the coast from Isken and beyond.

The day before, Tomas had reported to the castrum up near the forest gate, climbing the polished marble stairs to its arches and domes and vaulted halls. He had waited dutifully, sweating in the cold with worry about the satchel left in his rooms at the keep, below a floorboard. They had tersely updated him as little as they politely could on their progress with the runewands he had delivered – metal rods with faceted gems at their tip, each gem incised minutely with runes, the patterns calling to the deeper pattern beneath. Some would shoot beams of pure force; others could cut like a razor or send forth sheets of flame. The wand he had held back from his supposed superiors was now snug up his left sleeve in a custom holster, tight against the flesh of his wrist. The update had been brusque, with no progress of note to report. He was not a researcher of the castrum, nor an instructor. He was primus of a stormcastle, but the clout that would bring him within the Stormguard was held in low regard by the abstract skein-researchers of the castrum.

Up their own arses, he thought, and grimacing he spat in the street as he slowed to enter his target store in the east ward. The store's sign was a chisel crossed with a hammer surrounded by a filigreed wreath of ivy. With a quick glance to check the street was empty, Tomas ducked into the shop and in less than a minute was back on the cold street, a thin box of smoothed and varnished wood clasped in his hand. It was a foot and a half in length, the wood dark and thickly grained, but perhaps only two inches deep. Heavy hinges of iron played along one long edge, and on the other a metal rectangle with no hole or marking whatsoever.

Grinning, Tomas briskly walked to a side alley and turned to face the corner of a chimney flue at the back of some noble's townhouse. The alley was empty save a sprawl of litter, scraps of rotting food and torn paper and cloth. With a wrench Tomas pulled back the goggles covering his eyes, and he blinked. He could let nobody see his eyes, not since he had focused on the dagger of Varratim, the god-killing blade once wielded by Tullen One-Eye himself. The blade honed with the death of an unknown number of children, sacrificed on Varratim's black stone altar deep in the mountains.

In the gloom of the alleyway the pupils of Tomas's eyes spiralled and split and reformed and danced, growing, shrinking, multiplying then merging, an endless dance. He could always see the skein now, and when he looked at his reflection in the mirror of his rooms his eyes glowed like stars, so much denser than the pattern of life around them. In the alley, staring down at the box, he could see that the metalsmith had followed his instructions and fashioned him a skein-lock. The metal latch was inoperable from the outside, and could only be opened with a push of telekinetic energy through the skein. *Should be enough to keep Artollen out, at least,* he thought, his mouth twisting at the thought of her.

Floré Artollen had left him crushed beneath a tree bough, pinned to the remnants of a crashed and cracked orb of light they had piloted from the Blue Wolf Mountains. She had left him to burn in the wreckage, unable to lift the bough, and while he could not argue with her results, Tomas was finding it difficult to be wholly magnanimous with her. *I would have done the same thing,* he thought to himself, *but that doesn't mean I need to forgive her.*

Tomas didn't remember forcing the bough from his chest with the skein, didn't remember Orubor hands dragging him free from the burning wreckage. He remembered the pain in his ear, his jaw, as he awoke broken and bloodied and burnt. He remembered lying close to death, his mind latched to the pattern of the skein, and not a hundred yards away a brightness, a pattern so large and complex and insane that it had sent his mind reeling, panicking, away. *Anshuka*. A judge: a god. Asleep, but still so much more than he could have fathomed.

He had awoken in the back of a cart, days later, on the rough road south from Orubor's wood back towards Undal City. He had awoken scarred and pained, but better than he had any right to be – when he investigated himself in the skein, focused deep on his bones and flesh, he could see where he had been mended. Burrs and eddies and concentrations and links in the pattern, little recurring patterns. He remembered laughing for a long time in the back of the cart, laughing until he was coughing, laughing until the girl Yselda came and pressed a cloth to his head and told him to be still. *They stitched me with the skein!* Tomas had been injured before at the Stormwall, and the whitestaffs there could speed along healing, perhaps staunch a wound or knit a bone, but nothing like what the Orubor had done. Nothing with that level of subtlety. He had thought himself nearing the peak of what could be known for a skein-mage, but the Orubor, the Orubor and the image of Anshuka, resplendent, were enough to make him realise how much further he could go.

In the alleyway, Tomas unclicked the skein-latch and the front latch of his box with a thought, and it fell open. Inside, a layer of thick, padded cotton over a layer of lead. After unclasping the three straps on his satchel Tomas drew the knife of Varratim then froze at a sound to his right. Turning with a snarl and brandishing the dagger, Tomas faced... a kitten. Black and flea-bitten, eyes crusted and whiskers on one side singed, the kitten took a step from the pile of refuse and mewled at him. Tomas let out a breath and laughed, and slipped Varratim's dagger into the case, the black blade of obsidian and the hilt of worn bone, the pommel stone a faceted emerald the size of a knucklebone. It was cosseted close in the cotton padding and he could not bring himself to look directly at it with the skein – he had to hold it in the periphery of his vision. Lying in Anshuka's meadow close to death, grasping at the skein desperately, Tomas had sought to escape the inferno of Anshuka's sprawling complexity and the dagger had been there, left in the grass.

It was a nexus, a point, a full stop. It was a concatenation of pattern, a drinker of complexity. The absolute enemy of entropy, it would take pattern and movement and distil them to a final point of energy. There was no disorder in the blade, no randomness. It was in itself absolute, so different to the variegated patterns of living beings. Next to Anshuka it seemed so quiet, but around the blade Tomas could sense chaos as order broke down, as the very fabric and laws undermining the universe failed as they grew close to it, as they spent time close to that ultimate concentration. So close to such order, their own patterns could not but fail. If Tomas looked at the blade in the alleyway he might stay all day, might awake soaked with rain. *I must stay the course,* he thought. *I've miles left to go.*

With a start he stumbled back. The black kitten had stepped forward and stood on its hind legs, its forepaws pressing at the tops of his boots, claws extending, eyes wide. With his skein-scarred eyes he saw the shape of the hidden mechanism below the simple metal clasp, the lock with no key. A mote of pressure and strong pins slid into place, and the dagger was safe. The researchers at the castrum seemed to think a thin layer of lead might dampen the ability of someone like a whitestaff from being able to track an object or a person, but with his skein-scarred eyes he could still sense the way pattern altered around the knife, even through the lead. *Perhaps more dimly. Would I have been able to see it before?*

The kitten mewled wetly and Tomas pressed the knife box into his satchel, slipping the straps closed. With his goggles still raised he stooped down and in one hand scooped the kitten up, bringing it close to his face. Their eyes met, Tomas's pupils dancing and breaking and spinning, coruscating, bursting to fractal geometries and condensing again. The kitten's eyes were yellow, their pupils clear slits of blackness. Through the grime he could see a patch of white in its black fur at its chest. The kitten stared at him and he drew it closer to his face and with a quick lunge it bit the end of his nose, a playful nip.

In the skein it was a little thing, but still so complex. The more he stared the deeper the pattern went – its thought, its potential, its past, what was inside and out and around, its connection to the world and the forces around it, a million trailing links outward. Before his eyes had changed, if he had focused Tomas might have seen the strongest of those links, the brightest of those patterns, but now he could see so much more. *Such depth.* With a shudder he pulled his mind back, forced himself to concentrate on the layer of normal vision below the dancing web of the skein.

'Ha!' Tomas said. 'A mighty beast indeed! I have killed Orubor in the shadow of their own trees, have ridden the mad orbs of Varratim, have fought demons in the rotstorm and in the caverns of their ancient masters. You must fear me, beast!'

The kitten tried to bite him again but Tomas held it firm in his gloved hand and pulled his goggles down. Glancing down the alley he could see no other life, no mother, no brothers or sisters. The cat was alone. At his hip, the satchel with the dagger hung heavy. Tomas had been so sure when he decided to take it. *What would the Orubor do – lock it away?* It was a weapon, and his people were at war. *I could save them all,* he had thought, and he had believed it. Now with the dagger in his possession he did not know what to do. *I must learn to unlock its power.* Already he could see more than any skein-mage alive. In his room at the keep when he reached for the patterns he had learned, he found them faster, and though they still took so much from him, his paths to the pattern were so much more efficient. *Is this what a skein-wreck feels?*

Tomas took a last glance at the alleyway, and in his hand the kitten mewled again piteously.

'A worthy foe at last, perhaps, and one I'd happily dance the dance of magic and death with,' he said, and held the tiny cat close to his chest, turning to the cold streets and the gusts blowing in from the salt black sea, 'but for today we've a ship to catch.'

~

'Why would they try to kill the knight-commander?' Yselda asked. Her new commander sniffed and ignored her, perusing her knapsack with her good hand, the other wrist bound tightly in a sling and held close to the chest. Commander Arfallow's rooms were the same in size as the rooms Commander Artollen shared with Marta, but the walls were bare and no rugs broke the cold of the flagstone floor. Yselda shivered and let her hand trail to the hilt of her longsword – *no shortsword now, not for a private.* She blushed at the pride of it, the softness of the silk sword-knot trailing between her fingers, its green so vivid. Her tunic was the blazing red of the Stormguard commandos. After Starbeck's guards had dragged away poor Banner and the knight-commander had left, Commander Artollen had taken her and Cuss to the quartermaster. Tomas had made his excuses, and Floré left Benazir behind in case Marta awoke.

'Two new commando privates, Hollow and Grantimber,' Floré had said, 'to steward for myself and Bolt-Commander Arfallow. Tunics, blades, boots, bags. We leave in the morn so I'd appreciate your help, with apologies for the hour.'

The quartermaster in Protector's Keep was a grey-haired woman with a long nose and twinkling eyes who held her hands out to the two cadets and bowed her head to Commander Artollen with a smile. The garrison stockrooms were laid out behind her, shelves and piles and racks, weapons and shields and tabards piled high.

'*Bolt-Commander* Artollen, my dear, of course,' she said. 'With my congratulations on your promotion. I've a package for you as well, courtesy of the boss!'

She passed Floré a paper-wrapped bundle, clearly a scabbarded blade and some other item, and a letter attached. The commander grimaced as she took it.

'My thanks, Marsen,' she said, and then had left Yselda with Cuss and the quartermaster with instructions to fetch their things from the cadets' barracks and meet back in her rooms straight away. Marsen had hurried to and fro, collecting boots, measuring arms and hips and legs, piling the kit high as Yselda had looked on with a mix of horror and pride. *Do I want this?* She had responded so quickly to the knight-commander. *But what was I meant to say? Salem Starbeck, the leader of the whole protectorate!*

'Do you want this?' she had said, her voice a whisper as Marsen searched for knapsacks, and Cuss had looked at her in the dull glow of the room's candles and shrugged.

'Commando seems a good step to putting down some more crow-men,' he said, lifting the silver-bladed dagger from the top of his clothes pile. 'What else is there? Da is dead. Ma is dead. Petron is dead. Little Jana is dead. Everything I know is gone, Yselda. What else can I do but fight? Where else could we go?'

Yselda had stared at him. Cuss who had never killed a chicken, kind Cuss who never had a bad word to say of anyone and loved to swim and climb trees and row his little boat out onto Loch Hassel to fish. Big Cuss who was still big, but harder now, his face strained, his eyes dark. Cuss had looked at his dagger and had not met her eye.

'A Hawk dagger, that,' Marsen said, returning to them folding a shirt made of stitched panels of boiled leather. 'Silver blade, tapered point, skull-cracker on the pommel. Perfectly weighted for throwing, sharper than Anshuka's claw – mark me on that!'

Cuss held the blade reverently, but Yselda primly pushed hers back to the quartermaster.

'I've my own,' she said, and bared enough of her own blade that Marsen might see the silver sheen.

'Aye indeed, young miss,' the woman said, her face inscrutable. Cuss had lost interest in his dagger only when Marsen measured and fit him for his own steel gauntlets, heavy fists of dark iron with a snug leather glove within, a ridge across the knuckle for slotting silver coins when the fighting grew close. Only silver or fire would kill a demon; Yselda had seen that much for herself. As Marsen cinched them tight across his wrists and Cuss flexed his fingers, Yselda saw the look of fear that crossed his face as quick as the shadow of a bird on water. She thought of the questions she knew she should ask herself. *What are you afraid of, Cuss? Where you've been or where you're going?*

The next morning, waiting for Benazir – *No, Commander Arfallow*, she scolded herself – to head for the docks in the dawn light, Yselda felt the weight of her own gauntlets at her hip, hooked on her belt. Her hands felt clumsy when she put them on, as if everything was at a remove. The clothes didn't feel right, not the new supple leather armour, the fresh shirt beneath. Not the longsword, despite her pride in its weight. The red tabard felt gaudy with its gold trim and lightning bolt compared to her simple green rough cadet's tabard of the Forest Watch. *Am I a commando? I've never even seen the storm!*

'Decapitation works well,' Benazir said, slipping her bag up onto her good shoulder. Yselda started.

'What?' she said, and Benazir sniffed.

'Decapitation. Why would the reformists try and kill the knight-commander? Judges' girl, you asked *me*.'

'Yes, of course,' Yselda said, flustered, and swung her own pack with its spare clothes on her back. She had nothing else, no memento of home. In her room at the Goat and Whistle Inn in Hasselberry, there was the locket her mother had given her, a charm of carved wood on a knotted cord. She never wore it for fear of breaking it, but kept it hidden beneath a floorboard. *Is it still there? Will I ever see home again?*

Home. The pines of Hookstone forest grew straight and true, north of Loch Hassel, not the twisted trunks and gnarled limbs of the woods twisted by the winds closer to the Star

Coast. Yselda's mother and father had raised their cottage themselves, seeking the peace and quiet of the forest. Her father hunted mushrooms in the dank undergrowth and stickling pine needles of the forest, his slender hands plucking tender stems. When he returned from the forest he would bring her wood sorrel and dew-wet bluebell flowers, gently presenting them between rough fingers. Her brothers Robern and Fraser had no interest in plants, only the little boat moored on the loch's bank, but Yselda would stare with utter concentration, trying to see every part and intricacy of each plant. She liked the unique configuration of each one, every blade of grass its own thing. Her brothers would drag the boat down the shore and paddle in the shallows of the bay, but Yselda would help her father sort his bag of mushrooms on the grass in front of their house and he would smile.

'Not that one, love,' he would say, taking a mushroom that to her was identical to a dozen others he had approved of. He would point to a frill, a discoloration, a worry, and grind the offending stem into the dirt with his heavy boots. His explanations used words she didn't understand but she followed his word as law. When she roamed the woods near the cottage with Fraser and Robern, they carelessly plucked graystems and tawny dancers as if they were horse mushrooms, and laughed at her and pulled her braid when she tried to stop them.

Her mother hunted deer with her longbow, ranging away for days at a time and returning with skins and butchered meat. She didn't speak much, simply worked, correcting any mistake or trouble with a gentle hand rather than a word. One Deadwinter she had given Yselda a locket of carved wood, a simple oval of smooth oak with a char across it, a stain of black down deep that had been polished smooth. 'From a lightning tree,' her mother had said, all of them warm in the cottage. They could hear the singing from Hasselberry, across the loch, and in the depths of that cold night they had stepped out onto a dusting of snow when the bells rang and the villagers sent a thin paper lantern up to the sky.

'Praise Anshuka,' her father had said, and her mother had held Yselda and Robern close.

Yselda remembered wolves and ice and snow, the frozen loch. Blood on white. The last Claw Winter was now eight years past, but Starbeck said it was here again. Clutching her sheathed sword to her hip, Yselda ran the silk of the sword-knot between her thumb and the wrapped leather of the hilt. *I can never go home.*

In the dark of Protector's Keep, Benazir whistled sharply and motioned to the door.

'You need to wake up, girl,' she said, and Yselda hurried to open it. As they marched from the castle into the diffuse dawn light she realised she hadn't eaten breakfast. The sun wasn't visible and the sky was a pale grey that seemed to pull the colour from everything, even her new tabard so freshly dyed.

'Did you want food, Commander? I can fetch some from the kitchens.'

Benazir shook her head. 'Bakery,' she said. 'Might as well enjoy it while we have the chance.'

They walked in silence through the labyrinth of Protector's Keep, from the castle at its centre through courtyards and stables, soldiers everywhere nodding to Commander Arfallow with respect or saluting her with fingertips to forehead. Yselda felt a damn fool, her hair too short, clothes that weren't her own, and the longsword kept swinging behind her and catching on doors. They walked out through the gates and into the quiet cold of Undal City, and she felt a sense of utter fear at the warren of streets in every direction. *The buildings are too tall to see landmarks,* she thought; *how in the blazes do they ever find their way?* Benazir strode on, no taller than Yselda, slight and weakened by her terrible injuries, and yet swaggering forward as if she owned the city. When they reached the nearest bakery she sent Yselda in with a handful of copper pennies and they walked the last few streets eating fresh loaves stuffed with a sharp goat's cheese.

'The reformists want less power to the Stormguard on the Grand Council,' Benazir said around a mouthful of bread, and Yselda hurried to keep up with the older woman's quick march. There was no sword at Benazir's side but Yselda could see four of those black-handled Hawk knives sheathed at her hip, another at the top of each boot. One of them had a hilt of wrapped red leather where the rest were black.

'Kill Starbeck, they send a message that the miners, farmers, fishers, *whatever*, aren't to be put aside. The council must direct the blade, not the other way round and all that. Given that we face powers utterly beyond comprehension, ancient magic and technology that defy our every defence, and a literal invasion of storm-bred monstrosities slavering to rip our little country to shreds, I'd say they can fuck off, to be honest. Reform when the war is done.'

Yselda chewed on her bread and fell back a step to let a woman pushing a cart laden with broken crab pots wheel past her. Rushing her feet, she caught up to Benazir.

'Haven't we been at war for three hundred years?' she asked. Benazir stopped short and turned to face her, locking her gaze.

'There is guarding the borders, and there is *war*, Private,' she said, her tone rigid. 'We never push them further than the line we drew. We never take what paltry resources they have past there. They attack us, *we attack them harder.* The only force that violence respects is itself.'

Benazir swept her arm behind her and Yselda realised they had reached the east harbour of Undal City. Where dozens of trading cogs and caravels should have been there were a scant half-dozen bigger ships. Of the smaller fishing ships many were tied up tight under taut tarpaulin, and entire arms of dockyard and pontoon were abandoned.

'*This* is war, Private,' Benazir said, and shook her head. 'They are blocking the waterway south to Riven, yes, but also east to Isken somehow. Rumours of beasts in the water. Wyrms, perhaps. Half our trade comes along the Star Coast, the other half the Star Coast road. Now boats that sail out don't return, even if they hug close to the shore and far from the wild reefs. The rust-folk are tightening a noose. Have you seen the refugees?'

'Yes,' Yselda said, and swallowed. 'Cuss and I went to the forest gate. We saw the camps outside the walls. It is good they escaped, I suppose.'

Benazir laughed and threw her head back.

'Good?' she cried, '*Good?* Do you think mercy stayed the rust-folks' blades? You think those folks *escaped*? They can shoot fire from the sky, girl; they can wreak death and destruction at a scale not seen in our lifetime. They did not let them flee through some mercy, Yselda. Every refugee is a tale of horror about their dark magics and monstrosities to undermine our resolve, a tale of walls battered down with beams of light, of Stormguard hung from every tree as if nooses were going out of fashion. Every refugee is a mouth we must now feed, with our farms empty, our trade half lost, and a Claw Winter looming. No late harvest, not this year. The rust-folk have finally picked up a bloody book of their own history. We have had three hundred years of holding back monsters and the occasional band of desperate rebels or opportunistic fools. A rotsurge every year or two and the scum that it spawns to put to the sword. They took Fallow Fen, we took it back. This is different. This is *war*, Private. The reformists need to stay the hell in check or they'll be routed and hung for no other reason than to remove the distraction.'

Yselda bit her lip but before she could respond she saw Commander Artollen and Cuss emerging from a street parallel to them, each clutching a loaf of bread in one hand. The four of them gathered and Cuss chewed at his bread. He looked tired, dark bags under each eye, but Yselda couldn't help but smile at the sight of him in the red tabard, a longsword at his waist. *Cuss from Hasselberry,* she thought, *commando of the Stormguard.*

'You went to Gerren's?' Floré asked, and Benazir nodded. Floré shook her head. 'Amateur move, Bolt-Commander. Every cadet in the keep could have told you Bellentoe is the better baker. I thought you were meant to be the master of the Balanced Blade, of strategy and information? I'd have thought you better informed.'

Benazir leaned forward and peered at Floré's twisted brown plait of bread and raised an eyebrow, sighing in disapproval. 'You must learn not to take all your direction from cadets, dear Floré.'

Distracted, Yselda looked out at the ships. One was taller than the others, with two masts, one of which was as tall as any building surrounding the harbour. *Basira's Dance,* she thought. The water of the harbour was grey verging on black, gentle waves lapping. The east harbour was protected from the wind by the high city walls, and a few hundred yards of walled waterway curved from the harbour to the ocean to keep the worst of the swell at bay. The tall ship bobbed and it was the only craft Yselda could see that was alive, with sailors calling to each other, fussing with ropes, climbing the... *rigging? Is it called rigging?* She gave a start when Commander Artollen suddenly placed her hand on Yselda's shoulder and stared down at her, stone-faced.

'Tabard suits you,' she said, and Yselda eventually managed a smile and followed the rest of them down to the docks, the remains of her breakfast loaf twisted tight in her fist.

6

The Wind Sea

'Knight-Commander, we followed Captain Sorren and his troop west towards Garioch. We found fresh graves a day onward; appears to be two of his men – potential in-fighting? Several farmers passed him without any severe issue, only questioning on the land and their heritage and origin. He offered all he passed a gold piece to inform on any suspected rust-folk in their midst. All we spoke to claimed to have known nothing, and said nothing, but this evening we came across a crossroads with four corpses, and Lothal's eye daubed once more: ⟨. *Sir, we estimate his strength at forty men or more. Arrest seems unwise. We will dispense what justice we can, but may require further aid.' – **Second report on the massacre at Crowpit**, Agent Haysom, Third Moon Trading House

When they reached the ship Floré found their reinforcements assembling at the quayside: Stormguard commandos bundled in heavy cloaks, laughing and comparing gear. Set slightly apart, Tomas stood clutching... *is that a kitten?*

Floré shook her head. With Tomas stood Voltos Thirdskin, the Antian who had been her friend, had been *Janos's* friend when they were at the wall. The Antian who advised first Starbeck and then Benazir as commanders of Stormcastle XII on tactics and lore, who provided a version of enemy eyes on every plan. Voltos was covered in black hair – the Antian were stocky dog-like creatures, though Floré was never sure if a mole would be a closer approximation. Short and furred, with streaks of grey through the black of his coat, and spectacles perched on his muzzle and held safe by a thin chain, Voltos looked up. When his blue eyes caught hers he grinned.

'My dearest captains,' he said, and Yselda muttered, 'Commanders.' Voltos's ears twitched and he waved a delicate hand, his sleeves of silk emerging from below a heavy cloak lined in fur. '*Commanders*. Tomas has been filling me in. I must say, I did not think to see either of you again after Ossen-Tyr, Cuss and Yselda. I am glad you are safe.'

Floré lowered her pack to the ground and rolled her shoulder, remembering the violence of Ossen-Tyr. She and Tomas and their companion Heasin the Tullioch had been abducted into one of the orbs of light there. According to Yselda, when that happened Voltos had learned of the assaults on the Stormwall and hurried west to reach Benazir.

'It seems you missed the fun in the mountains *and* the fun at the wall, my friend.' She reached a hand to his shoulder and drew him close for a moment. 'This time you will need to stay closer.'

Voltos patted her arm and drew back. 'Your daughter does not join us? I thought we were seeking her salvation. Should she not be with us?'

Floré kept her face passive even as her heart wrenched. Marta had wailed that morning, had wept, had screamed in rage. 'I'm going to find a cure for you,' she had told her, 'to make you all better.'

Marta heard none of it. She was inarticulate in her rage, eyes straining in their sockets as she screamed and beat her fists against her mother's legs. The furniture of Floré's room had shattered to flinders as the girl reached for an outlet to her rage and poured energy into the skein, before collapsing. Floré had fetched the Whitestaff Mallendroit, and Marta had been pale and listless and weeping when Floré finally left, utterly shaken. She had entrusted the girl to the orphans' barracks, with a dedicated guard and the whitestaff ready to run to her at any hour. *What else can I do, my love? Janos, is this right?*

The kitten in Tomas's arms mewled and he started speaking to it in low tones, his goggle-covered face pressed close to it. 'Yselda,' he said suddenly, not looking up, 'can you run and fetch me a skin full of milk for the wee one? I'm not sure she should be on to human scraps just yet.'

Floré shook her head at Tomas and turned back to Voltos as Yselda ran back up the quayside, her long scabbard swinging wildly behind her.

'Cuss, go with her,' she said, and once he had started jogging in that direction Benazir stepped forward and shook Voltos's hand formally.

'You were missed at the wall, my friend,' she said, 'you and Tomas both. Yet we prevailed, though the cost was great.'

Voltos bowed his head to her. 'I heard about your hand, I...'

'*No,*' Benazir said, her voice suddenly steel. 'That is a price

I would have given any day since I put on my tabard, Voltos. You think a hand makes me less able to serve? There is always work for the wounded, work for those who can't swing a blade. There is honour in service, Voltos, whatever form it takes. I speak of the dead. A heavy weight.'

Voltos bowed his head again. Floré scratched at the scars on her right cheek, the rune-scars left by Varratim, and glanced over at the commandos awkwardly waiting nearby, clearly watching them all. Shifting her cloak back, her hand fell to the hilt of the sword at her waist, the sword Starbeck had the quartermaster give her. The pommel was a simple weight worked with the design of Anshuka's claw: Y. The hilt was straight and newly wrapped in red leather, the cross guard a gentle arc of black steel curving towards the sheathed blade, turning the sword into an echo of the god-bear's rune. The feel of it made her arm twitch. *This will serve you better than I,* Starbeck had said in his note. Ever Undal, incapable of saying what he wanted to say in words, only ever in gesture and furtive glance and inference. Floré knew this was Starbeck's own blade, the blade he had won fighting deep in the rotstorm decades before. A Ferron rune-blade to make Benazir's old dagger pale in comparison.

A line of runes was repeated twice, once on each side of the long fuller groove that ran down the centre of the black steel of the blade: ᚷᚦᚴᚴᚦᚷ ᚹᛁᛗᛏ ᚠᚒ ᚠᛁᛏᚷ ᚷᚴᚴᚴᚷ. Floré did not know the meaning of the runes, or the dozens of patterns surrounding them just below the surface at the metal, ghost shapes that caught the light. She knew their effect.

She had tied the green sword-knot with the white stripe to the hilt and feeling the eyes of the waiting commandos she swung the scabbard under her cloak to hide its intricacies, the gaudy runes and patterns embossed along its length, red leather into black. Benazir glanced down and saw the hilt and her mouth twitched into a smirk.

'*Somebody* got a nice present,' she said, and Floré rolled her eyes and stepped forward and to attention.

'Form up,' Floré called, and as one the commandos dropped what they were doing to stand in a rigid line. Tomas had put the kitten down in a small empty crate and was tamping tobacco into his pipe, leaning against a pile of crates, expression inscrutable under his heavy goggles. Benazir and Voltos came to stand next to Floré.

There were ten of them, and a quick glance told Floré Starbeck had done them a kindness. These were no green recruits. Six corporals, lean and weathered, a sergeant with a face that betrayed no hint of emotion except simmering anger, and three mages who stood slightly apart.

'I am Bolt-Commander Artollen,' she said. 'This is your mission lead, Bolt-Commander Arfallow, formerly of Stormcastle XII. Tomas-Primus will lead our skein-mages, and Voltos Thirdskin is adviser to Commander Arfallow.'

Floré strode up and down the two loose ranks the soldiers had fallen into and felt warm as she inspected them, a hand going to straighten a buckle, a lingering gaze on a dagger sheathed somewhere unorthodox. *This is who I am,* she thought. She felt a prickle in her eyes as she pictured another life: Hasselberry and Janos and Marta, warm porridge and a village kept safe. Picturing Marta brought her calm today. *I am a weapon. I must be a weapon for her.*

Stepping back from the ranks Floré saw the sailors of *Basira's Dance* had stopped in their work and were leaning on the rails, watching them all. Amidst them a man with a long, intricately embroidered coat and ornate tricorn hat stood pensively. *Captain Muirgainas, I assume.*

Floré glanced back at Benazir, who nodded to her and then stood impassively at ease.

'The *words*,' Floré said, inclining her head to the waiting soldiers.

As one they replied. 'Stormguard, preserve the freedom of all people in the realm. Suffer no tyrant; forge no chain; lead in servitude.'

Floré nodded and flexed her right hand and gripped the hilt of Starbeck's sword. On her other hip Captain Tyr's old silver knife from Hasselberry was tucked safe. She stepped back and bowed her head to Benazir. *She must lead, and I must fight.*

Benazir took a step forward and ran her gloved hand over her scarred cheek slowly. 'Know this: Knight-Commander Starbeck himself passed us this mission. As we stand here the rust-folk are driving our people from the Northern Marches. Their orbs of light mutilate our livestock, send columns of troops fleeing for their lives. They build their defences and harvest our crops for the winter to come. Your people flee from their homes, hungry and afraid.'

Floré noticed Yselda and Cuss arrive back, stepping slowly to the side of the quay to avoid causing a scene. Each clutched a skin, presumably of milk, and they stared at Benazir. Yselda's eyes were fearful, but in Cuss Floré saw nothing but anger, and it broke her heart.

'Know this,' Benazir continued, her voice steady. 'We will drive them out. We will make them pay in blood for every drop they have spilled, tenfold. This is war, and for now we must take the longer view. Today we go south to Riven. Our mission, to free the whitestaffs from whatever barrier is holding them from their *duty*. Duty to the people of the realm. Duty to Anshuka. Duty to the fallen.'

Benazir trailed off and Floré saw her eyes move from the commandos to the middle distance. With a swift step she was in front.

'You heard her! Get the ship loaded, full briefing when we clear harbour. Captain!' she called, turning to the ship. 'We would discuss our plans if it would suit.'

From the railing of *Basira's Dance* the captain stared down at them and nodded dourly. Gesturing with one arm to the gangway from quay to ship, Floré saw that where his hand would have been instead a dull hook of metal wrapped in corded twine emerged from the sleeve of his jacket.

'Welcome aboard,' Captain Muirgainas said.

As the commandos trooped onto the ship Tomas puffed on his pipe and lifted the small crate the kitten was in, twisting the knapsack at his waist around to his side. 'Do you think the food on this tub will be anything good?' Without waiting for an answer he stepped away and took his turn climbing the steep gangplank up to the ship.

Voltos snorted a laugh and watched him walk with Floré. 'You know,' he said, 'for some men, fighting demons and defending gods, crashing through the sky in orbs of blazing light, finding ancient magics... for some men I think that may have changed them.'

Floré pictured Tomas pinned beneath a tree bough against the dark stone of the crashed orb, flames all around, the fear in his eyes and the hate in his voice. A shiver ran up her spine and she simply shook her head and gestured for Voltos to head for the ship. When Voltos, Benazir, Cuss, and Yselda had mounted the gangway she made to follow and then stopped.

'Artollen!' called a voice. 'Artollen!' Floré peered up the dock and saw a boy of perhaps ten summers running towards her.

'Here!' she called, and the boy slowed to a walk. When he reached her at the dockside he was still red in the cheeks, the red clashing with the pale of his skin and the black of his hair. The boy was clad in tattered clothes. *Too thin for this weather,* Floré thought, *boy and clothes both.*

'What is it, lad?' she asked, and with a flourish the boy produced a letter from within his shirt. It was crumpled, plain brown paper tied with twine and sealed with wax. No sigil marked the seal. Floré reached out her hand but the boy snatched the letter back.

'Fella said you'd give me a gold coin for this, and you weren't at the keep, but they said I might catch you, and I ran all the way!' he said, and Floré's arm snapped forward and gripped him by the shoulder. As he yelped she snatched the letter from his hand and then shoved him back gently and checked it. No name, no address, no markings at all. Ignoring the boy, Floré opened the letter and within saw two items. There was no note. A knot of red silk with a strip of white in it, a familiar knot: her sword-knot. With trembling fingers she reached into the envelope and felt the dampness of the silk. Silk cut from the robes of Mistress Water. Silk awarded to her for gallantry in the rotstorm, for fighting demons in the shadow of the Ferron god-wolf Lothal himself. *With Janos at my side.* The sword-knot was held in a little loop of rough string tied tight, one tail of string trailing.

Floré let the envelope drop and clutched the silk. Peering

at the string she could see it was knotted complexly, a dozen turns… *a hangman's noose.* Floré shivered, and she pictured the noose hanging over the inn in Ossen-Tyr. *The inn where I lost my sword.* She could picture the leader of the gang who made their base there, a woman in a blue dress with a cruel mouth and a tumble of red hair. *A woman I beat into the dirt.* She stared at the boy.

'Who gave you this?' she said, and he shrugged, feeling at his shoulder where she had grabbed him. Floré knew this could only mean trouble. *But trouble for my return,* she thought, *not for now.*

'Fella,' he said and Floré blinked and stared up the quayside. The docks were silent in the morning light, the only sound her own breath and the lapping of waves and the creaking of ropes and wood. Floré bit her lip and dug a gold coin from her belt pouch and pushed it into the boy's hand, ten times the amount he should be getting for delivering a simple message.

'Buy a warm hat,' she said, and grabbing her bag of gear from the dock she stalked up the gangway and onto *Basira's Dance.*

~

'I just sail,' Captain Muirgainas said when Floré introduced herself. 'I sail you to Riven, I wait, I sail back. You keep your soldiers away from the sheets and sails, and we'll do fine. No pirates this far west – nowhere to go after Undal City but the Stormwall and the blight-waters, and pirates won't risk the reefs between here and Iskander. Heard about the boats not coming back. The *Dance* will outrun anything this side of Carob's Strait, and we know paths through the reefs that the Undal haven't dreamt of. We run fast; we run quiet.'

The man was surly and dour-faced and Floré was more than happy not to get involved with the crew of *Basira's Dance*. As the ship left Undal she stood at the rear railing and watched the city walls recede. She couldn't remember if the back of the ship was named the bow or the stern. She had been out in the small boats on Loch Hassel a handful of times, once to check sabotaged fishing traps in a dispute between neighbours, once to cross quick to an outlying farm where screams had been heard – a woman beating her wife bloody with an iron pan, it turned out, after she caught her with one of the farmhands. The waters of Loch Hassel were calm and blue, not this iron-cold nightmare of white-tipped waves and endless horizons.

The rolling of the ship in the waves made her stomach ache and she was gripping the railing hard, but the whole world still seemed to sway. Yselda stood a few paces from her looking similarly troubled, but Cuss was at the front of the ship with a few of the corporals, no doubt listening to their stories as they bragged about the rotstorm. The ship passed the old Ferron lighthouse just outside the harbour, a mirror to the one in Dal a few miles up the coast closer to home. This one the Undal sailors called *False Friend*. Like the lighthouse at Dal it rose from the waves, a sheer column of seamless black stone a hundred feet straight up. It was the same dark seamless stone as the Ferron overseer forts, including the fort that made up the foundation of Protector's Keep; the same dark stone as the Ferron slave roads that Undal still used for trade with Isken. *The same dark stone the orbs are made of,* Floré realised. Of all Undal perhaps only she and Tomas had been inside one of those orbs of light and lived to tell, but they were the same seamless dark stone as the lighthouse, with a crystal strip bisecting horizontally, the interior a mix of metal and crystal and stone that should be too heavy to exist, let alone fly.

Floré stared at the lighthouse. It still called true of a safe passage to harbour, but a century back it had acted as a beacon to the Isken navy when they had assaulted the city under the rule of their now dethroned princes. A hundred years may pass, but the Undal could hold a grudge. A hundred foot up that shaft of dark stone was an opaque glass orb that shone all night with a warm yellow light. In the cool of the morning, the glass or crystal of the orb was dim. Floré shook her head. Tomas knew all of what she knew, and likely more. The mysteries of the orbs were not her mission. Her focus needed to be sharper. *Marta is all that matters.*

The air seemed even colder out there at sea, as the coast fell away from them. Floré pulled her new commander's cloak close – the shoulder was trimmed in fur, the interior lined with thick fleece. Marta's fingers had pulled at the fleece that morning when she said farewell, when she handed her daughter to the orphans' barracks. The Stormguard had always taken orphans, given them hearth and home, trained them into soldiers for the protectorate. Floré felt a flush of shame. Marta had lost her father, and now her mother was abandoning her. Floré knew it had to be done but she could not convince Marta of that – Marta so young, so frail.

Whitestaff Mallendroit had promised her to check in on her every day. The children's barracks were painted in bright pastel colours, yellow and blue, and some children played games even so early in the morning. Floré had forgotten the children playing games. The orphan barracks in Undal were a far cry from the austere barracks she had called home as a child, but the games felt the same. *Run for the bear; spear in the mud.* As she sailed from Undal City, she remembered Marta sullen and silent in the arms of a member of the keep staff, and the other silent and sullen children in the barracks beyond – new orphans of the fighting in the Northern Marches, or the attacks of the orbs before that. Only a few had been playing games, those who had been there long enough to forget where they came from.

Will she forget me?

Floré let her tears flow. There was nobody to see them save Yselda, and the girl seemed lost in her own troubles. As the cold bit at her fingers Floré reached beneath her heavy red cloak and unhooked the gauntlets from her belt. New gauntlets. A gift from Starbeck, wrapped up with the sword, passed to her by the old quartermaster. She pulled the gauntlets on. They were black steel, truly black, and where most Stormguard gauntlets had a ridge to clip in a silver coin in case of a last desperate fight against a demon, these gauntlets had an entirely silver knuckle ridge protruding outward, and on the back of each fist the claw of Anshuka was embossed proudly: Y. The gloves below the metalwork were a supple red leather.

Floré sighed. She hated them. She liked her own gauntlets, the gauntlets that had seen her through storm and strife – no ornamentation, only pure utility. These were for show. She had no trust that the silver ridge would last more than one fight. Her own gauntlets were at the bottom of her kitbag.

With her hands covered, Floré wiped her eyes on the back of her sleeve and checked on Yselda.

'All fair, Private?' she asked, and the girl came to from her stupor with a few blinks.

'Aye, Sergeant. *Captain.* Commander! Sorry.'

Floré smiled at her. 'Nash and Esme would be proud of you, Yselda,' she said, 'your parents as well. The commandos are the best of the Stormguard.'

Yselda shrugged awkwardly, her fingers running against the trim of her tabard. Her new gauntlets were hooked on her belt.

'I'm not sure I deserve it,' she said at last. Floré eyed her up and down. Yselda had ever been her most dutiful cadet but the girl had seen horrors in the last Claw Winter, her family taken by the wild wolves that had descended to Hookstone forest from the Cimber hills. She had seen worse since then, her adopted family lost in the orb attack on Hasselberry. *There is fear in her,* she thought, *perhaps too much.*

'Put on your steel,' Floré said, tapping the girl's gauntlets, 'and remember the knot on your hilt. It is time to learn the Gauntlet. Benazir will show you some of her tactics and strategies of the Balanced Blade, but one without the other is useless. You need the strength to back up your cunning.'

The two spent the morning going through defensive and offensive use of the gauntlets and the new longsword at Yselda's hip. Cuss joined them when he saw what they were about, and the handful of corporals not set to watching the seas as well. Floré knew that, since the burning of Urforren and the campaign before, her own actions in the Stormguard had become something of a tall tale to the newer recruits. They did not work on footwork or sparring, with the roll of the deck below them, but stances and posture.

'Is it true you flew an orb?' one of the corporals asked as she corrected his knife grip, and the rest fell silent.

'If you're stabbing someone in the chest, hold the blade horizontally – it's less likely to stick on a rib that way,' she responded, then scratched the scar below her right eye. It was itching. They were heading west along the coast, hugging close so the reefs wouldn't bother them. Once they were in line with the island of Iskander they would head south. She presumed the captain knew some waymark to pick his way through the brutal reefs. It was a longer course than the other ships had taken, a course that seemed at first to lead them away – *but none of the other ships returned*. High above, the clouds were a pattern of herringbone blowing from west to east, herringbone against a pale blue. Across the deck sailors dutifully fussed with ropes and sails and all sorts, all of them wrapped up tight against the cold.

'Sir?' the corporal said. Floré drew her own dagger and showed him the correct grip for stabbing.

'Don't just thrust,' she said, 'use their weight against them. If you can get them falling onto your blade, all the better.'

She demonstrated with a piece of wood in her hand, pulling the corporal down towards her, getting her front leg amongst his to scupper his attempts at righting his balance. They went through the motion a few times, and then she had him try it on her. The dull piece of wood had been slotted into a hole in the railing for no purpose she could see, but it was roughly the right length.

The next corporal along was a thin woman with pale skin and a tight braid of brown hair. Her eyes were a watery blue, her mouth wide. Floré nodded to the woman and she dropped into a knife-fighting stance. Floré circled her looking for flaws. With her foot she tapped the woman's left toes.

'Turn them out a little further for balance,' she said. The woman nodded and complied then came back to a standing position.

'I heard you flew an orb, crashed some other orbs, killed a dozen crow-men, and saved Anshuka all by yourself, sir,' the woman said with an almost hidden smirk. *Cocky,* Floré thought, *but was I any different?* The Stormguard commandos were the best of the best, and they faced hell in the rotstorm. If she had made it to corporal, the woman was probably right to be confident. Floré stared out at the sea to the south. The water was dark save for white-capped waves that seemed always to press against the ship. Floré turned and stared at the woman until the other's gaze dropped, then she leaned forward and straightened the corporal's tunic and tugged her gauntlets tight.

'Nonsense,' she said quietly, though she was sure the other commandos training with them could all hear her. 'I wasn't alone. Cuss and Yselda were with me.'

With that she gave a curt nod to the assembled troops and descended from the rear raised deck. *Is it the aftcastle? Is that what it's called?* The sailor at the helm stared after her as she left, and as soon as she dropped out of sight she heard the excited chatter of the corporals. She focused on her breathing, and allowed herself to think of Marta. *Would you like to sail, little one, across the ocean?*

Standing for a long moment in front of the closed door of her cabin, Floré closed her eyes and pictured the beach north of their house in Hasselberry, through the woods, the old rough pine trunk that served as a bench as they swam and played and built castles. In her mind it was crystal clear. Marta slept on a thick blanket and Floré lay where the sand met the forest grass with her head on Janos's leg, staring up at clouds above, no sound but the lapping of water and the fingertips of the towering pines lingering on one another as they swayed in the breeze, that faintest rustle of contact.

~

A day before Ashbringer entered Undal City she repeated her ritual, singing to the melody underlying the world, asking it a question. She sought the pattern of the blade, Varratim's blade. When last she had sought a vague suggestion of this the direction had come to her, but now she felt nothing, only cold. She had nestled herself high in an oak tree, a tree left by the Undal in one of their fields in the farmland surrounding the city. They left a solitary tree in each field – when it was used as pasture, the animals could shelter below its boughs. Ashbringer had thought it sad, a tree with no community around it, but as she dropped her mind into the pattern of the world and pressed herself against the trunk she felt the strength in the tree. It was still connected, root to soil, leaf and twig to air. It was still part of the cycle and the myriad dance of pattern.

Ashbringer let her focus deepen, let her senses expand until she could see no specifics in the pattern but great currents cutting across the world. Undal City to her south was a tangled morass, a village a mile west a smaller mote of complexity. A herd of deer in a copse a few miles north. A flock of sheep closer, and stray points of light, the creatures of the night. If she focused, any one of those would have an incredible complexity to it. The more you look at something the more you will always see, a recursive observational loop she had to avoid lest she spend the night focusing on a ladybug. The wheat in the field around her faded to a gentle haze, but she could have spent a day studying a single stalk.

Wherever you look, she thought, smiling, *there is something further to learn.*

She drew her eye further and further back and pushed to the limit of her senses and thought of the knife, that oddity in the skein. She focused on it, let the part of her mind that found patterns, the legacy of predation, hunt it down. If she looked at a tree twitching in the breeze her eyes would find the squirrel sat still on a branch; this was the same, on a much grander scale. The dagger was an oddity in the skein, and she would seek it. *Where does it come from, so different from everything else?* She could not begin to guess.

She did not find it. She could not feel it. She had almost closed off her connection but she felt a familiar presence, somewhere in the tangle of Undal City. *Deathless.* High in her oak, Ashbringer had pressed her palms together and blown out a long breath. *Tullen One-Eye is in Undal City.* The mad skein-wreck of the Ferron Empire, perhaps the greatest manipulator of the skein to ever live, Anshuka had cursed him to watch his people fall, to wander for eternity. He seemed unable to interfere, only able to wander and watch, unchanging, undying. Her charge was to kill him, as Anshuka bade her ancestor, but no blade or spell would bring him harm. *Anshuka tests my faith,* she thought, *and I must be true.* In the mire of Undal City she could not sense anything specific – only that somewhere in that throng, Tullen One-Eye was hiding.

Ashbringer entered Undal City the next night by the northern gate. The forest gate, they called it, though trees were in scarce supply. She had slipped boots over her feet so close to the city, and long gloves to hide her blue skin. She looked strange still, but a tall willowy woman clad in a dark cloak and carrying a pack and staff was not enough to warrant comment. It was cold enough that her scarf and hood looked like measures against the bite of the air, rather than attempts to hide her serrated teeth, the sigils scarred on her flesh, the taper of her ears. The Undal would think her a mad barbarian who ate human flesh and read minds. The thought made her smile.

When she reached the looming gate the guards were checking entrants in a random manner, opening carts and bags of any they thought looked suspicious. The gates were tall and wide and heavy, banded wood and iron below a rampart of stone and well-lit braziers. Everywhere there were Stormguard, patrolling. Ashbringer hung close to a cart and then cut behind one guard as he questioned its owner, leaning heavily on her staff and affecting a limp. The staff was simply her bow unstrung, the silver of its wood dulled with muck from the road. Her bristling quiver was slung beneath her cloak along with her broken sword and one of the wands taken from Varratim's corpse – a faceted gem of blue at the end of a simple metal rod.

Entering the city, Ashbringer saw the truth of the refugees. At the forest gate, in what had been the market square when last she visited, an impromptu tent-town had sprung, and people gathered around communal cookfires. She could hear children crying, could see wounds and fear. Stormguard were there in the severe grey of the City Watch and the vibrant blue of the Lancers, distributing food and warm clothing and blankets. Ashbringer stepped lightly from the market square and, along the avenues, the evening streetlamps flickered against the dark and cold. She felt cold stone through the thin soles of her boots and she walked fast.

The city had a pattern but Ashbringer loved the trees of the forest, and couldn't but pity those poor creatures straining for light and space amidst storeys of industry and the tumult of human life. She loved the calm of the forest, the exultation of the moor. The pattern of the city was a febrile thing, pulsing with life and chaos. The pattern of the forest was a quiet beauty, a moment measured in seconds and centuries. *I will never live in a city,* she thought, and laughed to herself. She knew as an Orubor she would never truly live anywhere outside of the wood surrounding Anshuka's sleeping form. She might leave, but ever it called to her.

Making her way through the northern ward of the town Ashbringer stopped for a moment at the base of the castrum, the protectorate's skein-mage centre for training and research. Eight years before, she had broken in there and spent a long week living in the attic, perusing tomes of research she thought might unlock the secret of killing Deathless Tullen One-Eye. There had been nothing to help. Most skein-wrecks seemed to heal better than other humans, but they still died, and normally if someone was in the process of murdering them, they certainly made sure. She passed the castrum with a little bow and made her way to Protector's Keep seeking the advice of the new Orubor ambassador there, Highmother Ash.

She did not make it.

She was still many streets distant when the orb of light came. It flew in low, from the north, a brilliant white light pouring from it in all directions, obscuring the form beneath. It was the size of a lumber wagon, an ovoid of light that cut through the sky as fast as any bird but unperturbed by currents of wind. Ashbringer heard the screams around her, and the few people on the street so late began to run for cover. She peered upward. The orb traced a lazy arc around the city then began to dance over it, cutting back and forth.

Falling behind it like autumn leaves, something trailed and flittered down to the ground. Ashbringer ran two streets to where it had passed and saw them on the ground. *Paper.* Twisting her head in confusion, she picked up the paper and read. On one side a map of the protectorate with NEW FERRON scrawled across the Northern Marches, a border drawn in stark ink. On the other side, three statements in neat type:

URFORREN AVENGED
Undal skein-wreck and war criminal THE SALT-MAN
has been killed
FERRON REFORGED
The rust-folk claim the Northern Marches of the
protectorate as our haven from the rotstorm
PEACE IN OUR TIME
No Undal shall enter the Northern Marches and live

Ashbringer licked her lips and glanced up at the orb, running a few steps to gain a better vantage as it flew over the city. All around her were cries now and shouts. The orb was circling the three tallest structures in the city in a lazy spiral: the dome of the castrum, the ramparts of Protector's Keep, and the sharp bell tower of Undal City's central shaman temple. As it circuited again, bolts of purple light flew from the orb and smashed into first the dome of the castrum, then the tallest tower of Protector's Keep, and finally the shaman temple spire. The orb slowed at that last and the beam of force was followed by a gout of white flame spewing down from the orb. For long moments, the stream of flame held and then the orb was rising upwards into the night. Ashbringer listened to the screams and curses, and watched the shaman spire burn. Slipping into an alley she huddled low and opened herself to the skein. *I must find the dagger. It is our only hope.*

She was not safe in an oak as she was the night before – she was squatting in the dirt and refuse of a side alley, the screams of the city all around her, cold stone and dead wood and fear everywhere. Still, she fell into the skein, and kept her breathing slow. She was in the storm of Undal City, the pattern of tens of thousands of human lives, the plants, the livestock, all of it a tumult of chaos as the orb took its leave and the city succumbed to fear.

She widened her inner eye further still until she could sense the city, and she felt her body trembling as her viewpoint expanded to cover the Star Coast. She sent an astral form of herself high into the sky to gain better vantage over the vast swathes of land below. The energy projecting like this took was immense, even for one as experienced as her. She felt as if she were flying high above the world: she could see the rotstorm in the west, picked out in the abstract geometry of skein-sight. It was chaos. Anshuka was an anchor to the north and west, and elsewhere cities and towns faded to blurs of light and pattern.

The dagger, she thought again, *I must find the dagger.* She still could not feel it. She felt for the trace of Tullen One-Eye again, yesterday somewhere so close to her but lost in the stream of complexity that was the city. She could not find him. She focused again on his pattern – a skein-wreck was something so different than a normal human. Instead of the infinitely complex loops and connection and potential and history that made up a person, a skein-wreck was at once more concentrated and porous. A pinpoint of much higher complexity that was itself connected more strongly to the universe surrounding it. She could sense him, focusing on that pattern. She knew him so well. He was not in the city – *somewhere south?* A pinpoint in the ocean, almost alone. She could say no more than that. Her view of distances was abstracted. He was gone from the city; that at least was certain.

Resigning herself to failure, her astral form began to shrink back from its overview of the world, still suffused in its net of nodes and knots and connections. She stopped sharp and began to hyperventilate.

She could sense a skein-wreck. Not Tullen One-Eye. South, further south in the sea – *an island?* Iskander! She focused in on the pattern, even as it sat beyond the limit of her sight, even as her strength failed, only a hint.

With a cough Ashbringer slammed back to her physical form and she sprawled in the alley, utterly exhausted. She convulsed alone, long minutes in the dark. Her nose bled and her bones ached as her limbs flailed and contracted, and when finally her muscles relaxed and she could curl herself to a ball she began to laugh and cry and smile all at once. High above, clouds of black and purple began to coalesce over Undal City and lightning began to crackle...

INTERLUDES: OBEISANCE TO THE MOUNTAIN

THE APPRENTICE AND THE BLACK IRON SEA

'The whitestaff must steel themselves to be kind, whatever is necessary. A bud must be pruned sometimes for the plant to thrive. We must be the guiding hand against hubris and ego. The Stormguard will keep us safe, but we must balance them. We must heal where they hurt, share knowledge as they guard their intelligence close. This balance is not antagonistic – we are symbiotic. They thrive as we thrive. We are not apart – we are of one protectorate, and one people, regardless of our disparate origins.' – *The Way of Riven*, Mistress Water

Hove tried not to die. Port Last was aflame, from the fishing docks pressed against the churning ice water of the Storm Sea to the stout castle that sat atop the blunt bailey hill. The castle was stone ringed in stone but black smoke spiralled from every arrow-slit and doorway, stark against the frigid autumn blue of the morning sky. Hove's gaze did not linger long on the castle; his eyes cut from shadow to shadow. It didn't seem right, the screaming, the death and blood, all right after breakfast. *This should be happening at night.* He cut down another side street, stumbling past a burning stable and pausing a half moment to listen for pursuers, feeling bile in his throat. He couldn't tell if the goblins or the rust-folk or the demons commanding them had seen him run. Over the port, an orb of white light burned, a second sun hanging so close to the towers of the keep.

Everybody in the castle was dead already; Hove had slipped down to the kitchens early to try and nab a fresh loaf before they ran out again. He'd snuck past the cooks and filled his mouth and pockets with bread when the yelling began, and then the servants and cooks were swarming the passage up to the courtyard. Hove had hung back, slipped another loaf into his loose cassock robes, and then moved up the back passage to the courtyard just in time to see everybody die. So he ran, and ran again, sobbing and slipping over muddy cobbles down through the back gate of the castle and out onto the streets of Port Last. The streets were full of yells and smoke. *Where had the fire come from?* Hove didn't know, but suddenly it was everywhere: the smithy roof was ablaze, and something near the west gate was throwing up great torrents of sparks and flame. That orb hung there, unmoving, over all of them. *The orbs.* For spans they had been seen, distant motes at night. Rumours from traders, of cattle left mutilated in their fields, horses desanguinated or burned to cinder... and of children taken. News was slow to reach Port Last.

The boats, Hove thought desperately, pushing his legs to move onward, forcing himself into the present; *goblins can't use boats.* Hove didn't know if that was true but it *sounded true. Who had ever seen a goblin use a boat?* If he could push out one of the little sailboats from the dock east of town, he could follow the coast east to Nullen or Sparrowpit and tell the fishers there to flee. *I could flee with them.*

A scream sounded from the harbourfront street ahead. Hove pulled back and pressed against the wall of a cottage. A man clad in linen with a simple leather cap sprinted past him towards the screaming, a wooden staff in hand, and disappeared around the corner. The scream ended in a wet staccato gurgle, then a chittering laughter, high-pitched and alien, and grunts and thumps. Hove realised he hadn't breathed in a long moment and sucked in a lungful of cold morning air, coughed at the taste of smoke. Around the corner, another scream, this time deeper, and more of the horrible laughter. Hove shook his head and backed away, pushing into the cottage door, and falling into a simple stone kitchen. He scrambled to a low table of rough driftwood and crawled beneath it.

'I'll just wait here, and they'll leave,' he said, repeating himself over and over, and realised he was speaking aloud, realised he was breathing heavy and soaked in cold sweat. Desperately he clutched at his plain white robes, splattered with mud and blood and worse, and grabbed the amulet his mother had given him. It was a simple circle of wood with Anshuka's claw burned in: Y. Hove always wore it under his robes, even when he became a whitestaff proper and they gave him the jade stone of Riven; he had promised his mother he would always wear it. He gripped the amulet and stared at the cottage door, waiting for monsters to break it down. He couldn't fight goblins and rust-folk and demons. He was a *whitestaff*, not even a true whitestaff: an apprentice! He just wanted to study the rock pools and the crabs of the northern shores, to read the old scrolls. He wasn't a skein-mage or a warrior.

Hove shut his eyes and bit his lip, feeling the cold of the floor seeping through his thin shoes, through his robes to thin knees.

'Mother, give me strength,' he said at last, unsure himself if he meant his own mother or the great god-bear Anshuka. He pushed his mind out in the skein, focused on the pattern within himself that could hook onto the pattern above and below and through everything.

Hove felt his sight drop away as a tangle and morass of light of every hue slid over his vision. Every object, every sensation had a pattern to it, and all of them appeared before him. He felt his breath catch at the calming immersion, so familiar from his studies. Slowly he pushed out his sense from the table, feeling the rest of the cottage for anything alive. He felt a scurrying knot in the skein five feet to his left and let out a low moan, and then a snorted exhalation of relief. *Mice in the pantry,* he realised, feeling the shape of them, as if he were seeing the mice inside and out and a moment before and a moment after, their intention, their past, their potential. Alive things were always easier to sense, little bundles and knots of complexity against the subtle backgrounds of air and earth and stone.

For a moment he saw himself within the pattern, the thrum of his own heart, could see the pale of his skin and the green of his eye and countless layers beyond. He shivered and pushed outward, feeling the strain in his temples and burning in his stomach as he forced his sense further. He breathed deep and felt warm again with the exertion. Master Wall was said to have been able to sense the skein for a mile around in its entirety, and Mistress Water had pioneered the paths to follow a single thread or connection an endless distance, focusing and pursuing that narrow link at the cost of the wider view. Hove couldn't do that. Hove could just push out, perhaps thirty feet—

He dropped his link to the skein as violently as he ever had and his vision cut back to the kitchen, the stone floor, his own scrawny hands coated in mud. He had sensed something... a chaos in the skein, somewhere behind the cottage in another building. A break in the pattern that lay beneath all things. His master had told him of this: a tempest. *Demon. I must run.* Hove breathed in three times fast and ran to the door and flung it open. Demons, *crow-men*, dark skein wizards of the storm. They would sense him, would hunt him, would kill him for sport – drink his blood and make dice from his bones. He felt it in his heart as sure as night follows day, as sure as stone.

Squinting in the morning light he ran headlong down the mud of the alley, away from the demon he had sensed, and then turned a sharp left and sprinted towards the harbourfront. *Goblins can't sail, goblins can't swim,* he thought, refusing to think of anything else. He did not try to be quiet. If the demons were in the town, hiding would do him no good. They would sense him. *I must run!*

When Hove emerged on the harbourfront he didn't slow down to glance at the harbour wall, the watchtower, or the fishing port. He determinedly didn't glance left at the Lover's Wings Inn where shapes lay on the cobbles of the road unmoving. He did not look down as he lengthened his stride to leap across the body of someone in a grey tabard, armoured, and he did not think about their blood soaking into his cheap cloth shoes. Hove ran and kept his eyes on the horizon. East of the fishing docks past the harbour wall he knew there were a half-dozen small boats with single sails for picking up crab pots.

He heard a yell and something clatter behind him but he was running and running and not looking and then he was almost at the wall. To his left the harbour and miles of choppy black sea and towering clouds, to his right the costermongers and warehouses of the seafront. The chandlery was ablaze, the usually neat coils of ship's rope scattered to the mud. Hove kept running.

As he reached the edge of the harbour and moved to run through the open gates, a goblin lurched out from around the harbour wall and Hove yelped, leaping to his left and slipping on the cobbles. As he scrambled to his feet it yelled out something but he pushed his hands into the cobbles and threw himself away. The goblin was perhaps four foot tall, clad in a ragged pelt wet with blood, and Hove heard himself screaming as it ran at him, brandishing a club of dark wood. Still scrambling on the cobbles, he threw up his arms. Its skin was a pebbled and rough grey, and as it smashed the club into his arms he saw its black orb eyes and its jagged rows of teeth. A slavering tongue hung from its mouth, sinuously twisting as the goblin hit him again and again. Each blow was a violation, explosions of pain reverberating down to his bones. He curled in on himself, tried to become stone, felt his chest burning from lack of air as he struggled to breathe and cry and plead and scream all at once.

'Please!' Hove managed to say at last, his arms over his face, and then there was a crunch and the blows stopped.

Shaking, he lowered his arms from his face and looked up to see a City Watch guard looming over him. Her helmet was gone and her grey tabard was soaked in black blood, her face dripping red from a vicious cut that ran from temple to jawline. Her hair was plastered with sweat and ash and mud and her eyes were wild.

The guard hauled Hove with one hand behind the harbour wall, then leaned out around to look down the street. She spat a mouthful of blood.

'You're an apprentice,' she said, and not in the tone of a question. Rolling her shoulders she started to look around them, the cottages and long racks of drying fish and nets to be mended, the high harbour wall. From their hiding place behind the wall, outside of the harbour and town proper, Hove couldn't see the keep but he followed her gaze and could see the dark torrents of smoke reaching up to the sky. In one hand the guard held a woodcutting axe, her grip halfway up its leg long handle.

'What did you see, boy? Are any alive in the keep?'

Hove pressed himself down closer to the wall and the shaking began again. He pressed at his fingers and face and arms. They hurt; they bled. One of his fingers was skewed off at an angle he didn't dare think about, and the world was fading around him. His breath was ragged. The guard gripped his face with her hand roughly and turned him to face her. Hove shook his head slowly. Her eyes were wide and her breathing fast.

'I saw them. Demons. Rust-folk. Goblins. They had everyone gathered in the courtyard but I was out. When I came back through the kitchen nobody was around. I saw them...'

Hove swallowed and closed his eyes again, clutching at his amulet with blood-slick fingers. He pictured the other apprentices, Rhona and Gallen and the girls from Aber-Ouse; he pictured the old cook Huren's beard and the carpenter Noak's gnarled hands. The guards, the cooks, the servants, the City Watch commander with his slick hair and scarred face. The two whitestaff masters had left in the night a span past, with no note or explanation, so they were absent.

Rust-folk clad in leather wielding jagged spears were holding them all in a circle, and then from the shadows a dozen demons with hooded cloaks had stepped forward. They were taller than any man, long arms bent too many times, gloved hands curled into claws. Their hoods covered their faces. Nobody spoke. Rhona made eye contact with him, her desperately seeking eyes meeting his as he had watched from the kitchen corridor door off the courtyard, pressed tight against the stone. She had been crying.

A creature stood above the others, stepped up onto stone. She was as crooked and bent and gaunt as the rest, her hair a shock of red, cut short at the sides and back and tied in a knot above, her eyes a piercing blue. Bone plugs filled her earlobes, and around her right eye the Ferron rune for salt was tattooed in vivid black, the bisecting line crossing her eyelids: Ø.

'I am Ceann Brude,' she had called out in Isken. 'I killed the Salt-Man. Most will be allowed to flee, but some must be made example. The wolf will take its meat, for hunger, and for vengeance.'

Huddled against the harbour wall Hove dug his nails into his forearms and concentrated on that sharp pain, tried not to allow himself to picture it, but he could see the demons raise their hands and black fire pour forth. He could see rust-folk stabbing with wicked spears, goblins slavering at their heels. He could hear the screaming.

High above the harbour, a gull cried out and next to him the City Watch guard nervously fingered the haft of the woodcutter's axe she had saved him with.

'Everyone is dead,' he said at last. 'We have to get out. Nullen or Sparrowpit, we must warn them. *We have to get away.*'

The City Watch guard stared at him for a long moment and then nodded slowly, wiped blood from her chin with the back of one hand. She peered around the harbour wall again and then along the coast.

'Into the dunes,' she said at last, gaze distant. 'We follow the coast to Nullen, and then cut south to Garioch. They need to muster the legions.'

Her eyes seemed to focus as she hauled Hove to his feet, and he felt his jaw quivering as he met her gaze.

'What's your name, lad?' she asked. 'I'm Cora.'

Hove felt his mouth opening and closing but he could think of no words, not even his own name. '*We have to run,*' he heard himself say, and then he was sobbing in her arms and Cora was gripping him tight. After a few of his broken sobs she cupped his chin with one hand and held his head up, opening her mouth to speak, but then she was pushing him behind her and drawing her axe to bear. Through the gate a goblin, another, a third. They jabbed with crude spears and clubs at Cora, but she would not be baited. She bided her time, Hove scrambling back behind her, and then she stepped forward and sank her axe deep into the first goblin, wrenching its body into the second.

Hove heard noises coming from his own mouth, screams

or cheers or *something*, but then through the harbour gate people came. Rust-folk, clad in leather, hard-worn capes slung around their shoulders. Faces scarred and pocked, the men bearded, all with wild tangles of hair in intricate braids. Cora backed up and the third goblin scrambled back. There were at least six rust-folk Hove could see, but they did not step forward.

Ceann Brude did. Through the rust-folk she stepped, clad in strange black material, a flowing cloak. She was grinning as she turned her head to look at Hove, and he felt his breathing quicken. Her hands were overlong, the fingers stretched and many-jointed, and even with her back hunched she was taller than anyone else there, a broken heron crouched amongst crows.

With one hand she clenched a fist, and the axe tore from Cora's hands and flew to the demon's hands. Cora swore and stepped back.

'Leave the boy be,' she said. 'He's only an apprentice. He's innocent.'

Ceann Brude stepped forward, the heavy axe hanging loosely from one hand.

'There are not any… *innocents* here, Stormguard,' she said, and then quickly spoke some words in a tongue Hove didn't know to the rust-folk warrior to her right. He murmured something back and Ceann Brude smiled.

'*Innocents*. Yes. This trade tongue has many new words for me. There are not any innocents here. He touches the storm, so I think I will have him. We killed the rest, but I could do with a… *witness*, and one who touches the storm will perhaps understand better than the rest. You can die or flee – that is your choice.'

Cora looked down at him and Hove heard his own voice say, 'Please.' But then she was stepping backward with hands raised.

'I'm sorry, lad,' she said, and then she was running for the dunes. One of the rust-folk started to move after her but Ceann Brude called him back with a barked order. She said something Hove didn't understand and the gathered rust-folk laughed. Turning to him, she stalked forward and reached down one hand with its horrible fingers and traced his jawline. Hove felt sick.

Ceann Brude shook her head at him slowly.

'There are no innocents here.'

'...GIVE THE SISTERS MY REGARDS'

'If one considers the estimated pre-collapse size of the Ferron Empire, interesting questions are raised. The land they covered was perhaps thrice the size of the Undal Protectorate, with at least five cities and many sizeable towns and villages. After the Judge Berren fell, they spread east in search of arable land, and workers to till it. To the north the islands of the Storm Sea were inhabited, and to the west the Iron Desert was home to sporadic communities. How many remain, three centuries from the fall? We only know the conditions of the rotstorm within seventy miles of our border. To probe further is death. Are there pockets of calm, further west? Where does Anshuka's wrath end? We can only estimate, but we must always be aware of our ignorance. Once there were lands there, people beyond the Ferron. What became of them?' – **Report: An estimate of the Ferron problem**, Whitestaff Hillenstole, Riven

Two willow trees bent with age intertwined in the centre of what remained of the park, where Benazir had played with her brother, where she had walked with her parents, where she had sat alone. Night cosseted the park and surrounding city, a heavy weight of cloud and dark that blocked out all stars beyond, and a swirling drizzle that soaked the broken stone and ruined soil. At the south edge of the park, a lone sentry stood in a decorative stone alcove in the ruins of what had once been ornate gates, shuffling their feet against the damp and cold and leaning heavily on a long spear. They gazed down the avenues of Fallow Fen, dutifully scanning the darkness for any threat. They did not see Benazir. She stepped lightly from the shadows next to the alcove and grabbed the sentry's shoulder and pulled them back sharply. They started to yell out but all seven inches of Benazir's dagger pierced through their back, the point snagging on ribs for only a moment before slipping into their lung, driven by their own weight onto the narrow blade as Benazir pulled them back with a shiver of satisfaction.

She felt the sentry's legs give out and lowered them slowly to the ground before twisting the blade of the knife with a sharp jerk and removing it. Crouched over their twitching form, Benazir licked her lips and stared out from the alcove through the darkness at the empty streets of Fallow Fen, before turning back to the park and the Sisters. The willows were in blossom, and long before she had been born their canopies had grown together. In the darkness the blossom was nothing but grey shadow, but she could picture it, pink and white. Beneath the Sisters, where Fen folk had once lain on blankets and laughed and kissed and lived, the dirt was churned to mud and four rottrolls slept. Rottrolls the size of oxen, rottrolls with hide like armour and claws and teeth that would rend flesh like soft cheese.

Benazir glanced down briefly once the sentry had stopped convulsing, her eyes flitting across their form. A woman – thick-set, dark hair in a tumble of matted curls. Benazir's eyes moved from face to clothes to spear in three heartbeats. *Ugly, ugly, poorly made.* She wiped her dagger on the rust-folk sentry's sodden cape and slipped it back to its sheath on her belt, ran her hand across the other dagger next to it, and then checked the two daggers sheathed on her right, the dagger in each boot. Starbeck had said, *Take whatever tools you think best.* Benazir's sword and shortbow were abandoned back at camp, but she had six Stormguard Commando Hawk knives, each identical save the red leather hilt of the blade in her right boot. They were engineered to bring death – the prize of Undal City's forges.

As she stood from her crouch and stared at the rottrolls in the park through the haze of the Fallow Fen drizzle, she took comfort in the weight of them. She shook her head quickly, whipping her black fringe out of her line of sight.

Benazir's father's dagger with its rune of burning flame and hilt of worn antler was sheathed at Floré's hip, two streets north, and she did not allow herself to miss it. Wiping rain from her brow, she drew a knife from her belt, and in her gauntleted hand she held it behind her head by the tip of the silver blade. She waited, tasting rain on her lips, until from the mist and drizzle she saw the faint glow of a covered lantern. Benazir smiled and felt her pulse quicken, a shiver of anticipation running down her spine. The rust-folk might not keep to any rigid patrol routes or idea of discipline, but they were predictable enough and Benazir had been watching this end of the park for an hour as she waited for her comrades to move into position.

When the patrolling guard approached the alcove through the slick of rain, the faint glow of his lantern began to spill over her. *Not his lantern,* she thought, grimacing, *the lantern of some dead Fenner.* Benazir inhaled deeply, the scent of the rain and the sweetness of the willow blossom of the intertwined trees ahead of her in the park filling her lungs, and then flicked her arm forward.

The knife spun beautifully, the silver tapered blade catching the glow from the sentry's lantern, but her distance was off. Instead of sinking seven inches of silver into his chest, the weighted pommel cap of steel struck the guard and he let out a cough of pain, his lantern falling from his hands.

Before the lantern reached the cobbled path at the edge of the park Benazir was moving forward like a hunting cat, drawing daggers across her chest, and raising her right hand to throw again. From twenty yards Benazir loosed a second dagger, but the sentry caught sight of her and twitched to the side. The lantern broke on the cobbles at his feet and as the Hawk knife sailed past into the park beyond Benazir started to sprint. At the feet of the guard, lamp oil spilled forth in a pool of flame. From the darkness she rushed towards the curling flames, and when she closed on her opponent he drew from his back a rusted scimitar and yelled out something in old Ferron.

Benazir could only hear the blood in her ears, the rush of water over rocks, could only smell the flowers and blossom of the willow trees of Fallow Fen, not the stench and shit and blood, the rancid stink of the rottrolls. She did not try to listen, or translate. She feinted another throw with her dagger when she was only a few steps out and then when he raised his scimitar to block she closed: with her left hand she reached for his sword arm, gripping with gauntleted fingers at rough cloth slick with rain. He jerked it free, but her right hand was already snaking forward and plunging half a dozen quick jabs with the brutal Hawk knife. None would be fatal, but she didn't need that. She just needed to cut him enough that he fell back, or made a mistake.

Jumping back to avoid a slash from the rusted scimitar, Benazir slipped on the wet cobblestones of the path lining the park, and her other boot crunched on broken glass from the fallen lantern as she tried to catch herself. *Shit.* She stepped back thrice more, her left boot now coated in burning oil, and the sentry advanced. He was bearded, taller than her by a head and heavily muscled. Through his cloak and tattered leathers she couldn't see how many of her strikes had been true, but he held his right side back a little, and behind his black beard she thought she saw a wince.

'This is *my* town,' Benazir said, stamping her boot to quench the last tongues of flame from the lamp oil, but the guard did not respond to her with words. Instead he spat and charged forward, and Benazir drew another dagger in her left hand. With a blade in each hand, she met his charge with a quickstep forward. As he swung his scimitar for a heavy overhead strike, she ducked down to one knee and spun back around, her dagger catching behind his right knee, tearing deep. Benazir rolled forward and away, scrambled to her feet and shook her head to get her rain-slicked fringe away from her eyes.

'*My* town,' she repeated, her heartbeat a staccato rush. As the sentry turned back to her she flung another dagger. This time, the blade sank deep, biting into his shoulder. He screamed as his scimitar fell from limp fingers and he dropped to his knees. Benazir circled slowly, and cast one eye back at the Sisters. Beneath the canopy, the four rottrolls were bellowing as they rose to their feet, and a half-dozen rust-folk were gathering, yelling orders. Arrows split the darkness from the north of the park, peppering the rottrolls, and the rust-folk scrambled to the boles and roots of the Sisters for cover, even as one fell limp; what was a man now only a quiver.

Benazir killed the sentry. He tried to resist, but she circled him quickly and her gauntleted hands ignored his desperate fingers as she pulled his head back. She plunged the tip of her dagger deep into his neck and punched it forward in a gout of blood, a pulsing spray. Benazir let the man's body slump to the dirt and she tasted bile in the back of her throat. She gathered her fallen knives and turned a quick glance to the centre of the park, to the rottrolls. Janos and Floré were there now, along with the rest of their squad.

Floré was orchestrating a half-dozen commandos clad all in black and grey and darkest green – no tabards for night work. As they distracted the rottrolls with yells and snaking swords and swift bowshots, Benazir saw Janos standing back, flanked by two commandos with swords drawn. The skein-mage was wearing the same faded grey and black as the rest of the squad, but his hands were clad in black leather. Unsmiling, Janos watched the fray and started to move his hands.

Benazir focused back on her mission. Breaking into a jog she began to circle the park. The rottrolls were chasing the squad now, who darted between the statues and fountains that dotted the once peaceful garden. Benazir kept to the crumbled low wall of the park, glancing down the side streets and up at the roofs of the tall houses surrounding the open space. Nothing. She kept moving, kept moving when she heard a scream from one of her comrades, kept moving when in the centre of the park one of the trolls was consumed by a pillar of white lightning piercing out from Janos.

On the fourth avenue cutting out from the park to the east, she skidded to a stop. Racing towards the park down the torn and ruined street was a crow-man: *a demon*. Taller than any human by at least a head, limbs long and oddly bent, this one had the face of a young woman, hair flowing back in wild locks of blonde and gold. Her skin was pale and she flew over the ground, her feet a yard up from the churned earth and broken cobblestones. She was clad in armour of tight, banded leather, and a cloak of ragged black billowed behind her as she flew arms raised towards Benazir, face a mask of anger.

Behind the crow-man, at least two dozen goblins scrambled over broken earth and ruin and rubble, diminutive grey-skinned monsters, black tongues slavering over serrated teeth as they screamed towards her. Benazir could see light spilling from a doorway further down the road where they must have been barracked. Turning back to the park, she saw that two of the rottrolls were piles of black blood and charred flesh, the third hauling chunks of broken statues at Floré and the squad as the fourth pounded a commando into the dirt. Floré ducked the hurled chunks of masonry and statue and was hacking at the armoured hide of the beast with her sword, and thirty yards back Janos stood implacably by, his hands ever moving, a charge of white static building around his hands, his eyes blank. The rust-folk were all dead to the blades of her squad.

'Floré! Demon!' Benazir yelled, and then she turned back

to the approaching torrent of goblins, the demon. She had to keep the demon from getting close to Janos. Crow-men projected chaos through the pattern of the skein, the pattern Janos used to practise his magic. He could burn trolls all day long, it seemed, but if the demon got close Benazir knew he would be useless. She grimaced and took stock. She had six knives. There were at least two dozen goblins, and the demon. Benazir ran a quick hand over her knives, loosened them in their sheaths, and stepped forward into the road. She remembered her father in this park, the sombre deference afforded him by the other Fenners, dutiful nods and bows of respect to their commander.

'Demon!' she cried out, her voice a brittle, wounded thing. 'This town is *mine*.'

The crow-man stopped twenty yards from her and rose another three feet into the air, and with a snarl threw a bolt of black flame, a roiling spear of liquid fire that burst from her palm. Benazir rolled to the side easily, stood, and sneered. Beside her the stone of the road sizzled and spat sparks as the sticky black flame thrown by the demon burned down to the earth below.

'My town, demon,' Benazir shouted, holding one fist to her chest.

Even as she spoke the goblins were advancing, a ragged horde of slate-pebbled skin and black eyes, row after row of ragged teeth in wide mouths that seemed to nearly split their skulls, nightmares made flesh. They chittered and gibbered, and Benazir could see on them the loot of the fallen city; instead of animal skins and loose rags, they were clad in soiled and stolen clothes. All of them held some sort of weapon – daggers, cleavers, crude cudgels made of table legs.

One clutched a stuffed bear in one hand and in the other a meat hook. They edged forward, nervous, and the demon above yelled down at them in Ferron.

Benazir cocked her head. *Kill?* She thought she had picked up the word *kill*. She shrugged and took another step forward, ignoring screams from the park behind her. A goblin with a table leg broke from the pack and sprinted at her as the crow-man sent another bolt of black fire. Benazir hopped back from the flame and sent one of her daggers spinning. It sank into the goblin's torso, the force of it sending its frail body to the dirt of the road.

'My town, crow-man,' Benazir said, drawing another knife, feeling rage roaring in her breast, picturing her mother walking the swept avenues of Fallow Fen, the painted shutters of the houses, the flowers in the window boxes. 'The Sisters are for lovers, for families. Not for monsters. Fallow Fen is for Fenners, not *Ferron.*'

Another two goblins ran forward but before they had made it a step Benazir had sent a knife spinning into the gut of one, and the other sprouted an arrow from its eye socket. Floré appeared at Benazir's side, clad in black, slick with gore and rain, a wild look in her amber eyes. Floré's usual crop of ashen curls had been shorn back to stubble for the campaign, and Benazir felt a shiver of relief at the presence of her friend looming at her shoulder, muscled and armoured and ready for trouble.

'This demon giving you any trouble, sis?' she said, and Benazir grinned and twirled the knife in her right hand, catching it in a reverse grip.

'Not at all, dear Captain. Deal with the children of the lightning, and I'll finish my lesson.'

Floré nodded and nocked another arrow, and the crow-man screamed with rage.

Benazir closed the distance fast. She relied on Floré to keep the goblins off her, and as she ran three of them fell to her comrade's arrows until Benazir was within six feet of the floating demon. She dodged another gout of flame, this time a continuous stream of red and black that spewed forth in a ragged cone rather than a burning bolus of energy. With a gauntleted hand she grabbed a goblin by the scruff and hauled it at the demon, and the cone of black and red fire sputtered out as the goblin fell into it and began to shriek. Another goblin, the one with the stuffed bear and the meat hook, yelled something she didn't understand as it swung for her, but one of Floré's arrows split into its side and sent it sprawling. Benazir focused.

With her left hand she grabbed the ankle of the floating demon and yanked down hard, and with her right she skewered upward with her knife. She felt a hand with claw-like fingers raking at her face as she did but the blade sank deep, and then the demon was a whirlwind of thrashing limbs as Benazir clung tight, her left hand finding purchase on one of the straps in the banded leather armour of the demon. The silver of her blade was like the touch of acid to the demon, and it wailed and convulsed. Benazir pulled it close in until they were face to face, black blood streaming from its mouth. She pulled at the armour and pushed at her dagger. The demon let out another cry and fell slack in her grip.

Benazir let the demon drop and blew a breath out through her nose. *My town,* she thought once again, and suddenly Floré was next to her, a brutal downward slice of her dark grey sword blade bisecting a goblin who was scrambling up to Benazir's unguarded side. The goblin halves fell into rubble with a spray of green blood and Floré held her sword out in a high guard, the red and white knot at its pommel twisting in the breeze as wind coursed down the avenue.

The dozen remaining goblins were fleeing back down the avenue, and Benazir slowly nodded her head. Another dead crow-man, another step towards the liberation of her town. Glancing back at the park she saw the last of the trolls were down, one a pyre of sparking red flame, the other a misshaped pile of salt that the rain was quickly washing away. She grimaced. The idea of a mage turning her skin, her bones, her every organ to salt was enough to make her stomach twist. Benazir crouched down to the fallen demon and stared at her intently – the woman with the wild locks of golden hair, her pale skin contrasting so sharply with the black blood that covered her mouth and chin. Her face was young and unlined and she had green eyes, and Benazir felt for a vertiginous moment that she was looking in a reflection, despite the stark differences: long golden waves to her utilitarian short black, skin a cold white rather than warm brown. *The same green as my eyes, though,* she thought, and again felt bile in her throat. Reaching down she pressed her dagger blade between ribs until she heard the pop of the heart bursting. *Best to be sure.*

'Nicely done, Benny,' Floré said above her, relaxing her guard and leaning down to wipe the blade of her sword on the shoulder of the crow-man's tunic. 'But I think we really have to run.'

Benazir turned down the avenue of Fallow Fen, and saw the wyrm.

The Hammer of Poetry

'Melt in spring, river rose, ice and ice.
I saw you, oaken char, silhouette.
Cavern paint, mountain queen. Evermore.'

– #17, *Sea Collection*, Yggrid the Bloodless

Janos slept and dreamt of a storm, and in his dream he remembered other storm dreams, a fractal of dreamscapes. Always a storm, juggernaut clouds like elemental gods clashing above, the sky churning and the wind howling. The rain over the farm in Garioch, heavy as sling stones; the acrid mists and tearing gales beyond the Stormwall stealing breath and sight and sound; the blizzard of the Claw Winter against the holy roof of the shaman monastery in Inverbar, a creeping cold; the wind tearing through the pines of Hookstone forest, pressing at the walls of home. Janos did not know how long he slept but he dreamt of storms, as he had before. In darkness he twitched, and a voice called to him as through dark water. Hands pulled at him, tore at the seams of him.

Before, Janos dreamt of the rotstorm every night. It didn't matter what he did beforehand, if he drank hard liquor or meditated; sex, exercise, combat training. Every night he dreamt of the rotstorm, of Urforren. He would wake up shaking and screaming, and Floré would hold his shoulders and in a low voice tell him to calm. *Be calm, my love.* He would sleep again, sometimes. A sleep without dreams. A blackness that would envelop him and let him rest. Once, he awoke and found himself immersed in the skein, the pattern and the pattern below it, and for a long exultant moment he felt the pattern of the world, all Undal City spreading out around him: their room in Protector's Keep, the barracks below, the docks, the harbour. He had let his connection linger but then he felt a shivering sickness. *I cannot do this. Not again.*

When he woke the next day Floré had already left their room to drill the Lancer and City Watch cadets in the barracks. He ate a bowl of salted porridge and stared listlessly out at the blue skies over Undal City and the Wind Sea beyond. *Blue skies.* No storm here, no fractal lightning, no mist that would burn your throat to gore, no arcane winds that would peel skin and flesh from bone. Seagulls were wheeling.

Janos finished his porridge and read a collection of Huna Droll's new poems. Droll was Caroban, that far-off land beyond the Wind Sea and the Carob Strait. Hot jungles of verdant lush greenery, hunting cats the size of bears. His latest collection was ostensibly a list of every bogle in Caroban, to each an ode. Janos flicked through, stopping whenever a phrase caught his eye. In Caroban they called the bogles Relu, and from the introductory note in the Red Desert Press edition, the word could mean *ghost* or *spirit* – they seemed to think bogles were spirits of individuals, rather than the spirit of a place like most Undal believed.

Janos put the book down by his porridge and stared at the wall. *There are no bogles in the rotstorm, no little godlings, no spirits,* he thought, and then he stared up at the wheeling gulls through the window. *Is that true?* He wasn't sure. Any moment in the rotstorm was one spent fighting to survive, and the Stormguard had scarcely made it more than fifty miles west of the Stormwall in the three centuries since Ferron fell. *What lies in the storm beyond? Or where the storm ends?* Janos read the poems again.

He finally set the book down, dissatisfied. The poems were structurally excellent, empathetic and evocative, but he preferred Droll's earlier books railing against the corrupt merchant princes of Caroban. Those had an energy behind them, a weight of emotion. The book of Relu felt light somehow, separate from the world even as it described it in vibrant tones.

He dressed and packed his satchel with notebook and quills and inks and made his way out of the keep, but on his way he stopped by the training yard and peeked in. Floré had thirty cadets doing body-weight exercises and balances, all their weight on one palm, jumping on and off the stone benches lining the wall.

'Enough!' she yelled, her voice a whip-crack. The cadets sprawled in the dirt and breathed heavily, every one of them sodden with sweat and covered in dust and grime.

'Swords!' she called, and pacing the pentacle courtyard she caught his eye and flashed him a quick grin, before assuming her brutal persona once more.

'Faster!' The cadets who weren't already scrabbling with

training swords redoubled their efforts. The training swords were bundles of bound ash rods soaked in water so they wouldn't splinter. Janos had spent only a little time training with swords, but it was still more than he had wanted to. The cadets formed two lines and under Floré's direction began running through guard postures, the poses and fighting forms and concepts of the school of the Gauntlet. She cut through the line and came to him where he waited in the shadow at the edge of the courtyard. Her hair was as long as he had ever seen it. Since Urforren and the end of the campaign she had been growing it out, tumbles of ashen curls trailing to her shoulders. She was in her training kit, thick padded cotton trousers and shirt in faded blue, knuckles wrapped in layers of cloth.

'Headed out?' she asked, and he grinned.

'Going to see if I can interest Red Desert in my latest poems,' he said, and broke eye contact. They had been there a season, a winter of him writing his poetry as she drilled her cadets, and the relief at being away from the wall was so incredible to him. A whole world where the rotstorm was a story, not an ever-present reality. A span ago he had tried another publisher, a span before that another. He thought his poems might be good enough. He needed to write them, to have something to fill his mind, his hands, without the skein. She had stood with him at Urforren, had told him to do it, held him firm. *She understands why I can't go back.*

Floré kissed him on the cheek and squeezed his arm.

'Perhaps the harbour, and fish tonight?' she said, and he nodded and watched her work her way back through the cadets. Two were sparring fully instead of practising their guard forms and Floré waded in and snatched their practice swords from their hands and began to give them an awful bollocking.

'Did I give you permission to fight, you fucking sandbags? Get running!'

The cadets started to sprint, Floré trailing them, matching their pace even as she bellowed insults. Janos could still hear the yelling when he was many corridors away, headed out into Undal's streets.

The city was full of carriages and horses, market stalls and traders, people bustling everywhere. The planters lining the broader avenues were in full flower, and Janos trailed his fingers through the petals as he walked along. *Red Desert Press,* he thought, *but first I must see the kitchen.*

He headed west through the city until he reached the fishing harbour, and west further to the market square. This was the poorer end of the city, the houses lower, the streets narrower and with more scattered rubbish and stray dogs. The prevailing wind blew in from the east, and so the stink of industry and cookfires and chimneys found its way to settle over the fishing port and the scaleways around. Janos walked through thick air and past fish slick with fish scales and half-sluiced blood. He was dressed in simple trousers and shirt and boots, but the red jacket Floré had given him as a First Flower gift was embroidered at its seams with golden thread, the cut of it far too fine for streets like these. He wandered on, his hand tight on his satchel. Another dozen streets deeper and he came to Owl's kitchen.

'Morning, Owl!' he called with a knock on the door, and from within the closed shopfront there was a shuffling. A large woman with thick black hair opened the door.

'The martyr,' she said gruffly, and turned away, leaving the door hanging open. Janos felt his mouth twist in a frown as he entered after her. He closed the door gently. Inside Owl's kitchen were long trestle tables and low stools, and past that the kitchen itself, a series of low range fires and huge stew pots and a few counters.

'Come to feel better about yourself again, have you?'

Janos ignored her barbed comments and went to the book that sat on the low table. It was a thick book, full of cheap paper, and a stub of pencil sat by it.

'How many yesterday?' he asked, flipping open the pages, and she took up a large kitchen knife and began roughly chopping onions from a pile.

'More than the day before,' she said, and Janos nodded. Owl's kitchen served any who came. There weren't many truly homeless in the Undal Protectorate, if not by choice. Always there was work needing to be done, and a space to be given. Those who couldn't work due to illness were provided enough to live on, though most conditions Janos had ever heard of were not enough to allow for that. *No arms?* the joke went. *You have legs and a mouth. You can be a crier.*

Those who truly could not work could always receive food from places like Owl's kitchen, funded by the state, and there was always a warm patch in a Stormguard barracks. *But not everyone wants to be spending the night in a barracks,* Janos thought, *and not everyone trusts the Stormguard.*

'Can I give you some money?' he said, as he always did. 'For extra food?'

Owl shook her head and kept chopping onions.

'Ain't your place, lad. Charity's a failure of the state. What're they for if not to provide for those that need? Chop those carrots, peel those potatoes, then piss off unless you're willing to stay and look them in the eye this time.'

Janos chopped the carrots and peeled the potatoes and pissed off. He couldn't face the veterans that inevitably came, hungry. Scarred. Some from the Tessendorm raids, some from the old Antian war. Most fresh from the summer's campaign to take back Fallow Fen and destroy Urforren. *How many would have been saved if I told them I couldn't do it? How many would have been doomed if we let them be?* Janos left Owl's kitchen and was back on the streets long before the lunch crowd arrived, and he walked himself up to the forest gate. For a copper penny he got a cup of hot apple cider and a seat inside an inn. He spent an hour going through his poems, ordering them one way then another, removing some from the pile and adding others in.

Am I good enough? He didn't know. He was too close in. His poems were not the abstract imagery of Huna Droll or the emotive simplicity of Yggrid the Bloodless. He imagined what he was doing fell more in the recent school from Uradech, the naturalists. Ever he described nature as best he could with all the love he could muster. He could not describe people. They were beyond him.

Thrice he removed the poems describing the rotstorm from the pile, and thrice he returned them all. *Is it nature?*

He had written about the rotstorm, about the skein. He had written about turning Urforren to a circle of eternal burning salt. The feeling when you looked at the pattern of a human being, their past and present and potential, their entirety and... *simplified* it to mineral. He had written poems about the flush of blood to his fingers when the battle was pitched, streaks of lightning and sheets of flame pouring from him, tapping into the energy that was *everywhere*. Between each point of being and non-being, in every change there was, deep in the liminal space between chaos and order, pattern and noise. He had found that potential, and he did not write how. *How could I when I barely know myself?*

He wrote a poem about the view of Urforren through an eyeglass from a half-mile away, when past the accreted hordes of goblins and rottrolls, wyrms and demons, he saw gates closing on a *town* of living people. *Once living people...*

Janos had written many poems that winter but in the nameless inn by the forest gate in the north of Undal City he did not shuffle those and peruse them. Most were ash, committed to flame for the truth they carried. His shame. He focused instead on the nature poems. A page about a flock of sparrows, a murmuration twisting in the twilight. The stars above, the movement of clouds. *Everyone understands these things,* he thought; *I am putting names to what everyone feels in their heart.*

He had the idea that his other poems, now burned, about the hot flush of joy he felt when he destroyed a city with the wave of his hand, were not so universal. *Or perhaps the emotion is, if the action is not.* Janos ordered his poems and drank his hot apple juice and after a long minute staring at the wall he did not think about the skein, or the children of Urforren. He thought about a gull in flight past his window against a perfect blue sky, the twist of its head. Packing his poems carefully, he headed to Red Desert Press.

They ate fish that night at an inn by the harbour, the one with the miniature ship's prow jutting from above the door. The fish were sardines grilled with lemon, served on a bed of hot buttery potatoes. Floré waited until the food was served to ask him how it went. Janos picked up his glass of wine, a sour red from somewhere in northern Isken, and looked at her from the corner of his eye.

'A collection,' he said, trying to slow himself, trying to savour the announcement, 'two hundred to be printed initially, half the profit to me, half to them.'

He tried to raise his glass but she was across the table and hugging him. They drank that night and danced, and as they walked home she squeezed his hand. The oil lamps were lit on every street corner, and the sound of the Wind Sea beyond the city walls was a constant murmur, a soft reminder of a world beyond.

'I told you we'd be able to move forward,' she said, and he smiled at her and she leaned her head on his shoulder as they walked, but as soon as she looked away he felt his smile go cold. *A poetry collection. How many dead at my hand, and I write poems?* They entered the keep and the sight of the uniforms and the weapons left him queasy.

'Have you thought about the Forest Watch?' he said that night, when they were alone in the dark and he could not sleep, and Floré grew still.

'Would it help?' she said, so earnestly. Janos closed his eyes and dreamt of the storm. Janos dreamt of the rotstorm. Janos dreamt of lightning, of a voice, dreamt of runes burning. The lightning cut through black cloud and a rain that slicked him to his bones, and he could hear only thunder. Janos dreamt of the storm, and he tried to scream but the thunder was too loud.

Janos dreamt...

ACT 2

THE FROZEN BLADE

Pattern is a lie. For all of history across Morost, practitioners of the skein have fallen into the trap of all living creatures: to seek pattern and within it comfort. The truth is the chaos, not the pattern we dream.

Doctrine of the silent mind, Ihm Phogn of Cil Maric

7

The Weight of the Dead

'The Tessendorm reliance on slave soldiers is a wonderful advantage to us. Thrice we have, through the simple offer of freedom, turned armies against their masters. They are not, of course, free to come to Ferron or the territories; they are not of the soil, and could not walk free in our lands. General Garanad told them to take their spears and head to Isken, and a gold piece for each who walked away. Some even took employ as a mercenary force. We are stretched thin so we have left them guarding their former masters to the border of the territories, and the mines within. Easy work, for which they are motivated. There is no fear of them striking against us – even those who have kin in the territories under shackle and whip have now seen what our wolf-touched legions can accomplish. They fear us, of course. As it should be.' – **Commentary of the Ferron-Tessendorm campaign**, Consul Semphor, year 627 Isken reckoning

Night on the ship was endless waves, the smell of salt, the stink of the sailors and commandos thronging the lower deck. The upper deck was no longer a place of quiet contemplation – the rain had started in earnest as dusk fell, black and grey clouds like mountains filling the sky. The captain had anchored them offshore a mile from the coast, and through the drizzle Floré could just see the lights of some fishing village. She retreated to the cabin the captain had given to her and Benazir, an austere but reasonably spacious room with two bunks and a small table. Benazir and Voltos were drawing out the recent attack on Stormcastle XII with cutlery on the tabletop, and Tomas was sat on the lower bunk feeding drops of warm milk to the black kitten.

'That's my bed,' Floré said, and he looked up at her and smiled.

'She is quite clean, I assure you,' he responded, scratching the cat on the head. 'I have deloused her with the mighty skein itself. I'm not sure my instructors at the castrum would ever forgive me, but I think I could make a pretty penny in pest control if ever we find peace.'

Floré shook her head and sat down at the table. 'The cadets are down below with the troop.' Benazir nodded, clearing away her cutlery ramparts. Voltos cleaned his eyeglasses on his silk robe and replaced them, turning to Floré.

'How are you, my dear?' he asked, and Floré let herself slump back. 'Losing Janos, and your home. Marta's sickness. Many weights for one set of shoulders.'

Floré shrugged and scratched at the scars on her face, felt a tingle in her right arm as the bone-deep lightning scars joined the array of aches.

'We all lose people,' she said. Benazir's gaze fell into focus on her. Benazir opened her mouth to speak and then instead drank from her cup of wine.

'I might call the kitten Janos, in his honour,' Tomas said. Floré didn't bother rising to the bait.

'I lost Guil,' Benazir said, and they all turned to her. She met Floré's eyes. 'After you and Janos left, she and I took up. She died in the last attack. Rottroll.'

Her gaze fell and Voltos put a hand on her leg. Tomas scratched his kitten, his face turning between them all, expression neutral. Floré frowned. 'Guil with the *freckles*?' Benazir nodded glumly.

'Captain Guil, with hair like fire,' she said. Floré found herself nodding. She had always liked Guil, had known her for years, had ranged with her in the storm, fought with her at Fallow Fen and Urforren. Benazir had always had a soft spot for the girl, but Floré had thought her friend too much a stickler for rank to break that rule of fraternising with her own troops. She tried to picture Guil, freckled, red-haired, skinny and gangly but *sinewy*. Guil had done her hard yards in the rotstorm. Floré poured herself a cup of wine – some rough Isken yellow with a sharp scent – and raised it.

'Guil,' she said. Benazir and Voltos met her toast. Tomas lounged back on the bunk with the kitten stretched out on his chest.

'Always more to lose,' he said quietly. In silence they sat for a long moment. There was a knock on the door and Captain Muirgainas opened it abruptly, his hat and coat soaked.

'Commanders!' he called. Behind him oil lamps lit the foredeck, and he stepped back to show them the view.

In the centre of the foredeck under the beating rain stood three Tullioch, heavily muscled and scaled, long tails sweeping behind them. Their chests were all mottled a vibrant green, and each easily stood a head above Floré. Each of the three wore a bandolier and belt of hide or kelp with dagger sheathed, and the leader clutched a short spear of dark metal that ended in a brutal point. Floré's hand moved to her sword but she heard Voltos say, '*Wait,*' in an urgent low voice so she let it fall.

'Greetings,' Benazir called, striding past Floré, Voltos, and Captain Muirgainas to stand in the rain. The Tullioch were tall, with thick tails and clawed hands and feet. Their faces resembled a lizard's, an eye set on each side and a long muzzle with long nostril slits. They lived in the Wind Sea, and the wild reefs beyond.

'I am Bolt-Commander Benazir Arfallow. Welcome aboard. How may we help you? We seek to travel to Iskander.'

The lead Tullioch stepped forward and bowed its head.

'I am Leomar, son of Jalomar, of the Deepfarrow. We bear news, and seek news, child of Baal.'

Benazir bowed her head. 'Would you prefer to speak inside?' she said, and the Tullioch clicked its teeth.

'We won't be long, Bolt-Commander Benazir Arfallow. The news I bear... the concords do not hold south of this point. We can offer no safe passage to you and yours. Iskander is besieged by beasts of the blight-water, and none of your ships who have dared the journey have returned in two cycles of the moon. Each we have warned, and each has pressed on. Orbs of light harry the sky and hunt any ships that leave the island; aberrations hunt the water to the south and to the east, and hunt any ships that seek to leave your waters.'

Benazir lowered her head and Floré stepped from the cabin to stand at her side. They had spent hours the night before discussing what they could do if an orb came for them on the open sea. *We die,* had been the consensus.

'What beasts?' Benazir asked. 'We must press on, but any more you can tell us may grant us at least the chance to prepare.'

Leomar shook his head slowly and stared up at the rain and cloud above. Floré shivered as the rainfall made its way through her hair to her scalp and began to run down her neck. Next to her Benazir stood as still as a statue.

'Rottrolls,' Leomar said, 'stormblight and trollspawn. Goblins. Crow-men. At least one wyrm, though we think it east, for now. Blocking the Isken trade ships, though if this is by design I know not.'

The Tullioch spun his spear and bowed his head.

'I wish you safe passage, but I must seek news. Word from Undal is Heasin son of Luasin found battle with the orbs. Undal claim him as a hero in death and sent their thanks, gifts of steel, promises of friendship. He sought his daughter. Other children were with her. Sons and daughters of the Wild Reefs, my own daughter amongst them.'

Floré felt her heart ache as she pictured Heasin, the looming Tullioch who had helped her stop the orbs, and their mission to kill Anshuka. He had perished when their orb was forced from the sky, crashing into Orubor's wood. *My own daughter amongst them,* the Tullioch had said. Floré's mouth was dry, and she clenched her teeth.

'I travelled with him,' she said, 'and I know his daughter was killed. I am sorry, Leomar. None of the children taken survived.'

Floré knew the lie of it as she said it. Marta had survived. *But she was the last.* Leomar huffed and their shoulders heaved, mouth opening and closing slowly, clawed hands flexing in what Floré could only read as rage. Standing behind her she heard a cough, and in the doorway to the cabin surrounded by spilling light, Tomas clutched his kitten to his chest. It mewled against the storm and its claws dug at his gloves. With his free hand he slicked back his hair.

'Actually,' he said, water running down the opaque crystal of his goggle lenses, 'that isn't quite right. You should come inside.'

~

An hour later and Floré was sat jiggling her knee, trying hard to control the impulse to break Tomas's nose.

'Explain *again*,' she said, 'explain better.' Tomas sighed, rubbing his brow above his goggles. Next to him on the bunk the black kitten was curled in its box, asleep, and he turned to face it. They were back in the cabin, the three Tullioch now stationed at the prow of the boat.

'Look,' he said, 'we didn't have time to stop on the way out.'

'I know that, Tomas. Believe me I know. What I want to know is why in *six spans* you never felt it relevant to mention there were *children* left in that cavern. That cavern where we also left at the least a dozen goblins still breathing on our heels, and perhaps some crow-men.'

'Well that's it!' he said, face flushing. 'They're either dead from the goblins, dead from the crow-men, or *even* if the lizard kid did a number on them they're trapped in an utterly inaccessible mountain cavern in a range that has barely even been mapped. *Enough dead kids,* I thought. Let everyone move on. And since the Orubor won't even let us use the orbs we captured, what in all the hells is the use? No way of getting there.'

'Except you just told that Tullioch you could find his daughter.'

Tomas leaned back in the bunk and stroked the kitten and shrugged.

'Same as we did for you. His blood, a whitestaff. They can use it to track her down. It'll tell us where she is, direction and distance. The only thing missing is an orb to fly us there.'

Floré pictured Marta in those bleak caverns, Marta with Cuss's brother Petron chained and tortured for days on end. *Six spans.* The thought of sixty days in that cavern made her nauseous. Her own few hours there had been torture, physically and mentally. Without realising it her hand was rubbing her right thigh where Varratim's runewand had cut deepest, the muscle there now knotted scar. *I can still run,* she thought, *and I can still fight.*

'I will never forgive you for this,' she said at last.

Tomas shrugged. 'We keeping track now?' he said, and Voltos sighed. Benazir was stroking the scars at her jawline. 'Three Tullioch to help guide us through the reef isn't an advantage to be sniffed at. And if the crow-men had a full base there, there were probably supplies. They might be alive yet. Overall, we come out of this ahead in our mission. We can ask the Orubor for their aid when we have the chance to take an orb and seek the caverns.'

Floré shook her head and sank to her chair, wiping rain from her brow. *Maybe five or six children,* Tomas had said. *As if that's an acceptable number.*

'Get out of here unless you're sleeping here,' Benazir said, and Tomas and Voltos reluctantly stepped into the rain. They were sleeping in a small cabin in the lower deck. Cuss and

Yselda were in with the sailors and the commandos down in the open lower deck in hammocks strung between poles. As he left Tomas swung his cloak over the kitten's box to keep it dry.

'I did what I thought was right,' he said from the doorway, and Benazir waved him off. Floré just stared at her hands. *Every goblin a child. Can I judge him? How many have I taken?*

'Benazir,' she said, and Benazir paused, halfway through unbuckling her belt and kicking off her boots.

'This is about the goblin in the keep,' Benazir said, and Floré nodded.

'I have to tell you. All of it. It's worse than you could possibly imagine.'

~

Cuss swung in his hammock and tried to remember the commandos' names but they were all blurring except for the sergeant – Sergeant Buchan with his utterly terrifying face. A face of constant rage. Since they had arrived in Undal City, Cuss had spent every moment he had with the Stormguard commando cadets, even though he and Yselda had no official place until Starbeck invited them to the legion. Cuss shook his head. *Cuss Grantimber, Stormguard commando.* It was ludicrous – he was still useless in a fight. These six spans with the commando recruits had taught him that for certain. He was as old as their eldest members, and some of them had been drilling with the sword since they could walk. They were surly and harsh children, girls and boys with sinewy muscle and callused palms, always bruised, always tired and aching. He kept to himself, visited with Floré and Marta, or sat quiet with Yselda. Protector's Keep was full of places you could sit still and watch the sea. *I miss the forest though.*

Cuss pulled his cloak tighter and ran his fingers over the knot of silk Knight-Commander Starbeck had handed him. The hold was almost black, a single lamp lit in the centre by the stair to the main deck, and it was so *loud* with the waves crashing. He lay and thought about the distant stares of the commando instructors, the way they all had the same set jaw as Floré as if always bracing for a strike. *How can I ever be like them?* He didn't know. He only knew he had to try for Petron. *What else can I do?* He didn't think Petron would want revenge. *But I don't want them doing to anyone else what they did to him.*

The thought was enough to bring the tears again, tears and the tightness in his chest. Tomas had told him what had happened, back when they were both still injured, the two of them in adjoining beds in Protector's Keep infirmary.

'Bravest thing I ever saw,' he had said eventually, after a day of refusing to talk about it. He said it when Cuss thought he had been asleep. 'Your brother, tortured almost to death, nothing but cuts and dirt, he tells that lad Varratim to leave this kid alone. Your brother, he knows what that means. He *volunteered*, Cuss. Do you understand? They had him down there days, watching the others sacrificed. Tortured him. He knew what would happen. He knew Floré was about, knew we were there for a rescue attempt. Didn't matter.'

Tomas had stared up at the ceiling of the infirmary, and Cuss had seen that he was crying, tears soaking into the bandages coating his burned face.

'Why would he do that, Cuss? To save a child he didn't

know? Bravest thing I ever saw, your brother. Bravest bloody thing.'

Tomas had lain silent in his bed as Cuss wept. *Why did you do that, Petro?* he had thought, even thought he knew the answer. Petron would do it because it was the right thing to do, and Petron always had a sense of what the right thing to do was. Not what the rules said or what Ma said or the commander – what was *right. I can be brave too, Petro,* Cuss thought, and he tried to remember fishing with his brother, walking in the forest. He could not think of Ma or Jana – to think of them would be to lose hours to blackness, heaving sobs, a weight so great he couldn't bear it. After what must have been an hour with no sleep on the horizon, Cuss quietly swung down from his hammock and slipped on his boots, the new boots of supple leather provided by the keep quartermaster. He tiptoed to the door and headed up to the main deck.

The rain had stopped. Sailors were still up and around but it was almost pitch-black, the only light starlight and the reflected moon, nearly full. Cuss waved to the skein-mages and the woman Morag with the braided hair, who gave him a nod but didn't stop to talk. She was patrolling around the deck, and he could see another four commandos posted around the ship. Cuss stood by a railing and looked to where he thought land might be. He felt an ache in his stomach, a constant unwavering fear.

'A real ship, Petron,' he said quietly, thinking of his brother. 'A real ship and sailors, and I'm to be a commando. The sergeant is taking us to the island where the whitestaffs live, and we'll cure Marta and push back the rust-folk. I got a sword-knot...'

Cuss trailed off. His mother and sister had been killed by the orbs that stole Petron. His father had been gone so many years before that. Cuss was alone now, except for the sergeant and Yselda. *Yselda would tell me to call the sergeant the commander,* he thought, and sighed. Looking north – at least, he thought it was north – he scanned the sky for any glimmer of light.

'I have a silver dagger now,' he said, gripping the rail tight. 'I can fight back this time.'

'Who're you speaking to about daggers, lad?' a man said, and Cuss turned with a start. A sailor was there, a tall brawny man with dark skin, clean-shaven, a layer of black and white stubble cropped close to his scalp. He was wearing simple trousers and a long shirt, with a thick jacket over the top, the kind the sailors seemed to favour over capes and cloaks. A strip of leather was tied tight around his head, covering one eye. Cuss smiled.

'Sorry, sir,' he said, and the man snorted and joined him at the rail, leaning on his elbows.

'Nothing to be sorry about, and I'm not a "sir", lad. I work for a living,' he said, and Cuss settled back at the rail. Together they stared out at the lapping of the water. The rainclouds had mostly scattered.

'Talking to my brother,' Cuss said after a while, and the man pointed up at a constellation.

'That's Char the warrior,' he said. 'You see his blade, his horse?'

Cuss nodded and gazed up at the stars, thought he wasn't sure he could make out Char. He had never been good at spotting constellations.

'He dead then, your brother?' the man asked, his tone casual, and Cuss didn't bother to answer. He let his gaze drop from the cold stars to the railing, felt the itch in his fingers as the air stole warmth from his hands. He shivered. Every breath was a cloud, and it was colder than it had even been in Hookstone forest. *Colder than you ever saw, Petron,* he thought.

'He ever sail on a ship, your brother?' the man said, and Cuss wished he would leave.

'No,' he said, 'but we had a wee fishing boat on Loch Hassel.'

'Ah!' the man said. 'A lad from Hookstone forest! I've been there a time or two. Seems a good thing to speak to him then. Let him know how the sailing goes.'

Cuss looked up at the man, who was smiling back at him with an earnest face.

'Do you ever speak to anyone? Speak like this?'

The man's smile faded, and he turned back to the lapping waves.

'We all have someone we want to speak to, lad,' he said. 'I've more than I'd care to name.'

They stood together in silence and Cuss opened and closed his mouth. He had been too afraid to ask Floré, but maybe this sailor knew...

'Do you know the plan?' he asked, and the man tilted his head.

'Depends what you mean, lad,' he said, and gestured for Cuss to explain. Cuss bit his lip and stared back across the deck to where Morag the skein-mage paced, her steps careful, her eyes probing into the darkness.

'No ship has come back,' he said at last, not turning from Morag.

The man shifted his feet uncomfortably.

'No ship has come back,' Cuss repeated, 'and nobody knows why. Orbs or wyrms or demons or whatever else. We don't know why, but what's different about *Basira's Dance*? We have commandos on patrol but surely half the ships that left the last six spans had that. It isn't even a warship, just a trader! What do we do if we're attacked?'

Cuss turned to face his companion at the rail, and the man nodded and frowned and leaned his elbows on the smooth wood of the railing, clasping his hands.

'Orbs, we probably die,' he said, 'demons, we might survive. Water monsters, we could maybe take. A wyrm? If there is a wyrm in the sea, we are dead already. There's been maybe a dozen wyrms in the last three centuries, lad. You want to know the plan? *Basira's Dance* is a smuggler. Look at the sails.'

Cuss glanced up at the taut fabric stretching overhead, complex rigging holding each sail in place, sailors rushing to and fro below.

'Most ships don't sail at night,' the sailor said, 'and most ships aren't this fast. We've got four skein-mages, which is more than most legions in the Stormguard. I think the *plan*, if there is one, is to move fast and hope to luck. It's that or wait in Undal City for the enemy to come to you, no? The captain knows some routes, it seems. Perhaps he knows a way the rust-folk haven't guarded.'

Cuss nodded slowly, but wasn't convinced. He couldn't think of anything else they could do to prepare. *How could you fight one of those orbs without another orb?* With a clasp of his hand to Cuss's shoulder the sailor turned to leave.

'Don't worry, lad,' he said over his shoulder, 'your gang seem like exactly the people you'd want to be next to if things take a turn.'

He smiled and walked on, nodding briefly to Morag-Skein as he went.

'Wait!' Cuss called. 'Your name? I'm Cuss. Private Cuss.'

The sailor turned and touched his fingers to his forehead.

'A pleasure, Private Cuss. I'm Komende. Stay warm, and pass on my welcome to your brother.'

Cuss didn't know how to respond to that so he simply stood and watched the sailor retreat to the lower decks. Turning back to the ocean and the stars above he ran his cold hand across the railing and pictured his brother and sister and mother and father and the calm waters of Loch Hassel. Petron had always wanted to see the next village, the next meadow, Hookstone Town and beyond. *I'll see more, Petron. I'll see more and I'll let you know.*

He was about to turn in, to try and find some sleep and warmth, when he heard a wet slap behind him, across the deck. Turning, he saw a monstrosity. The deck was lit by a single oil lamp, and at the edge of its pooled light a commando was held two feet from the ground, twitching. Behind it a creature half-hidden in shadow was clutching the commando with one grotesquely muscled arm and clawed hand, the other hand reached up around the dying man's face, a palm of mottled green and grey knotted flesh clamped across his mouth. As Cuss watched agape it squeezed its claws closed and ripped open the commando's abdomen and face, his entrails and blood spraying across the deck in a burst of red. The creature let the dying man fall to the deck and Cuss saw it in its entirety: a lashing tail, a mane of matted hair, a lean crooked body leading to a flat face with black orb eyes and an impossibly wide mouth. *A rottroll? A trollspawn?*

It was perhaps eight foot tall with long arms and vicious claws, and as it stepped into the lamplight pooled in the centre of the deck Cuss saw into its bloodstained mouth, row after row of wet jagged teeth and a slavering black tongue like an eel writhing behind. Cuss reached for his sword and realised it was swinging safely in his bunk. To his right in the aftcastle by the ship's wheel a sailor was yelling, a bell was ringing. From behind Cuss, a burst of silver light crackled over his shoulder and he heard a grunt of effort. *Morag.* The beam of light hit the creature in the chest and left a charred mark, but the beast didn't even slow. He heard Morag curse behind him, but couldn't take his eyes from the creature.

I should be yelling, he thought numbly. *I should be running!* He had no weapon. The creature took two steps forward, the first foot crushing down on the ragged torso of the fallen commando. *Albverron,* Cuss realised. *I thought I didn't know their names but that's Albverron.* Albverron had shown him a tattoo of a skeleton on his wiry bicep when they were training on the deck, had made it dance as he twitched his arm. He had laughed, and corrected Cuss's stance with the longsword with a word and a quiet hand to his shoulder. Cuss forced himself to look away from what was left of the dead man's face and felt his lungs burning. He had stopped breathing.

Cuss's eyes were locked on the black orbs of the monster. All of it was slick with seawater and as it stepped to the centre of the deck it shrieked in a horrifying ululating yell, a warbling wail that sent Cuss to his knees. From behind the beast – *trollspawn, it must be trollspawn* – goblins were climbing the railing, first a dozen, then a dozen more. They did not look like any goblin he had seen. They had the pebbled grey skin and black orb eyes, the frail bodies and jagged nails and rows of serrated teeth, but shallow fins rose from the backs of their arms and legs and a crest rose from the top of their skulls. Each dragged behind it a thin lashing tail.

The trollspawn in the centre shrieked again, and Cuss forced himself to his feet. He grabbed a belaying pin from the railing behind him, twelve inches of solid oak. Taking a step forward he drew his fists up and screamed at the beast.

'Spit on you!' he yelled, his voice cracking. Morag stepped to his side, crackling green light playing over her fingers.

With a flurry of movement the door to the captain's cabin opened, and at the same time from the foredeck three figures leapt down, black shadows. *The Tullioch*! Warily they edged across the deck to Cuss. The trollspawn and goblins heaved heavy breaths and cast about. *What are they looking for? Why don't they attack?* Cuss didn't understand.

Across the deck Captain Muirgainas stood by his cabin door in only a long nightshirt, and began ringing a heavy bell that hung by his doorway. The next door opened and Floré and Benazir were there, Floré with her sword drawn and gauntlets donned, Benazir with one arm wrapped in a sling but the other clutching a dagger, both wearing shirts and trousers but no boots.

The trollspawn swung its head from Cuss to the Tullioch to the captain and Floré and Benazir, and with both clawed hands it reached down and picked up the body of the dead commando Albverron and it *wrenched*. The man split in two, his stomach and spine splitting with a sound that made Cuss vomit, a sharp acid spray that left him heaving. He heard a yell from the back of the boat. With a contemptuous flick the trollspawn threw the head and torso of the dead man at Captain Muirgainas's feet and made a strange chittering noise, and then the Tullioch next to Cuss stepped forward. He was lean and muscled, so similar to the Tullioch Heasin who Cuss had saved from the mob at Ollen. Cuss managed to stand up straight.

'Enough of this,' the Tullioch said in Isken, his black scales glistening in reflected moonlight. With an explosion of movement he hurled the spear of black metal he had held at his side, the point slamming true into the chest of the trollspawn. The trollspawn gurgled and staggered back and the entire ship held its breath, but then the door to the lower deck sprang open and a sailor ran out, screaming.

'The hold!' he yelled. 'They're in the...'

The first goblin on the deck threw itself at him, a dagger of black rock in its hand. The next three grappled at his legs and the man fell screaming. Still the captain rang his bell. Above the goblins and the dying sailor the trollspawn reached down to its gut and pulled out the four foot of black steel the Tullioch had thrown, holding the gore-soaked spear up to its eye. It shrieked again and from below decks Cuss heard an answering wail, heard screaming, heard crashing and breaking. *Yselda!* The trollspawn began to run at him, and the Tullioch next to him, then somehow Floró was there and her sword cut down hard into its calf, a mote of flame dancing along the blade where blood soaked it and flourishing into a blaze of red and white fire. The trollspawn stepped back from the flare, and Floró drew into a high guard as a ribbon of red and white fire danced along her blood-soaked blade.

The trollspawn roared and swung at her, and more sailors and commandos spewed from the lower decks, some bleeding, some dazed, some unarmed and others clutching bloodied blades. They emerged into the throng of goblins and everything descended into chaos. The Tullioch charged with brutal speed, two of them sprinting around the trollspawn to the throng of goblins and sailors, the other joining Floré as she baited the larger beast with darting strikes from her sword. Morag was climbing the rigging next to Cuss, and from her hands streaks of silver light crackled down and harried the trollspawn and goblins. Cuss found himself staggering back, belaying pin in hand, his breathing a rapid pant. Floré had put herself between him and the trollspawn. With every lick of her sword, the blood-soaked blade flared and danced with flame and the trollspawn reared and screamed.

'Here, lad!' someone said, and it was Komende the one-eyed sailor. He thrust a billhook into Cuss's hand, an eight-foot pole with a wicked hook on the end made for pulling flotsam and catching ropes. Komende held another, and as one they dashed forward and began to swing at the trollspawn, Cuss aiming lumbering blows at its head. It was swiping at Floré and trying to snatch up the Tullioch who was harrying it, the one who had been carrying the spear, but he danced amongst crates and rigging, always a step away. Every swipe at Floré ended with a hiss and a quickly retracted hand as she parried with the burning razor-edge of her sword. The blade was slick with gore now, and flame billowed around the dark metal and blood below. The flame had lost the tinge of red and was a furious glaring white, but Cuss could see runes and patterns carved on the dark metal within, glowing a vibrant red.

'The legs!' Komende called, and Cuss untangled the end of his billhook from a coil of rope and followed the sailor's lead. Together they swung, and the trollspawn fell to all fours as the hooks and poles tangled amongst its ankles. With a writhing twist Cuss's pole was wrenched from his arm, but Floré was already behind the beast, hacking down at the back of its neck with brutal short chops of her burning sword, her other hand gripping at its mane of hair. A taloned claw reached up to pull her free but the Tullioch grabbed it with its own claws. Cuss ran forward to help but then the trollspawn bucked and writhed and Floré was thrown clear. Her sword fell across the deck, the flame on its blade guttering out as soon as her hand left the hilt. Wrenching to its feet the trollspawn bit down on the arm of the Tullioch and shook its head violently, wrenching and tearing the flesh below. From the goblin melee behind, Benazir emerged with two commandos.

'Legs!' she said, and the two commandos leapt forwards with no hesitation at the trollspawn legs, hacking away. Cuss managed to get close enough to grab the blood-slicked Tullioch's unchewed arm and he pulled them back, staggering under their weight, as the trollspawn let go its writhing bite to scream in pain. One of the goblins came at Cuss and he kicked it, sending it sprawling, and he caught a flash of silver as a dagger flew past his head to sink into its neck. The goblin screamed and then it was burning, fire spreading from the blade of the dagger and out into flesh. Benazir was next to him then, and she eyed the Tullioch.

'Pressure on the wound!' Then she was turning and another knife was in her hands somehow, spinning in at the trollspawn bearing down on Floré, who scrambled across the deck and swept up her sword, the blade igniting into a plume of white flame that she moved in a series of heavy blows that the trollspawn furiously swatted against. Benazir's silver knife bit deep in the flank of the beast and the creature howled once more, a variegated cry that pierced Cuss down to his core. Floré did not flinch. Cuss fell to his knees as the decking beneath him smashed upward, and a clawed hand the size of his head broke through the debris. More screaming came from below decks. Human screaming. Goblin screaming. Trollspawn screaming.

Cuss fell back on the deck and scrambled, gibbering. *I can't do this. I'm not a commando. I need to go home! We need to go home.*

Ahead of him the beast screamed in pain and anger, swung its claws wide and reached for the silver dagger stuck in its leg. Floré stepped into its reach and, with a single movement that seemed to carry all her weight and energy, she thrust her burning sword into its neck and spun her body. A spray of green-black blood covered her as the trollspawn fell.

'We need to go home,' Cuss heard himself say, and then the battle before him drew into focus. The goblins, the screaming. *We need to go home! We...*

'Yselda!' Cuss yelled, and scrambling forward and snatching up a silver dagger from the trollspawn's leg he ran towards the lower deck.

Tomas met him at the stairs and Cuss skidded to a halt. His goggles were lowered, even at night, and behind him Yselda clutched her own dagger. It was soaked in blood, green and red, and her hair was singed. Tomas held a wand of dark metal with a red crystal at its tip in one hand and in his other the black kitten clutched tight. It was mewling and clawing but he held it close to his chest.

'Lower decks cleared,' Tomas called, 'and I even put the fires out after.'

Yselda was staring at Tomas with wide eyes. Behind him the two skein-mages attached with Morag to the commando unit emerged, slim figures clad in black. Tomas gestured at the remaining goblins who were backing up to the railing. There were only six or seven left from the original two dozen but they gripped brutal stone knives, and the sailors and commandos surrounding them were unarmoured and largely unarmed. One of the goblins leapt the railing and disappeared, but the next to try it was snagged by a bolt of crackling silver light from the rigging above that burned the eyes from its head and sent it spinning back to the deck with a sickening crunch. *Morag.* Cuss glanced up and saw her hanging from one foot and hand in the rigging a dozen feet up, her other hand extended.

'Step back!' Tomas called, and the sailors and commandos began to move away, leaving a circle of bloodstained deck, the corpses of more than a dozen goblins and six or seven humans. Cuss couldn't tell if the dead were sailors or commandos. The two Tullioch who had been fighting goblins stepped back warily, but neither took their eyes from the beasts, and both of their claws were coated in blood. Tomas stepped forward and levelled his wand at the goblins.

'Orders, Commander?' he called, and Benazir came to his shoulder. She glanced at Floré who was kneeling by the dead trollspawn, breathing hard and staring at the sword in her hand that still burned with white-hot flame. Benazir shook her head.

'They are goblins,' Benazir said quietly. Floré hung her head and dropped her sword, the flame dying as her hand left the hilt, the intensity of the runes on the blade fading slowly from red to black. Cuss went to Yselda and stood by her, his hands shaking.

Benazir put a hand on Tomas's shoulder. 'Burn them all.'

8

A Witness in the Dark

'Since the founding of the protectorate we have faced war,
war with Tessendorm, war with Cil-Marie, war with the
princes of Isken before their own people cast them down.
War against the Antian below, war against the Tullioch so
many years ago when we sought to expand, heedless of
the lessons of the past. Civil war amongst ourselves, as
tyrants and despots and politicians sought power over the
people's needs – the Pathbreaker Massacres, the revolution
of the self-styled Council of Chiefs. Always we have
prevailed, and always at our western border the rotstorm
rages – the common enemy unites us again and again and
the descendants of Ferron pay the price for our stability.'
– **Break the Stormguard's chains!** Lillebet Arfallow, year
312 from Ferron's Fall (1123 Isken)

Ashbringer ran through the streets of Undal City, streets that
thronged with patrols of Stormguard City Watch and Lancers.
From the area of town around the central shaman temple
there were cries and bells, and chains of people strung from

wells headed in that direction, passing bucket after bucket of water. *The fire is spreading.* The orb of light had sped away into the night after its brief attack, leaving panic and chaos in its wake.

Ashbringer was winded and exhausted. She had searched further in the skein than she ever had before seeking the god-killing blade, and she had still not found it. *I found something else though.* She kept running, a steady lope, her unstrung bow light in one hand as the other kept her scabbarded sword steady. Her scarf blew off as she rounded a corner and she did not stop to retrieve it, and after that every few streets she raised a startled yell as someone spotted her blue skin, the red fractal rune-scars etched across it. Her face was coated in blood, blood that had poured from her nose, her eyes, her mouth as she reached too far into the pattern and it took its toll. She ignored the blood and she ignored the screams and she kept running until she reached her destination.

Protector's Keep was a riot of activity. The outer gates were closed, and every watchtower and wall was ablaze with lit torches, archers, skein-mages. The keep was a hybrid of castle, palace, and ancient fort, in some decades a utilitarian barracks, in others a retreat for a louche ruling class. Ashbringer turned her head to one side and took it all in. Her natural inclination was to scale a wall and take what she needed by stealth, but she was tired, and the keep was on such high alert that she had to admit that even she may fail. She stopped still for a moment and caught her breath, then lowered her hood and moved from her vantage in the shadows.

As she strode across the square she held her head high

and kept her hand clear of her sword hilt. She tried to meet the eye of as many Stormguard as she could, but there were too many; perhaps an entire platoon of City Watch was patrolling outside of the gate. *What would they do if an orb came, spewing fire and death?* From the look of their faces Ashbringer thought they might even stand their ground. The Undal were always tenacious. As she walked towards them there were shouts and muttering and very swiftly she was ten yards from their ranks, a dozen halberds pointed at her, a dozen swords drawn, and a rampart bristling with nocked arrows all aimed at her.

'Greetings, dear friends. I am Ashbringer.' She bowed fluidly and rose again. 'I come seeking the Orubor embassy. I am in something of a rush.'

It still took them five minutes to admit her to the outer gates, under armed guard. A woman with a captain's rank badge tried to take her weapons and Ashbringer gave a smile that showed every one of her serrated teeth.

'No,' she said, 'I'm afraid I cannot allow you to do that.'

'You can't come in with weapons,' the captain replied, but Ashbringer shrugged.

'I assure you I can. Please fetch Highmother Ash, and perhaps that Starbeck fellow. He always seems rather decisive.'

The captain paled at her informality with Knight-Commander Starbeck, and Ashbringer allowed herself a self-satisfied chuckle when the woman had left. She had never met Starbeck in her life, had still been recuperating from her wounds in Orubor's wood when the embassy returned Artollen and her brood of cadets and wounded to the south.

Ten minutes later she was ushered to a sparsely appointed room where Highmother Ash waited, her diminutive frame and flowing locks of white hair a welcome sight. Ashbringer embraced her.

'Is Artollen here? The daughter?' she asked, slipping into the forest tongue. Highmother Ash tilted her head and licked her lips.

'South, to seek their mages, though the daughter is here,' she said. Ashbringer felt her pulse quicken. 'What are you about, child?'

A door opened and a stone-faced man entered, lean and armoured with a sword at his hip. He bowed firstly to Highmother Ash, and then to Ashbringer, and she returned the gesture.

'How can I help you?' he said, and Ashbringer grinned at his brutal efficiency.

'A child is in your care. Marta, daughter of Floré Artollen and Janos the Salt-Man.'

Starbeck stood very still and his face betrayed no reaction, though Ashbringer thought his fists perhaps clenched a little. She bit her tongue for a moment.

'I need her blood.' Starbeck sighed and rubbed at his face with one hand.

'This,' he said, 'I'm absolutely sure will be good.'

~

Hove brushed his teeth with salt paste and a rough scrap of cloth and washed his face. His left hand was still throbbing, days since Ceann Brude had taken him from Port Last. *It will never heal now.* He had tried to straighten the fingers himself on the fourth day after the rust-folk took him, but it had been too painful. The pain was lessened now with time and healing, but the first three fingers of his left hand were a mangle and he could barely make a fist. *I should be dead,* he thought, and pictured his friends in Port Last burnt and skewered. He scrubbed at his face with cold water from his bucket. He scrubbed himself all over and then slipped on the shirt Ceann Brude had given him, the simple black trousers of strange material.

'Why do you want me alive?' he had asked, when she came to him with the clothes and a candle and flint and steel, and she had shaken her head.

'Hove.' Her Ferron accent clipped into his name, making it sound strange and wrong. 'I can touch the storm; I *carry* the storm. I have a job for you. I am going to take you west. First to Fetter-Dun, to see how we live. Then, to Urforren. To see how we died. Have you ever seen the rotstorm?'

Hove had shaken his own head, then. He had never seen the rotstorm, not in all his life in Port Last.

'You will be my witness. You will witness for me the way they want us to live, and I will bring you to Undal City itself to speak to your mighty council.'

Days passed, and Hove was forgotten. A rotsurge had taken his parents' farm, and he had grown up in the shaman monastery and orphanage in Garioch. They had sent him to be a whitestaff, but he hadn't yet made the trip to Isken for proper training – first, a few years as an apprentice at Port Last to learn his fundamentals. Alone in his cold cell, Hove reached for the skein but there was only chaos, the chaos of crow-men nearby, and he felt sick.

Is this Fetter-Dun? He had never heard the name before Ceann Brude had said it. He waited in the dark as long as he could bear – he only had one candle and preferred light when he ate, or when the fear took him. Someone would bring him food, someone else water. *If it is water.* The only water they gave him was rust-red and tasted like earth and metal. They had kept him hooded and bound when they took him aboard their orb, and then there were blows and darkness. When he awoke he was in the cell. *Fetter-Dun.* The air was oppressive, tinged with some acrid taste, and through the seams in his cell wall fronds and tendrils of green and yellow grew. One night he awoke with an itch and one of the fronds was caressing his bare toe, a tiny mouth full of serrated teeth open, chewing. The skin on his toe was a mangle.

Hove had used a whole candle that night, burning back fronds until his cell was clear, but in the darkness he swore he could hear them growing – a squeaking, stretching sound at the edge of his senses. As the days passed before someone with food threw him another candle, he realised he could not wait. After wrapping his shirt around his right hand he combed his walls in the dark and crushed the life from anything he found. Bugs crawled in, long centipedes and spiders through the bars of his cell door. He threw them out again, and when they returned he crushed them and smeared them in a line at his cell door in a hope it might deter their fellows. If anything, it drew more tiny beasts. He warred with them, long lessons in his favoured subjects of biology and ecology now made practice. *I am the one who will survive in here. I am the one who will survive.*

Through the bars of the cell door Hove could see only a patch of corridor and then another cell. His candle would not cast light into it, and he had no reason to think it occupied. Hours and days passed. He could tell day from night only because the faintest of dim light shone in the corridor during the day, gift of a distant window perhaps. Ever there was the sound of wind against stone, the sound of lightning, and for many hours each day the pounding of rain.

I am in the rotstorm, he thought. *Hell itself.*

The shamans of the protectorate taught that hell was the same nameless fire as the Baal worshippers of Isken or Tessendorm preached. Heaven was ascension back to the pattern, to Anshuka's dream, to walk with her and all who had gone before in verdant meadows. Hove didn't believe that. *I'm a pattern,* he thought, *an odd little loop. When I end I'll just end, same as everything else.* He always felt so bad for the shamans in the monastery at Garioch. The workers and the whitestaffs and the Stormguard all came together to form the Grand Council, but the shamans stood apart and below. Despite the generally devout population, most Undal saw the monastery monks as at best misguided in their attempt to replace hard work with prayer, and at worst viewed them with suspicion. Not like a village shaman who was likely healer and apothecary and teacher and sage; the cloistered brothers and sisters of the shaman temple monasteries were a breed apart. They came to the whitestaffs and offered tithe and tidings, information, help, assistance. Hove had hated it as a boy, the devout shaman always ready to jump to any whitestaff's bidding simply because they were closer to Anshuka than the shaman could ever be. *They all end up in the same place, whitestaff and shaman and Stormguard. We all end up dead.*

Hove shivered in his cell. He didn't want to end. He wanted to live, to study, to laugh, to heal wounds and speak to his friends. The thought of that made him weep again. All of his friends scattered from the monastery in Garioch, all the new friends in Port Last so painfully found and so quickly taken.

Hove sang to himself or mumbled, or practised the patterns he would seek in the skein if ever they grew clear. The whitestaffs had patterns made and ready, patterns you could study and bend your mind to, rather than hunting the way a skein-mage would. As the patterns were the same, two whitestaffs could work together if their understanding was close enough, if their mental pattern matched enough the one they were taught.

Hooking his senses to the skein made him feel sick with all the chaos around, but he could still practise the pattern within his mind. He dreamt of Riven, a citadel of learning, a fortress library against the Wind Sea that held a copy of every book in the world, a place where you could be healed. He dreamt of kindly whitestaffs with staves of silver oak and jade amulets. They would congratulate him on his bravery, they would fix his maimed hand. They would take his fear. He would wake shivering and alone, and press the walls of his cell in case a seeking mouth had grown bold as he slept and twined its way into his domain. *Rotvine.* He had heard stories about it, the kind of stories children tell with a stub of candle when they are meant to be asleep.

Ceann Brude came for him the next day, but she did not take him outside to the storm.

'History lesson,' she said, looming over him and shoving him along with her terribly strong arms. She was clad in black as ever, a simple dagger at her belt next to a wand. The salt-sigil tattooed over her eye was stark and black against her pale skin. She pushed him along to a low room lit by a dozen flaming torches, her twisted looming figure above and over him always. A single long table filled the centre of the room, and on it a huge old map and four wooden figures: a wolf, an owl, a dryad, and a bear.

Anshuka, he thought, *Anshuka be praised.*

'How much do they tell Undal, I wonder? Even little whitestaffs?'

Hove shrugged and held his left hand in his right. She waved a hand at him expectantly.

'Ferron had four Judges,' he said, approaching the table. 'Berren the dryad died in the desert, and Anshuka slept. Nessilitor was full of sorrow and left. Tullen One-Eye and the empress... I don't know her name. I'm sorry.'

Ceann Brude laid the dryad figure on its side far to the west of old Undal, in the vast expanses of the Iron Desert. Hove could see it was an old map of the Ferron Empire – the rotstorm and the protectorate were unmarked. She took the figure of the owl and moved it north to an island deep in the Storm Sea, and Anshuka she left where she was, next to Lothal, in the heart of the Ferron territory.

'Seraphina,' she said, 'daughter of the Eternal Emperor Ferron. What happened?' she said. 'I want to know your history.'

Hove flinched. *It is a test. But what is the right answer?* He could tell her the history as he had been taught it, could change it to reflect better on the Ferron... He could feel cold sweat running down his back.

'Berren died, Nessilitor left, Anshuka slept. The emperor... died, I think? Empress Seraphina and Tullen One-Eye needed land to feed their people because without Berren their crops failed, and I think there were floods. I don't know why. They pushed out. With the god-wolf Lothal they crushed old Undalor. They subdued Tessendorm. Isken and Kelamor and Uradech bowed. Cil-Marie traded them slaves.'

Ceann Brude moved the wolf statue east until it sat on old Undalor, where the modern protectorate stood.

'Slaves, mines, wonders of skein-magic,' she said. 'The Tullioch Shardspire broken in two and the capitulation of the clans of the wild reefs. Vassal states to the west, beyond the Iron Desert. All old Undalor turned to plantation and mine and crops to farm. An empire, for hundreds of years. What happened next?'

Hove looked at the map and remembered the words of his old schoolmaster Byronus at the orphanage. *Does Garioch still stand? Did they destroy the monastery, the orphanage?*

'No empire escapes justice forever,' he said, and made himself glare at her. *I will survive this. I will survive you.* 'Mistress Water escaped the mines. Organised the people. Woke the god-bear. We fought back against your whips and your chains. Anshuka killed Lothal. The bear killed the wolf, and the owl fell to your mad skein-wreck. We won.'

Ceann Brude walked around the table to him and slowly moved the wolf back to Ferron, placing it on its side, and toppled the owl statue as well. She stood close to him, her face inches from his.

'And your bear went to sleep in her forest, trailing a storm of ice and cold,' she said, moving the bear across to Undal and leaving it there alone. 'And in her nightmares she punishes Ferron. For three centuries. A century longer than the expanded empire stood. Three centuries of children and monsters wrought in the storm.'

Hove gripped his maimed hand and met her eyes.

'What do you *want*?' he asked, and she trailed her overlong fingers across the bear statuette before leaving it be.

'I want to be free of the sins of the past,' she said eventually, and her face, so human and so young, twitched with anger. 'But that is not to be, so I will settle for a river of blood and a ditch of fire. And a home for my people.'

~

Floré examined the goblin corpse in the light of the morning sun. She had not realised how far west they must have travelled the day before, but just on the edge of her vision at the horizon there was a blurring of black, hints of purple. *The rotstorm*. She had been away from it for years, hadn't had a glimpse except for the rotsurges playing over Hookstone forest and Hookstone Town, and they were pale imitations. Just the sight of it made her fingers itch for her gauntlets.

'These goblins are weird,' Cuss said, standing at her shoulder. He was eating a bowl of porridge he had gotten from somewhere, changed into dry and fresh clothes. The clouds of the day before were gone, and the sky above was a solid mass of pale blue. Floré rubbed her nose and clenched her fist. The sailors and dead commandos were overboard sewn in sailcloth, and the goblins as well – all save one and the trollspawn. She had commanded they be left for her to inspect in the light of day, and they lay dragged between stacked coils of rope and crates, not quite out of sight enough for everyone's comfort. Captain Muirgainas had demanded she remove them, still clad in his nightshirt, but she had stood with her bloodied sword and locked eyes with him until he broke her stare and moved off to give the orders she wanted.

'Get me Benazir,' she said, 'and then go find out when we expect to arrive. Offer the Tullioch some food, as well.'

Cuss bobbed his head and took another spoon of porridge before stomping off. Floré clenched and unclenched her fists. Tomas appeared before Benazir did, face freshly washed, his goggles pulled low and a scarf of blue wool around his neck. He held his small crate with the kitten inside and was patrolling around the deck.

'Where did you get a scarf at *sea*?' she asked when he drew close, and he shrugged.

'I was cold,' he said, 'so I traded a sailor for some coin. Can't say it smells spectacular, but there you go.'

He stood awkwardly. The kitten mewled and he idly reached into his box to scratch it.

'I'm not your enemy,' he said at last, and Floré turned from the goblin to stare at him. He held her gaze steadily.

'We both want the same thing. Whitestaffs supporting the Stormguard, a way to kill Tullen One-Eye if he still lives, and a cure for your daughter. I know we've our differences and our past, but we are allies, Floré. I was your ally then. I would ally with you. Truly I would. I want the protectorate to be free of Ferron. What else is there?'

Floré stared down at the dead goblin and slipped on her gauntlets. She reached an armoured finger into its mouth – at least a half dozen rows of teeth, and then a chaotic tangle of more teeth beyond that.

'I am your ally, Tomas,' she said, but as she thought of the children he had left in the sacrifice cavern, she knew it was a lie. *What else is there?* Floré thought it a good question to ask of its asker. Tomas scooped his cat from its crate and held it up to the furred collar of his cloak. It closed its eyes and pressed close to him.

'Does it have a name?' she asked, and he smiled at her.

'Not yet.'

He left her with the bodies, and eventually Benazir joined her, nudging the trollspawn with her foot.

'They aren't children, Floré,' she said, straight to the point. Floré stood and opened her mouth but Benazir shook her head.

'They might have been. You might be exactly right. But whatever they were, they're monsters now. And if you're right, nothing short of killing Anshuka herself would change that.'

Floré nodded but her eyes kept returning to the frail goblin.

'You ever seen one like this?' she asked, and Benazir drew her knife and used it to manoeuvre the fin crests on its head, the backs of its arms.

'Always some fresh hell,' she said, 'but this is known. They see them sometimes down at the port in Final Light, west of here a ways. Swimmers. You know as well as I that every trollspawn is as weird as the next. Guess we found a splashy one.'

Floré furrowed her brow.

'We're at least twenty to thirty miles from the nearest edge of the storm, where the blight waters might be. You think it's just chance we happen across "a splashy one" out here in all this blue?'

Benazir laughed and sheathed her dagger.

'Floré,' she said, 'where I'm concerned I'd say this seems about typical luck. We knew something was attacking ships. Maybe this was it, but I doubt it. Larger forces than ours went south – whole flotillas now vanished. If Leomar is right, there is a wyrm cutting off the route to Isken in the east, and an orb *or orbs* sinking whatever gets as far as Riven. I fear this is the first drop of rain before the storm. We might be headed to an isle of ghosts, where all that is left is another enemy.'

Floré ordered the sailors to dump the bodies, and then checked on the Tullioch. Leomar's wounds were bound in thick bandage of kelp held on with a leather strap that one of his comrades had produced from a pouch. He was clutching his spear of dark metal.

'Is your mage honest?' he asked quietly. Floré stared at him.

'He can do all he has said so far.' The Tullioch relaxed and clicked his teeth. 'Though we will need the Orubor to agree for us to use an orb to reach the cavern. I fear it is too high and too remote to find without one.'

'Have you visited the shardspire?' he asked, and Floré shook her head.

'One day, perhaps,' she said. 'I owe Heasin son of Luasin of Shardkin Tullioch a great debt.'

Leomar nodded and flicked his tongue between his teeth.

'What will you do if an orb comes for us, Floré Artollen?'

Floré smiled at the rigid formality of his speech and thought about Marta in the orphan barracks, shivering with fever. *No father, no mother, no chance.* She closed her eyes for a beat and then opened them and smiled at Leomar.

'Whatever I can,' she said, and bowed her head in farewell.

She left the Tullioch staring south and discussing paths through the reefs with the crew, and returned to her cabin. Voltos was there, reading a book, though he quickly tucked it away when she entered.

'What are you reading, my friend?' she asked, and he licked his muzzle and stroked down his whiskers.

'*Every tree a home*,' he said. Floré sat down and took off her gauntlets. 'I read it sometimes. To remember him.'

It was Janos's first poetry collection, a smattering of short verse, beautiful depictions of nature. In the collection were a handful of descriptions of the rotstorm. The juxtaposition, the horror of those brutal poems compared to the rural idyll he painted of Undal and the beauty of the nature he described had been enough to garner his following, sell his books, account him the chance for a sequel. Floré scratched at her head. It had always amused her. Janos was the greatest skein-mage of his generation, had tipped the balance in their favour to recapture Fallow Fen, had single-handedly razed the rust-folk fortress town of Urforren to burning salt. The Stormguard let it be known they had a skein-wreck in rumour alone, for his own safety. *The most powerful man in the country, and he is known only as a man who writes a pretty verse.* She smiled sadly. It was what he would have preferred.

'It's a while since I read it,' she said. 'Have you any advice, Voltos, for what we face?'

Voltos squirmed in his chair and wrinkled his snout. He cleaned his round spectacles on a silk cloth produced from a hidden pocket and returned them gently to his face. Floré knew he did that to give himself a moment to compose his thoughts. He always had.

'Benazir seeks whitestaffs,' he said at last, 'Tomas seeks a ghost and a mystery, but, Floré, you must know we *all* seek a cure for Marta. Benazir loves you as a sister – she would never harm the girl or let her come to harm. Tomas sees her as a future disciple, or the key to unlocking his own power. In either case, her survival is necessary. You three need not be unaligned, but you easily may become so. Keep your friends close. A single spark fades alone, but from many a fire will grow. Eyes sharp, blade sharper.'

Floré nodded and when he left he passed her the book. She held it close, the thin red leather of the cover, the spiky typeface and thick paper. She did not read it, but sat and thought. She knew the poems in there, the feel of them, the *taste* of them. They were too powerful for her to read; every word was a spell taking her to a memory. *I can't afford the luxury of suffering right now.*

When the call of '*Land!*' echoed through her cabin, Floré was geared and ready. Her kit was in a bag, Starbeck's sword cleaned and oiled with the damp red and white silk knot tied to its hilt. There was a hierarchy to the knots – in theory they were personal, reflecting a soldier's greatest accomplishment. Floré's old knot for her reckless foray into the storm, snatching a rotbud from overwhelming odds with only Janos on her side, still felt a true victory. The new knot of green and white Starbeck had given her was too fresh, a reminder of all they had lost. She kept it folded in her belt pouch. She still could not account for the return of her old sword-knot with anything other than a vague worry, but the presence of it reassured her. She wore the gauntlets Starbeck had commissioned for her with their ludicrous rune and silvered knuckles, and made sure her cloak and tabard were straight. She would not be cowed by whitestaffs who had run from the orbs, run from an unknown enemy. Benazir joined Floré in her preparations, and when they strode out together in their matching tabards and cloaks Floré felt utterly secure in herself.

I am a weapon. I tried to be a mother, and I will be again, but for now Marta needs me to be a weapon.

She scanned the water but despite the fervent movement of the sailors could see no sight of land. Cuss and Yselda were lined up with the other commandos, and Tomas was sat on a crate with his three skein-mages – Morag and Anderson and Ruul – all of them lean and serious-faced. Floré thought they looked young. Tomas still wore a knapsack pulled in tight to his hip, but the wand previously sheathed up his sleeve on his wrist was now prominently on display at his belt. The crate for his kitten was gone; instead a basket of ship's rope with a tight fitted lid sat next to him. The lid was off, but Floré could see a long rope that could be looped over a shoulder. The kitten's head was out. *Bloody fool and his bloody kitten.*

'A name yet, Tomas?' she called, and he grinned back to her.

'Jozenai,' he called back, 'first Knight-Commander of the Stormguard!'

Floré laughed despite herself. Jozenai, the commander who threw back Ferron, who raised the Stormwall. The cat had never so much as extended one of its claws for all she could see. As Tomas turned back to his kitten and his mages she stared after him a long moment, Voltos's words echoing in her ears. *There is no reason for us to be anything but allies.*

'Land!' the call came again, and Captain Muirgainas stomped across the deck and up to the raised forecastle. Floré and Benazir followed him, and there they found the three Tullioch. Leomar was hissing gently as he looked ahead.

'Berren's black blood,' Benazir spat, and called back down to the main deck. 'Bows ready, and blades sharp!'

Floré could only stare. Ahead of them, she could see the isle of Iskander rising in her sight, a lump of green and brown on the southern horizon. But long before then, the wreckage. She saw ship after ship. Masts stuck from the reef like the tops of a drowned grove, and between them and the island, spires of coral broke the surface of the water irregularly. Waves rolled in sheets and sets and then broke and scattered on unknown obstacles below the water. She saw no bodies, but hunks of sail and rope and rigging, barrels, boards, chunks of hull, a prow…

'How many ships?' she said, and next to her Muirgainas spat over the railing and slipped the knotted cord that covered his hook-hand free, unveiling a brutal point sharpened bright.

'All of them,' he said, swallowing audibly. 'It's a narrow run through the reef here. There are only two approaches to the island, and this one's the quieter normally. Coral like stone that'll tear you to flinders. If these ships were wrecked here, the wrecks wouldn't move far, not on these reefs.'

He shook his head and turned and began yelling orders. Floré pulled on her gauntlets and drew her sword. *I should have taken a bow. What could do this? A wyrm? An orb?*

Next to her Benazir gripped the railing with her hand and blew out a breath, the cloud of it dissipating upward and away on the wind.

'There's no going back,' she said, and Floré didn't bother to answer.

'For Marta,' Benazir said. Floré pictured her daughter, alone and afraid and sick, and she clenched her fists tight.

'Forward!' Muirgainas called, and the surly man's voice was thunder. 'We're running before the wind, my beauties. I want full sail, let out the reefs and tighten the halyards! I'll eat my dinner on a whitestaff's table, and we aren't stopping for any swimmers!'

9

Fractal Gallows

'Knight-Commander, Captain Sorren has hanged another dozen villagers, though the rest of the village appears to have been allowed to flee. There is no name for this place on our map. We met a tinker on the road. They claimed the Stormwall is under assault, and Fallow Fen has potentially fallen once more. Captain Sorren and his troop must have met the same news. They have stopped two days now in the nameless village, presumably deciding a next step. The self-appointed cleanser of the Northern Marches must now face his duty; he was sent to scout and report on rumoured rust-folk refugees farming and working amongst our own, and the trail of blood he has wrought is perhaps too strong for him to face his superiors in Aber-Ouse. Each night the strange orbs fly overhead, and the unease is palpable even within my own team. Of his forty men, I cannot say how many are loyal to him. My team is small and we must be surgical in our excision of this corruption.' – **Third report on the massacre at Crowpit**, Agent Haysom, Third Moon Trading House

The next hours of sailing wore on Tomas's nerves. The commandos had arrows nocked, and the sailors who hadn't perished in the attack of the night before wore heavy cutlasses at their belts. Artollen was everywhere, checking each commando, murmuring support. The three skein-mages he had been assigned asked him for orders and he drew his focus back to them. *All so young.* He couldn't remember their names. *Moira?* He was having trouble focusing. Since his connection to Varratim's dagger, being able to see the skein everywhere was endlessly fascinating but it seemed to take a portion of his focus, always. He would drift as people spoke to him, coming back to concentration with a snap having missed questions or whatever else they wanted. *I will learn to control it. I must.*

'One on the fore, one on the aft, one in the crow's nest,' he said, more to get them out of his hair than anything else. Little Jozenai was scratching at the top of his basket to be let out. *His basket? Her basket?* Tomas wasn't sure. He couldn't articulate the comfort the little cat brought him, and resisted trying. He didn't want to find a reason to let it go. *It was alone, just like me.* He clutched his satchel tight and went to Benazir, who was stood behind the captain at the ship's wheel on the aftcastle. She looked half-frozen, with heavy bags under her eyes.

'You need to get more sleep,' he said, and she curled her lip.

'That is the trouble with goblins,' she said, 'they never are considerate. I like your wand, by the way. Very shiny.'

Tomas smiled and cut a half bow. Benazir had never seen one of the ancient runewands in action until the night before, a sheet of flame turning goblins to char, a wave of his hand and a focus of the skein extinguishing where it might have caught the deck, the rigging. The captain muttered darkly next to her. *Probably not a fan of fire on his ship,* Tomas thought, and shrugged it away. The captain's thoughts didn't matter.

The ship was cutting through the clear water, the captain yelling indecipherable things to sailors who pulled ropes, sailors who hung from the prow and peered for jagged coral.

'You've done this run before, Captain?' he asked, eyeing the nervous sailors and the Tullioch who lounged at the forecastle rail, hissing to one another.

'Certainly,' Muirgainas said, 'but never with two dozen wrecked ships in the only clear channel, and no idea what wrecked them.'

He broke off their conversation to yell more orders and Tomas pulled at his goggles. The leather padding was soft, but it still rubbed at the skin of his face, especially on the right cheek where it overlapped the soft pink of the burn scars. *Burn scars courtesy of Artollen.* He ground his teeth. Benazir reached into the rope basket, scratched Jozenai's head and smiled. Taking Tomas's arm she led him to a patch of the rear rail.

'Do you have a plan if one of those orbs shows up?' she asked and gave him a grin. He thought it was a grin. He could only see with the layer of the skein forever over his eyes, and the subtleties of facial expressions were hard to pull forth from that spinning complexity of pattern and abstracted connection.

'I do have a plan, as it happens,' he said, 'but it will put me on my back for a few days if it succeeds or fails, I think, so I'd rather hold it in reserve. But I don't see what other option we have. Silver pays gold, but in this case, *iron.*'

Benazir patted his shoulder.

'I can always rely on you, Tomas. You've been a good friend. You would have been proud of them.'

Benazir's voice caught on that last phrase, and Tomas blinked inside his goggles, glad she couldn't see. *Proud of who?*

'Lady Kelvin and Nostul and the entire cadre did wonders during the attack. I could not have asked for more. Their deaths weigh heavy, Tomas. I did my best. I hope you know that.'

Tomas turned his face to an expression of sorrow. He'd entirely forgotten his cadre of Stormcastle XII skein-mages. *On to bigger and better things.* Nostul was always scheming and bitter that he didn't have Tomas's role as primus, and Lady Kelvin was a child – a precocious child, but still a child. *Which ones died?* He couldn't ask, was certain she had already told him.

'Lead in servitude,' he said, short of anything useful to say, and Benazir nodded along, staring behind the ship at the churning wake. 'Actually, I've been meaning to talk to you. Your trick with the rune-dagger and the wyrm. I have some ideas.'

Benazir's hand went reflexively to her left hip where the runed dagger was sheathed. Her belt had four daggers and her boots two more, identical save for the red leather wrapping of one hilt at her left hip. With his skein-broken eyes Tomas could see the pattern for fire, that thirst for blood and heat etched on the blade – a crude imitation of his wand. *I could craft such a blade, now, perhaps. Could craft something even greater. I just need time.* There had been no time, no moment since he was back from Orubor's wood with the blade. The castrum wanted him to talk of wands and orbs; Benazir and Starbeck wanted him to plan this fool mission after the simpering whitestaffs. *I could do a lot, with the right dagger.*

When they had finished discussing his plan he retreated to his quarters, asking Muirgainas to send him a sailor. *I need the anchor chains set right if this is to work. Silver pays gold.* It was an old skein-mage commando trick, damned hard to pull off. Throw as much kinetic energy as you could into a small object like a silver coin, and send it hurtling faster than an arrow at your target. Most people missed, and the energy and pattern and focus required for such a move was complex and utterly fatiguing. Tomas had been within the orbs, had seen one cracked by a hard enough impact. If he got it right, he could save them all. *And if I get it wrong,* he thought, *instead of a skein-mage primus slinging fire and death and wonder, they'll have me passed out and shivering for the day when they need me most.*

He fed Jozenai some milk and removed his goggles for a few minutes, enjoying the soft padding of the kitten's paws on his cheeks as they played on the bunk, enjoying the air on his eyelids and not the press of the goggles tight to his face.

'You don't think me a monster.' Jozenai mewled and took more drops of milk from his clay saucer.

'Many would,' a voice said, and Tomas snatched for his goggles and reached for his wand. *How could I not hear the door open? Nobody can know!* A sailor was in the doorway, closing it gently behind him. A broad man with long sleeves cinched tight, a closely shaven head and a band of dark leather over one eye. From the corner of his eye, with the fraction of his eyes that still saw only reflected visible light and not the endless other patterns around them, Tomas saw he had dark skin and his remaining eye was a rich brown, wrinkles surrounding it as he smiled at Tomas.

'Jozenai is a name that would get a cat killed, in the rotstorm,' the sailor continued, and Tomas slipped the kitten back into her basket, still facing away from the man, one hand fumbling to pull his goggles on.

'There are no cats in the rotstorm,' Tomas replied. *Did he see? Do I kill him? How would I get rid of the body?* He turned, but his eyes glanced off the man and he found himself looking at the wall instead. 'You will speak nothing of this.' He felt queasy, and the broad man stepped forward and spread his hands.

'Look at me,' he said, and Tomas could not, could not make his eyes settle. *What is happening?!*

'Look at me, Tomas-Mage, Tomas-Primus, burning blade of the Stormguard.'

The man's voice was deep and strong, and Tomas forced his head with all his will and looked at him with his broken eyes. He saw pattern, so much more than in any man he had ever seen. Infinite concentrations and loops and swirls. If the skein was an ocean this man was a sinkhole on the ocean floor, an infinite depth of current, but... cut off. Surrounded by a space. *He is connected to nothing.* Surrounding him, another concentration – a bending of the world's patterns to shield them from him, and him from them.

'Who are you?' he asked, and the sailor stepped forward and took a seat.

'Guess.'

~

Hove couldn't help but be grateful when Ceann Brude asked if he wanted to go outside. *How many days has it been?* The food was not so bad – tough potatoes and miscellaneous beans cooked to mulch, no spice, but if they had given him maggoty bread or nothing at all he would have had no say. The water still tasted like rust, and he spent his nights pressing at the vines and creepers trying to snake into his cell. Twice more a vine took a bite from him when he was too exhausted to keep up his hourly checks. He practised his lessons and spent long hours having imaginary conversations with his friends that would never happen because his friends were all dead. Every few days a guard would bring him an extra ewer of water and in the cold damp of his cell he would strip and wash himself, wash his clothes as best he could and then sit naked until they dried, twitching away from any rustle or sound that could be another centipede or spider or strange little crab or biting frond. *She said I will be a messenger. A witness.*

He held that thought to his heart. A messenger would have to be kept alive. He clutched the wooden Anshuka amulet his mother had given him so long before on its simple cord, and traced the rune with his fingers: ᛉ. Anshuka's rune was from the Ferron script, not the long lines and slashes of old Undal script or the curling letters of the Isken trade tongue used for most everything.

For a whole evening he imagined what might have happened if he had chosen to be a skein-mage instead of a whitestaff, if he had learned the pathways in the pattern of fire and force and danger. He knew it wouldn't have mattered; all was chaos, so close to a demon, and he would be a skein-mage apprentice instead of a whitestaff apprentice. Still an apprentice, still lacking any knowledge that might be useful. The only patterns he knew were the first circle of healing and the first circle of growing. *I could heal my hand, and grow biting vines the size of eels.*

Ceann Brude took him outside. Hove thought he had grown used to the acid tang of the air, but out in the open it was worse. He stared up for long minutes at the storm above. Clouds clashed like titans, like mountains collapsing, an avalanche of black and grey and red and purple streaks, all of it illuminated from within by blue and white dancing lightning – sometimes clear bolts that split fractally and danced across the surface, sometimes faint glows from deep within. The thunder was almost constant, at the edge of hearing and then close, pressing down on his chest. There was no rain, only a light mist that felt cool on his skin but after a moment began to burn ever so slightly.

'This is the rotstorm,' he said at last, and she cutted his head and shook her own, clicking the joints on her long fingers, more joints than any human had.

'This is not storm,' she said, 'this is a place of calm. Why we live here. This is the quietest and softest it ever is, boy.'

Ceann Brude gestured around, and he saw a fort half eaten by bog and mangrove and strange fronds and tendrils, a squat stone tower, buildings woven from reeds. There were people in heavy oiled cloaks moving, and the ground was slicks of mud over hard stone.

'This is Fetter-Dun, but that is not today's lesson. Come.'

She led him through the square and down a narrow passage thick with vines that reached for him as he walked, and he rubbed at the burning mist on his skin. His left hand was still curled around the broken fingers, and he held it tucked to his chest, his eyes wide as he strained to take in whatever he could after so long indoors.

They emerged from the passage to a patch of open ground surrounded by twisted trees, sickly-looking leaves clutching limply to drooping branches. In the centre was an orb of dark stone with a stripe of opaque crystal around its middle. The stone was impossibly smooth, and the entire orb rested on three squat metal struts that seemed to have sunk into the soft ground below. It was huge, the size of two carriages next to each other, the size of a trade wagon. A crack of thunder rang out above and lightning touched down to earth at the edge of his sight, in what might be low hills out past the trees. Hove shivered and drew his feet closer together as a frond of grass cut at his bare ankles, a prickle of pain dancing up his leg where it had touched bare skin.

'Sleep,' Ceann Brude said, beside him and above him, looming, her wide mouth shaping the word so carefully, and there was a flash of green.

Hove slept and dreamt of his mother. They were home, before the rotsurge that took their farm past Garioch. They were home and she was cooking and he was meant to be helping but the table was too tall, the stone sink impossible to reach. He fetched pail after pail of water from the deep well outside but spilled each one before he reached the house. She smiled at him and told him not to worry. He dreamt of a dog and he dreamt of a storm and he dreamt of nothing, and for a time, he knew peace.

When Hove awoke the storm was above him, far worse than before. What had been mist was now rain. A tattered cloak was draped over him, half soaked through, and above him the sky was a churning mess of black and rough purples, a gale pulling at clouds that seemed to stir and shift of their own volition, the same gale pulling at his skin, his breath. He sat up and clutched at his amulet.

'I don't deserve this,' he said quietly, and glancing about he saw himself quite alone. The orb of dark stone was beside him, the two of them in a rocky crater or hollow of some kind. In front of him a rough trail was marked out. *Maybe.* It looked to be the same rocks and dirt as everywhere around him, but there were perhaps a few stones moved to give a clearer path out of the hollow.

Hove did not get up. He sank into the skein, waiting for the chaos to take him, and when instead he saw the web of the world, the connections and swirling patterns and abstract geometry and light, pulsing and dancing, he began to weep. Without saying a word he performed the first level of the first circle of healing, his focus on his hand. He found the pattern of his mangled hand, found the pattern that the hand remembered. *Please,* he thought, and felt the tissues growing stronger and fusing, pulling themselves, a deep inflammation fading as blood vessels found each other once more. The bones were too far. He tried to force them back, but already the strain of using the skein was casting sweat off him, and he could feel his blood burning with the effort. He stopped, but did not release the skein. For a long moment he just lay there and felt the pattern of the place.

It has a pattern, he thought, and he tried to extend his awareness upward to the storm above. As soon as his mind's eye grew close to the tumult of clouds, all sense of pattern left him. *The storm is chaos,* he thought, *but there is pattern down here. Life. There is still life, even here.*

Hove stretched his hand into the dirt next to him and

clutched at dark soil. He closed his eyes, but then there was chaos in the skein, a cloud of contradictory paths and impossible connections moving closer. With a sigh he released his hold and his view of the world returned to normal. With his left hand he clutched his amulet. It still hurt, but not so much, and with an effort he managed to bend his first two fingers to grip the amulet weakly.

'Thank you, Anshuka.' And then Ceann Brude was at the lip of the hollow, crouched like a gargoyle, her cloak billowing in the wind, the shock of red hair atop her head swirling around her.

'Come and see!' she said, a smile on her face, and she scarpered away. Hove frowned. *What is she? Where do monsters like her come from?* His mother had told him tales of crow-men, but never could he have imagined how alien she felt, her every movement wrong, a spider in a suit of human flesh.

After clambering to his feet he picked his way up the rocky path to where she had perched, and he found her a few steps further. Ceann Brude was stood with a woman, a woman not dressed like the rust-folk. She was clad in a heavy rain cloak, a scarf of patterned weave tied tight around her mouth. Below that, instead of the ramshackle rust-folk clothing, patched and repaired a thousand times, she wore beautiful black leather armour, embossed and embroidered with symbols he did not know, something like the jagged Ferron runes but with curls and weighted lines, with leather gauntlets covering her hands and wrists and boots to her thighs. At her waist where a belt dagger should be a small hammer hung in a loop, the head and haft of it a lustrous black metal incised with convoluted patterns of silver and gold. She stared at him with narrowed eyes when he emerged, then turned back to Ceann Brude.

'The fleet is ready,' she said, her accent like none Hove had ever heard, sharp and strong, 'if I have your permission.'

Brude cackled and gestured for Hove to join them.

'You have my permission, silent sister,' Ceann Brude said, and she led them a few steps to a knoll of twisted rock. A strand of kelp snapped at Hove's ankle but the strangely clad woman stamped down and twisted her heel, crushing the mouth of the vine. Hove joined them and looked down, down from the storm-ravaged lands to the sea below. There was a cove, and within it a dozen ships, ships with two masts each, a hundred foot long a piece. They were being loaded at a makeshift pontoon, and the pebbled beach thronged with goblins and rust-folk. Hove saw what must be a rottroll, a hulking creature twice the height of a man, and then more – dozens more of them, what he had thought to be a boulder field actually a mess of lounging monsters.

'What is this?' he asked, and Ceann Brude pointed down to the water. The sea below the storm was churning, waves crashing against each other in every direction to the horizon.

'This,' she said, 'is the next step of your journey home.'

Hove finally saw what her crooked finger was pointing out, there amidst the breaking waves and bobbing ships: *shapes in the water.* Long sinuous shapes, near as long as the ships above, like snakes. *Wyrms.*

Hove clutched his talisman and prayed to Anshuka. He repeated his mantra of survival, the will that burned in him to live his life and not submit to Ceann Brude. *I will survive this, and you,* he told himself over and over, but watching the fleet below he could not bring himself to believe it.

~

Floré kept her hand on her sword hilt and stared at the island growing larger ahead of them. Hours had passed, and no attack. Everybody on *Basira's Dance* was fraught, tension held barely in check. The Tullioch spoke amongst themselves in their own tongue, calling in rough Isken whenever they recommended a change in course or speed, and the commandos took breaks to eat and stretch in shifts, always most of them stationed at the rail with bows ready. Floré kept scanning the water for sign of some goblin or trollspawn, scanning the horizon for a mote of light that might grow larger until it was an orb of destruction against which they had no defence. *Where are they?* Tomas's skein-mages prowled the deck.

Tomas had reappeared on deck with a sailor in tow, and was directing the man to move anchors and chains around the decking, carefully spaced. Floré did not bother to question him. Benazir had told her the plan, and she doubted it had a chance but there was no reason to argue. Voltos and Benazir were with the captain, and Floré was left alone. She fingered the hilt of the sword and pictured the burning blade, the way the runes had caught on blood. She shivered. Benazir's old antler-hilted dagger that now hung at Yselda's belt and Benazir's newer dagger procured somehow from the armouries of the Stormguard carried runes for fire and burning. They would catch on flesh and blood, and the fire would spread through the flesh they found. Benazir had killed an eighty-foot wyrm that way, finding a single soft spot and letting the magic do its work.

This is different. Floré frowned. Starbeck's letter accompanying the blade had mentioned no intricacies of its use. The fire on it died if her hand left the hilt, and the flame did not catch on flesh and propagate; instead, the blade itself just grew hotter and hotter. After killing the trollspawn the night before, she had barely been able to hold the handle of the sword, and her final cuts had burned the creature as much as they tore flesh. Floré shook her head. The intricacies of rune-magic were a lost art. The Orubor could supposedly craft rune-blades, and Ferron had the knowledge before they fell. Rumour was that the insular island of Cil-Marie to the south had perfected not only rune-blades but many other applications beyond warfare, but the rumours were vague, and short of shipping slaves to whoever would buy them the Cil-Marie seemed to have no interest in trade or diplomacy. *Slaves like my ancestors.*

The island grew, and the sky stayed clear. To the east a commando was pointing at something and arguing with a sailor, and Floré joined them.

'What's the problem?' she asked, and the commando twitched his nose. He was a burly man, long moustaches drooping down to his chin. He stood a foot taller than the sailor he argued with, and the shortbow in his hands looked like a toy.

'Iskander lighthouses,' he said, pointing east. Floré could make out a faint vertical line on the horizon.

'Not a problem,' the sailor said. Floré clenched her right fist and glanced across the sky in all directions. *No orbs,* she thought, *not yet.*

'If the lighthouses are north of the island, and east of us, how can the island be south of us? This is the wrong island!'

The sailor rolled her eyes. 'We did a loop, big man,' she said. 'To get by the reefs, you can't go to the lighthouses.

That's what they're there for. A lighthouse isn't a beacon to call you home – it's a fire to flee from. We're approaching from the west, and then we'll follow the island's north coast to Riven.'

The commando grumbled and stalked off, and Floré stopped the sailor with a raised hand.

'How long?' she asked, and the sailor sighed and ran a hand over tightly braided hair.

'Few hours?' She squinted up at the sun and then back out at the water and seemed to feel the breeze on her face for a moment, then shrugged and walked away.

The sailor was right. They reached the west coast of Iskander a few hours later, and no wyrm or orbs attacked, no swimming goblins or trollspawn. The island seemed to be two huge mountains that rose from the sea, a belt of thick forest at their base before the dark water. The forest climbed down ravines and canyons and up the mountainsides, but the top of the two peaks were both bare. They skirted the north coast, the Tullioch calling directions to the captain and suggesting paths. He seemed happy to follow their lead.

'If an Antian tells you where to dig, that's where you dig,' he said when she asked how he fared, and left it at that. Benazir joined Floré and Cuss and Yselda and they watched the dark forests roll by, stands of tall pine and old oak mixed through with sharp rock.

'Anyone ever been to Iskander?' she asked idly, and the sailor who had been following Tomas around earlier stepped to her side. He was coiling a rope around one arm, palm to elbow and back again.

'I went once,' he said, 'a long time ago.'

'This is Komende!' Cuss said, smiling, and Floré nodded.

'My thanks for your aid last night,' she said. 'I'd appreciate it if you'd join us on shore. An eye familiar with the place might spot something we miss.'

Komende smiled and bowed his head to her and then nudged Cuss in the shoulder.

'Maybe I'll join up,' he said, 'if you can get me a tabard.'

They sailed on and on, and finally as the afternoon faded into early evening, they rounded a bay and on the far side it was there. *Riven.*

The citadel of the whitestaffs was a fort built into the side of the mountain, its base a hundred feet up from the churning sea below. The citadel was entirely white stone, and the side they could see that faced the sea was smooth and unbroken, a perfect drum, a bulwark against any possible storm. From it, on the island side, a thick wall spread out and the peaks of towers and slanted roofs could be seen peeking above the ramparts. A road travelled down from the citadel to a small town with a few docks that sat in the sheltered bay, and everywhere between the citadel and the docks the trees grew thick, even amongst the houses of the town.

There were no ships at berth at the simple docks that Floré could see, only a few rowboats or single-sail fishing boats that had been made fast to the rocky shore or small pontoons. She could see no people.

'Orders?' Muirgainas called, and after a long moment of silence Floré nudged Benazir in the back.

'Take us in and make fast!' Benazir called back, her voice strong. 'Get her ready to leave in a rush. I want half the commandos and a skein-mage on deck. This ship is our only way home, and nobody sets foot on it without my permission. The rest, to secure the town.'

The commandos rushed to obey, Sergeant Buchan yelling orders as he split them into a shore crew and a ship crew. Floré shivered. It was as cold in the bay as on the open sea, and despite the blue sky it had been a freezing day. She stamped her feet, and pulled on her gauntlets, flexing her fingers. The joints were still stiff in the new armour, and she idly scratched at the rune on the back of each fist. The three Tullioch were content on the forecastle; none offered to accompany them ashore, and Floré did not ask. Benazir asked Voltos to remain with the ship and he retreated to their cabin.

'If you need me, call,' he said, but Benazir was firm. Floré saw the sense of it. *Voltos is here for tactics and intelligence, and this could be a knife-fight any second.*

Basira's Dance slowed to a crawl and the sailors leapt to their work, and within moments they were tied up and a gangway lowered. Floré led the landing party, drawing her sword as she walked up the pontoon. Tomas and Benazir were at her side and behind them the commandos with bows drawn, skein-mages alert and at the ready. Tomas clutched his knapsack.

'I left Jozenai on the ship,' he said, 'and if those sailors don't keep her fed and warm I'll scuttle the bastard thing.'

Benazir cuffed his shoulder and shook her head at him, and Floré rolled her eyes.

'It's too quiet,' she said as they stepped from dock to quayside, the blessed relief of dry land. 'Far too quiet. Buchan, take Morag and a squad and check the rest of the harbour. We'll rendezvous in the town square.'

'Path to the citadel is this way,' Komende said, gesturing up stone-paved street to their left, 'or at least, it was.'

High above them the citadel loomed, up on the cliffs

above the steep banks of forest growth. Floré licked her lips and kept her sword steady, walking quietly forward, eyes darting. Doors were closed, windows shuttered. No blood, no destruction. *What in all the hells happened here?* Cuss and Yselda kept close behind her and Benazir, blades drawn, eyes flitting from shadow to shadow.

Floré found out what was wrong when they reached the square. The towering dark pines that grew up between houses and along the streets were widely spaced and taller in the square, a patch of green grass long untended blowing and rippling in the breeze beneath them. From every tree, bodies were hanged. On each tree, each bough, each branch it seemed, a fractal gallows. A dozen bodies hung on the smaller trees, perhaps double that number on the largest. As they stepped into the square fully a flurry of gulls took flight from their feast, beaks dripping gore, calling in harsh cries to the wind as their black-striped wings carried them up. They did not flee, but circled above as Floré peered at the bodies.

The corpses were uniformly clad in white, and she saw the green glint of Riven amulets around necks, hanging loose below tight nooses.

10

The Citadel

'Where does your war end? Our war does not end. Endless war is the only way to keep the blade and mind sharp. If we fall into the trap of peace we will become the next fatted calf for slaughter. If we grow weak and indolent as the Tessendorm have, then all our nation's struggles are for nought. We do not make war for a love of it. We make war for a love of the home we defend, the home we preserve. A wolf that does not hunt is a dog, and nothing more.'
– Commentary of the Ferron–Tessendorm campaign, Consul Semphor, year 627 Isken reckoning

The little girl wept as Ashbringer took her blood. It was only a nick, a scratch to the back of the hand and a drop swept up onto Ashbringer's long blue finger, but Marta cried and cried. A man dressed in brown, some sort of child carer, held her close and said kind words to her.

'I am sorry, little one,' Ashbringer said, and with a flourish of her hand she went to hand the girl a flower from her coat pocket. Marta shrunk back, and behind her in the quiet of the chamber she could hear Starbeck muttering orders to one of his soldiers in the doorway. Even with her insistence, he had said she could only see the girl once the fires were under control and he could accompany her. Along with him were a dozen City Watch with long truncheons of dark wood, and they all eyed her warily. Highmother Ash, tiny and wizened, stood behind her, clad in a simple robe of green-dyed wool.

Starbeck stepped back into the room and stared at Ashbringer, his fingers flexing. 'Well?'

Ashbringer ignored him and focused on Marta. She opened her mind to the skein and probed at the girl, saw the tumult of connection, of concentration within her. *So much like her father.* The child was weak. With a spiralling bloom of energy she focused on the flower in her hand, a flower picked from a meadow days before as she walked the valley of Mother's Den on the edge of Orubor's wood. The wilted and dead thing responded to her prompting, and the petals flourished with new life. Marta frowned at her and reached forward to pull it away before retreating to her carer's side.

'You were very brave,' Ashbringer said, and then she nodded at the man in brown. He scooped Marta up and took her away, the girl glaring back at Ashbringer and Starbeck.

'*Well?*' Starbeck said again. 'What the hells is all of this about?' Ashbringer sank to the floor and sat cross-legged, turned her eye to the blood on her fingertips. She still held her connection to the pattern, and calling on the skein she focused. Traces of light across her vision, showing her a world of light and connection and possibility.

'Like calls to like,' Highmother Ash was saying. 'The

daughter of a skein-wreck may find a skein-wreck. Ashbringer has hunted Deathless Tullen One-Eye for many a year. If she asks for the blood of a child, know it is not done lightly.

Like calls to like. Blood calls to blood. If she could find a connection... The strongest connection was to Marta, only a room away, a link of bright pulsing light. She ignored it. There were more, faint threads that carried south. Ashbringer sighed. She was already so tired. She felt Highmother Ash's hand on her shoulder, and centred herself. With a focus of will she followed the threads, her living gaze seeming to flit along those wavering lines of light that were so tightly connected. Black water below, clear sky above, lights in the ocean. On and on. An island. She saw Floré with a naked blade, standing afraid but not alone. Clouded. *So far.*

The threads diverged. Tracking back she found where they split, so close, and a white drum tower flush against a mountainside, the inside and outside, the stones of it, people, the moss on its walls all at once. *The citadel.* Within it, a whirling storm of pattern, whitestaffs, humans, *something else.* She felt a presence there. Another, nearby, a concentration of pattern so familiar.

Tullen One-Eye. Deathless.

Ashbringer's eyes snapped open.

'Artollen and her comrades went to Iskander,' she said, and Starbeck stared down at her.

'Everyone out!' In moments they were alone. 'Do they live still?' His voice was tight.

Ashbringer nodded slowly and swayed on the spot. *So tired.*

'The island. Tullen One-Eye is there. I must go.'

Touching a finger to her nose she felt the free-pouring

blood. *I have looked so far today.* Starbeck opened his mouth and let out a soft curse.

'Berren's black blood,' he said. 'What can we do?'

Highmother Ash was holding her close, cradling her, and Ashbringer closed her eyes. The old Orubor answered the knight-commander in a tone as calm as a river breeze.

'Six spans, I have been here, Knight-Commander,' Highmother Ash said, drawing herself a chair and sitting gently and primly. 'Never before have we offered embassy or brooked contact. I am here as a sign of respect for Floré Artollen. I am here as a sign of the fear you *must* have for the god-killing blade, the ur-blade, the knife of knives. Do you understand?'

Ashbringer wiped blood from her face and stood and began checking her weaponry, but she was so tired, and then she was sitting down again. *When did I sit down?*

'For now,' Highmother Ash said, her eyes locked on Starbeck, 'she must rest. We must wait, we must hope, and we must trust to Anshuka.'

~

As the sun set the commandos searched the town and found no living soul. Floré stared up at the scores of hanging bodies. The gulls returned to them and fed, and some bodies had clearly been there many spans. A few had fallen to the soft grass of the village green, but most of the corpses still hung, swaying.

'I'm taking Komende and some commandos. He says there was a skein-mage who lived just south of town,' Tomas said, his voice strained. Floré waved her hand, her eyes still stuck on the bodies hanging from the trees. Benazir came to join her and together they left the green and sat on a stone bench outside a cottage, with a view of the forest road up to the looming whitestaff citadel. From this angle, the unbroken white drum tower that presented to the sea was more geometric, ramparts and towers and a large gate. There were torches lit up there, perhaps movement on the ramparts.

'You ever see anything like this?' she asked, and Benazir laughed.

'Floré, we spent a decade in the rotstorm.' She scratched at her scars. 'It'll take more than some dead whitestaffs to get me scared these days. Do you think any are left?'

Floré shrugged. *How many more people could even be here?* Sergeant Buchan approached and drew to attention and Benazir saluted from her seat on the bench.

'No sign of struggle, no sign of life,' he said. 'No animals, no plates of food left out. Villagers all gone but looks like they knew it was coming. Maybe by ship?'

Benazir nodded but Floré just stared at the hanging bodies. *Maybe by ship.* She pictured the dozens of broken ships, wrecks floundered on the reef. She had thought they had been wrecked trying to approach the island. *What if they were wrecked trying to leave?*

'Stay here with two men with torches lit for when Tomas returns with the cadets,' Benazir said, and Floré glanced around.

'He took Cuss and Yselda?' she asked, and Benazir shrugged.

'They have to learn eventually.'

Floré frowned. With the reserve left on the boat and Cuss and Yselda gone, in the village they had three corporals, Sergeant Buchan, and two skein-mages. With a few moments assessing she split them into two parties. A skein-mage – the blonde one Morag – to stay at the village with the sergeant and one corporal. Two corporals and the remaining skein-mage, Anderson, she told to follow her.

'Any problems down here, kick up some noise and we'll head back,' she said to Buchan, and then a voice was calling, a voice from the forest road to the citadel.

'Good evening!' Floré spun, sword in hand in a heartbeat, the strange heft of the unfamiliar dark blade making her frown as she drew it into a high guard. A grey-haired woman in white robes walked down the forest path, a staff of silver in her hand. The tip of it shone with a warm yellow light, and around her neck a jade Riven amulet. *A whitestaff.*

Floré kept her sword high and they walked to meet the woman, meeting under the swaying corpses and feasting gulls. She smiled at them beatifically and held out her hand, palm up.

'I offer you welcome to Riven, Stormguard,' she said, 'though I do wish it were under better circumstances.'

At her side Floré could see the two skein-mages frowning and flexing their fingers. The commandos all had bows drawn, but pointed to the grass below.

'We are here on behalf of the Grand Council,' Benazir said, and the whitestaff nodded.

'Of course you are. The master of the citadel invites you to dine with him. All will be explained there.'

The whitestaff turned and began to walk away and Benazir looked to Floré, eyes wide, as if to say *what now?* Floré licked her teeth and sheathed her sword.

'No,' she said, and the whitestaff turned.

'No? You won't be joining us for dinner? The master will be disappointed.'

Floré shook her head and stepped forward, snatching the staff from the woman's hand and throwing it behind her. She grabbed the whitestaff by her robes and pulled her close.

'No,' she repeated. 'No, we won't be waiting until dinner for an explanation. I see three score dead whitestaffs hanging like Flameday ribbons, an empty town, a dozen scuttled ships at least, and it's been six bleeding spans since the council had a report from the citadel. Talk now, or I'll arrest you and throw you in the hold and we'll go and put the question to the next fool in a white robe.'

The woman stiffened in Floré's arms.

'*Unhand* me, you lout,' she said, wrenching to break free. Floré held firm. 'I am *Mistress* Farrow of the Riven citadel. I am a *mistress* of the whitestaffs, you snivelling child. You'll spend the rest of your life scrubbing latrines. There are machinations at play a fool like you could never understand.'

Benazir placed her hand on Floré's arm, and Floré let the whitestaff drop.

'Dinner would be lovely,' Benazir said. 'We've many a question, and I'm sure you will be able to help us, won't you, Mistress Farrow.'

The whitestaff stooped and swept up her staff, her composure slowly returning.

'Follow me if you want answers,' she said, her face flushed and her hair a touch dishevelled. She did not meet Floré's eye. Floré took a final glance at the hanging bodies. *None of this is good.* Motioning for Buchan and Morag and their squad to stay put, she sheathed her sword but kept her hand on the hilt and tugged it to keep it loosed it in its scabbard. *None of this is good at all.*

The forest road wound for perhaps a half mile, a

well-maintained road wide enough for a wagon that slowly wound its way through switchbacks up to the citadel gates. The wind was blowing in from the sea, and the cold seemed to settle in Floré's bones. As they drew closer to the citadel wall Floré could see there were four posts driven deep into the earth and supported by struts a hundred yards from the gate. To each, a person was bound. They were all long dead. Two wore black robes, one wore white, and one wore what could have been a Stormguard commando tabard. All were decayed, and the birds had eaten their fill. Mistress Farrow eyed them as they approached the stakes, and all slowed their pace without discussing.

'Traitors deserve no better,' she said. Floré stared at the woman and felt her right arm start to shake and tremble and ache. She clenched her fist and her jaw.

'Who did they betray?' Benazir asked, and Mistress Farrow laughed and kept walking.

'The protectorate of course,' she said, and then the gates swung open before them, a black maw set in white stone and flanked by burning torches.

When Mistress Farrow was a few steps ahead Floré leaned in to Benazir. 'I might have to kill her you know.'

Benazir smiled. 'Get in line.'

~

'*Crúca*, they are called,' Komende said, 'hookstones.'

Tomas nodded eagerly. *I can show you things you have never seen,* the man had said in the ship's cabin. *I can unlock powers you don't even know you covet.* Tomas knew who he was dealing with. Tullen One-Eye. A legend alive. *Come to Iskander to discover how to track a dagger and track Tullen*

One-Eye, he thought, *and I already had the dagger, and Tullen One-Eye steps into my cabin!* He grinned and glanced back. The two cadets were a dozen feet back as he'd instructed, swords drawn.

'So you don't want your dagger back?' Tomas asked perhaps for the fifth time, and the man calling himself Komende shook his head. Tomas's head felt fuzzy, as if he was a bottle of wine deep into an evening with no dinner and the sun beating down. *When did I last sleep?* Whenever he closed his eyes, still he could see the skein unfolding before him. Sleep had come in odd snatches, moments when his mind felt calm. For spans. *When did I last truly sleep?*

'I've played that game,' Komende said, quietly, leading them along a small forest track through a copse of dense pine. 'I've killed a god, bedded an empress, won and lost an empire. I am *tired,* Tomas. So very tired. I will give you the secret of what it is to be a skein-wreck, but in return you must kill me. Why do *you* wish for this power, my boy? Why did you steal the dagger from the Orubor?'

Why did I steal the dagger? Tomas grinned to himself in the dark of the forest. His mind felt so addled, as if he were just waking up from a long sleep. *It must be the stress.*

'Janos is dead, so Undal has no skein-wreck. If Varratim could kill a god with that dagger, what else could we learn from it? Once I healed and learned that the Orubor would not grant us the orbs or the dagger that *we* captured, I took matters into my own hands. The fate of our people should not be decided by savages, detached from the world. Wands, dagger, orbs. If the castrum could unlock the potential of any of these, who would dare move against Undal? Freedom for the people of the protectorate.'

Tomas paused, and shook his head slowly. *Why didn't I take the dagger to the castrum then?*

'We would be truly free,' he continued, but his voice trailed off. He shrugged, felt a sudden wave of elation come over him. *Where did that come from?* He shivered and shrugged again but the emotion was there, a slick happiness. *Too good to be true, all of it,* he thought, *but either way I'll kill him, and I'll be the hero.*

'The crúca are nodes in a web,' Tullen said, his voice a mellifluous baritone that rose and fell in every sentence as if he were reciting poetry. 'They are the point where currents of pattern connect and diverge. Across the world of Morost they appear, these slick black stones. You have seen one before, I think?'

Tomas shrugged and scratched at the edge of his goggles. *Luck* stones, they were called in Undal. They were scattered about, and a farmer would plough around rather than digging one free. The sacrifice altar in the Blue Wolf Mountains came to his mind, that same slick black rock.

'The Luck Stone tavern in Aber-Ouse has a bar built around one,' he said, 'and of course that little number in the Blue Wolf Mountains with the runes, where your boy Varratim sacrificed those children to hone his knife.'

He waited for a reaction, but Tullen or Komende or whatever he wanted to be called was calm. Behind him he heard Cuss and Yselda arguing about why the whitestaffs would have betrayed the protectorate. They moved deeper into the forest, and though he could hear the two children stumbling behind him, with his skein-scarred eyes he could see perfectly, with maddening complexity in every direction at once. He blinked and kept walking.

'Varratim wanted to be a skein-wreck, to take from the pattern without giving,' Komende said at last. 'He took the dagger from me, though I did not try to stop him. He honed it with his sacrifices. I could not tell him what to do. Anshuka's will binds me to live forever, to provide no aid to Ferron. Even if I wanted to speak the words to him, they would fall as ash on my tongue.'

'Yet you can tell me,' Tomas said slowly, his grin fading a little. 'Me, an Undal. Me, a Stormguard skein-mage. Why would you do that? How could you?'

Komende turned to him in the dark of the forest and smiled.

'Only in my enemy can I find redemption,' he said. 'The blade has the power to kill a god. The power to do many things. Varratim was a simple man. He wanted to use it as a knife, to *kill*. I want you to use just a fraction of its stored potential to unpick a knot, for a moment, that I might die. The price for my death is the key to your ascension to skein-wreck. You are already nearly there, Tomas. Your eyes are scarred by the blade.'

Tomas removed his goggles and hung them around his neck. In the dark of the pine forest his pupils danced and gyrated and split and reformed.

'Your eye doesn't do this,' he said, and Komende laughed.

'No, it certainly does not. You know how I lost this one?'

Komende pointed to the eye beneath the leather strap. Tomas frowned as he remembered his children's stories.

'You traded it to an Antian witch for one of their eyes, to see the skein better,' he said, and Komende laughed deep and long.

'I always did like that story,' he said, 'but nothing as fun. I scarred only one eye with the ur-blade, Tomas. Eventually it was too much to see the skein forever. I took it out so as not to go mad, once I'd seen long enough to learn how to *look*.'

They entered a clearing, a break in the trees. In the middle of a meadow of long grass sat a slick black stone, absorbing the light of the first evening stars.

'The sun has set,' Tullen One-Eye said. 'If you are to learn the truth of how to cure your sight, and your mind, first you loosen the leash of the bear, enough that I might die.'

Tomas pulled his goggles back up as Cuss and Yselda entered the glade.

'Sir?' Cuss asked, his voice querulous. 'I thought we were looking for a mage's house, sir? Tomas?'

'Keep a perimeter around the meadow and don't bother me,' he said, but he did not take his eyes from the stone. The crúca. With his skein-scarred eyes he could see the knot there at its heart, the node of connection in the great currents that crossed the world, striations of connections spiralling out into the aether around them. He could see the pattern in a depth he never had before, for all his years of yearning and study. *If I followed the right path far enough*, he thought, *it would lead to Anshuka herself.*

Tomas clutched at his satchel and felt the hard case of the dagger beneath. *The ur-blade, he called it.* He could not look at Komende straight on; the man's pattern was too dense, the sun at noon. *What patterns dance on the sun's face?*

'What are you doing, Tomas?' Yselda called, and he blinked and looked back at her across the clearing and opened his mouth but didn't know what to say.

What am I doing?

~

They passed through the outer rampart wall and into a huge inner courtyard, paved with large flagstones and dotted with benches and small fountains and outbuildings. The citadel itself stood across from them, four storeys of worked white stone, stairways and arches. *A warren,* Floré thought, imagining having to attack or defend the place. She knew of no historical battles there. During the Tullioch war the whitestaffs had withdrawn, and the Tullioch had left the uninhabited island unmolested. The civil wars that had plagued the protectorate in its earlier days had left the whitestaffs carefully aside in their brutalities; the whitestaffs could advise, but not fight, and normally they sat stoic as Stormguard fought Stormguard. The entrance of the citadel was sparse and airy, the stone floors swept and the walls painted a bare white. Torch sconces everywhere threw light across the central courtyard, and in the centre an oak tree stood, its limbs spread wide, not a leaf to be seen over branches of silver-white.

'If you'll wait here a moment I'll announce you,' Mistress Farrow said, and wandered off towards the central drum tower.

'You know,' Benazir said with a sigh, 'I'd really hoped to get some nice cathartic rust-folk slaughter in on this trip.'

Floré flexed her fists in her gauntlets and shook her head. 'I'm not sure cathartic would be the word, anymore. Just you and I, born a hundred miles in the wrong direction. We'd be fighting just as hard. You getting anything, mage?'

Benazir stared at her sidelong and cricked her neck. 'Everybody makes a choice,' she said, 'and any who choose to take up arms against Undal will have me to deal with.'

They all waited in silence as the skein-mage Anderson squinted into the night for a few seconds.

'Whitestaffs in there, and others. A bunch of them.'

She nodded and turned to the two corporals, Halas and Bén.

'You two,' she said, 'stick on Benazir. Follow her lead.'

Both nodded and gave nervous grins. The woman Halas had two of her front teeth missing, and when she grinned there was a disconcerting gap. Noticing Floré's glance, she blushed.

'I usually have teeth, sir,' she said, and Floré left it at that.

'Anderson,' Benazir said quietly, 'remind me. Whitestaffs are not known for their… offensive magic. Is there any chance they might have some skein-spells we should worry about?'

The skein-mage nodded and tugged at his gauntlets, cinching them tighter. 'Growing and finding, healing, stuff like that. Something like fire can take years to learn. A few of them might have that one, for lighting torches and whatnot. I'd be more worried about those big sticks they carry. They tend to be on the slower side as well, not combat trained like our skein-mage cadres. They can link though: they all learn the same patterns, so they can link and amplify their spells. Useful for healing, I suppose. Skein-mages tried it in the past but it never seems to be worth the effort.'

Benazir smiled at him, and then Mistress Farrow was returning, her staff clicking on the stones of the courtyard floor.

'If you would,' she said, and then they were following her through yet more doors. They turned three corners and went through two more doors and saw nobody, and then they passed through an arch and a heavy curtain of black cloth was parted to a grand hall.

Shit shit shit, Floré thought.

'Shit,' Benazir said.

The space was a hundred foot long and perhaps sixty wide, and there was no ceiling – it was open to the sky. *Another courtyard*. Intricately carved arches lined the walls, and there were rows of seats lined against them. To their left, perhaps thirty shamans clad in grey and black robes sat, a mixture of men and women. All were armed, some with heavy cudgels, some with swords. They sat silently and stared at the incomers. To their right, the same number again of whitestaffs, each clutching a stave of silver wood at least five foot tall, all of them staring. Floré barely took them in.

Against the centre back wall of the courtyard, a Ferron orb sat. It lay at a slight angle, one of the metal strut legs broken off, but it had been landed on a pile of carefully placed stonework to keep it largely level. Above it was a long trail of debris and scarred stone where it had careened down the wall at some point, and its ramp was lowered, an entrance to blackness. In front of the orb a low altar had been placed, and on it the body of a crow-man lay, utterly unmoving. Standing over it was a whitestaff dressed in brilliant robes, his hair and beard lustrous and long. He was facing the orb when they entered, but turned when he saw them.

'Welcome,' he said, a voice rich and loud from years of oration. 'Welcome to the dawn of a new age.'

11

The Ur-Blade

'I ask you this, citizen of the protectorate. A child in a storm deserves what aid you might give it. Do you deny this of one born forty miles west of the Stormwall, even as you would give your life for one forty miles east of it? There is folly in this. It is the folly of the Cil-Marie placing their people into castes by the shade of their skin, or the barons of Tessendorm who care only for bloodlines. We are better than they – we understand the commonality of life, the shared burden of the protectorate. "From each their ability and to each their need" – so spoke Master Wall in the first days of the protectorate, when the blades of the Stormguard still served the will of the council and the people, rather than dictating it. We are a small nation, at the end of the world. If we open our arms to the children of the storm, we may save ourselves along with them.' – **Break the Stormguard's chains!** Lillebet Arfallow, year 312 from Ferron's Fall (1123 Isken)

Benazir stepped forward into the courtyard, confident Floré would be behind her with hand on hilt. She did not recognise the man in the centre of the courtyard. Master Vilni had presided over the whitestaff college for a decade, as far as she knew. She had met him once in Undal when reporting to the Grand Council, a man with amber skin and kind eyes who always spoke of balance.

'I am Bolt-Commander Benazir Arfallow,' she said, projecting her voice. She swept her gaze across the seated whitestaffs to her right, few that they were, and across the ominously armed shaman on the other side of the courtyard.

'I come from Undal City on behalf of the Grand Council. I come bearing the news that the Northern Marches have fallen to our old enemy. The orbs of light that stole our children attempted to kill Anshuka herself, but were repelled. They now harry our legions and drive our people from their homes. I come seeking the aid of the whitestaffs. I ask you, where is Master Vilni? Why did you flee? What befell those who came before me?'

The bearded man smiled at Benazir and pressed his hands down on the altar before him, the white stone with the body of the crow-man atop it. One of the shamans stood hurriedly from his seat and hurried to the master's side, whispered in his ear. The shaman was a tall thin man, thin-lipped and bald. He kept glancing back at them.

'What the piss is *he* doing here?' she heard Floré whisper behind her, and she frowned. The shaman ran back to his seat and lowered his gaze, a long dagger clutched between both hands uncomfortably.

'I am Master of Riven,' the man said, and with a delicate hand he stroked the face of the demon that lay dead before him. 'Master Deranus. I ascended after Master Vilni. The orbs attacked us here a span before they began to hunt across the protectorate, though we fended them off. We are not without power! I recalled our whitestaffs, our sages and philosophers, our researchers and healers. When the orbs came here I saw what they were, and my brothers and sisters heeded my warning. Technology not seen in hundreds of years, since centuries *before* the old empire fell. *Knowledge*, my child, knowledge to take us to the future, to change the world. All that was needed was to grasp it. I drew us back to best decipher how, without the confusion of the Stormguard involving themselves.'

Benazir shifted her feet and licked her lips. 'Where is Master Vilni?' she repeated, and the self-proclaimed Master Deranus shook his head.

'He did not agree with our course, and worked to stop it. Peace was brought to him. None could be allowed to stand between us and the chance of salvation for all our people.'

Benazir let her left hand drop to the hilt of her knife. Deranus was forty paces away perhaps. Not an easy throw, and he would see it coming. *But he is old, and I am tired of this.* Letting her fingers linger on the hilt she took a breath and pictured Guil, freckles and smiles and soft caresses. She made herself breathe slowly, made herself think of the mission. *If I fail, Guil will be one of the first of many.*

'You have captured an orb,' she said slowly. 'You have my congratulations. How did you manage such a feat?'

The old man laughed. 'Well, that's the trick of it! Two boons at once. You know that whitestaffs can aid each other, in the use of the skein? A circle of healers is far more potent than one whitestaff alone. This is why we formalise the patterns.

Any skein-mage could discover a pattern, but it would always only work for *them*. We learn the same patterns and we pool our power. This is how we heal those who would otherwise die. This is how we seek and we find and we grow our gardens. It is not easy, child. It works best if there is the energy of many, and the shared pattern of many. To capture this orb… we used a pattern. A pattern that came to use unexpectedly, a collection of patterns really. Energy and pattern. A source that may keep us safe yet, and take us to the future. Now, we can guide, but there is no cost. We can *fight*. And we will. Do not worry!'

'Enough riddles,' Floré said from her shoulder, but Benazir held her hand up for calm.

'We seek to understand,' she said. 'We are of the same nation. The same vow. *Preserve the freedom of all people in the realm. Suffer no tyrant; forge no chain; lead in servitude.*'

Master Deranus bowed his head. 'This is my shame,' he said, his mouth turning down into a grimace, 'but the chain had to be forged. The patterns and power could save us all. With those patterns and my focus, *our* focus, we can wipe the Ferron threat from the face of Morost. We can bow Isken and the slavers of Tessendorm. Is it so much to chain one man? All he knew, we can *use*.'

Benazir ran her hand through her hair and considered the ache in the stump of her other arm. *Always an ache, these days.* She pictured Guil smiling, Guil and her dancing in their rooms.

'If you've a weapon,' she said, and felt her mouth go dry, 'I'd use it. If it is a chain, I'd break it.'

The old master smiled at her.

'Perhaps. The others would not. They tried to leave, to

confer with the council. I could not let them, you understand. This weapon may end the war, may lead the protectorate to a generation of peace and plenty. I could not allow them to risk that with loose tongues, or risk the council delaying. We have delayed too long already.'

Benazir shivered at the thought of the sunken vessels, imagined an orb flying low, beams of force and fire. *How could a ship hope to evade that?*

'What happened to the whitestaffs in the harbour?' Floré asked, her voice ragged, and Benazir could hear the anger in her friend's voice. 'What happened to your brothers and sisters?' she continued, and Benazir made no move to stop her, felt in her own throat a twitching disgust. 'The healers and sages, the bright lights who were meant to keep Undal safe? To heal the sick, to raise us all up? What in all the hells have you done? Murdered any who dissented? What rule is this, Deranus? By whose voice do you make this decision?'

'They refused to lead in servitude,' the master said, and shook his head. 'They would not do what we must for the greater good. For the *future*. They spoke of chains and service and Mistress Water; they spoke of our oaths to do no harm with the skein. They could not be allowed to interfere. Thankfully, our shamans have ever heeded the whitestaffs' command. They have been loyal, and paid the price to keep our new mission safe. I'll not be lectured on morality by a *commando*. The Stormguard exact judgement where they must. We had to clean our house, that we might save you all.'

Descending from the raised altar he beckoned them to follow. Benazir laid her hand on Floré's arm and let the old man lead on, away from the courtyard and the shamans and the whitestaffs. *Why are the shamans here?* She did not know, did not know too much. *Patterns and energy, whitestaffs and shaman, broken hulls floating on the water…*

Benazir pictured Guil again, her freckles, her red hair cut close, the curve of her cheek. She imagined what revenge would feel like, revenge against the rust-folk. *They have taken everything from me. Is it so much to chain one man?* Benazir shook her head and her hand fell to her knife, the blade with the thirst for fire at its heart.

~

Ashbringer had awoken in Highmother Ash's chambers laid carefully in a *bed* of all things. She drank the water left by the bed and ate the tough strips of meat left for her, tearing at them with her teeth. She checked her gear. *Boots, cloak, bow, blade.* Under each eye she smeared a daub of ash from the dead fire in Highmother Ash's room, an oath to herself. *I will find him.*

'Your mission has not changed,' Highmother Ash said when she found Ashbringer sharpening her blade. 'You must hunt Deathless.'

Ashbringer smiled and embraced the old woman. 'There are dark forces in this world, Mother,' she said. 'I will hunt him: trust in that.'

'As it should be.' Highmother Ash settled down on the end of the bed, watching intently as Ashbringer prepared. 'I have rune-blades for the Undal,' she said, 'a gift to ease the pain that we have lost the weapon of the enemy, and the slight that we will not trust them with the orbs of light.'

Ashbringer frowned and checked the fletching on her arrows. 'Is it wise, to arm them so?' she asked, and Highmother Ash shook her head.

'The council do not think so,' she said, 'but my heart tells me this fight is far from done, and may be beyond us alone. I'd have allies here, not fearful neighbours waiting for us to falter.'

Ashbringer leaned low and pressed her forehead to the old Orubor's and closed her eyes. 'Obeisance to the forest,' she said, and the old Orubor smiled and patted her cheek.

'Anshuka guide you, child.'

Ashbringer drew in a deep breath.

She sang as she left, not bothering to hide the blue of her skin or her bald head, her long ears, her wicked smile serrated and sharp. She did not alter her gait to be lumpen and *human*; she strode from the keep with the grace she had been born with and the guards recoiled from her, or called out, but none stood in her way. Her quiver sat proud at her shoulder and her bow was strung. Undal City was dark and cold, bitterly cold, and as she sang she let her mind touch the skein and followed the melody. She needed to find a nexus, a place where the threads of the world pulled close. *A place that means something to people.*

She found what she needed at the east gate. *How many farewells, how many greetings?* It was a liminal space, not quite the city, not quite beyond. It was perfect. Even in the dark of night there were people everywhere, the streets abuzz with chatter after the orb attack. Over the shaman's temple plumes of smoke still poured into the sky. Ashbringer sang and the carts around her rolled to a halt. She stood in the street and paced slowly, and all around the people of Undal City stopped in their tracks and stared at her, guard and soldier and civilian, old and young. She sang the song of the city and the song of another place, a place she had only seen in her mind's eye.

A child began to sing with her, a small child, voice not yet constrained by the chains of melody. Ashbringer walked to her and sang as she walked and the child's father drew her close but Ashbringer smiled at him, and her gold orb eyes met his pale blue irises and he let the girl go. The girl sang, nonsense words, and Ashbringer touched a long finger to her face and then stepped back to the street. *It is near.*

The little god came from the alley. It had the body of a rat, a small rat. It ran from the alley and stood before her in the street and she went to one knee and placed a hand on her heart. The rat had a coat of shining brown, but swirls of green traced through it, and where a rat's tail would be pink this god's tail was a lustrous jade, a sinuous living stone. Its eyes were purest black, and its whiskers and nose and paws the same living jade as its tail. Ashbringer focused on her destination and asked a boon of the god. Most of them were in nature, places of beauty that drew the eye and thought, thought that formed a pattern, pattern that coalesced and warped and created something new – a god built of feeling. This was a city god, wiry and hungry, and it was wary of her. Yet she sang, and the people watched, and after an age the rat bounded in a circle that bloomed with golden light and where mud and horseshit had been was sparse heather and rock, a dusting of snow.

'My thanks,' Ashbringer said, and she stepped into the circle. Gazing back out she saw the rat bound away down an alley, followed by a hundred eyes. She smiled, and with a flash the circle closed on itself and she was high in the mountains of Iskander, staring down at a citadel of white stone that stood stark against the ocean.

~

Tomas called Cuss and Yselda to him in the meadow east of the Riven citadel. The hookstone sat black and squat behind him, pushing up from the earth, and now he had seen it he did not seem to know how to draw his focus away. He had slipped his goggles back on but Yselda had seen him from across the meadow. *Did she see my eyes?* He felt so terribly tired all of a sudden, the nights of poor sleep on the boat, the nights before in Protector's Keep spending long hours awake looking at the ur-blade.

'What are you doing, Tomas?' Yselda asked, and he smiled at her. *I took the blade from the Orubor. I took it, and I'll use it, and with their own weapon I'll end the war the Salt-Man couldn't.*

'I must perform a ritual,' he said. 'Skein-mage stuff. I need you two to guard the meadow, and under no circumstance are you to look inward. There are forces here that would tear your soul from your bones and turn your blood to snakes. Understood?'

Yselda nodded, and Cuss wrung his hands on his sword hilt.

'What about Komende?' he asked. Tomas smiled at the boy and gently turned him away from the forest clearing.

'He'll be looking out too in just a moment. I need his help with something first.'

Leaving them to their protestations, Tomas moved back to the crúca stone and drew the dagger box from his satchel, letting the bag and box drop to the ground after he unlocked the latch with a thought. *Think about this!* he seemed to hear his own voice say, but with the knife in his hand all he could think about was pattern, the currents flowing from the stone. His hands were freezing, the fog of his breath spreading wide as it flew from him in heavy clouds.

'All you need to do is push the power of the ur-blade into the crúca,' Komende said softly. 'That will break the network, for a while. Any long-term spells and effects may take some time to reassert themselves. I'll show you how to control the blade, and take without giving. You'll be able to kill me.'

Tomas ripped off his goggles. His eyes twitched and he couldn't seem to focus. *Does this make any sense at all?* he heard in his mind, but he swatted it away. *Tomas-Wreck. I could remake the Stormwall in sheer rock a hundred foot tall. I could bat orbs from the sky like fireflies.*

'It will have enough power, after?' he heard himself say, his voice a flat thing, and then Komende, *Tullen One-Eye*, had a hand on his shoulder. The man met his eyes, and with his skein-scarred sight Tomas lost himself in the depth of the pattern within Tullen.

'Just enough to disrupt the web for a few moments,' Tullen said. 'My truest enemy, I promise you. You will be able to control it.'

Tomas's hand was shaking but he held up the dagger before him, the dagger of black obsidian with its handle of twisted bone, the green faceted gem at its pommel. *Why did I take this from the Orubor?* With his eyes as they were it was a horrifying sight, a point of purest black, of *order*.

I could bring order.

With a stuttering step he went to the crúca stone and knelt upon it, one hand caressing the smooth blackness. He understood now. Varratim's altar had been a part of this network, a place where the world connected, a *focus*. *Did we lose this knowledge or did we never have it?*

As a boy Tomas had always been the smartest, always the first to get the joke or find the answer. The orphanage at Aber-Ouse was a cold and desolate place but he had thrived. The fact that people don't have to like you to do what you want was a lesson he learned early. Nobody there liked him. Nobody there liked anybody. *Through all that, here I am. About to become the first skein-wreck since the Salt-Man...*

The memory of Janos sparked something in him, and his head seemed to clear a little. *What am I doing? This can't be right.*

'I met the Salt-Man once,' he heard himself say, the dagger pressed up against the stone. 'When we took back Fallow Fen. We were pinned down by two dozen rust-folk archers. He collapsed a building on them and he wasn't even sweating after.'

Snarling, in a moment of clarity Tomas turned on Komende and pointed the knife at him.

'*He told me it couldn't be taught!*' he yelled, and at the edge of the clearing Cuss and Yselda were turning.

Tullen One-Eye stayed calm even as Cuss and Yselda started to yell, and his eyes never left Tomas's.

'It cannot be taught,' he said slowly, 'but it can be taken. The power from the knife, every drop left after you shatter the web. You plunge it in your heart and you *drink* it and you stop living in the shadow of a dead man.'

Tomas heard his own breath fast and Cuss and Yselda were running, running towards him, but Komende was heading them off. With a scream he plunged the dagger down, down into black rock. The blade sank true, up to the hilt, and a spiral of fractures glowing hot silver spread across the rock. In the skein he saw the fractures spreading, from there to another crúca, another node, another. *How many are they?* The currents were in disarray, the skein a mess of chaos as if a crow-man stood at his shoulder.

'What have you done?' Cuss demanded, but Tomas could only weep. With a jerk he pulled the dagger free, and turned to Komende.

'You lied to me.'

Komende smiled and reached down and with one strong hand twisted the dagger from Tomas's grasp. Tomas could see it perfectly in the skein. It was still a blackness, a point of perfect order in the messy tangle of the cosmos, but so much smaller now. *All that power, gone.* He slumped from the stone to the ground and felt a burning pain in his eyes.

'Good news and bad news,' Komende said, twirling the dagger absently, addressing Cuss and Yselda. Tomas writhed on the ground, the sharp pine needles of the forest floor pressing deep into his skin. He retched.

'The good news is your friend's madness should soon be healed if he lives. The blade is too much, too much for a human mind to hold. From the moment he tried to conceive it he has been slipping into abstraction.'

Cuss and Yselda stared down at him and Tomas saw the disgust and fear in their faces as they looked upon the fractal horror of his eyes, the dancing geometry of madness. *Is it disgust I can see?* It was so hard to tell, so hard to focus on the moment when he was so submerged in the pattern. He pulled his knees to his chest and closed his eyelids and pressed his palms to his eyes but he could still see, could still see pattern everywhere, through his eyelids and beyond. Tomas wept.

'Who are you?' Yselda demanded, and she drew her longsword and moved into a low guard. Komende laughed.

'You know, girl, that is maybe the first time somebody has drawn steel on me in a long time where they have a chance. Not a *big* chance,' he said slipping the dagger into his belt, 'but a real possibility.'

'Bad... news,' Tomas managed to say, and the man named Komende sighed and shook his head.

'I think you know that, friend.'

Cuss drew his sword and moved to stand over Tomas, shoulder to shoulder with Yselda. 'I recognise that dagger,' he said, voice hoarse. 'Are you one of them?'

Komende rolled back his sleeves to show a deep intricate framework of runes and geometrical patterns, whorls inked on his skin in vibrant red and blue and gold.

'I am not *one* of anybody,' he said, and his gaze grew distant and he stared up at the mountain peaks looming high above the forest. With a wave of his hand they both grew utterly still. Tomas drew himself to a knee. 'I am like nothing you have ever seen, or will again.'

Tullen One-Eye stalked from the clearing and a few moments later Cuss and Yselda fell to the ground, gasping, able to breathe again. Tomas could feel his head clearing as if a deep fog were lifting. *When did it descend?* He remembered taking the dagger from the Orubor deep in the wood, the fear. He remembered flashes: Undal City, a kitten in his hand, a black iron sea. *Jozenai.* Looking back at the hookstone, Tomas felt his head spin. The fractures of molten silver still glowed, and in the skein the currents were in turmoil, tendrils and light coiling back as if severed. Where once streams of connection had vanished beyond his sight, now they coiled around the crúca stone. *All the world connected,* he thought, falling back in the grass. *Anshuka, forgive me, what in all hells have I done?*

~

Floré followed Benazir and the master of the citadel up a winding staircase, towards the top of the white drum tower. She couldn't stop thinking about Jule. *Jule,* the village shaman of Hasselberry, here in Riven, the gaunt heron of a man always nosing after Marta, always chiding them for skipping his services. The man who she had left Janos with, when last she saw him. She clenched her fist tightly enough she could feel the silver of Janos's wedding band cut into her finger. She had broken Jule's nose or jaw, she couldn't remember which, on her way into the temple in Hasselberry after the orbs attacked. She had found Janos with wounds beyond any man, his abdomen torn so deep, clinging to life only to tell her that Marta had been taken. She had sat with him until he grew utterly still, until he was dead and gone, and then she had left the shaman temple. *Left to find Marta.*

Why would he be here? Perhaps the shamans had fled to Riven along with the whitestaffs. *Are the shamans and the whitestaffs working together?* The shamans of the protectorate were a shabby lot, normally found praying to talismans and interpreting books of scripture from those they claimed spoke to the four Judges: Anshuka, Nessilitor, Berren, and Lothal. Anshuka's prophets were of course most highly considered, but the others were seen as gods in equal might – *just not equal worth,* Floré thought with a sneer. She had seen Lothal's bones herself once, deep in the rotstorm, ribs like petrified trees, teeth longer than swords, and a skull that still appeared in her nightmares from time to time, backlit by lightning and roiling cloud. Even the memory made her arm ache. *Some scars never heal.* The shamans held no power in the council, no influence beyond what they could convince their parishioners of. They were a joke, a ludicrous attempt to pour liturgy and order over the chaos of faith and nature. They aided the whitestaffs in their ministrations, but she had no idea that the connection was so deep.

The old man was talking as he walked them further up. They passed doorways and corridors, cold stone oppressively weighing above them.

'I thought whitestaffs were sworn not to use the skein for violence,' Benazir was saying, her voice echoing off cold stone. 'Is that not what Mistress Water taught?'

Master Deranus stopped on the stair and turned to them, one eye twitching.

'You think you know her lessons?' he spat. 'You know *nothing* of her. She set down edicts to keep a peace, but that time is gone. We are in a new age. I have discovered a font, and with it the patterns that might free us all. We came together in conclave and fate brought us a boon. Anshuka be blessed. What could this be if not her will?'

He stopped in front of a wooden door and let his gaze pass over them all.

'I was a scholar,' he said at last, 'and I researched Mistress Water. I researched the skein-wrecks, those who could touch the pattern without suffering for it. Did you know she was one? The mistress? No, I see you did not. Few do. Who else could speak to a god, who else could throw off the shackles of an empire? A skein-wreck, but not a destroyer. She *built*.'

At Floré's side, Benazir rolled her eyes. 'History isn't

skein-wrecks and mages,' she said, 'it's people and politics and power. All empires fall, Whitestaff. If not her, someone else. If not Anshuka, something less dramatic. We would not be bowed forever.'

The master squinted at her slightly and shrugged. 'Perhaps you are right. But think on this. There are people in this world who can do so much more than others. Powers that are beyond our ken, beyond the reach of almost all. They are not the same as us. They are set apart. I studied for many years, seeking in my youth to follow her footsteps – a whitestaff skein-wreck! Imagine the good I could have done. It was not to be. In my older age I let hubris slide, and sought a way to bring together our numbers, to act as a greater whole, to immerse ourselves in the skein together, and follow and guide its paths as one. The focus of many, the energy of one. The focus of one, the energy of many. What could we achieve?'

He opened the door and a long chamber with a low ceiling appeared, lit by dim sconces. Inside a dozen whitestaffs sat on low benches, heads lowered, surrounding an altar of white marble.

'No,' Floré said, and then she was running.

Janos lay on the altar. She pushed through the whitestaffs, their voices muttering, and reached him. He lay cold and still, robed in white. No decay ate at him, no wounds marked his face. Floré pressed her face to his and it was *him*, truly. Janos. Her husband, Marta's father, the man who had burned Urforren to cinders and slain wyrms and devils beyond count. The greatest mage in living memory, who had abandoned it all to build a life with her in the forest. *My poet.*

'He's dead!' she screamed, and the words died in her throat as she repeated them over and again, hot tears springing to her eyes. She clutched at his hand. No breath moved his chest, no pulse quickened in his veins, and his flesh was cool to the touch but not *cold*. Floré stared, and saw his chest rise and fall ever so slightly. In a flash she turned and drew her sword. Benazir and their team of commandos already had their weapons drawn, but the master of the citadel watched them coldly, unfazed. The skein-mage Anderson's hands were wreathed in green flame and he was glancing fervently around the room as if desperate for answers.

'The man may be dead, or close enough,' he said, stepping gently around Benazir's raised dagger and steadying himself on the shoulder of a murmuring whitestaff with a bowed head.

'His *power* is not,' he continued, and slowly he walked to Floré and gestured down at Janos's chest and arms, the tattoos of vibrant red showing through the thin linen of the white robe.

'In our hour of need we had no pattern and no power, but with him by my side I can *use* what he found. The power of the spaces between, the power of what was and what may be. The liminal energy he tapped still flows – his sleeping mind seeks it as we draw from him, protects him from burning away. The patterns he sought are still remembered in flesh and spirit. Together we can guide that pattern and that power.'

Floré breathed heavy through an open mouth and drew her sword high.

'Wake him. *Now*,' she said, but the master shook his head and gently reached down and clasped the hand of the man before him. *Alive?* A rune on Janos's arm, a line with a curving hook at one end, flared with red light and with a jolt Floré was thrown across the room and slammed into the wall. As one the whitestaffs in the room moaned lowly. Her sword fell from her hand at the impact and it felt as if she'd fallen the twenty feet from the centre of the room. Slowly she slid from the wall to the floor and coughed, her hand grasping at her ribs. Her chest felt too tight to breathe. The master closed his eyes and the whitestaffs' chanting grew in intensity as Benazir and the commandos charged forward, but then they were all of them lifted from the ground, sparks of lightning playing over their armour and flesh, and the screaming began.

'He is a font,' the master said, his eyes still closed, 'and from him we will draw salvation!'

Floré reached for her sword but then the lightning was coursing over her, and from the doorway shamans clad in black and grey swarmed forward with sword and dagger and club. The last thing she saw was Janos, his tattoos burning with light, the master clutching his forearm and raising his other hand. She saw Janos's hand lying limp, but one of his fingers twitched…

A blow fell, and Floré saw no more.

INTERLUDES: OBEISANCE TO THE HIGHMOTHERS

AN EYE IN THE DARK WATER

> *'The kelp asleep!*
> *The crab alive!*
> *The clam so deep!*
> *The joyous thrive!'*

> *– Tullioch farming chorus*

Ruemar spoke to herself and to her broodmother and to her father. Ruemar spoke to the wand of cruel metal she found on the corpse of one of the storm devils, the *crow man*, and to the Antian children, though they could not comprehend her. The human children were no better but the Antian at least sat and listened, their furry little faces so strange and pensive. She liked the Antian. She was largest; she knew she must protect them all. They were not of the Tullioch, never mind the Deepfarrow, but she felt kinship in their shared horror.

All had been taken, and all had seen their fellow captives torn asunder one by one on the altar of black stone in the cavern they never went to anymore. She told them all tales of the wild reefs as they clung to her for comfort in the long cold nights in the mountains of the Blue Wolf. When she hunted the caverns for what scraps of food might remain, what tools, what comfort, she spoke of her fears and her hopes to those who were not with her.

'We will run out of food eventually,' she said to her father Leomar as she rummaged in crates, though he was many endless miles away in clear water.

'There are caverns I cannot access, doors that will not open,' she said to her broodmother, who would cock an eye at her in her memory as if to say, *You must not be trying hard enough*.

Many of the doors were coruscating strange rock walls that would open if you pushed at them in the correct way with the skein. She had discovered this after perhaps twenty days from the day of chaos, the day the orbs left and the demons mostly left. The warrior Tullioch Heasin, father of Hassin, had freed himself, had freed his frail human comrade, who in turn had passed her the key and spoken in his garbled tongue. She did not know what it was he had said.

How many days? She was no longer certain. Twice the moon had grown to her fullest, and Ruemar knew that at home the dancing would be sweet in the coral caverns of Deepfarrow, safe from wind and water, safe from beast and storm. She let out a keening note when she thought of the days lost. When the storm devils took her with their orb of light, she had seen fire rain down, great gouts of fire redder than the coral of the home cavern, beams of impossible purple light that broke apart whatever they touched as if struck by a thousand hammer blows all at once. She had hidden with her family, tried to stand guard over the little ones. She remembered nothing more, only a flash of light and blackness and then the cold stone of the sacrifice cavern.

Ruemar spoke to herself, and to her broodmother, and to her father. She did not know if they had survived the attack on Deepfarrow Hold but she held it in her heart that they had.

'I am Ruemar, daughter of Leomar, of the Deepfarrow,' she said to each goblin as she threw their corpses from the cavern mouth where the orbs had fled. It was the only exit or entrance to the cavern complex Ruemar had found in all her days searching, a wide-mouthed cave that opened onto sheer cliffs below, ice and rock above. There was no escape there. She had considered it for a long time. She could knot every piece of fabric in the cave complex to make a rope, but even if it held she would be up in snow and rock and death. She could see nothing but sharp peaks and snow in every direction. The children would not be able to join her. *I must protect them all.*

Ruemar had been a juvenile when she was taken but her purple headcrest was fading as the days passed. In her heart she knew the truth. The day Heasin, son of Luasin, freed her from her bonds she was no longer a juvenile.

She had guarded the children long minutes after Heasin and his human had left, hearing scream and clamour and great crashes, but then there was an interminable time where silence filled the cavern. Eventually she stepped out, with the human and Antian children wailing behind her. She allowed them to follow the first steps up into the long corridor leading away from the sacrifice cavern, but as soon as it opened into the wider complex she forced them to hide in an alcove behind some crates. She had tried to reassure them with language and gesture, and eventually the humans and Antian clung to one another in reasonable silence.

Ruemar had hunted.

She hunted first for Heasin, silently. She came across many dead – *so many!* Storm devils from the blight-water who had sacrificed so many on their stone were burned to cinders, goblins strewn and torn. From one she took a dagger of cold steel and with it in her hand she felt stronger. She stalked the corridors and amongst the dead goblins there were others, alive. The first she came across lunged at her with its hands, gibbering in a tongue she did not speak. She dropped her knife and with her bare hands wrung the life from it. Its grey skin was rough beneath her strong fingers, its muscles too frail to harm her or resist. She panted as she snapped its bones and threw it to the ground.

They will kill the children if they find them, she knew, and so Ruemar picked up the fallen knife and she hunted. She found the cavern with the open wall, and in it an orb of dark stone bisected by a crystal strip sat squat on three legs of stout metal. There were more dead in that cavern, more dead everywhere, and Ruemar added to the number gladly. She killed goblins, again and again. Every fallen crow-man, every storm devil she passed she made sure there was no twitch. After an hour she found she was looping back in the same corridors. She repeated her steps. She took different paths. She found goblins huddling behind crates or clawing at half-open doors. Some rushed her in a group of four so she used her claws, felt gore rise in her throat at the sight of the spraying blood as she shredded their frail forms. She had fought, in the wild reefs – you could not live there without fighting. This was different, she knew. It was a slaughter.

She found a storm devil, *crow-man*, still alive. It was a woman, taller even than Ruemar, limbs gangly and twisted. She was rushing down a back passage, gathering into a bag of dark cloth a collection of the wands the storm devils used, a dagger, some food. Ruemar followed the devil slowly, saw her stop and concentrate at patches of wall where the stone was lighter. Ruemar hung back, felt a prickle at the edge of her senses. The devil was using the true current, seeking pattern. In front of her the lighter stone melted back and an opening appeared. The woman entered, and emerged a moment later clutching a cloak and a book to her chest, muttering to herself.

Ruemar had seen the devils use their wands. She knew a storm devil could only be killed by silver or fire, and she had no silver.

She attacked like a maelstrom. In three bounds she was atop the crow-man, her claws reaching around to rip at her chest, her mouth clamping down where the devil's shoulder met her neck. Hot blood coursed into her mouth but it tasted like the earth, thick and mineral and *dirty*, not the clean taste of blood. She dug her claws deep and wrenched her body and spun to the ground, digging as deep as she could.

The crow-man stopped struggling, limply resisting but with no concerted effort, and Ruemar reached for the bag. With a scrabble she found what she was after: a wand tipped in red. Opening herself to the skein she focused on it, and even with the horrible confusion the crow-man exuded, the chaos in the true current, she found the pattern for flame.

Ruemar burned the storm devil to char and ruin, and on that day she was no longer a juvenile.

In the days since she had found many doors. Food to sustain them. Blankets to warm the little ones. She laboured long hours stripping the dead goblins and devils of anything that might be useful before she cast them from the mouth of the cavern. She wore a belt of black fabric now with a dagger sheathed and four wands topped with crystals of green, purple, blue, and red. She spoke to her father as she paced around her only remaining hope: the orb.

'It must be one of their orbs, Father,' she said, sat on the cavern floor staring up at the dark stone. 'I cannot find the latch, though I try. I try and try. Perhaps I am too weak. Perhaps I am a fool. What would you have me do?'

She tried to break into the orb but the dark stone resisted her strength. She could see seams where a ramp might descend, perhaps. She spent hours with improvised chisel and hammer, hours more sat basking in the waters of the true current. She brought the children with her sometimes, and they sat and played and sang in their strange tongues as she focused and probed. Nothing seemed to work.

She lost days to fear, a deep black fear that sat on her chest and made her blood run cold. *If they return, what will we do?* She tried to teach the little ones to run, to hide if ever the orbs came back. She prayed to the great whale, long litanies of the beauty of Deepfarrow Hold. She prayed to the bird, the great scavenger who would take her to the next life, return her to the ocean. *Will your wings find me here?*

At night she dreamt of the water. There was water in the caverns, true, a trickle down the walls of some rooms, a well dug deep in the heart of the cavern complex. She had brought herself great buckets of that well-water to bathe in, but it lacked the salt and clarity of the sea. It was a dark water – it tasted of the mountain, of minerals and muck and stone. Her dreams were always of the currents in the reef around the hold, where she would hunt with her broodmates, play at fighting, study the true current. She had toured the kelp farms and outlying settlements with her father, had taken her turn as apprentice to the guarding patrols, but the hold was home – a place where your family lived, all of them, old and young, close and distant. She remembered rueing the lack of privacy and longing for adventure, to cross the Wind Sea! She had not even left the Deepfarrow waters, not truly, before all of this.

The smaller Antian, the one she had named Jurren, began to cough. It was a little at first, but after a span she began to worry. Ruemar knew nothing of medicine. She had grown sick of not knowing names for the little beasts, the humans, the Antian, so she had named them after her broodmates. *Her* Jurren in Deepfarrow Hold was strongest and brightest, always first to leap to action. She bestowed his name on the more timid of the two furred creatures, in the hope his spirit might aid it. The other Antian was Gellen for her younger brother, and then the two humans she named Bullitar and Bollitar after the broodmates of legend, the pair who stole a feather from the bird's tail, who convinced the whale to carry them through the Fractured Sea. She did not know if the humans were siblings (or male, or female, or whatever it is humans were), but Bullitar and Bollitar always escaped whatever trouble they got into. She hoped to call on their luck.

Jurren coughed again, and Ruemar fretted. *Do Antians need warmth or cold? Water or meat?* They had long run through the fresh stores and for many days had been subsisting on stale bread and dried fruits, strange cured plants, and what she thought might be meat that had been twisted into a dry knot. The nights were growing colder and great flurries of snow blew into the mouth of the cavern, almost reaching her orb.

Ruemar spent the day with the little ones and the evening with the orb, sunk into the skein. She had learned much from her days forcing open doors of stone, no matter how long it took her. She had ventured back to the sacrifice cavern but it held no secrets she could comprehend, only the memory of horror, the nauseating twist of skein around the strange runes carved in the black rock of Varratim's altar. After another evening spent immersing herself in the current she went to the open cavern mouth and looked out to the south. The stars were dancing, more stars than she had seen from the reef where spray and glowing plankton stole starlight from view. She sat and watched the stars pass and when she walked back to the orb she held her hand against where she felt a door must be.

'Open,' she said aloud, and the orb did not react. 'Please.' She leaned her head against the cold stone. 'I cannot save them here. Please.'

She fell asleep on the floor and the next morning when she went to the children Jurren did not wake. Their breathing was shallow, their eyes unresponsive. The other Antian clutched at them and spoke rapidly but Ruemar understood none of it.

'It will be all right, Gellen,' she said. 'I will protect you.'

She left Gellen with Jurren and took Bullitar and Bollitar down to the orb and sat with them.

'We must open it,' she said, but they did not respond with words. *How many days since they last spoke?*

'If we can open it, we can fly down from here,' she said, her voice so quiet. 'I can fly the Antian to an Antian town. I can fly you two to a human town, where they will hold you close and treat you well. I can fly myself to Deepfarrow Hold.'

In her heart she knew it would not happen. *If I can fly this, I will take you to safety,* she thought, *and then I will hunt.*

The image of the crow-men who had done their sacrifices had not left her. None had returned. Had Heasin of Shardkin truly killed them all? She did not think so. *He would have come back for me. For all of us.* Her rescuers must be surely dead.

'I will be my own witness,' she said quietly, and one of the humans clung to her arm. 'I will be my own hero. I will not die in this place.'

Ruemar fingered the wands at her belt and stepped forward, drawing the blue wand, and pressing it against where she felt a seam must be. Opening herself to the true current she poured her energy into the wand. A beam of blue-white light shot out and dissipated against the dark stone, and she pressed it tighter and fired the wand again, and again. It took from her, as the skein ever did, but it was efficient, and when she held her eyes against the dark stone she thought she could see the faintest of scratches. She tried the other wands, even the green one that seemed to do little unless turned against a waking foe. It would send a waking foe to sleep, but against the austere stone its pattern faded and dissipated. A long evening she spent with the wands, and at the end the patch of stone was scorched and perhaps a chip or two had appeared.

Ruemar slumped to the ground on the cavern floor beneath the orb again. The humans had long since gone to the room where they slept, and she had failed them again.

Ruemar fell into the current and let it carry her. She felt the cavern and the orb, the intricacies of every stone. She could sense the faint presence of the sleeping children, but no other life anywhere near the cavern complex. She lay there, not probing, just letting the current wash over her, feeling its ebbs and flows and ripples. She lay utterly still and did not move her eye in the skein, simply let the world pass over her and tried to connect to the great whale, or the ocean. At the periphery of her vision the sacrifice cavern came into the current so she shifted her focus away from there, but still lay untethered, not looking. The cavern and the orb and the children, stone and air and snow above.

Wait.

There was a nodule. A knot. A tiny whirl in the current. An eddy. Ruemar felt her claws dig into the cavern floor but she did not allow herself to focus. She let the knowledge of the knot bring it into her senses slowly. Far from the door or its hinge and its lock, there were many strange patterns, but she felt one that was connected to it. Somewhere within the orb. It was a shape, but could be another shape if it just... *moved.* With only a mote of energy she slid the shape's conformation and there was a creak. Ruemar scrambled back out of the way as above her the ramp descended. She got to her feet and flexed her claws and let out a bark of exultation. She stretched out to her full height and her tail slashed behind her across the cold of the cavern floor, her tongue flitting between her teeth. She tasted the stale air spilling from the orb and flared her nostrils.

I will protect them all, she thought, and she pictured the children who had not been saved. She pictured Hassin daughter of Heasin on the black altar of stone, the human children, and heard in her mind the echoes of their screams and the burning stares of the warped storm devils. Ruemar pressed her fist to her chest and closed her eyes and prayed to the bird, the great scavenger who would take the dead to where they belonged.

I will protect, and then I will hunt.

A Rock, a Hook, a World, a Web

'We worship the god-bear Anshuka, and before us the Ferron worshipped four Judges: Berren, Lothal, Nessilitor, and Anshuka. The Tullioch worship the bird and the whale, though give us no detail. Are these perhaps judges, or abstract concepts like Baal and the nameless fire that so occupy the strait kingdoms? In Ona it is said they worship a great dragon who lives in the endless cloud above, but again it is unclear. A physical dragon, like the great Judge Anshuka? Or simply an idea, or a spirit? The Antian claim no gods, and the Cil-Marie have made their own in the Sun-Masters. Still odder sects persist across the world of Morost. What gods or judges are worshipped in the jungles of Caroban and Siobh, or the fabled isles of Lello? Ferron showed us the horror that can happen when a god is called to a mortal war. Let us hope none lurk in the far reaches of the world.'
– **Pantheon of the protectorate**, Campbell Torbén of Aber-Ouse

Torrenda was cold and wet but her stomach was warm, the wrapped brick of ever-burning peat held tight to her body under a thick jacket of oiled leather. She felt its heat prickling her skin, and could picture the spiderweb of broken blood vessels across her flesh where the heat had left its brand over the years. She held one arm to her stomach to steady her burden, and felt her shoulders ache with the familiar weight of the pack on her back. She wiped frozen rain from her forehead and forced herself to breathe steady. Already she had walked a dozen miles of rough track before finding the road, and she knew if she didn't find the wayhouse soon she would catch chill. *The crossroads will be soon,* she repeated in her mind over and over, and huffed through her nose. One foot in front of another she trudged on along the road, stepping through puddles. Her boots were already long soaked through. *The crossroads will be soon.*

In Ona, the air was always wet. The churn of clouds and water from the Wind Sea to the west combined with the gales and cold air from Caroh's Strait in the north. The storms grew in the endless islands of the Crowns, and then broke across the mountains and down into Ona bringing mist and rain. From the road Torrenda could see the rock chimneys rising a dozen yards to each side of the rutted track, which wended its way around and between them. Some fifty feet tall, narrow daggers of red rock jagging upward, and some three-hundred-foot columns pushing at the sky, vine and shrub trailing down their sheer sides. Further from the road there were thorny shrubs and cactus stands, and then more chimneys of rock, the occasional squat tree or clump of dark grass. Off into the distance through the rain and mist she could see the shadowy presences of more rock chimneys, obscured by more wet. *Always wet.*

Torrenda shivered and remembered home, a cave hollowed high atop a cluster of rock chimneys, connected to the hamlet by rope bridge. She used to run with Kaarle across the bridges, but Jussi was always too afraid. Torrenda smiled at the memory and caught her foot on a rock in the road and stumbled down to one knee, one hand pushing down into muddy cart tracks up to the wrist, the other clutching to her stomach. The heat from the burning peat through her clothes intensified, and she let out a gasp. Her trousers were already wet, but now they were wet and mudded and filthy. *The crossroads will be soon.*

It was ten more minutes of walking, wending through rock chimneys and cursing the rain, and then Torrenda saw the shrine and the wayhouse beyond. The shrine was a rock cairn atop a slick black stone, a dragon stone, with a sheltered hollow in the piled cairn pointing outward at the crossroads. Torrenda could hardly see the roads headed left and right, but could see the track going past the shrine and the low bulk of a wayhouse a few hundred yards on.

'Thank you, Father,' Torrenda said, and rushed forward. The shrine was well maintained. Within the wet stone of the cairn, the hollow held a dozen bricks of dry Ona peat, lustrous black with a few tendrils of roots from whatever moss once grew over it. Raising her jacket to guard against the worst of the wind, Torrenda reached a wet hand into the pouch held tight over her stomach and pulled out the brick of burning peat, slipping it into the shrine. Her brick was smouldering, letting off a musty rich smoke ever so slowly despite the damp, and she could feel her hand starting to burn but then the brick was safe and in the hollow and she breathed a sigh of relief and drew her hand back. She let her pack slip from her back, rolled her shoulders, and allowed herself to smile. She was cold and she was wet and she was so very tired and hungry, but she had made it to the shrine, and the wayhouse was near, and the ember was still burning.

Reaching back into the shrine she arranged her burning brick with a fresh one leaned against it, to catch, and then she lit a second dry brick at one corner. When curls of grey smoke started to spiral from its edge she drew it close to her, slipped it into the pouch at her stomach and pulled her jacket close. Tomorrow, another dozen miles, the day after perhaps a dozen more, and then there was the shrine at the waterfall below Tarran Point. Ever she would walk, ever she would carry the father's flame. Any traveller could take fire from the shrines on the dragon stones, fire to warm their village, fire to keep them dry against the endless mist and rain of Ona. As shrinekeeper Torrenda had sworn to carry the flame ever onward, an endless journey navigating the wilds of Ona. She carried no riches or weapon. No bandit would attack a shrinekeeper, few bandits that there were.

Stepping back, Torrenda closed her eye and offered a prayer to the father above, the great dragon: *I will carry your spark, and keep travellers safe from the cold.* She felt a shiver of warmth from the fresh brick of peat, and through the cold of the rain smelt the rich darkness of the peat smoke filling her lungs. With the lit fire now smouldering in the shrine above the black dragon stone, in the gloom of the afternoon she could make out a small bird hidden in a dense shrub nearby, watching her. Through the downpour it flitted, disregarding her, into the opening in the cairn, hopping close to the burning peat. Its feathers looked soaked through – a sparrow, or something like it.

'I'll keep you safe from the cold too, little traveller,' she said, and she hefted her pack and turned towards the wayhouse. Tea and soup and perhaps a bed, or at least a space on the dry floor. *I will be dry tonight.* She decided she would listen to the talk in the common room that night. Normally she paid it no mind, but at the last wayhouse there had been rumours and murmurs: *Cil-Marie are pushing into the Crown Isles, with magic cannons on their boats; the magic storm in the far west is growing, and spreading along the Wind Sea; the strait kingdoms are aligning to retaliate against Caroban's raids; Siobhen seen in the passes to the north of Ona, dozens, hundreds – armed and waiting for some order or sign from their dark god.*

Torrenda had walked the rain-drenched wilds of Ona for two decades. Whenever she passed Kaarle's home in the east valleys he offered her a place, but she always smiled and declined. *No roof for me, no stones in my pockets.* Ona was kept peaceful by the harsh geography of its coast and surrounding ranges, brutal columns of geometric basalt and granite that turned any thought of invasion sour, and by dint of having no resources worth taking. *Only rain, and happiness.* There was no great industry, and the only sizeable town, Wasserschild, faded and grew with the arrival and departure of the slow-moving caravans of livestock that grazed the canyons, village to town, town to village. The idea of war, of ships battling on the sea, of a magical storm, intrigued her. She could not imagine a war, so many people in one place!

Once she had seen Wasserschild when there was a break

in the rain, a long-predicted week of dryness. There had been so many people and caravans, animals, so much movement! Torrenda had danced with a boy from the southern mountains who kept llama, his hair braided, his eyes shining. He had said his pastures in the southern range were so high that he was above the rainclouds, that he lived in sun. She had laughed at that a great deal. *Deeply unnatural*, she thought, smiling at the memory.

Walking away from the shrine above the dragon stone, she tried to picture if Siobh invaded as they had in her parents' day. All had fled to the mesas and rock chimneys, and after weeks of being pelted with heavy stone from a great height the invaders had retreated, soaked, ill, broken. Torrenda had never seen the sea, had never left Ona, but loved tales of the endless blue with a clear sky above. The tales of Cil-Marie at war with the pirates of the Crown Isles, of a magical storm full of monsters at the far end of the world. They were stories that could keep her dreams filled.

She was happy wandering from shrine to shrine, lighting the fires above the dragon stones to honour the father, to provide light and warmth. It was not an easy task, but the joy she felt walking the canyons, watching the bloom on the cacti, the lizards crawling between the rocks, the sprigs of colour crawling up the stone columns – she would not trade it for pirates and *the sea*, little that she could even imagine the sea. It was nice to listen though, to hear of how wide the world was.

The sparrow flitted by her face and Torrenda blinked and halted, and then it was gone, gone to the drizzle and mist beyond. Torrenda went to step forward and there was a crack behind her, the crack of stone shearing. Instinctively she glanced upward and raised her arm. Any given year some Ona were lost to rockfall, the peril of living in the shadow of the towering columns that provided them shelter and safety and so much more. Above her was only stillness, the nearest columns dozens of feet away. Torrenda glanced back at the shrine and let her bag swing from her shoulders to the mud.

'Merciful Father!' she said, and then she was running to it. She stopped short. The cairn was still standing, but below it a web of glowing silver cracks covered the dragon stone, stark against its slick black. They glowed with a dull light and Torrenda felt her hand rising to touch it, but she stopped short at a growl.

From a stand of cacti not ten yards off, a tulka emerged. Every shrine had a tulka, and many other places besides. The spirit of a place, a piece of the world and all its connections and the prayers of its people incarnate. Torrenda bowed her head. The tulka at this shrine had come to her before, many years ago as she tended the flame, and had taken a scrap of cheese from her hand, had allowed her to stroke the static fur on its back. It took the shape of a canyon fox, pointed wide ears over a triangular face, sharp eyes, a slim body and a bushy tail. There were many canyon foxes in Ona, but instead of their dun coats and black eyes, the tulka was a creature wholly apart. Its eyes were glistening pearlescent orbs, its coat matte black streaked with whorls of shining silver. The claws on its padded feet were a shining onyx. The tulka fox growled not at Torrenda, but at the dragon stone, stepping forward and sniffing it gently.

'Spirit,' she said, 'what can I do?'

It made no response. In the cairn, Torrenda's peat brick

still burned. *Did I do this? No!* Countless times she had laid a brick of fire in the cairn above the dragon stones. Countless times she had prayed to the father. She had seen tulka perhaps a few times a year as she made her offerings, and twice beyond that far from any dragon stone, out in the wilds of Ona where no human dwelt: once a hallowed eagle with feathers of gold and a beak of purest white; once a beetle the size of her fist at the bottom of a waterfall, its horn and shells patterned in starlight, every leg the most delicate glass.

The tulka fox stepped back from the shrine and looked to her. *Is it afraid?* Torrenda lowered her hand to the tulka, felt the heat of the burning brick strapped to her stomach. It pressed its head to her palm and she felt the living heat of it. In the rain they stood together, staring at the dragon stone and the web of glowing breaks. Still it held together. *For how long?*

Torrenda wiped mist and drizzle from her face. There were shrines all across Ona, some clustered together, some many miles apart. Each shrine atop a dragon stone to honour the father above who flew in the endless cloud over Ona, the great dragon. *Is this happening here, or everywhere? What does it mean?*

'I will fix this,' she said, but even as she said it she knew it to be a lie. How do you fix a broken stone? *You do not.* Torrenda pressed down a final pat to the tulka fox's head and turned towards the wayhouse.

'I will find the truth of this, and see what can be done,' she said, and the fox trotted after her, sticking close to her heels. Never had she seen a tulka do that: stick so close to a human. Stooping down she stroked its back, marvelled again at the spirit made flesh.

'You will help me, perhaps,' she said, and she walked to the wayhouse, in her mind trying to judge the distance to the nearest dragon stone. Rumours of magical storms and pirate wars would have to wait. She had news of her own.

No Trial for Rust-Folk

'This war is the legacy we have been left. Three centuries since Ferron fell, and still the rotstorm rages, and ever the descendants of empire seek refuge or violence at our border. The rotstorm is a divine punishment. It is not for me to say when Anshuka's rage should wane. I must hold to the tradition of our people, and for Undal to be free, Ferron must be kept in check. The Stormguard do not wait passively. We do not hide behind the wall; we strike into the storm. If the boy can help us take Urforren, for a generation we might build and strive in peace.' – **Private diary**, Knight-Commander Salem Starbeck

Floré pointed her blade down the long avenue in Fallow Fen and Benazir broke eye contact with the demon corpse at her feet and followed the tip of her friend's sword. *Silverberry,* Benazir thought, *it's Silverberry Avenue where the booksellers were.* Fallow Fen was a ruin, left for a decade to goblin and rust-folk and worse, and they were there to take it back. She saw what was coming for them. At the end of the avenue was a wyrm, the wyrm that had been taking out their patrols for three weeks, that had cut a hole in the Stormwall, that had decimated Donegal's lancer legion in the northern quarter and eaten six skein-mages to date. The wyrm that defied all missiles and blades, that seemed to shrug off skein-flame and alchemist's fire and ballistae bolts alike. The creature that had allowed the rust-folk to take the city, ten years before. Benazir had never seen a wyrm before, and the sight of it made her pulse skip beats. *The wyrm of Fallow Fen.*

It was sinuous and long, perhaps fifty feet in length, its head as large as a bullock, head and body both covered in chitinous armoured scales that twisted as it swam through the air impossibly. Down each side of its body and in a stripe along the top were three chaotic lines of black eyes, orb eyes, pools of darkness. Its mouth was a horror, a threefold beak wet and lined with endless rows of jagged teeth each as long as a finger. Benazir saw the dozen goblins who had escaped Floré's blade and arrows running towards it, shrieking and yelling. The wyrm swam in the air ten feet from the torn ground of the ruined avenue and writhed and moved forward, letting out a shriek that made her bones ache, at once sickeningly high and heart-shakingly deep.

Benazir felt a twist in her guts. She could not kill this thing. Perhaps nothing could. In three hundred years of Stormguard history, the killing of a wyrm was fable – crushed by a cunningly triggered rockslide, chained by a thousand lengths of iron and burned by a phalanx of skein-mages working day and night. Hussain the Blue killed one, once, before another killed him. *The only reason we are alive at all is they are so rare,* she thought with a grimace. Glancing behind her she saw the remnants of their squad lining up, eying the side alleys, waiting for Floré's orders. Private Guil was there, and shot Benazir a quick smile, her cheeks flushed and red. Benazir didn't smile back but held the girl's gaze.

Janos walked forward and smiled at Floré and then at Benazir. He looked skinny, as if the fighting was burning away every last scrap of fat on him. His brown hair was knotted behind his head, and he scratched at a week's growth of beard with a gloved hand as he stopped beside them. Like the rest he was clad in black and grey leather, and in the darkness of Fallow Fen Benazir couldn't make out any nuance of his facial expression. With one foot he nudged the corpse of the crow-man and reached a hand out to Benazir's shoulder and squeezed it in thanks. Together they stared down the avenue at the writhing creature, ever so slowly moving towards the park, and it let out another shriek. Below it the dozen goblins echoed its cry, high voices cracking. Benazir pushed her hair back from her forehead and looked up at the sky. The cloud was breaking, and she could see starlight up above.

'This is the wyrm, then?' Janos asked, gently, and Floré blew out a breath.

'I would think so,' she said, 'but should we ask it?'

Janos smiled and Benazir looked back at the blossom of the Sisters, their branches intertwined, and remembered old Hovarth giving her a bottle of rum outside the kitchen of Stormcastle XII. '*Give the sisters my regards*,' he had said. She gripped her dagger.

'This is my town,' she said, and she could feel her voice breaking. She pointed her dagger at the wyrm, the silver blade slicked black with demon blood. She remembered her fear in the deep rotstorm, remembered her shame, remembered her father's thunderous voice, her mother's cold dismissal. 'This was my home.'

Floré put a hand to her shoulder and squeezed, but shook her head. 'This one isn't for us yet, mate,' she said, and Benazir pressed her tongue to her teeth and stared at the monster.

Janos sniffed, stepped forward and tilted his head. 'Benazir.' He met her eye, and then he stared at the wyrm. He raised both of his hands, and his feet left the ground until he was floating like the demon had been, three yards from the ground, and even through the black cloth of his tunic Benazir could see a glow as the runes tattooed on his arms pulsed with red light.

'Form up!' Floré cried, her face setting to stone the moment Janos began calling his magic. The commando squad surged forward to surround Janos and nocked arrows as the wyrm advanced, the dozen goblins cheering and screaming below it, the commandos knowing arrows could do nothing against the wyrm's armoured hide.

Benazir felt acid in her gut. They should run. She knew they should run. Nobody could stop a wyrm. *Janos is the best, perhaps the best in a generation,* she thought, *but even he couldn't believe…*

'Do we have a plan, Captain?' one of the commandos called. Floré held her grimace but then laughed and Benazir stared up at Janos, floating like a demon himself, like a skein-wreck from a storybook. They needed an army, a trap, siege weapons and every skein-mage. Starbeck was planning for it, the forges working day and night on chain links the size of fists. *Janos…*

She went to grab him and pull him back so they could leave, even as it broke her heart to abandon the Sisters, but she stopped herself. She had doubted him before, in the storm, and he had proven her wrong. Benazir checked her knives and bit her lip, but she held position and looked to Floré. Floré caught her gaze and smiled.

'We have a skein-wreck, my dear comrades,' Floré said. 'We have nothing to fear here.' The head of the wyrm was only thirty yards away, its three chitinous beaks snapping open and closed, that impossible mouth, the horror of its teeth curving back into a throat black as the nameless fire. Benazir thought she could see a tongue deep within, a pulsing movement in the darkness. As the wyrm lithely swam through the sky towards them, the strips of black and red eyes along its ridges and sides flickered with movement. *It's watching us,* Benazir thought, *watching its prey.* Janos was mumbling to himself, and then the wind around them all was whipping into a frenzy. Blossom from the Sisters fell, spiralling around Janos, around Benazir and her comrades, and the sweet smell of the twin willows' blossom filled Benazir's nose as Janos brought his hands together, and then violently apart.

The wyrm was rent; split; rendered in two. Its fifty-foot body was split longitudinally from mouth to tail tip, split with a perfect cut that followed its internal equator even as it had roiled and coiled towards them. For a moment the two halves hung in the air, and then a fountain of emerald blood from countless arteries and veins coated the street and the two halves fell from the sky with the noise of meat hitting the butcher's slab, a wet thud that reverberated along the street, an impact Benazir felt in her bones, crushing most of the frail goblins beneath its armoured bulk. Sheathing her daggers, Benazir stepped forward and, with Floré, took hold of Janos as he descended to the street and stumbled. He looked grey. A handful of goblins were scarpering away from the wyrm, those who had been lucky enough to escape its falling form. Guil and another commando stepped forward and with steady calm they sent a rain of arrows after them. Within moments each had loosed a handful of arrows, shafts sinking deep into the frail backs of the fleeing goblins.

'How did you do that?' she asked Janos, knowing the truth even as she spoke.

'I told you, Benny,' he said, voice shaking, 'I can take without giving. I can see the pattern beneath the pattern.'

Turning to face the fallen wyrm, he put an arm around her shoulder and pressed his head to hers. The commandos were cheering then, and Floré was calling sharp orders clear above the tumult. Benazir held Janos up and felt him shaking, shivering. *It still takes from him.* He was doing the impossible, pulling in energy beyond what any human could give, yet it was not without cost, not truly.

'This was your home,' he said, quietly. 'What else could I do?'

Benazir leaned against the skein-wreck, and glanced back over her shoulder. One of the willow Sisters was charred along its trunk where a burning rottroll had collapsed into it, and the other had lost one of its huge boughs in the combat. It had cracked, and dangled down from the trunk, trailing pink and white blossom flowers in the corpses and dirt. In the ruins of Fallow Fen the blossom of the Sisters drifted around them and the rain finally stopped; the night was clear.

They left Urforren a week later. With the wyrm dead and Janos growing in power every day, the rust-folk remaining soon fled west into the storm, harried at each step by Lancers and commandos.

'A great victory,' Starbeck said, Benazir, Floré, and Janos

invited to dine with him in his personal tent. Benazir raised her glass.

'What would you do next?' he asked, and the three of them exchanged eye contact. The food in Starbeck's tent was no better in substance than what was served in the mess, but his staff had plated it on fine porcelain and the rough measure of wine allotted to each soldier every day was in a goblet of carved wood instead of a cracked clay cup. Benazir sipped her wine and considered, then allowed herself a grin. *Fallow Fen is free.* Her father had lost the city, Commander Hallfast in all his temper and his bluster. Benazir had left his name for dirt. *And I'm the one who took it back: Benazir Arfallow.* She raised her glass to the memory of her mother and her brother and waited patiently for one of the others to fall into the trap.

'I suppose secure the city, and shore up the Stormwall,' Janos said. 'Then the job is done.'

For someone who can do magics beyond anyone alive, Benazir thought, *he's always been rather dense.* She smiled at him though. He was trying, and Floré was happy. And he certainly was acting less of a fool since he and Floré started spending time together. Starbeck turned to her but she inclined her glass to Floré who frowned and rubbed at her nose – it had been broken a few days before by some Ferron's fist.

'We stopped them this year,' Floré said, 'but there will be rotsurges again next year. If their demons can harvest the rotbuds from wherever the hell they come from, they can kindle them and send storms across the protectorate, spewing monsters as they go. We should fortify and rebuild the wall, but also send patrols to see if we can stop the next rotsurge.'

Starbeck nodded indulgently and Floré drank her wine and rubbed at the lightning scar up her right arm – a scar she had gained chasing a rotbud, just as she suggested. Benazir met her friend's eyes and nodded encouragingly. Starbeck skewered a lump of potato with his fork and took a bite, chewing carefully. The rotbuds were the worst of the enemies' weapons – motes of pure rotstorm, strange arcane artefacts or seeds that in the hands of a demon could spawn a storm, a *rotsurge*, that would cut across the protectorate. Not only would the storms ruin crops and batter buildings, but they would also send bolts of lightning and arcane seeds burning to the ground, and from those goblin and rottroll and rotvine and worse would sprout, strange aberrations and beasts. The Stormguard Forest Watch and Lancers would spend a season hunting down whatever hell came. Dozens or hundreds would die, at the least.

'Well?' Starbeck said at last, and Benazir put down her glass.

'We burn Urforren to the ground.' She stood up and she crossed her arms and began pacing the tent. Floré rubbed at her nose and Janos laughed but Starbeck kept eating his dinner.

'How would we possibly do that?' Janos asked, and Benazir cocked her head at him.

'With our *skein-wreck*, Janos,' she replied acidly.

He leaned back in his seat.

'Every year they push out. They raid, their crow-men send rotsurges to cross our country and terrorise our people. They have only one city: Urforren. It is seventy miles into the storm if we cut straight. I say we force-march it. In five days we can be at their city walls. All we need to do is get you close enough to see it, and hold the crow-men back long enough to let you do the thing.'

Janos and Starbeck both narrowed their eyes, and Floré spat wine.

'You promised not to tell anyone,' Janos said, staring at Floré. She shrugged and twisted her mouth in apology.

'What,' Starbeck said carefully, 'is the *thing*?'

Benazir sat back down and gestured to Janos.

'Salt,' he said, his voice suddenly flat, his eyes still. 'It has a pattern to it that always calls me. I could turn all of it to salt. I've done a field before. I tried it once in the storm, to see how far I could extend. I can go further. Burning salt, a salt forever imbued with fire. Nothing would ever grow or live there again.'

'What of the army, and town, awaiting?' Starbeck said, and Janos shook his head.

'All to salt,' he said, his voice a small thing, and then he drained his wineglass.

'A forced march,' Benazir said, more forcefully this time. *I can end this war.* 'Commandos and Lancers both. Janos surrounded by every skein-mage and archer we have. We march, we kill anything we find. They'll settle in for a siege, but we won't come with siege engine and ram. We come with one aim. We end this.'

Starbeck sipped his wine and stared at Janos.

In the end the march took seven days. The rotstorm threw everything it had at them. Rotbud and biting vine took their victims, mainly from the Lancers who had no experience in the strange hell of the rotstorm, didn't know the esoteric and nightmare rules that must be followed to survive. Above them a roiling cloud of purple and red and black, an endless tempest crackling with lightning. Occasional bolts would crash down to earth, seeking the fastest path. Three Lancers around a campfire were struck, all dead within a moment. Mooncalf white crocodiles, huge and ungainly, ambushed any who lingered too long by open water. Then the goblins and the rottrolls came...

The first attack was at night, and then again before dawn, and every night after. They began to camp in rigid rows, every third man on watch, everyone clutching their steel. A few of the Lancers got rotsick, fevered and maddened by the oppressive storm. They were far enough in that Benazir couldn't send them back, so she had them bound and gagged and carried on poles like goats to a roasting fire. Their supplies were what they could carry on their backs, and even before they reached Urforren some had worked through their water ration, trying to wash away the acrid mists.

Always Janos stayed far from the edge of their small column, Floré next to him with her eyes sharp, eight skein-mages and two dozen archers and then a ring of commandos. They marched on Urforren and Benazir led the way.

'It's your plan,' Starbeck had said when he gave her the command. She had felt sick then, felt sick ever since. A thousand of them marching into the storm. It hadn't been attempted in a generation at least. *There must be enough of us that they choose to meet us at Urforren.*

They flew banners, marched tall. The clouds of red mist came and six breathed too deep, despite all they'd been told. They coughed blood for a night and a day before they died. Everyone else coughed only a little blood, and kept their scarves high. Benazir felt each death as a stone in her heart. *They are only here because of me,* she thought. She clutched at her arms in the night, dug her nails into flesh, kept her face still. *To act is to court death, but to wait is to accept it.*

Guil was there with the team surrounding Janos, Guil and the stoic Yonifer. *I've led them into the storm and out again,* she thought, and did not let herself think of her first command, of Fingal and the crocodile, Orun and the rotvine, Myte and Frolley swarmed by goblins. She had run dozens of missions since then, had lost people, had saved others, but when she slept under a thick tarp, pressed close to the dark peat of the Ferron wastes, it was those faces that came to her.

They reached Urforren and she sent for Janos and Floré, and together they stood on the brow of a hill. It was a squat town, low walls of stone and palisades of scavenged wood, no towers to catch the wind, no flags flying. The size of a market village in Undal, but *dense*. She could see that, how narrow the streets were, and the throngs of people at the gates desperate to get in. *Rust-folk*. They were trying to press in before the army reached them, every farmer and eel-eating scavenger for a dozen miles if she was to guess. From the vantage of the hill, she could see the warren of streets and the low roofs and make out tall bent figures stalking the wall like herons in a stream, gazing out at them. *Crow-men*.

'Is it time?' Janos asked her, and she handed him the eyeglass.

'It will take me a while,' he said, his stance unsteady. Floré gripped him. 'Are you sure about this, Benazir?'

Benazir drew a knife and hefted the weight of it, glanced back over their ragged column. *How many dead on the march alone?* High above them the madness of the rotstorm raged, thunder moaning across the land. It started to rain and the endless wind picked up, a gale that carried wisps of acid red cloud twining through the sky.

'We end this here,' Benazir said, and down at the city the

rust-folk gathered at the gate split and fell back, as from the city the first hordes of goblin and rottroll spilled out, and began to run to meet them.

ACT 3

THE BURNING BLADE

Orbs of fire
None to save
Ferron's ire
Seek the cave

Sop for the mewling ones in the darkness that
they might know hope, Antian children's rhyme

12

APPLIED CHAOS THEORY

'Six more dead to in-fighting, so only thirty-four Lancers remain with Sorren. There are clear dissenters. I've sent Rikard to make contact. From what we have heard in our scouting, they plan to continue through the villages as they loop back to Aber-Ouse. Tomorrow we will strike; we cannot risk another massacre. We are sorely outnumbered. These Lancers have broken their oaths. By the bond placed in our house, as independent arbiters of corruption, find enclosed my full judgement. The sentence will be carried out blade and bow, by your command.' – **Fourth report on the massacre at Crowpit**, Agent Haysom, Third Moon Trading House

Ashbringer stared down at the white walls and towers of the Riven citadel from high on the mountainside. She was stood in a clearing amongst the scree and boulders at the base of a shallow ridge leading up to the peak of the taller of the two mountains that loomed atop the island of Iskander, and her boots crunched in a layer of thin snow. Above her the moon was fat and yellow, its face and edges sharply delineated against the endless black beyond. Ashbringer stared at the moon, and then at the twinkling souls of her ancestors. Focusing in on herself, her heartbeat, the feeling of the cold air on her skin, she breathed deep and she pushed her awareness out to the skein, that pattern underlying all the world. She fell to her knees.

Chaos. Ashbringer felt bile rise in her throat, her bare hands scrabbling at rock below. *What is this?* It wasn't the chaos of a crow-man, a demon. Not that chaos those creatures of the rotstorm carried with them, surrounding them like a cloud of foul gas, a chaos of impenetrable shapes and shadows that drowned all pattern. She made herself focus on this new strangeness. The pattern was still there, she could feel it in herself, could feel it in the rock below, the nearby sprigs of heather, the air around her. *What is missing?* It took her long moments to understand.

The currents underlying the world were altered, circumscribed in strange ways. Normally in the skein always there were tendrils of connection that trailed off to the edge of her senses, and barely hinted at broader connections below and above and around her, barely noticeable or noticed. Just the background of the universe, the stitching that held the fabric of the world in place.

Gone, she thought, and then realised her mouth was open and she was still clawing at the earth with her hands.

'Not gone,' a voice said from behind her. 'Broken.'

Ashbringer rolled forward and drew her broken sword as she sprang to a crouch, swirling to face her old enemy. *Deathless.*

Tullen One-Eye stood a few feet behind her. No footprints

marked the ground around him in the snow, and he was clad only in a simple shirt and trousers. At his belt, the black-bladed dagger that had almost killed her god. With a snarl Ashbringer drew herself upward and took three steps back.

'Have you broken her bonds then, that you struck at my kin, that you took the blade?'

Tullen smiled at her, and with her senses still locked onto the skein she had to glance away from him, the strange concatenation that he was, the depth of pattern... *wait*.

'You are connected to the world once more,' she said, and a thrill of fear ran through her. Anshuka's curse had kept Tullen apart, kept him from ageing, from injury, kept his tongue from aiding the Ferron as they rotted in their storm, kept his magic from doing anything but the most meagre of tricks.

Ashbringer levelled her broken sword, the silver blade intricately rune-carved, the hilt the antler of a stag whose like would never be seen again, the antler of a little god. *Anshuka's work undone... Is the mother safe?*

'How have you done this?' she said, breath fast. Tullen began slowly moving his fingers and in the air in front of him a circle of red light appeared, bisected twice, and at the end of each straight line one of the runes of the Ferron Judges: XYFꞱ, *feather, claw, flower, and eye.*

Ashbringer took another step backward. Ever she had failed in her quest to kill Tullen One-Eye, but if the disconnection imposed by the mother had failed, even as his powers returned so too would his human frailty. *Will the broken blade cut true?*

'Strength and art and justice and love; Anshuka the bear; Berren most Fair; Lothal the Just; Nessilitor the Lover. Community and solitude, and violence and compassion.'

Tullen's eyes locked on hers as he spoke, his expression utterly still, his focus absolute. Around them the sky felt taut, and Ashbringer tried to focus on the skein again.

'What has happened to the currents?' she said, and he smiled at her.

'Berren died,' he said, a flower composed of green light blossoming on his palm, 'the great dryad of the Iron Desert. The artist of flowers, the dreamer of green fields. He died and we starved. Anshuka wept, and then went to her long sleep. Nessilitor retreated to the Storm Sea, the cold and the ice. Lothal stayed true. Do you know what a Judge is, Orubor?'

Ashbringer sprang at him and swung her sword low. With a raised finger Tullen summoned a wall of red light. Her sword clashed against it and the blade shattered entirely, shards of silver exploding back and sinking into her cheek as she ducked her head away. Ashbringer staggered back and raised the hilt with one hand. Perhaps an inch of blade remained, star-metal coated in the slick shine of silver.

Tullen shook his head and suddenly his hands were weaving and she felt her body leave the ground, and manacles and shackles of red light encircled her ankles, her wrists, her waist, her neck.

'*Listen to me*,' he said, and his voice was thunder. The sword hilt fell from her hands to the snow. He came in close and met her eyes, his stare intense, his mouth twitching. Ashbringer felt the hot trail of blood down her cheek, felt the biting cold of the winds whipping around the peak above.

'Three hundred years I've been bound. My tongue has been held, tied by that inscrutable curse, to mutter in shadows, to watch. Three hundred years I've plotted revenge, escape, death, glory. You will *listen*, Orubor Ashbringer. This time, you will listen.'

Tullen began to pace around her, kicking at snow, flexing his hands. As he walked he wrung his hands, flexed his fingers, rolled his shoulders. *A caged wolf,* she thought, *who sees the open door but does not yet believe it.* He stared down at the citadel far below, a faint smile passing across his lips.

'I was born *after*,' he said, not turning from the citadel, 'but the Undying Emperor Ferron told me the truth. I would tell it to you. Anshuka was a place-spirit. A bogle, a Relu, a little god, a tulka: a thought form. A place has a spirit; a spirit can be fed; what is fed will grow. Tullioch or Antian or human, wherever there is a focus of will and energy, a snag in the world for whatever reason, over enough time the will brought to bear on that place will alter the pattern, create something to reflect those feelings. The Tullioch have their whale and bird and a thousand lesser manifestations. The Antian presumably have their own subterranean spirits, and we have the bogles and little gods. All across Morost, they are manifest. Some are large, some are small. Anshuka was the great bear of Orubor forest, worshipped by the *humans* who lived there. So she grew. When the Undying Emperor found her she was thrice the size of any natural bear.'

Anshuka. Ashbringer could not move, could barely breathe, and yet managed a growl at his blasphemy. *Anshuka is everlasting, and Orubor have hunted the woods forever!*

Tullen paced the high clearing, eyes flitting from the citadel far below to the peak above, then resting on a point out to sea along the coast. Dark shapes above the water, shadow against shadow, the merest flit of what could be lamplight. *Are they ships?* Ashbringer tried to reach for the skein but the manacles of light seemed to pull all pattern and thought from her. She slumped against them.

'Nessilitor, the owl of the Storm Sea, from her island home. Berren, the green man of the western grasslands, the steppe beyond the Iron Desert. Anshuka, mother-bear of the forest. Lothal, Ferron's own wild wolf. The emperor took them home, and he raised them up. The will of a nation, the will of the greatest sorcerers of the age. They transformed to what you know as Judges. Gods. Creatures capable of altering the world around them profoundly, unendingly. Spirits with physical form, who can lay their thought on the balance of the world, and its currents. Wilful spirits.'

Tullen drew close to Ashbringer and stared long into her eyes.

'There is more, young one,' he said, 'but perhaps you would benefit from discovering it yourself. Perhaps it is time to understand he who you have hunted so long. Do you know how long I spent examining the walls of my cell, the confines laid upon me? Anshuka's wrath has no limit; it is not circumscribed. Across continents it reached. I have broken her grasp, at least for a moment. Consider this a taste.'

Ashbringer tried to scream as Tullen One-Eye laid a hand on her brow, but then she was in the skein and the world was folding inward, and she saw nothing but black, and felt nothing but pain.

~

Cuss was breathing heavy long before they reached the harbour town and its horrible trees full of horrible corpses. Tomas was slung over his shoulder, weeping, and Yselda stuck close to his other shoulder with her blade drawn, knot of green silk flitting in the gusts blowing up from the sea. It was so cold that as they marched through the dense pine the dead needles below crunched like shards of glass, his boots sinking deep into mulch below, a frozen top over wet mud. He slipped, he fell, he dropped Tomas, and he got back up. He dragged Tomas to his shoulder again.

'Got to warn the commander,' he kept saying, expecting Yselda to tell him off for his repetitions. Instead she would only nod, her skin pale aside from flushes of red in the centres of her cheeks. He was sweating under the weight of the skein-mage and shivering as the freezing air seemed to take all warmth from him. The pines here were dark and tall, not the twisted trunks of Hookstone, or the wider new growth that surrounded Hasselberry village. These trees were old, old and salt-cured and swaying ceaselessly in the frigid gusts that blew up through Riven village. Cuss was cold, his shoulders hurt, but he could feel a hot coal of anger at the back of his throat. *Pretended to be friendly,* he thought, and as he took a heavy step through a bank of dying bracken fronds he bit his lip and clenched and unclenched his fists, even as they gripped Tomas's tabard to hold him steady.

He had liked Komende. Komende had reminded him of the woodsman Nash in Hasselberry, someone taking him at his value, measuring him as a grown person and not a child. *A damn fool, Cuss Grantimber,* he said to himself, imagining his mother saying that to him so many times softly, with a smile. When he brought home a bucket of frogs, when he ate the next day's bread without thinking, when his eye was black and blue and he was inarticulate in sadness.

'Is it really him?' Yselda said, when the first buildings of the harbour came into view. Cuss could only grunt in acknowledgement. *Komende is Tullen One-Eye.* He pictured the tattoos of red and blue and gold, the way the man used the skein as if it were nothing, the daze Tomas seemed to have been under. *He said he'd teach me to juggle when we sailed back.*

'He must be the one who stole that dagger from the Orubor,' she said, 'and tricked poor Tomas to use it.'

'Poor Tomas,' Cuss said, slipping the skein-mage from his shoulder to lean against a woodshed. The dark crystal goggles were gone, lost in the forest. Cuss stared into Tomas's eyes and his lip curled in anger. He had seen eyes like that before, broken by magic, dancing and strange and alien. *Varratim's eyes.* The man who had killed his brother Petron. The man whose campaign of terror had killed his mother and sister.

'Maybe *Tomas* stole the dagger,' he said, turning to Yselda. *Maybe.* 'He's been acting weird for a span at least.'

She frowned at him but took a step back from the skein-mage, appraising him. Tomas was clutching at his knees and muttering to himself.

'He helped us before, Cuss,' she said eventually, 'and he's always been weird.'

Cuss nodded. *Fair enough.* Tomas had sat with him, spans before when Cuss had been still recovering from his wounds in Protector's Keep in the city. Tomas had been a wraith shrouded in bandages, but he had lain on his hospital bed and spoken to Cuss and told him how Petron had died. *Died saving a wee kid,* Cuss thought, with a smile. *Bravest thing Tomas ever saw.* Petron had taken the place of a little child, choosing to be sacrificed instead of them on Varratim's dark altar. Choosing death rather than letting another be hurt. *Tell Cuss I love him; tell the sergeant I did my best,* were the words Tomas said were Petron's last before the crow-men took him for sacrifice. Cuss pictured his brother, curls of brown hair, a crooked grin. He did not picture him in a dark cavern, did not picture the knife with its obsidian blade. He would not. Petron on the boat in Loch Hassel, throwing worms for the old man of the loch, the bogle that twisted in the depths somewhere, always hidden. *Love you, Petro.*

Cuss sat down on his haunches and slapped Tomas in the face hard. Yselda grabbed at his shoulder and cried at him to stop but he didn't. He shrugged off her arms and slapped again, and again, and after long moments Tomas blinked and stopped muttering, and the hands at his knees stopped clutching and started to tremble. His broken eyes focused on Cuss.

'What have I done?' he asked, and Cuss took the water skin from his belt and passed it to the mage.

'Cracked a big black stone,' he said, 'but it doesn't matter now. Tullen One-Eye is here, with a knife that kills gods, and he was headed towards the commanders maybe. You need to wake up. Are you hurt or are you injured?'

Tomas blinked at that and met Cuss's eyes, then he smiled and drank the water deeply.

'I think maybe both, Private,' he said, and then held out an arm. Cuss and Yselda both pulled him to his feet.

'Artollen's words suit you,' he said, after a few seconds of brushing dirt from his robes and tabard. 'She and her disciples at the wall have asked me that enough times. I had perhaps not... appreciated their meaning until now.'

'We need to get to the commanders,' Yselda said, swinging her sword in slow arcs. Above and beyond the small cottage they had stopped in front of, Cuss could see the whitestaffs hanging from the pine boughs, swaying in the wind. He tightened the wrist straps on his gauntlets and closed his eyes for a second, then snapped them open and gazed at Yselda. She looked scared, but she nodded.

'Eyes sharp, blades sharper,' Tomas said, and drew himself to his full height and blew out a long breath. 'My mind is certainly a lot clearer now. I'm sorry, Yselda, Cuss. I am. I don't know what he has done to me. We need to get to the commanders, get the whitestaffs, and potentially get the hells out of here. If Tullen One-Eye is back to his full strength then there is little we can do to fight him.'

Yselda drew her antler-hilted dagger.

'Silver and fire for demons, sir?' she said, and Tomas shook his head and began walking away, up along the edge of the town towards the forest road and the Riven citadel.

'He is no demon, Yselda,' he called back, and Cuss put a heavy hand on Yselda's shoulder as her head drooped. 'He is something far older and far worse.'

~

Floré woke up with blood in her mouth, her eyes fluttering open. Her head was in Benazir's lap, staring up at her friend's face in a gloomy cell of stone.

'Hey there, sister,' Benazir said smiling, and Floré groaned and closed her eyes. Her spine ached; her ribs drew a sharp pain on her left when she breathed. She opened her eyes again. Benazir was smiling down at her still, her eyes red and full of tears.

'*Where…*' she said. And then she remembered. *Janos.* 'NO!'

Benazir held her as she wept and wailed. Floré had left her husband dead in the shaman temple at Hasselberry, and he was impossibly here, across the Wind Sea and the wild reefs, lying on an altar in the whitestaffs' citadel, warm to the touch and barely breathing at all. *Six spans he's been dead. Is he dead?* Her heartbeat would not slow.

'He was *dead*,' she said at last. She drew herself away and pressed her palms against the wall of their cell. Her gauntlets were gone, her sword belt and tabard. They had left her boots and shirt and trousers but that was it. Slipped on the index finger of her left hand, Janos's silver wedding band was still there below her own. They were in a cell perhaps ten feet long on each side, the floor covered in old straw, one wall a series of iron bars with a simple gate in it and a heavy lock. Floré ran a hand through her hair and licked her teeth, tasting the iron of blood. *He's alive.*

Benazir got to her feet and handed Floré a handkerchief. She had similarly been stripped of weaponry, sword belt gone, daggers drawn from boots. A shirt with one sleeve cut off at the shoulder where the bandages wrapping her right arm began, the sling hastily retied to hold it close to her chest.

'You hurt?'

Benazir shrugged, eyes focusing on Floré's face. Floré turned away from the scrutiny, turned to the bars of the cell. She began to shake them, one by one. They held firm to her grasp. Her head pounded.

'Not injured, mate,' Benazir said behind her. 'Is he alive?'

Floré shook the gate in the cell bars, rattled the heavy lock on the other side and felt at it with her fingers. *Some sort of dungeon.* She stuck her face as far as it would go between two of the bars, casting her gaze left and right. A flickering torch somewhere to the left, and only darkness right, nothing but more cells within sight, all of them empty.

'Where are the others?' she said. *Is he alive?* 'Halas, Anderson, Bén?'

'Dead,' Benazir said. 'I think we would be too if Deranus hadn't called off his shamans. I hadn't realised the clergy were so deep in the whitestaffs' thrall.'

Floré shook her head, and a blossom of pain flourished in the back of her head.

'None of us did,' she said, pulling her face back and sitting down heavily in the straw. 'These bars are strong.'

Benazir stood over her silently for a long minute and then crouched down in front of her, her hand on Floré's shoulder.

'*Is he alive,* Floré? He could cast back the Ferron. He could help us hunt Tullen One-Eye. You said he could help Marta, before. He could control it. If he can be woken, there is *hope.*'

Floré hung her head between her knees and rubbed her thumb over the silver wedding band. She pictured Janos holding Marta close when the girl had her fevers, her coughs. He swore he never touched the skein, not since Urforren, but something he did always brought her strength, brought her calm. *Marta. Janos.* Floré's hands balled into fists.

'He was warm,' she said, 'he was not… decayed. I think he was breathing. He must be alive. But I swear, Benny, he was dead.'

Benazir stood and began wrenching at the bandages on her right arm, first pulling the sling free and then unwrapping the long lengths of overlapping bandage below. Floré watched and squinted but did not comment. *Benazir does nothing without reason. The balanced blade always knows the smart move.*

13

BLOOD AND TEETH

'The local peasants are a weapon. Send them fleeing before you, and the masters of the land must feed them or face revolt. Seed sickness in their ranks, and they will take it to the hearth of whatever boot they lick. Seed rumour in their ranks, and watch it taken for gospel by wide-eyed fools in power. Seed horror in their souls with a few choice examples, and it will spread like a flame on dried grass through the populace. In Tessendorm we decided to focus on the horror and the sickness. In the desert campaigns of my youth in the west this failed for General Noruno when the horrors drew the populace together against him, against all sense. In Ossenya, the sickness spread to our own ranks due to poor handling of the entire affair. In Tessendorm General Garanad sought to combine these tactics, and it must be said his results speak for themselves.' – **Commentary of the Ferron–Tessendorm campaign**, Consul Semphor, year 627 Isken reckoning

It took a minute to unwrap the bandages starting just below her shoulder and running down to the stump of her wrist. Floré realised what she was about when three-quarters of the cloth was gone. Benazir's arm below was scarred deeply, fresh marks bright against her brown skin, muscle and tendon pulled tight in strange directions. Floré shook her head and grinned as the final layers of bandage fell free and the shape she had seen pressed against Benazir's forearm came clear. Floré pulled herself up to her feet as Benazir drew a blade from her dressing, hidden below the bandages.

The knife was simple: a wooden handle only a few inches long, the blade short but flat and thick and curving to a cruel hook. The sharp edge under the hook gleamed in the faint torchlight of the cell, and Benazir smiled at Floré.

'Call someone down,' she said, 'we want to talk to the master.'

Floré scrambled to the bars, felt the spike of adrenaline in her blood.

'Guard! Shaman! Guard! We need to talk to Master Deranus!'

She yelled as loud as she could, and then turned fast to Benazir.

'What is the plan?' she asked. Benazir nodded to herself as she wrapped her injured arm in bandages again. She left the sling on the floor, and only made a cursory wrapping of the end of the wrist. Flexing her wounded arm and rotating it she met Floré's eye and shrugged.

'Kill everyone.'

Floré raised her eyebrows. 'Kill everyone is the plan?' she asked, and Benazir shrugged.

'Fine. Kill everyone, don't let that bearded arse do whatever skein thing he did before with Janos. Seems to need a group of them to channel our boy's powers. So kill everyone, and he won't be able to.'

Floré yelled again for the guard and rolled her shoulders.

'Your tactical mastery never ceases to amaze me, Bolt-Commander,' she said, and Benazir came up behind her and tapped her on the shoulder with the blade of the knife.

'Says the person without a knife,' she said.

Floré allowed herself a grin. *He's alive.*

From the end of the corridor there was noise, footsteps. Two shamans stepped into view, and Benazir was close to the bars, knife somehow disappeared into the waist of her trousers. The shamans were both clad in grey robes, one holding a long wooden truncheon, the other a rapier, the kind of narrow blade the nobility in Kelm…or used in their duels. Both were men, young men with no heft to them, and Floré could see no hint in their movement at any surplus of dexterity or strength that might worry them. The shaman with the rapier had keys openly on his belt, and stood only a foot from the bars of the cell. *Amateurs.*

'We need to speak to the master,' Benazir said, her posture slumped and her voice quiet. The shaman with the wooden truncheon came in closer.

'What do you have to say?' he said, nervous. He was a pale man, long hair lank and greasy. The shaman with the rapier was also pale, a sparse beard covering his chin, the crown of his head completely bare. Floré kept her shoulders and gaze low and folded in on herself, made herself look as small as possible.

'I saw Anshuka,' she said, low and quiet, and the two

shamans grew still. 'I went to Orubor's wood and I stood before her, in all her glory. The mother herself, the one who has taught us so much. The one who freed us and keeps us safe.' Her voice grew quieter as she spoke, and the shamans both leaned forward.

'She lies,' one said, but the other was tilting his head.

'No,' he said. 'The last ship, they spoke of a commando riding the orbs of light, fighting alongside the holy guardians. Was this you?'

Floré shrunk down even lower and then raised her head to the man, her eyes wide and unblinking. She leaned forward.

'Aye,' she said, not breaking eye contact, 'I rode the orbs of light; I fought demons at her very feet. Do you know what she said to me?'

The shaman with the rapier was close now. *Close enough.* He mumbled a prayer to Anshuka, praise to the mother. Floré flexed her fingers.

'She said,' she began, and then with a lightning grasp she had his robes and pulled him towards her, her grip iron, throwing her whole body backward. Her arm wrenched as the shaman slammed into the cell bars and wailed, his rapier falling to the floor. To her left Benazir had dropped to a knee and her arm snaked through the bars. The shaman in front of her collapsed as her blade sank deep into the top of his thigh, near to his crotch. It tore back towards Benazir with a spray of red.

Floré surged forward and had both arms through the bars even as the shaman was trying to thrust himself away. She gripped his head between her hands and wrenched her whole body, twisting with all her might as her hands gripped his skull. There was a wet snap as his neck broke, and he slipped to the floor. Benazir was standing, looking appreciatively at the knife in her hand. The shaman before her was already dead, his life's blood pouring out in spurting sheets of red across the cell floors. Floré pawed at the dead man in front of her, pulled free the loop of keys and started working on the mechanism. Within moments they were standing in the hallway. Floré waved the thin rapier around then threw it down, picking up the blood-slick wooden truncheon instead. It had *heft*.

'Femoral artery on the first try?' she asked, glancing down at the pooling blood beneath them, and Benazir cut a bow.

'What can I say?' she said. 'I take pride in my work.'

Together they moved along the corridor, past guttering torches, and at the end of the dungeon Floré slowly opened the only door. It swung quietly, opening to an empty guardroom. None of their gear was there, and Floré swore. There was small window set high in the wall, and she glanced out, catching hints of low pine. *We're lower than before.* They kept moving, down one corridor and another, and then there were stairs. Floré gestured at them and Benazir nodded, and together they climbed upward, emerging at last on a thin rampart overlooking the central courtyard with its huge silver-barked oak.

Floré glanced back down at Riven Harbour, and saw *Basira's Dance* bobbing in the dark water, lanterns spilling light across the deck. She could see motion. She went to turn back to the citadel, to seek her next entrance back into the labyrinth, but her eye was drawn. Out, past the harbour, past the dark breaking waves, a fleet of six ships, each easily as large as *Basira's Dance*. They each had two masts and high sides, galleons in the style of Cil-Marie, their decks aglow with lantern light. Floré gestured for Benazir to look and Benazir followed her gaze and swore.

'Lothal's bones,' she said, 'look at the water.'

Floré looked, and saw in front of each ship a writhing ahead of their prow within the water, long sinuous forms cutting through the darkness, the glitter of innumerable red eyes. Starlight reflecting on cruel teeth. *Wyrms.*

~

Yselda knew something *else* was wrong long before they entered the citadel. Four corpses nailed to high posts outside the open gates, *how welcoming*. When they entered there was no staff, no retinue of servants. No whitestaffs. Only a vast courtyard surrounded by high walls, a grand silver oak at its centre, fountains and flowering shrubs and benches all around.

'Hello?' Cuss called, and Tomas shushed him. Yselda swung her sword in a low arc. She had spent the last six spans training every day, her bow, her sword, her mind. *I'm ready this time.* She had killed goblins in the meadow next to the god-bear Anshuka, keeping the mountain-sized deity safe as it slumbered. She had held her nerve and faced up to Varratim when he came for her and Cuss, but it hadn't mattered. *I still fell to the ground like a child. I landed no blow against the crow-men.* The crow-men who had burned Hasselberry, who had rained death on her home. *Who killed Esme and Shand and Nat and Lorrie.*

Yselda stalked forward into the courtyard and glanced around at the myriad gates and doors, arches, entrances and exits.

'Which way?' she asked, and Tomas looked at her, his

strange eyes glittering. He gazed around them, seeming to focus, and then he smiled and gasped.

'Tullen isn't here!' he said, darting forward and pushing at a door. 'This way!' he called back. Yselda, and Cuss hurried to follow him. 'Tullen isn't here, but we have to go this way!'

As they followed him down corridor after corridor and then up winding stairs behind Yselda Cuss kept a running tally of his questions and concerns.

'A minute ago he was addled, now we're to chase him headlong. Where are the whitestaffs? Where's the commanders, the commandos? Why all the hanged folk? Can Tullen One-Eye even *die*?'

Yselda didn't answer his questions. She kept her eyes sharp on every corner, and held her longsword in a low guard close to her waist, ready to lash out at any sudden threat appearing close by from the shadowy corners. *It's so cold.* Even with the gauntlets and the thick cloak the quartermaster in Undal City had given her, she felt chilled to her core. *A Claw Winter.* She felt sick.

Yselda had lost her family to the last Claw Winter. Mother and Father, her brothers. Yselda and her brothers had played in the forest in spring and summer and autumn and winter, but their world was circumscribed: 'From the loch to the burn by Hozen's place, to the big rocks along the beach. And no further north than Nan Shepherd's pastures.' It was enough. The burn by Hozen's was perhaps five foot wide and shallow most of the year, and they built little weirs and bridges, piled stones. At Nan's pastures they clambered the fallen drystone walls, stones thick with moss but sharp underneath. The old woman sang songs to them, teaching them the words: 'Three children of the mist, unkind'; 'Tollen's Folly'; 'Six birds'.

They would fetch her water from her well or eggs from her chickens and every now and then she would present them with a treasure: a button, a shining stone, a twisted knot of fabric. To Yselda she gave a bear, a little beast stitched from black-woolled goatskin, with button eyes. 'Anshuka!' she said, and Yselda held it close. Robern and Fraser were jealous of the bear, but they all shared the same big bed and she shared it freely.

The year the Claw Winter came, the leaves on the rowan in the garden froze right on the branch. After three weeks of freezing winds the pines were the only green remaining, every fern and flower freezing green and then white. It had been summer, and then came the freezing wind from the north and they were suddenly plunged into what felt like the depths of winter or beyond. A wrong wind. Nan Shepherd's goats kept close to her paddock, or spent their nights huffing and stamping their feet in a huddle in the lee of Yselda's family's cottage.

Yselda shuddered at the memory of the fear in her parents' eyes as much as from the cold, and the memory of the cold. That year, the usual slow fade from summer to winter through a season of changing leaves and preparation was not to be; only the abrupt chaos of rushed provisioning. Her mother stayed out three days and came back with a doe and a mouthful of curses.

'Nan is gone,' she had said to Yselda's father, her voice low, 'the goats as well. Blood all over the paddocks. Wolf sign.'

Her father had made a move as if to quiet her but Yselda's mother shook her head.

'You'll frighten the children,' he had said, and her mother had left the cottage into the freezing air and returned with their wood axe. She closed the door and leaned the heavy axe up against it.

'They need to be scared.'

Her parents spoke long into the night in muttering voices. Yselda slept with her brothers in their bed pulled close to the fire, and dreamt of Nan Shepherd's bitter tea, and goats with rough wool.

When they woke, the decision was made for them. They woke to snow, a foot of fresh cold powder that clung to the pines. The freezing wind was gone, but heavy black clouds towered in the sky. To the south, the calm waters of Loch Hassel were still and strange, light catching and bouncing from a thousand points, swathes of white and grey cutting across the water in unmoving swirls. It had taken Yselda a long minute to realise the loch was frozen, and she had laughed. Their little rowboat was buried in snow. Her father came to her with a cloak and lifted her up, then pulled Robern up as well.

'A Claw Winter,' he had said, and Yselda had shaken her head in confusion.

'It's frozen!' Fraser had called, already running for the shore.

'There'll be no autumn, no harvest, no time to prepare,' her father had said, his voice strained, 'only snow and cold. We need to get to Hasselberry.'

His voice was muted by the still-falling snow, and Yselda had watched Fraser run down to the loch, saw his footprints sink deep. Her mother had stepped from the cottage in her heavy coat, axe in hand. From the shadows of the snowy forest, an explosion of snow and movement. The wolf took Fraser at the shore, and Yselda remembered screaming.

I'm ready this time.

In the courtyard of Riven, Yselda did not allow herself to think of Fraser, of Robern, the run across the frozen loch with a pack at their heels. Captain Tyr finding her on the banks wreathed in frozen blood, alone.

Yselda breathed out as Tomas looked to the ground, as Cuss looked at her for direction. She kept her breathing slow and when the fear began in her mind to surface she concentrated on the words of Commander Artollen in the pentacle courtyard of Protector's Keep: *Focus on the wolf nearest to your door.* She let one hand rest on her belt pouch, where she kept her whetstone and cloth for maintaining her blade. Below all of that lay a neatly folded scrap of grey cloth, cloth torn from the commander's own cloak, after Yselda killed a timber wolf in Hookstone forest. *Focus,* she thought. *The forest is full of wolves, but for right now, focus on the one in front of you.*

They kept moving, Tomas turning left and right, always climbing. After a minute of walking upstairs he opened a door and inside a shaman and a whitestaff stood, two women with haughty looks. Tomas stopped suddenly, Yselda and Cuss with blades bare at his shoulders. The whitestaffs stood over a table covered in gear – *the commanders' gear,* Yselda realised. The whitestaff was holding the longsword Knight-Commander Starbeck had given to Floré, the silver sword with its intricate runes, the upswept cross guard, the curved handle with its pommel bearing Anshuka's rune: Y. The shaman was examining Commander Benazir's knives – six of them spread out, all with blades of gleaming silver, one etched with runes. Next to the weapons were armours, pouches, belts, and two tabards of red trimmed in gold, with rank badges sewn in.

'Who are you?' the whitestaff asked, and drew Commander Artollen's sword up in a clumsy imitation of a high guard. Yselda stepped past Tomas and pointed her own blade. *Neither of them would give up their blades, let alone their belts and gauntlets.*

In her mind she heard Floré's voice: *We are Stormguard, little sister. We don't fear wolves, or demons, or the dark things of the storm. They fear us.*

'In the name of the Stormguard,' she heard herself say, her steel as firm as her voice, 'lower your weapons, back away, and tell us where our comrades are.'

The shaman picked up a knife and waved her hand wide.

'Where do you think you are, girl?' she said, her voice a snarl. 'This is Riven. The whitestaffs command here. Address the mistress with respect or I'll scrub your mouth with soap.'

Tomas was muttering behind her, and as she glanced back his head was turning in all directions, eyes open but unseeing. *What does he seek?*

'That's my commander's sword,' Cuss said, and the whitestaff twitched her nose.

'No longer. Your leaders are now in the dungeons, and you will join them. Lower your blades. I don't want to have to call the shamans and the whitestaff council, but I certainly will, child. This is beyond you.'

Yselda found herself smiling, and even gave a laugh. The whitestaff swung the runed blade through the air.

'Enough!' she yelled. 'Lower your blades now! Shamans! Guards!'

Yselda rolled her wrist, sending the point of her sword in a lazy circle.

'I was unsure what to do next,' she said, drawing the sword

back so the pommel sat by her hip, the blade a straight line from her waist to her cheek. *For close work,* Floré had taught her. 'Thank you for bringing me clarity, Mother.'

Yselda charged the whitestaff. She ignored the shaman. *Cuss can handle her.* The whitestaff swung a heavy blow with Floré's sword, but it was slow and with a flick of her wrist Yselda added her own momentum to her enemy's sword, and then she was close, inside her guard. With a punch she smashed the hilt of her sword, her gauntleted hands, into the woman's mouth. The whitestaff reeled back but Yselda followed close, inside her reach now, shoulder blocking so she could not swing the stolen sword. Again she punched, and then pulled her arms low so the blade of her sword was pressed against the woman's neck as the whitestaff was pushed against the wall. She leaned on the blade and a stream of blood began to pour.

'*Drop it,*' she said, and there was a clatter as the rune-sword fell to the ground. Across the room she heard a crash and a wail. With one hand she grabbed the whitestaff by her hair and threw her to the floor, spinning to check on Cuss. His sword was sheathed, and on the floor in front of him the shaman was collapsed under fragments of what had once been a chair.

'A chair?' she said, and Cuss shrugged.

'Seemed easier than swords and things. It was a big chair.'

Yselda shook her head and smiled. *Sweet Cuss.*

'Tomas,' she called, 'what the nameless fire are you doing?'

Tomas was staring fixedly up and above them, to the left.

'I've found him,' he said, and then he was pointing to the door. Yselda backhanded the whitestaff in her grip with her sword hand, and the woman crumpled to the floor.

'Get the stuff,' she said to Cuss, and she sheathed her sword and picked up the runed sword. It felt light, the curve of the handle a little strange compared to the utilitarian steel at her hip.

Up they moved, stairways and hallways, until they entered at last a low chamber lit brightly by dozens of braziers and torch sconces. A dozen whitestaffs were sat bowed in prayer or meditation. They did not look up when Tomas swung open the door. Cuss was behind Yselda, nervously casting glances back down the stairs with every few steps.

'She shouted for shamans,' he said. 'Where are they?'

Yselda couldn't answer him. She had seen the figure on the marble altar in front of the whitestaffs. *Janos.* Janos the poet who lived in Hasselberry. Janos, Marta's father, Floré's husband. *I thought he was dead.*

Tomas strode past the rows of seated whitestaffs and she hurried to follow, Cuss next to her. The whitestaffs' eyes were closed and they chanted in a tongue she did not know. The three of them backed around the altar, and Tomas laid his hands on Janos's head and chest.

'Is he dead?' Yselda asked, and the skein-mage next to her focused, his eyes closed.

'He is… chained,' he said, eyes opening and blinking, hand going to the wand at his waist. 'Chained by these *dogs*!'

Ripping the wand from his belt, Tomas leapt the altar and a raging red-white cone of flame began to spew from the wand across the praying whitestaffs, great arcs of fire covering all of the benches. Yselda found herself clutching Janos, pulling him from the altar and down behind it. Cuss hunched over her; his cloak spread around them all. There was a long moment where the only noise was the sputtering flame, a roar of visceral heat, and then whatever meditation or reverie the whitestaffs had been in was lost to them, and the screaming began. Yselda pressed her hands to Janos's face.

'Wake up!' she screamed, and all around her the stench of burning flesh, the smoke. She felt the panic begin to take her. *Focus on the wolf.* She shook Janos, grabbed his head and pried his eyelids open.

'Wake up!'

~

On the rampart Floré and Benazir stared down at the Ferron flotilla. *Wyrms.* It had to be Ferron. *Where in the hells did they get those ships?* There was a dull hum and then silence flooded over them, an ominous silence of a too loud noise, the pressure on her chest that was now so sickeningly familiar. The noise of the ocean, the rustling of the branches, her own ragged breath, all fell away. Floré spun and drew up her truncheon. From a courtyard amid the mess of walls and towers below, the captured orb rose. It was an oblong of white light, incandescent and glaring. Floré stared up at it as it rose twenty feet over them, and then she caught movement to her right. From the drum tower of the citadel, a door had opened to the thin rampart where they stood. From it, the shamans poured.

There were perhaps thirty of them. The rampart was only wide enough for them to stand two abreast. They were clad in the full greys and blacks of their order, some clutching talismans or tomes, all armed. There were swords and daggers, a hatchet, one with a spear. One of the first clutched a mace, a short steel haft ending in a weighted steel head covered in three-inch spikes of black metal. The shamans began to walk towards them, and overhead there was a lessening of pressure as the orb flew outward, towards the harbour. Sound returned, and following the orb Floré felt her heart hammer as it hesitated over *Basira's Dance*, but then it was away, heading out towards the incoming fleet. *Fine by me.*

'I think these boys and girls think we want a lesson, Floré,' Benazir said, and Floré rolled her shoulders.

'I always hated shamans.'

Together they walked forward, stopping fifteen feet in front of the advancing shamans. Floré peered but could not see Jule, the gaunt heron of a man.

'You can't fight thirty people,' the first one said. A man, burly, wide shoulders under a black robe worn to grey. He held a woodcutting axe in his hands, a long two-handed piece with a thick wedge-shaped head, made for splitting logs. Floré glanced down at the dark of the pine forest, and then back at the citadel. *Janos.* She could see red light flickering and smoke pouring from a high chamber ahead and above. *How can this be it?* They could not fight thirty people. After all of it, after every scrap, she would die on this wall and Marta would sit in the orphans' barracks and learn to play games, and each night she would reach for the skein in her dreams until her strength fell away to nothing.

After losing Janos, to find him here, held from her by the machinations of fools. Floré bit her tongue until it bled and touched her wedding ring and felt her right arm twitch as the scars shook, as they always did when she was nervous. *My love, so close, after so much. How dare they?*

Benazir came and stood at her shoulder, one-armed Benazir not two spans from her sickbed, Benazir who'd been pulled from the maw of a wyrm, already half chewed. Her fist pressed against Floré's shoulder. A simple motion, but Floré knew what it meant. *We die here. I love you.*

No, Floré thought, *I'll not have it. None of it.* Snapping her head up, Floré let her mouth open and started to breathe deep breaths. *I'll not lose Janos. I'll not lose Marta. I'll not lose Benny. None of it.* She felt the rage build in her, the rage she so often held in check for years and years, and fire that started in her stomach and spread until every part of her was shaking, and she let out a huff of air and scrunched her nose.

'You can't fight thirty people,' the man repeated, louder, his hands wringing the shaft of his axe. *Nervous.* 'I'm not fighting thirty people,' she called, and spun the truncheon smartly, then smacked it against the stone of the rampart. It was heavy wood, and the report was loud.

'I'm fighting two of you fuckers until you die, then the next two, then the next two.'

She raised her truncheon and pointed to the shamans, the rage in her breast building with every moment until she felt she might become a pyre, might set alight like Starbeck's burning blade.

'You, then you, then her, then her, then that big fella. Then whichever fool wants to get between me and that door. No trial for traitors and dogs. Flee, or die screaming.'

She didn't wait for an answer. The big man at the front charged forward and she dodged his swing and shinned him with the truncheon, stepping back as a swing from the shaman with the mace followed close. Benazir was behind her, snaking forward, and the big man dropped his axe as her knife scored his arm. Floré pushed him back into his fellows, the press of them forcing flesh forward for her to destroy. Again and again she blocked and parried and the truncheon lashed out, driving away glancing blows, breaking wrists, smashing teeth. The shamans surged forward.

'Back!' she called, and Benazir was next to her and they fell back a dozen steps. As the shamans clambered over the writhing mass of six of their comrades screaming and nursing wounds, Floré charged them at the moment she judged their footing was at its worst. One of them landed a blow to her side, a lance of pain, but she felt it turn on her ribs and crouching low she drove upwards and pushed the woman over the ramparts, sending her crashing twenty feet to hard cobbles. The shamans all stopped for a moment, the front ranks breathing hard, and in the pause Benazir stuck her hooked knife in her belt and snatched up a hatchet.

'You can surrender any time,' she said, and then with an explosion of movement hurled the hatchet. It buried itself in the neck of a shaman who fell back and tumbled off the rampart down to the courtyard below, an arc of blood spiralling as he fell.

'Not that guy,' she said, and she pointed into the throng of shamans, 'but *you* could.'

Floré stepped back quickly as two of them rushed forward, both armed with swords. These women were young and fit and fast but had no skill with a blade. Floré left herself open and when the big swing she was waiting for came she sent the woman spinning with a grab of her arm, and toppled her into her friend. The truncheon cracked out, split the first skull, and then the wood of it splintered as she sent it crashing through the second skull and it hit the hard rampart beneath. Floré flung the brain-slick truncheon shards at the next shaman, who screamed, and then she threw a man behind her for Benazir to deal with as she focused on the next, dodging a jab from a short spear. Behind her a scream, and then behind her and below a thump. Benazir was death. She stalked the rampart behind Floré, and anyone Floré sent spinning back met the hooked blade in the leg, the arm, the neck, the groin. Some vessel vital for living, some tendon vital for standing – they would be ripped away methodically and left to bleed out below the stars or kicked and rolled to the ramparts below.

Floré batted the spear ahead of her twice and then gripped it suddenly and kicked off the rampart wall to her right. The momentum carried up the spear, and the haft of it was held close to the left of the shaman's torso. Floré let go of the spear and skidded to a halt at the side of the rampart, the shaman spinning down to land with a wet crack on the ridge of a tiled roof below. From the mess of bodies Floré grabbed a sword, at last. It was cheap iron, poorly weighted, but she swung it in flowing arcs. She was coated in blood, bleeding from a dozen wounds, and could feel every muscle shaking. She blinked blood from her eyes and drew back.

'Flee, or die screaming!' she yelled, glaring at the remaining shamans, punctuating her point by driving her sword down into a writhing shaman at her feet, a man clutching at his bleeding wrist. He stopped writhing and slumped still and she pulled her sword from his chest. She twitched to the side as someone in the second row hurled a carpenter's hammer. It sailed past her shoulder and she heard a thump and Benazir swearing.

'Which of you did that? That bastarding hurt!'

From the doors behind Benazir, far around the ramparts another half-dozen shamans emerged, led by Jule, the fat yellow moon reflected on his bald head, his steps careful as he advanced towards them, a quarterstaff in his hand. Floré let her guard sag. *So close*. There were still another dozen shamans at least in front of her, and the effort of fighting however many she had already sent to the ground had her heart beating brutally fast, her breathing coming in sharp stabs. *So close*.

The shamans in front and behind were not advancing. They drew to a stop and one by one were staring outward from the ramparts, their faces lit by a flickering yellow glow. Floré took another step back, bumping into Benazir, and allowed herself a glance.

Silent chaos. The orb the whitestaffs had captured from the Ferron using Janos's hard-won skein-spells hovered over a burning ship, a second ship aflame to its left. Figures dove from the burning ships. Floré knew they would be screaming, though of course she couldn't hear it through the horrible silence of the orb. Gouts of fire and purple beams of force shot out from the orb. *It's not enough*.

The wyrms were attacking the orb. Six writhing serpents, each fifty feet long. One was wrapped around it entirely, its chitinous beak jabbing at the white light of the orb's surface that was now striped with darkness where it was covered by the armoured and hellish serpent body embracing it. The wyrm opened its beak and then its whole body contracted, and the stone orb clasped tight in its grasp seemed to stutter, to crumple. The white light flickered and died, and suddenly the world was a chaos of screams as the voices of the six wyrms cut clear through the night, throaty ululations of arcane horror mixing with the roar of flame on the ship below and the wails of the burning sailors and goblins leaping from the blazing decks. The orb of broken stone slipped from the wyrms' grasp and fell to the ocean, but the noise of it hitting the water was lost below the screams. *Would the master let anyone else fly his orb?* She wasn't sure he would.

Even a mile from the scene, with the sea wind whipping, Floré heard the screams of every wyrm as they spiralled in the sky. *Somebody's child once?* Floré had spent hours thinking on the physicality of it, locked in her room in Protector's Keep. *How could a child become a wyrm?* The transformation to goblin was a horror, but the shape was the same, the same essential plan. The wyrm was utterly alien, like nothing on Morost. Floré had not liked the answer she had come to: *Janos can turn a man to salt. Anshuka can make a storm last three hundred years; if she wishes a child a wyrm, what could stop her?* Floré clung to Benazir's cold certainty that the goblins and the wyrms, even if they had been children, were nothing that could be saved. *If they could be saved,* she knew, *then what in the hells have I done? What in the hells should I do?*

The other wyrms surrounded their champion, spiralling and dancing in the starlight, as below them the sailors on the blazing ship leapt to the blackness of the water below.

Floré turned to the shamans in front of her, spat, and grinned a feral grin, feeling the sticky residue of blood in the cracks between her teeth. She bounced on her feet and flexed her shoulders, opened her arms wide. *Not enough.* She knew she would not survive this.

Floré took a step forward and raised her sword.

'Flee, or die screaming, fuckers.'

14

DRAW A LINE AND BURN A DITCH

'I have fought for the Stormguard. I have lost my home in Fallow Fen to the crow-men, the goblins, the rottrolls. I have seen blights of rotsurge roll across the sky, monsters clawing from the lightning strikes. I have seen this and despaired, for there are monsters in the rotstorm. This is true. But, sisters and brothers, I have also seen the starving and the weak, the people forced to live in the storm! The rust-folk. I do not blame them for following the demons and monsters. What choice do we leave them?' – **Break the Stormguard's chains!** Lillebet Arfallow, year 312 from Ferron's Fall (1123 Isken)

Yselda and Cuss pulled Janos from the burning room, Tomas hot on their heels. Tomas looked haggard and drawn, sweat pouring off him. They headed out of door after door, fleeing blindly, and found themselves on a wide roof – the roof to the drum tower, that semi-circle with its curve facing the brutal winds of the sea, a flat face towards the inner courtyards.

'Chained him,' Tomas said, breathing heavily, and the

four of them moved twenty yards from the tower door. The roof was studded with small towers, trees in wide pots, low benches. *This is not meant to be a place for war.* Yselda helped Cuss lower Janos gently to the ground and then she surged to her feet as three whitestaffs ran from a nearby tower door, heavy staves in their hand.

'Heretics!' one called, and Tomas's hand went to his wand but Yselda waved him down.

'Wake him,' she said, grim-faced. 'We've got this.'

Together with Cuss she advanced. The whitestaffs ran to them across the roof, and when they drew close one opened his mouth to speak, but Yselda gave him no chance. Screaming with rage she launched herself forward, and the rune-sword cut deep into his side, the blade blossoming with flame. The man fell back, but Yselda found herself on her back as a sweeping staff from the woman to her right took her legs out from under her. The breath blew out of her but she brought the burning blade up in time to intercept a heavy two-handed blow from the third attacker's staff.

The whitestaff she had cut was screaming in pain, clutching at his ribs. The man above drew back to slam his staff down but then Cuss was there, his sword skewering into the whitestaff's side a moment before he slammed into him, full body. From the floor Yselda rolled and swung her blade in an arc to her left, and the whitestaff who had tripped her fell to her knees cursing, her calf slick with blood, her robes charred. Scrambling to her feet Yselda batted the woman's staff away and sank the sword deep into her skull with the backhand, watching in horror as the blade burned so brightly, as the woman's eyes met hers, as she gasped and slipped from the blade to the cold roof. Yselda stared down at the woman, the jade amulet of Riven on her chest. *What am I doing?*

Cuss gave a startled shout and it brought her from her reverie. The man he had skewered was down, but had rolled away with Cuss's sword as he died and now Cuss was facing off against the man Yselda had first scored a hit against, Cuss with only a slim dagger against the brutal oaken quarterstaff the whitestaff was clutching. Cuss was dancing back, but twice he was hit, his thigh, and then his shoulder, and he fell to a knee. Above him the whitestaff reared back, quarterstaff raised above his head, face a mask of rage.

No.

Yselda threw the dagger before she finished thinking the word, the hilt of antler slipping into her gauntleted palm and then shooting through the air as she flung her arm forward. The blade bit deep, deep enough for the rune at its heart to feel the blood, for it to pulse and burn. The whitestaff clutched the dagger and pulled it out with a scream but already a burning hole a foot wide from the wound had spiralled out and charred his flesh and clothing, and he coughed smoke. He fell face down and the dagger slipped from his grasp.

Yselda stood and made herself stretch her arms, her feet. She picked up the dagger and sheathed it and pulled Cuss to his feet and gazed down at the burning blade in her hand. It still flamed, flamed wherever blood had touched it. Even through her gauntlets she could feel the heat of it, could feel the sting in her own hand. *Who would make such a thing?* She held it away from her body.

'Look,' Cuss said, and she followed his gaze. At sea, across the outer wall, two ships burning bright and four in full sail just in front, six huge creatures flying in the sky above them, serrated serpents fifty foot long, studded with rows of red orb eyes, thrice-beaked mouths opening and closing. They were almost at the harbour. Running, the two of them went to the inner side of the roof where they might look down over the courtyard and the harbour below. *Basira's Dance* was emptying out, and she could see the Tullioch and sailors and commandos fleeing towards Riven town, towards the citadel. *There is no safety here.*

'Sergeant!' Cuss yelled, pointing. Yselda followed his gaze: forty foot below their roof on a narrow rampart wall thirty feet from the ground, Floré and Benazir stood, six attackers on each side, the wall covered in dozens of corpses.

'No!' Cuss screamed, and Yselda covered her mouth with her hand when she saw. From each end of the rampart, more were coming. A dozen more at least, in each direction.

'Floré!' she yelled, because she could think of nothing else to do. *No!* The commander was all she had left. *I can't lose another family.* Desperately Yselda searched for a way down to the ramparts, but there was none to be found. Below them on the rampart, Benazir and Floré were back to back.

'No!' she yelled, and she could feel the burn of the sword in her hand, the burn of tears in her eyes.

'Floré!' Cuss yelled.

Behind her she heard Tomas muttering, heard him scream in pain.

'Floré,' Janos said, his voice so weary. Tomas pulled him up, face strained and nose bleeding, and the two of them stepped to Yselda's side. Yselda stared at him, mouth wide. He was clad in a simple white robe, his eyes dazed, his breath coming in heaving gulps.

'How?' she asked, and Tomas spat blood.

'They had him in a cage. A cage of pattern. I had... I had to break it.'

Tomas slumped down to the rooftop, and Janos was left swaying gently in the freezing night breeze. Yselda gripped his arm and held him steady.

'Floré,' Janos said again, and she saw his eyes focus, saw him blink, his jaw set, heard his breath catch. She saw a dead man find his family.

~

Floré screamed as the blade sliced deep at the back of her left wrist, felt her grip slacken on the sword as tendons tore. She headbutted the shaman wielding the dagger, and as he reeled she kicked him in the chest. He flew from the ramparts. Another was there, always another. Long had the fight moved from grace, if ever it had been there. She threw herself into every movement. She knew if she gave less than everything, her limbs might not even respond. She took wounds, so many wounds, snaking cuts she could not deflect fast enough, rough blunt blows that left her shaking and numbed. She could hear Benazir panting for breath behind her, hurling weaponry, throwing anything she could find at the shaman advancing on their rear. They seemed content to watch their comrades do the butchery.

'Do you surrender?' the shaman in front of her said. Floré batted away the shaman's guarding sword and elbowed her in the face, and then skewered her lungs through her ribs as she turned to flee.

The next shaman landed a blow to her left shoulder with a rapier, another of those thin, measly Kelamor blades. It sank three inches into the meat of her shoulder and Floré screamed as the point scraped bone. She smashed her own blade down, snapping off the foil of the rapier. With her left hand she pulled the blade free from her shoulder and flung it at the woman, and when the shaman flinched and raised her guard she swung a low slice across the woman's stomach, an explosion of entrails sending the next ranks of shamans scattering back.

Floré slipped, and brought herself to a knee, managed to turn a falling blow from a sword, scrambled backward. *This only ends one way.*

'Floré!' Benazir called, and Floré spun from her own foes and ran. Benazir was pressed back to the rampart wall, a shaman grappling her as another drew back his blade, Jule looming behind them, uninjured, clean and whole. Floré hurled her sword, an ugly throw, and it slammed into the shaman's sword, throwing his arm back. He grunted and drew the blade back again. Jule stepped to the swordsman's side and levelled his quarterstaff at Floré.

'First her,' Jule said, his eyes ice, 'then *you.*'

For Floré, the world went quiet. *Am I dying?* The shamans clutching Benazir, those beyond, they all fell still. She heard no movement behind her. Absently she clutched at her stomach, her face. Slick with blood. *Which wound killed me?* To her left the dark sea of pines swayed, and high above the looming mountain seemed to envelop most of the sky, as if it reached upward, consuming stars.

The sea wind tore at the rampart, a gust of ice. In front of her, Floré watched the shamans move from still to utterly unmoving, as they turned as one to statues of salt.

'Salt,' she heard herself say, before she could even process the thought, and she felt herself begin to weep, her breath coming in sharp bursts. *Janos*. Floré had fought creatures from the storm, rogue mages, war wizards from Tessendorm, but never had she seen a man turned to salt, save by Janos. Her poet.

Blades fell to the gore-wet rampart, or were turned to blades of white crystal. She turned and, behind her, a dozen shamans or more, now statues. She pulled Benazir away from the men, held her close, and then the winds gusted again and the features of their attackers began to swirl as the currents of storm pulled them away, salt drifting to sky. Jule was screaming, but he wasn't turning to salt, was whole, surrounded by his comrades turning to nothing, held as if in an iron vice. Floré drew Benazir away from him, pulled her close. She trembled, and then she was rising from the rampart, her feet no longer touching stone, Benazir clinging to her.

Together they floated upward and towards the roof of the citadel, where Yselda awaited with a burning blade, Cuss and Tomas eyes wide. And in robes of white, sigil tattoos burning with red light, was *Janos*. He smiled at her as she descended to him. Yselda and Cuss took Benazir's weight from Floré's shoulder and lowered her to the ramparts. Benazir was coated in blood, wick-thin and grey and wild-eyed. Behind them with a crack Jule fell from the sky.

Floré and Janos held each other for a long time, a grip of iron, and then she kissed his face, his eyes, his mouth.

'You were dead,' she said at last, face wet with tears and blood and worse, and he smiled and stroked her cheek with his thumb.

'I think I was, or so close as makes no matter. Jule must

have taken me. He's been watching us for them since the day we arrived, I think. I remember some. Shamans directed by whitestaffs, circles of mages pooling their energy. I'm sorry.'

She kissed him again and pressed her head to his.

'Wyrms,' Benazir said, and she slumped down even lower. 'Hi, big man. Wyrms.'

She pointed out towards the docks, though the rampart wall blocked her own view.

'You wouldn't fight,' Jule said, his voice a wheeze. He was slumped on the ground, legs twisted.

'When the chance came, what would you have me do? With you the masters *captured* an orb, lightning and force! Master Deranus—'

Jule fell silent as Yselda backhanded him.

'Cuss,' Yselda said, 'get the folks from *Basira's Dance* inside. Tomas, can you help Benazir at all? We need to fortify if we're going to hold against those things.'

Janos smiled at Yselda, and Floré clutched at him. She did not look back at the harbour, though she knew four ships of Ferron, rust-folk, goblin, crow-men, perhaps rottrolls and worse awaited. *He's really here.*

'Marta needs you,' she said, the words coming out in a rush, 'the skein-sickness. It's worse. The whitestaffs, the skein-mages. None of them can help.'

Janos's expression dropped, his brow furrowed. He was down on his knees with Floré now, but still swaying gently, blinking too often. He twitched his head and pushed at his skull with his hand, as if trying to force himself into some sort of focus. Floré cupped his face in her hands.

'Janos,' she said, 'she needs you.'

'Only a skein-wreck could help her,' he said, his voice

growing stronger with each moment. '*I* will help her, my heart. I promise.'

Floré closed her eyes, swayed, spread her bare hand across his chest. She felt exhaustion crashing over her. *Alive.*

'You wouldn't *fight*!' Jule said again. 'I have my holy purpose. The whitestaffs are the mother's will on this earth. The skein is *her* gift. Who are you to spurn it?'

'Yselda is right,' Tomas was saying. 'We can't fight these wyrms. Perhaps one or two I think I could manage now with Commander Arfallow's example, but beyond that we haven't the material. We need to hide, or figure out how to flee.'

'Calm.' Janos rose from his knees and stepped to the rampart. He did not let go of Floré's hand. 'I spent years fleeing; I spent years hiding. When they came for us in Hasselberry I realised that until the war is done for all of us, it will be done for none of us. We must draw a line and burn a ditch, as Commander Jozenai said. We must end this once and for all.'

'Yes,' Jule was saying, and then Yselda grabbed him with one hand and hit him once, twice, *thrice* with a brutal crack, and she dragged him to the rampart edge. Floré stared wordless, and Janos frowned. Jule opened his mouth to speak but Yselda held him at the edge for a long moment before pushing him hard back down to the floor of the roof and smacking him a final time with the hilt of her sword. She turned away from them all, staring out across the sea, breathing hard. Jule lay still. Floré shivered, and Cuss was there suddenly next to her, slipping her own cloak around her shoulders, a pair of black gauntlets with silver knuckles and thick leather gloves into her hand.

Janos stared down at the harbour of Riven, and Floré

followed his gaze. His face was set in stone, no trace of a smile, and he looked worn and aged. Down in the harbour the four remaining galleons were drawing close to Riven port, and above them six wyrms writhed and swam in the air, twining together. From this close she could see the decks now, make out the hulking figures of rottrolls amongst others. *Where could they have gotten ships?*

Yselda pressed the hilt of the rune-sword into Floré's hand.

'Get the folks from the ship assembled in the courtyard,' Floré said, 'and get the outer doors closed.' Yselda nodded and left in quick order, Cuss hot on her heels. Tomas was crouched by Benazir, tying cloth tight around a wound, pressing at another.

'What happened to your eyes?' Benazir asked, and Floré turned to look at him. He turned his face to the ground. Next to her, Janos focused on the harbour, his fingers tracing shapes in the air that lingered for long moments in red light, runes and geometric patterns linked by tendrils of pulsing light.

'Bad things,' Tomas said, turning to face Floré. His pupils danced and split, broke to fractals and coalesced to odd circles, ever moving, ever changing. *Eyes like Varratim's.* Floré opened her mouth to ask, felt her face twist in disgust, but Tomas held his hand up in a sign of peace.

'Please,' he said, 'I must tell you.'

~

Ashbringer stumbled down the slope, following Tullen. She was sure he had not walked up the mountain to find her, but now he seemed to be revelling in every twist of the trail, his hands lingering over leaves and branches as they descended into the treeline lit only by starlight and the fat yellow moon above, close to full. She felt a deep uneasiness in herself as she walked, and she dared not touch the skein. The broken antler hilt of her sword was tucked in her belt, and he no longer seemed to deem her a threat.

She didn't seem to be able to even think of hurting him, of killing him. She tried to, but always her thought would flit away and land elsewhere. *Locked. Cursed.* She had awoken with his hand pressed to her brow, her mind steeped in the skein but only in her own pattern. She pushed outward but it was like trying to hear through water, trying to see through thick painted glass. Shadows and hints on the other side, utterly beyond her effect. She was alone, isolated. No longer a part of the world. She stood when she was told to stand, and walked when she was told to walk.

They climbed down the mountain and she thought of feeding him to wolves but then she was thinking, *What is this mountain called? How do mountains get their name?* She let him lead by a few hundred yards and tried to sing, but without dropping into the skein she could not find the song of this place, this mountain valley. She considered *looking*, extending her thought and feeling to that comforting current, but the fear in her was a tangible, guttural thing. *It will be hidden. If I have lost that, who am I? If I am not part of the pattern of the world, what can I be? A wraith. Lost. How will I find my way to the stars, if I cannot sing their song?*

They walked and they walked, the deep pine above hiding the citadel and the sea from view. The trees had thick trunks, pinecones littering the forest floor and the trail they walked, pinecones the size of her closed fist. Some had been chewed by squirrels; others were still sleek and wet with sap.

Tullen was mostly silent, occasionally humming to himself. Ashbringer could not take it, could not take the questions in her heart.

'What will you do?' she asked, gnashing her teeth and wringing her hands, and he turned to her and smiled.

'Oh,' he said, 'after three hundred years, I've some ideas. Oh yes indeed. There are places I would see again that have long been forbidden to me, and people I might speak to. There is a *wolf* I must find, you know. An ember in need of a soft breath and a cupped hand so it might grow. I also must say, intentional or not, I've felt a little... disconnected from the world. Set apart. I think it might be good to find connection, don't you think?'

They walked on. She did not answer him. She was so very cold. She considered driving the broken hilt of her sword, that nub of silver-coated steel, into the soft flesh of his neck, but then she was looking at the stars and trying to remember the constellations the humans named amongst them. They were thick tonight, shining strong over the clear waters of the Wind Sea. *I have failed you, Highmothers.*

'I have travelled far,' Tullen said as they descended a series of steep switchbacks cut into the mountainside. 'I have seen Cil-Marie, and Ona, and the Crown Islands. I have stared out at the waves of the Last Ocean and wondered what lies beyond. Uradech and Cinnae, I spent a few decades there. I learned to play some instruments; I learned to cook. I found solace in items, in riches, in flesh, in the drug distractions of the lowest and highest echelons of different societies. I grew bored, and disconsolate. Always I wondered, what is happening to my home, the nation I built? My dear Ferron?'

They stopped and he reached a hand out to her. Ashbringer did not flinch or resist. Tullen cupped her chin and grinned at her, his cheeks tight.

'I could never tell,' he said, 'what of that was me, what of it was the compulsion *she* put on me with her curse. I have passed no such burden to you. I have locked you away, so you might understand. You may not harm me, and you may not touch the pattern. Aside from that you are free. You are my only friend. One day I will free you.'

Ashbringer stayed silent, and Tullen walked on. They reached the final ridge before the citadel and he clapped his hands in joy.

'Oh, *fun!*'

Over the harbour six Ferron wyrms danced and writhed and twisted into one slithering scaled mass, impossible to tell where one began and another ended. Below them, four ships were making anchor, small boats thronging with goblin and rottroll and crow-man and rust-folk were beginning to make their way to shore, the first few landing parties spreading out across the docks, goblins crawling up the gangway of a tall ship docked at the tiny quayside.

Tullen closed his eyes for a long moment and then they flashed open.

'The young pup is up and about,' he said. 'You asked him for help once, did you not? To kill me. He gave you nothing but sadness and platitudes if I remember rightly.'

Ashbringer bowed her head. *If he is awake, there is hope. What one does, the other might undo.*

'He is a man sickened by so much war, so much death,' she said and Tullen sneered.

'War he made. Death he dealt. I've no time for the mewling

of children who are too foolish to think of consequences before they act. Shall we go to him? Would you like that?'

Ashbringer could not bring herself to speak, but she knew her eyes betrayed her longing for an ally, any ally in the straits she found herself. Tullen nodded.

'Very well,' he said, 'let us seek the fabled "Salt-Man".'

15

The Salvation of Flame

'*Knight-Commander, Captain Sorren and his troop are dead. Despite the disparity in the strength of our forces, we suffered only one loss against thrice our number. We struck at night, and gave no offer of clemency. This was my decision, and I will happily report more fully. Sorren has murdered children and civilians with bare nods at due process under the assertion they were rust-folk, or somehow descended from or related or sympathisers to rust-folk. As per our edict to investigate and judge suspected corruption of Stormguard duty, so we have fulfilled our contract. The bodies have been buried in a pit outside of town, and rank slides and personal effects will be returned to the commander in Aber-Ouse along with my full report.*' – **Fifth report on the massacre at Crowpit**, Agent Haysom, Third Moon Trading House

The first afternoon the rotstorm had been hell around them, black and red and purple lightning finding the metal rods at the top of the masts and running down thick cables to the sea below, the wind blowing in every direction at once. Hove spent the entire day clinging to the rail and weeping in between bouts of sickness, spewing the little food he'd been given in his cell over the side. The contents of his guts fell into the churning sea until there was nothing left to give, and then he heaved and heaved and heaved. The spray of the saltwater was a blessed relief from the burning of the rain and mist, teams of rowers pulling with all their might to get them clear of the storm.

'Home, after this, my witness,' Ceann Brude had said. She was not on his ship. He did not know the ship's name, if it even had one. His left hand still ached so much. Once they were out of sight of the shore the rust-folk seemed content for him to have free rein, but all he could do was clutch the rail. As night fell, the waves stayed wild and the winds strong, but they kept a more constant easterly direction, and the black and purple bruised clouds of the rotstorm slowly faded to wisps and then clear sky above. Sails were raised and the goblins that mobbed the decks corralled by rust-folk and shepherded into the holds below.

Hove spent the night huddled against the rail; he could not face descending into the darkness of the lower decks with the goblins. Deep in the blackness of night he was shivering, awake, and weeping, and one of the sailors laid a blanket over him with a look that might have been utter sorrow. He could make nothing of their language, nothing of their expressions. *Is it hate, when they look at me? Is it pity?*

The next day Hove explored where he could, but the aftcastle was full of crow-men and the officers and the deck bustling sailors. The forecastle was where the rust-folk had set themselves, sharpening blades, chatting to each other in old Ferron in thick accents. They were more recognisable to him than the sailors, clothes of heavy wool, hair braided and long, some with heavy beards thick with wax. They stared at him whenever he came close, whistled, made low jokes to one another.

He ended up climbing down a rope ladder past the prow of the ship to nestle amongst the rigging below, two large nets spread under the bowsprit. He did not know the purpose of the nets, but they supported his weight. The mast and crow's nest were occupied by sailors who shooed him or kicked him away, and the lower hold was now full of goblins and rottrolls. As he tried to join the back of the line for the pots of steaming hot grain mush that passed as lunch, one of the rust-folk had held him over it by the ankle, a hundred goblins chittering and screeching below. Hove had screamed and fainted, but when he woke he was safe on deck with a bowl of hot mush next to him.

'Mother,' he prayed, clutching his talisman over water more grey than blue. 'Mother why have you forsaken me?'

The sailors eyed him with suspicion and perhaps pity when he ventured back on deck. They were all amber-skinned, their heads shaved clean except for the officers. All of them were uniformed in the same style as the intricately embroidered outfit of the woman who he had met with Ceann Brude – long sleeves and trousers, a thick embroidered belt. The officers' and the captain's uniforms were marked with the same swirling language as that woman's tunic, and each of them carried a similar small hammer to her at their belts, though none were as deeply or ornately carved.

Hove spent most of the day in the rigging below the prow, watching the wyrms swim ahead of the boat, their long bodies cutting through the water just ahead of the bow where the water parted. *The sea is beautiful,* he thought, when land was a distant memory. He had sailed in the little boats at Port Last, played in the estuary in rowboats and single-sailed dinghies. Never had he seen an ocean like this. He thought of his proud mother and father, six children and never enough food or money but who sent him off to be a *whitestaff*, to cure disease, to research, to think, to predict storms and help shore up the protectorate. *I still will. I must.*

On the second day he tried talking to people, but nobody seemed to know the trade tongue of Isken. It began to rain, a long day of it, and he sheltered under the eaves of the aftcastle, close enough to hear the tread of the crow-men's feet, close enough to hear the muttered orders of the captain to his sailors. *Who are these people?* Port Last was close enough to the storm that he knew plenty of lore and rumour about the rust-folk, but never had he heard of them sailing. He knew they must be sailing the Wind Sea from the faint sightings of the sun to the north. From Port Last, you could sail west to storm, east to the endless ice floes, or north to nothing but the endless dark water of the Storm Sea, sailing over the watery grave of Nessilitor the Lover. *If it is south,* he thought, *where to? There is only Iskander, then Cil-Marie beyond.*

Hove knew almost nothing of Cil-Marie. He thought they worshipped the sun, or someone called the Sun-Master. They were a distant thought, beyond the wild reefs of the Tullioch clans, water normally impassable.

That second day they passed wrecked ships, perhaps a dozen of them. The rain eased in the afternoon and Hove watched the spars of broken wood, the barrels and crates and ragged sailcloth tumbling past them, bobbing in their wake.

The wyrms were unperturbed. A sailor sat on the prow now, calling back in a language Hove didn't recognise whenever the wyrm altered course. *Are we following the wyrms?*

Another bout of the sickness hit him, and he managed to sleep. When he awoke it was dark, and clambering to his feet he went to the rail. *Five other ships.* There had been a dozen ships that set off from the makeshift harbour in the rotstorm. *Where are the other six?* He could not spot Ceann Brude or the woman with the engraved hammer, could spot nothing familiar at all. *She has forgotten me.* Hove wept behind a crate, clutching his blanket. Behind him, an island loomed, two mountains sewed together with forest, dark and stars beyond. *Another place I don't know, full of people I don't know. Is it Iskander?*

He longed for the dull warmth of familiarity, of *knowing*. He had not realised how much simple uncertainty could eat at you, cutting away at your resolve and your mind. *I should be tallying soldiers, getting names, intelligence I can report back,* he thought at one point, but he shrunk back in on himself as a sailor clad in black rushed by, yelling. *I'm not a soldier, or a hero.* He pictured Cora, the Stormguard who had defended him and then fled Port Last at Ceann Brude's command. He hoped she had made it. *She must have. She will have made it, and I'm going to make it.*

The first Hove knew of the orb of light was a yellow glow on his cheek, his hand. He stared at his fingers dumbly. At the shout of a sailor he looked up and there it was, an orb of glowing light pouring fire in a stream down on the next ship along. The sails were ablaze, the deck a riot of colour and motion as crow-men shot beams of lightning and flame upward, as sailors rushed to pull ropes, to throw burning sailcloth overboard. Hove could hear the sound of the water around his ship, the steady creaking of wood and rope, the chittering of the goblins below, but no sounds came across the water from the ship the orb attacked. A pulse of purple light fired thrice from the orb into the hull and with the next wave the ship began to list, tilting heavily to one side, burning even as it did.

Hove screamed, his scream lost amongst all the others, and the orb was spewing flame at a second ship now – *not mine, Anshuka please not mine next* – but then from the water the wyrms came. All six of them crashing into it, all of it unfolding in perfect silence except for the screams and moans of his shipmates, the yells of the captain and crew. *Be a witness,* Ceann Brude had asked him, and so Hove gripped the rail and he screamed and he gibbered as the wyrms battled the orb and were victorious, and as its light failed and it fell to the sea the sky was cut with the screams of wyrms, the screams of the dying. The survivors swam water thick with blood and wood, seeking refuge on the remaining ships, and through the darkness on the coast Hove could see it, and he would have wept if he had tears left to give: *Riven.*

Since he had known it existed, Hove had dreamt of studying in Riven. The accumulated knowledge of three hundred years, a fortress library undaunted by storm or war. A place to think and understand the world in silence and peace. He looked up at the white towers and drum wall of the citadel, gleaming silver-yellow in the moonlight, a hulking imposition on the side of the mountain, and he felt a sickness deep in his bones: hope. *Please, Mother,* he prayed, *you must save them from us.*

~

Janos swayed on the roof of the citadel, his cheek twitching as he completed another pass with his hands, and another rune flared into light alongside him. Floré stood at his shoulder and held him with one hand, and he leaned on her when it all threatened to overwhelm him. *It has been so long.* He remembered the orbs, the red-haired demon cutting at his stomach with her knife in that awful silence. *The beach.* They had taken Marta away. The beach had been the worst moment of his life. Janos kept his hands moving, kept on tracing runes in the air in front of him. It was so cold, and he had to hook his awareness into the skein to do the work. Below, the ships came towards Riven, the wyrms winding above them, closer and closer. With a shiver Janos traced another rune, remembered lying on his back on the beach by Loch Hassel, coughing blood, remembered the pressure lifting on his chest and the noise of flames and chaos coming from his home, from the village beyond. Hearing his own voice screaming as he watched the orb cut through the sky, his sight fading to black, every star dimming. *I failed her.* He had thought it then, and shivering on the roof of the citadel he thought it again and he knew it to be true.

I failed Marta. I failed Floré. How many others died? He wasn't thinking about Hasselberry, not just Hasselberry. Janos was thinking of the years in the forest, the years where he could have ended the threat of Ferron forever. *I could have done anything.* Starbeck had come to him with plans, plans to use him non-militarily. Roads, walls. Refining ore, prospecting in the hills. Janos had refused them all. What would the protectorate have looked like with a half-decade of a skein-wreck's power, even if he refused to kill?

We could have been ready. I could have been ready.

Janos leaned into Floré and paused, in front of him a jumble of glowing runes and symbols hanging in the air unfinished. In the skein he could feel her, from her skin to the marrow of her bones, every inch of her. He remembered the shaman temple, and Floré, and then stillness and silence for a long time.

'I hope you aren't dead,' Jule had said to him, dragging him from blood-clotted sheets and straw to the back of a wagon not two days later, 'for I've my orders, praise to the mother.'

He remembered the road. *Was I breathing, then? What am I that I can't die?* He had some idea. He was a pattern; all life was pattern. He had studied and changed himself; any thinking on a pattern would change it. He had drawn connection to himself, linked himself to the liminal energies of the world, the potential in everything, realised and unrealised. He had done so to wield fire and hell, but in doing so he had perhaps made himself harder to kill than he could have imagined. *The other patterns feed into me, reinforce me.* He frowned and formed another sigil with his hand, a tattoo on his shoulder burning with heat and light. With a thought it went to join the others, a glowing constellation of symbols interlocking, circling him and each other, each in their place, each with their connection. *Focus. I cannot fail them again.*

It was so hard to focus. He spoke as he worked, distracted mumbling to Floré, who clutched at his shoulder, hot blood streaming from her wounds and wicking into his simple white robe.

'You found her,' he said, and she laughed.

'A fine fight, that,' she said. 'Their crow-man, their chief Varratim. He had Tullen One-Eye's knife, the blade that killed Nessilitor the Lover. It drinks pattern, or something. The orbs were taking children who could touch the skein, taking them back to the Blue Wolf Mountains, sacrificing them to charge this knife with power. They killed Petron.'

Janos let out a breath and turned, turned to the stairwell where Cuss and Yselda had descended. Benazir slumped close to them, the skein-mage hastily trying to staunch her many wounds. Janos stared at him for a long second. *That man saved me.* He knew it in his bones. He remembered so little of the last spans, but he remembered feeling chained, caged, as if every connection between him and the world was passing through a filter he could not control. *What did I do, while I slept?* He remembered whitestaffs chanting around him, images of an old man, and pattern being called; pattern reaching through him, power pouring through him. Then blackness. *Which pattern?* They had yoked him like an oxen.

Janos forced himself to stand upright, kept tracing the runes. *Six wyrms, four ships...*

'He wanted to kill Anshuka,' Floré said, her voice thick. 'I don't understand the magic of it. We gave chase, but they found us first. He used Marta to trace us. He wanted *me*, so I could tell him how to become a skein-wreck.'

Janos left his constellation of runes hanging in the air, turned to her and smiled – a wide grin at the insanity of it.

'What did you do?' he asked, and Floré shrugged and grimaced, averted her gaze from his.

'Escaped, stole an orb, beat him to death in Anshuka's shadow.'

Janos shook his head, eyes fixed back on the harbour. His breath faded and he just felt tired, so tired.

'I failed you,' he said, 'but I should have known it wouldn't matter. You always were the strong one.'

Floré gripped him close. 'There's more, my love. Marta…
the whitestaff has barely been able to help. The skein-mages
of the castrum are useless. She reaches as she sleeps, touches
the skein and it takes from her. Every day she is weaker. If we
don't do something soon…'

'They could not have helped you,' he said, 'only a skein-
wreck could. She is something new, perhaps. None before has
had a child. We should have paused at that, perhaps. But a
skein-wreck can help. I can help. I know I can help her.'

Floré squeezed his shoulder and then ripped another strip
from her shirt, mopped at the blood on her face. He could
sense her pattern of course, so familiar, could feel the ragged
burrs of wounds, as well as the changes since he had seen her
last. *I slept so long.*

'You said you would never touch the skein again,' she said
quietly, and behind them Tomas was squinting at the symbols
around Janos, trying to fathom what he was doing.

'No,' Janos heard him say. 'That can't possibly be right.'

'When they came for Marta, I reached for it,' Janos said,
'and when I saw fear in her face all my convictions fell away.
I'll burn the world for her if I must. I'm sorry for all you had
to bear alone, my love. But I'm here now. I'm here and I can
do this, and I will keep doing this until Marta is safe. I was a
coward. I ran, because I could. How many would live now if
I'd been strong enough to do my duty?'

Floré leaned into his arm and held his hand in hers, and in
his ear she whispered, 'The crow-man told me something. In
the rotstorm, Anshuka's spirit hunts. When it finds a child, it
changes them. That is where they come from, my love. Every
goblin a rust-folk child.' Janos stopped moving his free hand
and held his breath. *Every goblin a rust-folk child.* He fell to

his knees on the rampart, and above him the pattern blazed with heat, a growing flame constrained within it.

The pattern was complete, an orb of sigils and runes pressing at each other sparking, hovering in the air above him, a flame in its heart brighter than any made by man. Something unseen in Undal since Hussain the Blue. The weapon that kept the borders of Cil-Marie and the Sun-Masters clear of any enemy for time immemorial, as the disciples of Ihm-Phogn held their secret state away from the hells of the world. Janos had read of the theory in Hussain's notes, but never dared attempt it. *The burning sun.* On his knees he gazed down at the harbour, the four ships and the flood of goblins and rottrolls and wyrms and crow-men.

'What would you have me do?' he asked, and Floré shook her head. In front of them the intricate fractal geometries and arcing connection of the weapon pulsed with a burning light, hues of red and yellow and orange fading into one another. *Like a rotbud,* he thought, but he couldn't bring himself to concentrate on that. *Every goblin a rust-folk child. How many have I killed? How many patterns cut short?*

'What would you have me do?' he asked again, his voice shaking as he turned to Floré, hands clawing at the stone of the rampart below him. *What can I do? What have I done?* Janos felt himself hyperventilating, and his grip on the skein began to waver, the burning sun above him flickering as connections within it bent and frayed. Floré gripped his shoulder hard and he focused and the sphere of runes held strong.

'Now?' she said. 'We must survive. We must *fight*. For her.' Her voice was strong, despite the blood caking her face, her hands, despite the cold he could sense threatening to consume her. With a nudge of pattern he warmed a spiral of air around her, and she smiled at the wave of heat.

'This is incredible, Janos-Wreck,' Tomas said behind him. And on his knees, tears streaming down his face, Janos turned to him. *A Stormguard skein-mage.* Janos did not recognise the man but could see his eyes were broken, skein-scarred, the pupils dancing. He did not know what could cause such a wound but he could feel the pattern of it, the odd wrinkles and eddies in the current, a concentration.

'You broke the chains,' Janos said, and still immersed in the currents underlying the world he shivered and focused. He rose to his feet and held a hand out and touched Tomas's brow, focused. *Changed* what lay beneath. Tomas swore and fell back, clutching at his eyes, swearing and cursing as he fell to his knees.

'What have you done!' he yelled, but Janos ignored him and turned back to the pattern held in stasis in front of him, to Floré next to it, her face illuminated by the burning flame.

'I wanted to be better,' he said, 'for her. I didn't want her father to be a killer, a monster. I've done such things, wielded power I think perhaps no man should have.'

Tomas opened his eyes and coughed and blinked, and Janos and Floré turned to him. He rubbed at his eyes, blinked again. A clear crystal blue, his pupils wide and fixed.

'If you did not have this power,' Tomas said, 'we would all die now, and your daughter soon after. Undal would fall, and once again we would see chains and a cruel hand. The world is moved by power. You have it, and you must act, or be damned regardless.'

From the nearest stairwell Yselda and Cuss emerged, the Tullioch Leomar with them. He dragged the master of the citadel, his beard wild, his eyes wilder. Janos recognised him, the face from his dark dreams these long months. When the old man saw Janos he began to scrabble and push at his captor but the Tullioch Leomar held firm.

'We thought you dead!' the master said at last, mouth opening and closing rapidly, eyes darting to all sides and then settling on the glowing sphere of runes that still floated over Janos's head, that sphere so bright with flame. 'We thought only...'

Janos turned away from him. He did not even know the man's name. *You thought only to use the power I found.* What had they done with it? Captured an orb somehow, burned ships in the water. Janos had tried fighting an orb himself, but in the brief moments before the chaos of the crow-men's aura overcame his ability to manipulate the skein, he had failed utterly in his attempts to damage it. The idea of this man using *his* pattern, using the connections he had spent so long growing to slowly understand, made him feel sick to his core. *A conclave,* he thought, *some whitestaff trick of joining hands and bolstering each other in the skein-sharing pattern.* The idea revulsed him instinctively, but he did not understand why. *How could they know my pattern? How could they see what I have seen?*

'What are you going to do?' Floré asked, and Janos sighed deeply and held her hand. With the other he sent the burning sphere of runes forward and down, down towards the harbour. It seemed to trail light, a red glow ever so softly following. Janos did not answer Floré's question, only shook his head.

In the harbourfront the wyrms began shrieking to one another, dark cries that carried to the citadel roof. Janos shivered and watched. The wyrms were keeping pace with the ships, dark wood on dark water, and ropes were being thrown and the first rust-folk and black-clad sailors were leaping to the harbourside. Goblins were clamouring at every railing, and the bent and stooped figures of crow-men. The rune sphere came to a halt in front of the wyrms, hovering out over the water between the ships, and a wave of fear passed through the sailors. Those ashore began sprinting from the docks, and those aboard the ships began flinging themselves into the icy water. The crow-men twisted and crooned to each other, and the wyrms wailed and writhed, beaks probing towards the approaching sphere of burning runes and snapping at the air.

'Turn away,' Janos said, and when Tomas did not comply he twisted the skein around him and turned the man.

Behind them, light and heat and noise. Even turned away with his eyes closed, it was a long moment before Janos was blinking, seeing again. He was the first. His ears were ringing. The rest of them were on their knees. The old whitestaff was spewing, sick, the Tullioch making keening cries and gripping at its head. Tomas was huddled in a ball, and Cuss and Yselda both pressed against a tower wall, holding tight to one another with a hand each, their other hands on sword grips, Benazir stoic next to them, head turned to the wall, scarred face a grimace of pain. Janos tried to picture them as he had last seen them, Cuss and Yselda children in Hasselberry, Benazir newly appointed to her command at the Stormwall. *So much I've missed.*

Janos reached down to Floré and pulled her to her feet. Together they looked down at the harbour. The sea was rushing to fill in the hole where his orb of flame had burned away the water. The quay, the ship Floré had called *Basira's*

Dance, the four Ferron galleons, the wyrms, the thronging goblins and rust-folk... all were gone. A circle of fire had burned clear down to the bedrock, soil and stone and house and ship and flesh burned away to nothing. *The burning sun.* Janos slumped on the railing.

'They may have been children once,' Benazir said from behind them, her voice a fragile thing, as if she was pleading, 'but they are goblins now. We can't undo what is done.'

She pulled herself up and the three stared at the ruination below, the charring at the edge of the circle of destruction. The nearest pine trees and houses were ablaze, the whole harbourfront smouldering. *We can't undo what was done,* Janos thought, *unless...*

'That was a surprisingly good one,' a voice said beside Janos's ear, and Janos felt a prickle of pain as a knifepoint pressed against his ribs ever so gently. Benazir and Floré were looking at him, frozen mid-motion as they turned and reached for him, Floré's eyes running with tears. Janos blinked and reached for the skein, but what he saw instead of pattern was concentration, a point of fullest density held on a blade – the blade against his ribs.

'Let us see what the young pup knows, shall we?' the voice said, and then the dagger was gone from his back. Janos twisted in place. He could see Tomas and Yselda and Cuss, the Tullioch and the whitestaff, frozen in place just as Benazir and Floré were. Nobody else was on the roof.

Janos sank into the skein and let that web of light cover his vision, the pattern of everything – its potential, its past, its capacity, its complexity – articulated in a dimension beyond normal sight. He turned slowly across the roof, scanning... there!

'I can see you,' he said, even though it was a lie. He could see a ruck in the skein, as if someone was pulling it around themselves to shield their own pattern. *A pattern shield.* Janos had never heard of such a thing and a dozen implications flooded his mind at once, even as the shield dropped and in front of him two figures stood. One was Ashbringer, the Orubor who had once asked him to help her kill an invincible man. The skein was shaded around her, her connection to the outside world beyond her own body dimmed and blocked in a thousand thousand ways, tendrils of light curtailed and snipped. *Chained.* She was shaking her head at him, and slowly she walked to where Floré stood frozen and sat cross-legged at his wife's feet.

The second figure was hard to look at. A man, and so much more. Connection in such depth and infinite subtlety it made Janos's eyes itch. Concentration of pattern like stars behind stars, like a layer of constellations, every layer giving way to another. Tullen One-Eye. The unkillable man, the ghost who wandered helpless to watch his people's downfall. Janos's hero, Janos's inspiration; to be a skein-wreck, like Tullen One-Eye, so he could save his people. The man who rode Lothal the wolf into battle; the man who broke the Tullioch Shardspire, that holy place of coral and rock tended for a millennium and broken in a heartbeat. *Tullen One-Eye.* The only man to kill a Judge, his knife cutting to the heart of Nessilitor the Lover, the great patron of generosity and love, the owl with eyes like starfields and a beak of crystal and wings of night itself. The skein-wreck who wrought the Ferron Empire, more than five centuries ago.

'We don't need to fight,' Janos said, but a stream of flame was coming for him. Janos parted it with a wave of his hand, the simple dancing geometry of progressive fire dissipating into the diffuse movement of steam.

'Why wouldn't we fight?' Tullen asked. 'Don't you want to show me your skills, Salt-Man? It has been a long time since I was unfettered, *unblinkered*. I am eager to see.'

The mocking tone Tullen used set Janos's teeth on edge. He felt so tired. With a thought he took flight, away from Floré, moving himself into the air. Towards Tullen he began to probe. It was a rapid series of exchanges as he arced in a slow loop through the sky to the far end of the citadel roof, away from his love. Janos sent streams of lightning, and Tullen dodged and then intercepted the crackling beams with a shield of shimmering red light. Tullen dashed back and forth, sending strange spiralling flames, and Janos was soon sweating as he flew between the twirling snakes of fire that hunted him as he flew above the citadel.

'I don't want to hurt you!' he called, desperately, and Tullen tutted.

'Enough playing, Salt-Man. Fight me properly, or I'll turn one of your little friends into lunch for my pet Orubor.'

Janos swore and swooped low, and as he moved his eyes flashed and his hands spun traces through the air. Tullen frowned as a cage of blue light surrounded him, wrist-thick bars that hummed with power. The cage began to shrink closer, and the humming grew as Janos threw more and more energy from the liminal space between chaos and pattern into his creation.

'So the idea is this gets smaller and butchers me?' Tullen taunted. Janos ignored him and grew still, hanging in the sky, the patterns tattooed in his skin and etched deep in every beat of his heart all burning with black light. He could see the pattern over everything – the citadel, the great tree, the harbour and the burning ash floating down over it. Janos held himself still in the air high over the roof and focused on the cage. The bars were contracting, so close as to almost touch Tullen's skin. He had imbued the cage with an immense amount of energy. Tullen grinned and sent a spewing crackle of lightning from his palm and the cage bars drank it in, humming even louder, steadily contracting inward.

'Very nice!' Tullen called, and then he waved his hand and the bars were smoke, and Janos had lost them. The pattern around him fell to chaos and suddenly gravity had him, a pattern asserting itself. Janos slammed into the roof of the Riven citadel and felt the air push from his lungs, the wet crack of a rib against stone. He stumbled to a knee but righted himself quickly and sprinted across the rooftop, trying to keep distance from Floré and the others. Tullen paced after him and with a lazy gesture one of the decorative trees from the rooftop wrenched free from its planter and flew at Janos. Janos exploded it with a beam of white lightning, and a shower of splinters fell across his frozen comrades. Another tree followed, and another, and then a slew of dozens of decorative roof tiles that he deflected with a long burning arc of black flame.

In the corporeal realm their battle was an intense flurry of light and energy, deflection and attack. Through the skein, it was something else entirely. It was pattern changing, and being changed again. Rival weavers picking at a tapestry, responding to one another's changes in a heartbeat. In the skein Janos could see the chains so intricately woven around Floré and Cuss and Benazir and Yselda, weaves of gravity and air and weight and force holding every limb and muscle still. Floré strained towards him and Janos rolled behind a low bench and tried to focus on Tullen. The man was stalking across the roof courtyard, his cloak trailing behind him, and a faceted dome of light surrounded him. Within the dome, Tullen's skin glowed black as he called on his own remembered patterns, and a gout of boiling acid spewed forth from an outstretched palm. Janos rolled away, the stone behind him sizzling and melting as the acid ate at it. *Focus*.

With a sustained effort of will and lightning, his own energy blasts probed at the imperfections in the pattern of Tullen's protective layer. 'Damn you!' Tullen cried when Janos broke through the shimmering field of red light, one of his bolts snaking through and burning into Tullen's shoulder. Tullen stepped back sharply, face no longer calm, eyes blazing. Lightning met lightning in an explosive burst, from each mage a beam of opaque light burning with energy. Janos could feel his own energy slipping into the skein and spreading his awareness again to the space between chance and order and pattern and chaos, potential and stillness. *The space between*. He found the energy there, and as the beams of crackling lightning pushed at each other, Janos tore one hand free and reached for salt.

It always came easy, the salt. It was a pattern he could always reach, a recurring structure that called to him; the first he had found. Breaking off his lightning beam, Janos dove to one side and then began with a distraction, a spume of burning acidic green flame that Tullen would have to focus on to deflect. Even as the first mote of fire left his fingertips, Janos was changing the air around Tullen, the air, the ground, the gases and vapour and every mote of matter in a great column surrounding the skein-wreck. Changing them to an ever-burning salt. In a moment it was done. Atop the rounded citadel of Riven, a column of salt ten foot wide and thirty high stood, throwing off waves of heat and light as it burned hotter than any flame. The column burned and Janos slumped, holding himself up with one arm on a decorative stone bench. He turned from the pyre of flame, turned to Floré and—

A cold pain slipped up between his ribs, a sickly sharpness, a taste of iron, and a hand grasping him and pulling him back. He felt a concatenation, a point of utter concentration and order in the skein, mapped to the form of a blade, and he felt it deep in his chest. His own patterns whirled and flared and broke and sank into the nexus. He felt the knife-bearer lift him physically with the blade, balancing him, lowering him down gently to his side.

'Please,' he said, and Tullen One-Eye leaned over him. With his plea a torrent of hot blood poured from his mouth. *Let me see her,* he thought, tried to say. With a wave Tullen One-Eye dispersed the flaming salt pillar Janos had built behind them, motes of flame spiralling out towards the sea.

'If I can make the pattern cover where I am,' he said softly, 'I can make it show me where I am not. I'd call it simple misdirection if it wasn't so terribly complicated to do.'

'Please,' Janos said again, feeling another gout of his pattern flood into the knife.

'Please?' Tullen let go of the hilt and kicked Janos over onto his back, the roof pushing the blade deeper. Janos could see Floré, unable to move even her expression. He stared at her. *I love you. I'm sorry.* He tried to speak the words and his lips moved but no air came from his lungs. He could see in her eyes that she understood. Ashbringer was there as well, standing now next to Floré and touching her cheek,

Ashbringer weeping herself but not intervening, only standing at Floré's side and watching, mouth downturned. *I died once already,* Janos thought, and again he reached for the skein.

Janos was the first Undal skein-wreck in more than a generation. His mastery of the pattern was unparalleled in the Undal Protectorate, perhaps even further. He fell into the pattern and even as his own deep currents were torn away one by one, he looked around him. Tullen One-Eye was another skein-wreck, a density of pattern and current, a depth of connection to everything far greater than his own. *A one-eyed skein-wreck.* He did not linger on the man who had killed him. He could feel, could *see* the skein in the blood leaving his body, his limbs shutting down, his organs failing. Could see the patterns and connections that had saved him once slipping away, consumed by the nexus of the blade, a dark singularity that grew as it fed on the depths of his connection and pattern. *No.* He could not stop it.

Janos focused on Floré. He looked in her, her past, her present, her future potential, every connection she had made and every connection she had broken and torn, every ragged wound. He found a place, a space in her mind and her heart where his pattern and hers intertwined and he reached inside himself and drew out a thought and placed it, and he saw in her eyes a twinkle. An understanding.

I love you, Janos thought, but then the patterns were fading, and he was so cold. *I must... what must I do?* Thought slipped away leaving only feeling, the cold on his fingertips, clouds gathering above. Janos stared up at the stars that shone around the thick clouds above. Snow beginning to fall, ever so softly...

Janos died, utterly.

16

CLAW WINTER

*'Let me tell you a secret, or perhaps you already know? The rust-folk live amongst us, even now. Do you think the Stormwall impenetrable, the ring of steel our masters claim so perfect? Expect no perfection from imperfect beings such as we. The Stormwall is porous. Refugees flee. Some are caught and killed, or forced back to the storm. Some maraud and rampage and are eventually hunted down. Others pass through Undal like ghosts in the night, seeking the freedom of fairer lands beyond. Yet some stay. They work the farms and mills; they keep their heads down. They work, and do they not deserve this chance? We are a nation of slaves risen high.' – **Break the Stormguard's chains!*** Lillebet Arfallow, year 312 from Ferron's Fall (1123 Isken)

Cuss watched Tullen One-Eye stab Mister Janos in the back. The man was dead, a tower of burning stuff burying him, and then he was standing behind Janos with that long knife drawn, and Cuss couldn't move, couldn't think. He tried to scream, tried to weep, tried to fight, but he could do nothing. He watched Mister Janos die, and he planned. *I have a silver dagger now.* As soon as he could move he would skewer Tullen, and then skewer him again. He would cut him down to nothing, and break that blade, and leave the corpse for the crows.

Cuss railed in the stillness, expecting to find calm eventually, but the anger grew and twisted in his heart with every moment. He pictured his brother's face. *What can I do, Petron?*

'Well,' Tullen said, retrieving his dagger from Janos's back and smiling. 'Isn't that just lovely. A nice little something to whet my appetite. Now what to do with all of you? You all seem upset. Good. Sit with that a little.'

The man strode amongst them, stopping to look at each. Benazir and Floré he frowned at, Tomas he ignored. The Tullioch he appraised with a long glance, and when he reached the whitestaff master he knelt, patting the old man's head. Yselda he looked over quickly and shrugged, and then he met Cuss's eye.

'Oh dear,' he said, 'I think I taught the pup what hate is. I'm sorry, pup. It is a hard lesson we all must learn, but hatred can be fuel. Fuel for transformation, for greatness.'

I know hate, you bastard, Cuss thought, never for a second ceasing to strain for his dagger. *I know hate and I swear you'll know mine before this is over.*

'So,' Tullen said, gesturing for Ashbringer. She walked to him, crestfallen, and took his hand. Cuss wanted to scream. *What are you doing?!* She was his *friend.* She met his eyes and he saw the pain there. *What hold does he have on her?*

Tullen drew Ashbringer close to him and they both rose

from the ground, little stones kicking up beneath them as currents of air pushed away from their floating forms.

'A Claw Winter is coming,' he said, smiling. 'You have no ships; you have no skein-wreck. You have nothing. I have – let me see – my power, my knife, and an Orubor to keep me company. Shall I kill you all, or let the snows and slow starvation drive you to feed on each other's corpses, so that when you die it is with even more shame in your hearts? Hmm? Yes, I think that works for me. I bid you farewell.'

Tullen, Cuss thought, *Tullen bastard One-Eye.* The skein-wreck floated upward, Ashbringer at his side, and then they were a streak of light headed north across the darkness of the open sea, impossibly fast.

Cuss felt his hand jerk to his dagger and then Floré was crouching over Mister Janos and screaming *no,* over and over. Cuss sat down on the roof of the citadel and he burned with such hate he could not even breathe.

'Heal him!' Yselda was saying to the old whitestaff, the master, her dagger against his throat. 'Heal him now!'

The old man spluttered and crawled forward. He closed his eyes and turned back to her, hands raised.

'There is nothing left to heal!' he said, and then Floré was on him, fists swinging, heavy blows, and she sat astride his chest and hit him again and again.

'Stop, sister!' Benazir said, slumped against the rampart, but Floré did not stop. Yselda made no move to intervene, and Cuss sat and stared at Mister Janos's body. Finally Tomas pulled Floré back, the old man unconscious on the ground, his face a mess of blood.

'Anshuka's tears,' he said, 'we may all of us need a healer before this is done. Yselda, gather the sailors and commandos.

We need to secure the citadel. Send out teams of five, to capture any shamans and whitestaffs they can *alive*. Cuss, Leomar, get those tower gates secured. Some goblins or rust-folk might have got into the woods before Janos burned the port.'

Cuss looked up at him and realised the mage's eyes were clear.

'Your eyes,' he said, and Tomas raised his eyebrows and glanced at the body of Janos. His cheek twitched and mouth parted and Cuss could see a cold clarity in his gaze.

'Indeed,' he replied, his voice as gentle as Cuss had ever heard it. 'A gift from our skein-wreck. You need to get those gates secured, lad. Don't worry. I'll watch her.'

Tomas let Floré go and she went to Janos, and then Cuss watched as he shook his head and closed his eyes for a long moment. Opening them, he followed Floré and put a hand on her shoulder, and then he was at Benazir's side, the two of them in hurried conclave.

Cuss got to his feet but before he went to the tower he too went to Floré, who had pulled Janos onto her lap and was cradling his head, weeping silently as she held him close. Cuss had no words for her, but he put his gauntleted hand on her shoulder and stood for a moment with the snow falling all around them, and then he got to work.

'They're over the south wall!' someone yelled, and Starbeck dashed to the windows of the war office, high in Protector's Keep looking south over Undal City. *Six ships.*

'Berren's black blood,' he said, his voice lost in the clamour. He could see three of the ships still hanging back in the bay off the Star Coast, out beyond the lighthouse *False Friend*.

Lanterns lit on their decks, they were motes of light against a black sea and a black sky. Three more were closer than he could see, hidden by the dark bulk of the city walls. Starbeck peered and was about to yell back orders when he saw them, first one, then another, lit by the rampart braziers, heralded by screams of fear. *Wyrms*.

They spiralled over the city walls and writhed through the air, descending into the night streets, lost to his view. At least four. *Four wyrms*. A single wyrm at Fallow Fen had held back the combined might of the Stormguard for five spans of bloody fighting, until Janos had destroyed it with a wave of his hand. *Where are you, my boy?*

'Bring me Captain Nintur!' he yelled, and then the chaos fully began. The Commissar-Mage Inigo and his cohort were yelling at each other, the commander of what remained of the navy demanding he be heard. Starbeck listened, gave order. *Evacuation*. From the east gate to Hookstone village, from the north and west up to Overton. Skein-mages went to try and snipe fireballs at the hulls of the ships before they could disembark whatever troops or horrors they held. Ballistae and catapults on the walls were even now raining bolts and rocks and flaming tar at the nearer three vessels, aiming at dark targets on dark waters.

'Six ships aren't an invasion,' Starbeck heard someone say; 'it's a distraction!'

He snatched the young officer and ripped his rank buckle from his tunic and grabbed him by the throat.

'Get a blade and go get yourself a wyrm,' he snarled, 'if you want to see your rank restored!'

The young captain ran from the room.

'Six ships aren't an *invasion*,' Starbeck roared. 'Six *wyrms* could be the end of us. Unchecked they will destroy the city if it takes them three days or three weeks. Commissar. Options?'

Inigo gripped at a fistful of beard with one hand as he spoke, scratching and pulling at his cheek, his eyes staring out into the night. His other hand was free, the fingers twitching and moving rhythmically. Behind him his mage cohort were arguing with each other in hushed voices.

'Four wyrms,' Inigo said, still staring out at the city below. 'Hussain the Blue killed three, in his life, and the last of those took him with it. Janos destroyed the wyrm of Fallow Fen, and perhaps more in the fortress of Urforren. Commander Benazir Arfallow killed a wyrm at Stormcastle XII with only a rune-dagger and a sure hand.

'Your mages?' Starbeck asked, but he already knew the answer.

'We have no magic that will assail them. Our fire, our force, it rolls off their hide like water. Silver will wound, but at Fallow Fen we threw ingots faster than crossbow bolts and barely left a mark. They are engines of pure destruction, creatures of utter capability. The castrum will stand, Commander. We will fight. But the okçin will not win this battle, not today.'

Starbeck pulled his tunic straight and gazed from the high windows down into the city below. A fire was spreading in the scaleways, the warehouses and salthouses and smokehouses of the fishing port at the west end of Undal. The dancing red of the flame competed with the soft pale glow of the *False Friend* lighthouse in the water off the eastern trade port. *Is this the end?* Starbeck could only think of Benazir's dagger.

'We must hope the ballistae combined with my mages are up to the task of delaying the beasts, or drawing them away,' Commissar-Mage Inigo was saying, and Starbeck nodded.

'Do it,' he said. *It will slow them, at least, so we can evacuate.* 'And bring me the prototypes from the castrum smithy – every rune blade that holds an edge. We shall see if we can recreate Benazir's miracle. The balanced blade may save us yet. Send me your ten best combat mages as soon as you can, and the rest to the ballistae.'

Turning to the assembled officers and runners, Starbeck fell into the cold surety of action. There was a plan, and there was work to be done. 'We need every runed weapon in the city, in this room, now. And get me Captain Nintur of the Lancers, and the thirteenth commando regiment!' he ordered, and then waved a dismissal. *It will work.*

Bells ringing below in the shaman temples, screaming filtering up from the streets. Starbeck closed his eyes and pictured the tree-lined streets of Undal City, the parks and squares, the people dancing in the streets at High Harvest. *I will not let them end.* Every moment brought a new report, and his officers dealt with every runner, sifting the information into intelligence and bringing him only what was actionable or important.

'Captain Nintur, sir,' an aide said, gesturing to a man to his left with a face like a hatchet, nothing but sharp lines. Nintur wore a heavy chain shirt and plate armour below his blue Lancer tabard, and at his waist a heavy-headed war axe was slung in a loop. In the distance there was a crashing shriek, then a low-pitched guttural howl that cut through the clamour and screams.

'They've reached the keep,' someone said.

'What can we do?'

Starbeck bade Nintur to wait with a wave of his hand and kept his orders flowing. *Seal what gates they could. Send riders and Lancers to harry and distract. City Guard to evacuate where they could, and run interference and reports. Every skein-mage assigned a six-man Lancer guard. Any reports of crow-men to the commissar-mage. Field hospital below the keep, in the barracks next to the infirmary.*

Rune blades were stacking up, four on the table before him, and two blades from the castrum's experimental runesmith project, blades with no hilt but wrapped leather on dull black metal. The thirteenth commandos marched into the room, a troop Starbeck had once led into battle himself, on rotation back to the capital. They were a lean group of men and women, tough and grim and scarred. Starbeck had Commissar-Mage Inigo and his chosen combat-mages join him and the thirteenth commandos.

'Commander Arfallow killed a wyrm at Stormcastle XII not seven spans back. She is not a skein-wreck, or some hero from a forgotten age. She is a commando of the Stormguard. She stuck a runed blade in its gullet, and let the magic catch and do the work.'

He motioned at the table before him, four blades: three daggers and a sword. Two had runes of burning like Benazir's dagger, one blade was wet with a tacky green substance. He had seen one like it before, knew it would pulse acid whenever it had contact with blood or flesh, and would not cease. The final blade was something new to him, the patterns on it not runes but geometric, the hilt and blade new.

'What is this one?' he asked, and his aide dashed across, clutching maps to her chest.

'Lightning, sir,' she said, 'gift from Highmother Ash of the Orubor, from the bladesmiths of Elm, she said, sir. She is outside, sir; she had it and you said...'

'Bring her in! Commandos, grab a blade. Split into squads. If your blade-carrier falls, you pick it up, and so on until you are dead or the wyrm is dead. Understood?'

The commandos looked at him with utter stillness in their eyes, and then their captain gave a soft salute. It was Hallen, a lad who had been a cadet at the wall when Starbeck had led the thirteenth. He stood fair and tall and his face betrayed no fear as he bowed his head to his commander.

'Clear, sir. See you after.'

The commandos began pushing at the different weapons and each other, one of them laughing a manic cackle, all of them in awe as they hefted them. Hallen gripped one of the burning blades, his face set. *My dearest ones,* Starbeck thought, and committed their faces to memory. Outside, the wail of a beast far closer than below in the keep.

'The window!' someone screamed, and with a crash the panes of the war office windows facing south smashed inward, a chitinous three-way beak snapping and tearing at masonry, a maw that could swallow an oxen whole. The stone wall of the high tower windows pulled away and apart with each wrenching bite, and Starbeck could see eyes running down its flank, red eyes that glowed like burning crystal. From the commissar-mage a burst of white lightning flew, striking the beast, and then the other mages were joining him and aides and officers scattering for cover as fire and force and lightning ripped through the war room and tore at the wyrm. It coiled back from the tower and then threw itself forward again, shrieking.

'Saves me a walk,' a commando said, and then she was running, the blade in her gauntleted hand wet with green acid ichor. The wyrm smashed its beak forward again and managed to get its head wedged into the window arch, and the commando did not hesitate. Around her the lightning and fire of the castrum's finest mages flew and she dashed and leapt to a table and then up into the creature's mouth and the beak closed around her and with a spray of blood her severed leg was falling back to the command table below. With a crash the wyrm was twisting back, writhing in the sky, shrieking and shrieking, its beak opening and closing as it backed away and writhed, but the commando did not fall clear from its mouth, even as its beak chewed open and closed. She had struck true, and she held fast.

The wyrm fell suddenly, whatever arcane horror that held it aloft failing, and it came crashing down to the roofs far below and the room fell still, the burn of magic and the copper stench of fresh blood thick in the air.

'Suffer no tyrant,' Starbeck said, his arms pressed hard against the map table. Freezing gusts blew in from the sea through the now broken window of the command chamber, and he shivered.

'Forge no chain,' the commando Captain Hallen said, testing the edge of the fire-sword with his thumb.

'Lead in servitude,' Starbeck's aide said, her face a mask of fear.

'Let's go, team,' the captain of the thirteenth commandos said. 'Can't let Cal have all the glory. Blades and teams, form up!'

With crisp salutes to Starbeck they left the room at a run, the commando mages of the castrum keeping pace. Commissar-Mage Inigo collapsed into a chair, his face ashen. *I can't even remember the captain's first name*, Starbeck thought, feeling a familiar acid ache in his gut. How many years had he known

Hallen? It had only ever been Hallen. The fallen commando – *Cal* – had a face Starbeck hadn't even recognised.

He went to the window and stared down at the chaos below. Captain Nintur approached.

'You wanted me, sir?' Starbeck stared south. On the harbour wall a crow-man perched, backlit by the fires of a catapult station that she had destroyed, the heavy siege engine a bonfire at her back. Her black cloak billowing in the wind, a shock of red hair above – *or does the fire just make it seem so?* He could see no more detail, only the hunch of her back, the long shadows of limbs oddly bent. She dropped like a phantom into the streets below. *Four blades are not enough.* If even one of the commandos failed, if even one blade was lost to crow-men or demons, it would be disaster. *Even if they all struck true, how long to retrieve the victorious blades and strike again?* The reports had told him there were six wyrms. *At least six.* There had never been more than one wyrm together, not since Hussain the Blue put down the Talpid invasion and fought two, to the death of all on the moors of Aber-Ouse.

'There is a child in this city who must be gone, safe, to the north,' he said quietly. 'Her survival is more important than my own, or yours, or any other's.'

Nintur stared down at him, and Starbeck sighed.

'I will explain everything,' he said, 'but for right now have your troop ready to leave within ten minutes, and send someone to the orphans' barracks for Marta Artollen.'

~

Ceann Brude saw the wyrm fall. She had called him Arun, named for the brightest star that hung in the sky on the western horizon. On those rare nights when the rotstorm calmed and the winds fell still, perhaps once a year, Arun was the only star whose light might shine through the weakening tempest and down to those poor fools below. *Poor fools like me, and like him.* She had found the wyrm in the ruins of the tree city of Hunesh, where once Berren the Fair had built a utopia for the Ferron: a city built in trees as tall as the hills, a place of vine and flower. Ceann Brude had not seen it so. Before the rotstorm, before the Ferron Empire had expanded into Undal in the east and past the Iron Desert in the west, with tendrils across the world, the great Judge Berren had died. His works were undone. The valleys of the Iron Desert fell fallow, and the tree city of Hunesh collapsed and died.

Brude had taken her orb – she thought of it as hers, now, she felt so familiar with it, her bond so strong even as it drank at her energy and left lines on her face, aches in her bones. She had flown across the rotstorm and found the wyrms, solitary and woeful creatures, and with the storm kindled inside her she had spoken to them with emotion and with thought. She had found so many, hiding in the ruins of the end of the world, in the far places where even the rust-folk would not tread. They hungered and they pained and they remembered before, before the god-bear had transformed them. Brude shuddered as she stared at the castle, the imposing keep of Undal City. She moved from shadow to shadow, ducking into an alleyway as a patrol of blue-clad Stormguard rushed past.

'Where are the goblins? Are there trolls?' she heard one say. Another street, another moment. 'Are the rust-folk through the walls?'

Brude smiled in the darkness. Her soldier had advised, and Brude's thirst for revenge against the Stormguard and their god had not abated, but there was a greater desire. Glancing up, even with the glare of the oil lamps and the burning of the siege engines she had destroyed entering the city, she could see stars, hundreds and hundreds. *They are the eyes of the gods,* Brude's mother had told her. Brude moved in the shadow and though she hated them, she did not slaughter the Undal as she went. Cloaked and hunched she stalked until she stood in an alley, flexing her long fingers. Across from her the hulking fortress of Protector's Keep, black Old Ferron stonework with fresh masonry above, a thousand soldiers manning every conceivable point, groups of commandos and mages scurrying.

Brude sank back in her alley and pressed her aching back against the cold stone of the building behind her. Closing her eyes she fell into the storm within, the tempest of chaos and connection and pattern and disorder. Sweat beaded on her brow as she pushed outward, feeling for the wyrms. *Four.* She could only sense four, where there should be five with Arun dead. Through the whipping winds of pattern and scything arcs of connection she could not tell who else had fallen. Brude sank to her knees and sent a thought to her brothers and sisters, those changed so brutally by the god-bear. *To the ships,* she thought, and felt their understanding. There were no goblins or rottrolls, no stormblight or the odder creatures of the deep rotstorm whose changes held no coherence in their pattern. There were no rust-folk. There was only Brude, and the soldier and her sailors out on the ships, and the wyrms of the deep storm.

'Show yourself!' a voice called, and Brude's eyes snapped open. At the end of her alley, four commandos stood, a mage behind them who was squinting anxiously. Brude unfolded herself from the floor, her overlong legs and arms stretching out, and the commandos did not hesitate. They ran at her even as the skein-mage recoiled and began desperately retreating. He must have reached for his precious pattern and found only her storm. The lead commando threw a dagger at her and Brude twitched to one side. Then in one swift movement from her waist she drew her first wand.

The commandos burned. The wand was black metal tipped in a faceted red gem. The metal of a fallen star, Varratim had said. The kind of unworkable black metal rocks that littered the Star Coast and gave it its name, which had fallen throughout Ferron just the same, once upon a time. It felt cool in Brude's had even as she found the connection in a heartbeat to the pattern in the flame and sent her energy to it. It took only a scant racing of her heart and there was an inferno, the alleyway filled with a brutal cone of red and white flame. The commandos did not live long enough to scream, and through the charnel smoke Brude stalked forward.

The skein-mage who had been back-stepping now turned to run, screamed in horror, and with a call to the storm Brude raised a tempest around him, dragged him back towards her waiting arms. He was young, and now she was out of the alleyway and raising him with one long sinewed arm, her hood falling back. She glanced at Protector's Keep, and smiled at the mage. He reached for a dagger at his belt and with her free hand she slapped it away and hit him thrice about the head, desultory slaps.

'You will be my messenger,' she said, and from her robes removed a fist-sized jagged crystal of amethyst, shot through with veins of black.

'Do you know what this is?' she asked, and the skein-mage's eye went wide with fear. His hair was cropped short, and he was clean-shaven. *He looks a little like Amon,* Brude thought, and smiled at the thought of her friend.

Brude threw the mage to the cobblestones and glanced across the wide plaza to the keep. Figures running everywhere, chaos, but the wyrms would be retreating. With a moment of concentration she rode the storm in her soul, funnelled it, gave it every mote of her energy, and the crystal in her hand began to pulse and glow.

She threw the glowing crystal to the ground next to the mage. She knew it would not break.

'A rotbud,' she said, 'a little piece of my home. My gift to your leader. Tell him Ceann Brude sent this.'

The energy of igniting the stored hell within the rotbud had been enough of a toll to make Brude reel, but she stayed on her feet as she stared down at the skein-mage.

'The Claw Winter is upon us,' she said, feeling the icy chill of the wind whipping through the streets of the city. 'We hold the Northern Marches. We will hold them with fire and storm, by blood and by magic and by blade. We have wyrms, we have orbs of fire and death, we have the wands and weapons of our ancestors. We will not go back to the storm.'

With a brutal stamp Brude brought her boot down on the skein-mage's face. Stooping over him she drew her face close to his and forced the rotbud into his hands. She heard shouts nearby and running feet, and knew her time in the city was at an end. She gripped the skein-mage's face with her twisted fingers, long and strong and crooked and alien.

'Tell them I killed the Salt-Man, tell them I burned their city, tell them I brought them this storm. *Make them understand.*

The north holds nothing for them now. The north belongs to the storm.'

Brude slammed the mage's head back into the cobblestones and then she ran, ran to an alley, another alley, and she kept running.

In the plaza outside Protector's Keep the young skein-mage lay dazed, his skull bleeding, his face a mess of wounds, his comrades dead. His breath blew out in puffs of steam visible in the freezing night air, and all around him he heard screaming. Looking up he could see patches of stars but the clouds were thick and dark, and from them snow began to flutter and spiral down, fat flakes of it.

The mage let out a gasp of pain and drew himself up.

'Help me!' he called, but his voice was lost in the screaming and yelling and clamouring of bells. He did not know how long the bells had been ringing.

In his hand, the rough crystal of the rotbud twitched and then cracked and split, the throbbing purple and black light bursting out, and for a moment there was silence. Then thunder rolled across the burning city and the clouds above lit with streaks of red and black lightning, forked fractal beams scattering through the cloud and splitting the air.

The rotstorm had arrived in Undal City.

EPILOGUES: OBEISANCE TO THE FOREST

WOLF MOON

'I do not care if they are prostrate in love or fear or weakness or injury. All I care is that they bow. In time we will liberate them from their worst tendencies and educate them. It may take generations to break the bonds of blood and culture, but we will be tyranny and desolation and duty and peace. We will settle the barbarians of Undalor so that Ferron may flourish. Do not mistake me for kind. We will inculcate a seed in their breast, a longing to be better. To be Ferron. Make them bow, and when that seed sprouts they will serve us in heart and soul.' – **Declaration to the nobles of Talpid,** Empress Seraphina of the Gilded Spire

Tullen sat at the edge of the pool in Hookstone forest. *Black Dog Rocks,* the locals called it, a deep series of pools with steep rounded edges perfect for diving. Children from nearby villages would trek there in the summer. Tullen smiled and prodded the fire in front of him with a stick, the smouldering log casting flickering shadows around the forest. The trees here were crooked, bent by the constant wind from the Star Coast, and the forest was short and dark. With the Claw Winter upon it, the snow lay thick on the pine boughs above but Tullen sat below the shield of an older tree, the blanket he sat on folded over a thick layer of cold needles, but no snow. *Not that it matters now.*

With the skein returned to him, his connections spiralling outward, he could warm himself at will, could have cleared the snow away. He did not. He wore his heavy cloak and scarves and a hat with flaps that tied under the chin, bought from an Isken trader. He stared at the rock in the central pool and drank from a cup of wine, though he did indulge himself by sending a little heat into it until it steamed. *Perfect.*

The rock in the centre of the largest pool had sat since time immemorial. A crúca stone. A hookstone. A node in the web of the world, a knot in its tapestry. Tullen stared at it, at the thick hot-silver cracks spreading across it. In the skein, he could see where the currents that would bind it to the larger world were curtailed, where they spiralled in on themselves or trailed away to nothing instead of connecting further, thinning to nothing at the edge of his perception instead of continuing onward. He did not know what breaking the nodes had done, even partially cracked as they were, except from free him from Anshuka's curse. He had his theories, but was not sure.

His own isolation of the Orubor Ashbringer was a simpler thing, a direct connection from him to her, a wall thrown around her, a suit of armour between her and the world.

Because I am a man, not a spirit. What other effects wrought in the skein held true only because of the intricate span of nodes and connections? *What else has been set free?* He smiled at the thought.

Nobody understood the Judges as he did. With a sigh he drew with his smouldering branch a circle in the air, prompting with the skein to make the symbols last those few moments longer, to hang glowing in the air. He bisected the circle twice, ending each line with one of the runes of the Judges: XYFⳑ, feather, claw, flower, and eye. Nessilitor the Lover, Anshuka the Mother, Berren the Fair, Lothal the Just. Smiling he began to draw lines out from the circle, and other runes and symbols, small runes for all the little gods he had met, the eel writhing in the loch a mile to the north; others, so many. He drew larger runes and symbols for true Judges like the bird and the whale of the Tullioch, the father dragon of Ona who swam the clouds above the rain-drenched canyons of that distant land. He drew for long minutes and looked at the madness in front of him, a mess of lines and connection, runes and symbols and letters and names from a dozen languages, some overlapping. Tullen blew out a breath and let them all fade away, and threw his stick onto the fire.

'Lothal,' he called, 'it is time, my love.'

The wolf came to him slowly, stepping from the forest. A black wolf taller than a horse, twenty hands high, streaks of silver that shimmered in the moonlight dancing through its fur. Black eyes, deep pits that drank light, looked at him. Framed against the tangle of bough and branch it was a nightmare manifest. Tullen smiled at the wolf and licked his lips, tasting the sweet wine lingering there. He savoured it, savoured the sight of the godling before him, the bite of the cold on his exposed skin. It was a freedom of sensation – *I had not realised how dulled my senses had become, under Anshuka's yoke.*

'Come, my friend,' he said, and he drew the ur-blade. 'It is time you returned to yourself.'

Lothal came to him and lay low, head nestling at his feet, and Tullen smiled and stroked the thick fur of the wolf's muzzle. He had seen Lothal's bones, deep in the rotstorm. After Anshuka struck him down, Tullen had thought the wolf lost. Nothing is ever truly lost. He knew that now. Judges were thought made flesh, intention and will and presumption and bias and prayer and fear and hope all rolled into a spirit, a beast. The Ferron had guided thought so that each beast might embody a different virtue, but they were as flawed as the people who made them.

Tullen had found the pup. It had taken decades, fallen from grace as he was, but he had tracked the histories, pored through the tomes in the ruined libraries of fallen cities deep in the rotstorm. The places of the rotstorm still had their little gods, frail as they were, though with each year as less thought was bent on the memory of those places they faded to shadow. Tullen walked the rotstorm and no acid mist burned his skin, no lightning charred him. Anshuka kept him safe even as he worked against her. Watch them suffer, he could almost hear in the back of his mind. Not the words, the feeling.

Enough people remembered Lothal that, even centuries from the fall, that echo was there, that sentiment of awe so close to worship. Tullen had found the pup. Once it had been the point where a spring-fed waterfall poured down arid rock, where packs of lean wolves would rest on their hunts. The locals had paid homage with gifts of meat, and the spirit there was a little god, a wolf with black eyes and silver-streaked fur. A place has a spirit; a spirit may be fed; what is fed may grow. Tullen had found the place where that spring had once poured forth, found a foetid pool of acid water and bite-kelp, bulrushes wavering in endless winds as above him the rotstorm raged. He had found it as a heavy rain fell, a cold rain, cold even through his dulled senses. Amongst the choking weed and blackened peat, under skies burning with lightning that never truly ceased, only ebbed and flowed, he found the pup. Lothal had been so small, sickly and thin, nestled deep in a bed of broken reeds. Tullen had stared at him and felt an ache in his heart. He was not sure then how far the bear's edict went. He knew he could aid no Ferron, in deed or word, but the pup... He reached for it and drew it forth and then he had walked from the storm.

In Hookstone forest, the hulking shape of Lothal stood and circled Tullen and then howled at the full moon above. A wolf moon, his mother had called it, centuries before. A full moon in winter, the best chance for the wolf to hunt in the hungriest season. Deep in Hookstone forest the reverberating deep howl of Lothal was echoed by packs of roaming wolves, first one then another and another until the forest was a cacophony. Tullen held his head back and howled too, and then with a move as swift as he could manage he plunged the obsidian dagger, the ur-blade, deep into Lothal's breast. The wolf made no move to dodge him. It whimpered and slumped against him, and Tullen fell back to his knees, but kept one hand on the dagger and the other gripping Lothal's thick mane of fur.

Tullen focused. All the pattern, all the power, all the possibility collected in the ur-blade from the skein-wreck Janos, distilled, he poured into Lothal. Nothing but pure power – the potential for pattern. Varratim had sought to unleash that power in destruction; he had seen a weapon. Tullen knew a blade was a tool to create as much as destroy. To prune, to direct, to carve shape. Finally the dagger was nothing more than a mote in the skein, a black speck of concentration, and Lothal burned with light and current and potency. Tullen stepped back and stared at the wolf as it began to writhe and growl and grow and flex. *What will you become?* When old Ferron had raised Lothal to become a Judge there had been ceremony and concentration, the will of a thousand minds. Honour, they had thought. Justice. As Tullen watched the wolf writhe and grow he did not seek to impart his will or his influence. *What are you going to become, little pup? The shadow of honour? Or a light of your own devising?*

Across Hookstone forest and across Undal and along the Star Coast and through the deep forests and wild places of Morost, the wolves howled at the moon, howled with their hunger, and something else beyond.

Duty Ends with Death

'Kiss your daughters, count their toes, hear the daughters,
wail and woe;
Kiss your daughters, sing so sweet, sate the daughters,
peace for meat.'

> — *Chorus, 'Three daughters of the mist,*
> *unkind', Undal folk song*

The snow lay thick on the roof of the citadel, and in the courtyards the paths and benches were picked out in the differences in its depth. The great white oak of Riven had shed the last of its leaves, and a layer of inches-thick snow sat on every branch spiralling out from its twisted trunk. Floré crossed the courtyard and swung open the wooden door to what had once been a guardhouse, perhaps. There was no lock. Floré did not let the others torture the man, or kill him. *He may be our only route to answers.* The sailor was well fed, as well fed as the rest of them as they rationed the whitestaffs' provisions.

'We do not keep prisoners,' she said, and the man stared at her from behind the bars of his cell. The cell door hung open.

Floré glanced around the cell. The sailor had a bunk, a

blanket, and a bucket. *More than he deserves.* Floré swept snow from the shoulders of her cloak and stamped her boots.

'The door is open,' she said. 'You can walk off into the snow any time you like. Swim home, maybe, to Cil-Marie?'

The sailor shifted on his bunk. He had given no name. Four spans he had sat in the cold of the guardhouse cell, its door unlocked, warmed only by blankets and a bowl of hot porridge Floré brought once a day. One of the commandos had found the sailor washed up on the newly made beach at what had been the quayside as they searched for any wreckage from *Basira's Dance*, any food or supplies. They had dragged the sailor up to the citadel and dried him off, but four spans later still he would not speak of their mission. He spoke the trade tongue, Floré discovered, when after a span living in the guardhouse he came to the citadel and asked for a blanket and food.

'You aren't my prisoner,' she said, 'but you are certainly my enemy. Tell me what you are doing with the rust-folk and I'll get you firewood, more food perhaps.'

The sailor looked fixedly at the wall, and Floré stared at him for a long moment before she shrugged and left the room. Every day she tried. *The rust-folk have no fleet.* Floré knew that, as well as she knew the sun rose in the east, and the winter brought the wolves. *Who are these sailors?*

She walked from the cell he had chosen, an old guardhouse cell separated from the citadel by the wide spread of the central courtyard. Tomas and the commandos had suggested interrogation, perhaps torture. The man wore the ragged remnants of what could be a uniform. *Is he from Cil-Marie? Kelamor? Caroban?* She had asked him, and he had ignored her, clutching his blanket. She saw in his amber skin traces of the people of Cil-Marie, that secretive land south of the Wind Sea, but she did not know what to make of it. She had more than a share of that look to herself, and for a sailor what did it mean? *Not Undal,* she thought. *No Undal could ever sail with the rust-folk.*

Slowly Floré paced the courtyard until the cold in the air started to burn her lungs, and then she returned to the central halls. She passed long-empty halls and corridors until she reached the small section of the citadel they had decided to inhabit. When she broke into the hall of the old master's wing, warm air hit her. Cuss and Yselda were stacking firewood by a large central hearth. The old whitestaff Master Deranus was huddled in a corner reading a treatise on something, and his surviving disciples were spread out across this entry hall and the library next door. Benazir had let them know that the slightest misstep and she would take their heads, and after a span and an execution when one of the younger whitestaffs tried to slip them a sleeping draught at dinner, they obeyed her meekly.

Deranus had lost the power that had driven his schism and his followers were dissolute, left with nothing but their guilt for the lives they had taken in their fervour to be a vanguard of the future. Floré glared at the old man as she passed him. *I'll have his head, when I don't need it.* The old master was a resource she couldn't waste yet.

Floré swept through the hall and did not stop to talk to Cuss and Yselda. She did not want their glances and their worry. She kept going until she reached what had been the master's study, which was now where she and Benazir and Tomas and Voltos held their meetings and made their endless plans. The room was a wide circle, lined in tall bookshelves, with a comfortable table and chairs in the centre over thick rugs patterned with the complex heraldry of Tessendorm.

Tomas was clutching the black kitten Jozenai, who mewled and stretched on a cushion on his lap. He stroked its ears gently, leaning back in his chair and glancing up as she marched in. Captain Muirgainas had rescued the kitten in its rope basket when he ordered the ship abandoned, and ever since they had been reunited, the mage and the cat were scarcely separated.

'Any news from the sailor?' he asked. Floré shrugged off her cloak and sword belt and hung them on a peg, sitting heavily in one of the carved chairs and rubbing at her cheek absently.

'Only silence and mystery,' she said wearily, and Benazir poured her a cup of tea from the pot in the table's centre. Benazir was thickly wrapped in layers of shirts, and at the end of her right arm the rough hook Captain Muirgainas had one of his sailors make was cinched tight to the stump at her wrist by three leather straps.

Floré drank her tea and listened to them talk. *No ships,* Voltos reported; *food running low,* Benazir said; *whitestaffs have been directing the Shramana for maybe years,* Tomas said. Floré frowned at that last piece. She listened to it all and she drank the tea and she smiled and frowned when it made sense to do so and she did not think about Marta, about unknown leagues of ice and snow over water between them as the early winter winds whipped the Wind Sea.

'I'll see you at dinner,' she said, and Benazir frowned. Tomas just stroked his cat and stared into the middle distance, one hand tracking sigils in the air. Since he had seen Janos drop the rune-sphere on the harbour he spent many spare moments tracing runes and fractal shapes in the air, traces of light lingering behind his fingers as they moved. Floré left them and sought out Leomar.

She found the Tullioch on the roof of the citadel, as she had for many days previous. He spent long hours in the lee of one of the squat towers that emerged onto the drum tower roof, a heavy cloak draped around him. He stared out at the sea, where his two comrades had returned spans before, promising to summon any ship they found, promising to report to the Deepfarrow Hold.

'She is closer, this morning,' Leomar said, 'perhaps within the Wind Sea. Perhaps as close as the Deepfarrow Hold. She moves quickly.'

Floré sat next to him on a stone bench, swinging her scabbard out wide. Her new gauntlets still felt strange, the black metal and silvered runes and knuckles gaudy and impractical. She longed for the familiar heft of her old battered gauntlets, but they were gone – melted away, turned to fire with *Basira's Dance*.

Floré sat next to Leomar and gazed at the grey sea to the north, tried to picture the snow-covered forests and moors of Undal, where Marta must be. *Where are you, my love?* The whitestaffs performed the second circle of finding every day for Leomar, and every day for Floré. With a drop of their blood they traced their daughters: Ruemar, daughter of Leomar. Marta, daughter of Floré. They could answer direction and vague distance, and Floré plotted their guesses on a map of the protectorate she kept tucked in her shirt, over her heart.

They sat long into the evening, despite the snow. Floré had dressed for the weather, layering shirt and tunic with heavy cloak and scarves. She concentrated on the last gift Janos had given her. As he lay dying, he had reached for her and found her image of him, the copy of his pattern she held in her mind, her memory and interpretation of every moment together. He had *nudged* it, given it a little spark.

Hello, my love, she thought, and felt his presence at the back of her skull, as if half asleep, as if the sun had just kissed his face and woken him up.

It felt as if he was smiling. She spoke to him, little things. As the last traces of evening light played over the restless sea she told him Marta was further, north and away, but she didn't know where. She told him about Cuss and his anger and his training, Yselda worrying over all of them, Tomas and his long silences and small kindnesses, so different than before. Benazir and her sharp edge returning as she found a target for her wrath.

She felt as if he was frowning, staring at her intently, though she could not see him. She couldn't describe it. It was the emotion she would have if she had seen his face, heard his words, but he wasn't there. *How are you, my love?* he seemed to almost say, and on the roof of the drum tower of Riven citadel she cried a little. Leomar did not comfort or acknowledge her, keeping his own vigil and counsel. She told Janos about her sadness and her fear, her endless anger like a frozen blade clutched in her hand. Being able to sense his feeling calmed her. She did not feel the same fiery rage as she did when she took him for dead in Hookstone forest, that inferno that tore sense from her mind and kept her heart burning. *I grieved you once, my love,* she told him. *Now I will live for her.* Floré's anger was a cold thing, a patient thing. A frozen blade, sharp and waiting.

After the sun set fully and the stars above filled the sky,

across the wild reefs to the north they saw it. An orb, dancing, spiralling as it flew, first low and then high, darting left and right through clear skies. Floré reached to her sword hilt and she stood but Leomar held out a scaly hand and stilled her.

'That is not Ferron,' he said, his voice eager and she turned to look at him.

'What do you mean?' she asked, and he shook his head and clicked his tongue.

'In the summer when they took the broodlings, I was watching. When they scouted and attacked, I was watching. Never did I see an orb fly like this, not the Ferron, not the whitestaffs who flew the orb here.'

Floré watched as the orb danced closer and closer, now darting high, now skimming low over the water, low enough to send up a spray of choppy wake, disturbing the pattern of the waves below.

'Like hunting blazefish on the reef,' she said, and pictured Heasin, her friend, her ally. 'I think you are right, Leomar. I think a Tullioch flies this craft.'

The orb came to them, and stark against the white of the snow-covered roof they stepped out and waved to it. It descended to them, the oppressive silence, the white noiseless glow casting over them and reflecting from the snow until it seemed all was white light. The orb descended to them. Floré clenched her fist on her sword hilt. If she was wrong, they were dead. *I'm not wrong.*

The light faded, revealing an orb of black stone bisected horizontally by a strip of dark crystal. The underside of the orb was scored with deep scratches, the upper half draped in fronds of seaweed. The orb settled onto three spindly legs of metal that seemed to fold out of nowhere, hidden within the stone. Noise rushed back to the world as a ramp lowered from the orb, the crashing of waves far below, the sway and dance of the towering pines surrounding the citadel. Floré heard her own breath, thick and fast. Down the ramp stepped a Tullioch, a burly female with chest scales the same deep emerald as Leomar. She staggered, holding herself up with one arm, eyes sunken and jaw wide as she fell to her knees. At her belt Floré saw runewands, black metal tipped with crystal.

With a hiss Leomar lunged forward and embraced the fallen Tullioch, clutched her tight to his chest in the snow as he spoke, a susurrus of alien dialect that Floré could not begin to comprehend. Floré flexed her gauntleted hands, clenching her fists. She stared at the orb, stared at it hard. She pictured Tullen One-Eye. *How do you kill an unkillable man?*

Floré had stood silent and frozen as Tullen murdered Janos, took her love away from her. *Took Marta's best chance away from us.* She had stood helpless as a child. Now she could feel the flames of anger building inside of her, a deep and true hatred she had tended these long cold nights.

How do you kill an unkillable man? You go north, and you cut out his heart.

THE END OF BOOK TWO

Floré will return in… *THE GAUNTLET AND THE BROKEN CHAIN!*

ACKNOWLEDGEMENTS

Thank you for reading this book and joining me on another adventure.

Eternal thanks to Abigail as ever for her lessons on asymmetrical warfare and her utter patience. Without her this book wouldn't be here. Thank you to my mum and dad – this book is dedicated to you, for all the love and support (and books!) you've given me over the years. Thank you to my alpha and beta readers and the whole of 'Third Moon Trading House' – Rich, Anthony, Adam, Erick, Abi, Anna, Simone, You are absolute rock stars. Thanks to Holly, for starting the storm and for her insight on this chapter of it – a sword-knot well earned. Thank you to Clare for her guiding hand and eagle-eyed edits, and to all the amazing team at Head of Zeus – sales, marketing, design, and production – the care you've put into every element of this is a joy to see. Many thanks to Helena Newton for her patient and excellent copyediting. Special thanks to Oliver Cheetham – your steadfast and eminently sensible counsel is always spot on, and a keen eye to windward is a wonderful thing to have on your side.

Finally, thank you to everyone who read *The Gauntlet and the Fist Beneath*, and has now joined me again for this adventure. There are roads left to go, and battles still to be fought – I'll get to take you there in part because of the wonderful reaction and enthusiasm readers, booksellers, bloggers, and reviewers have had. I'd especially like to thank all those booksellers who've gone above and beyond any expectations simply for the joy of it – notably Goldsboro Books, The Broken Binding, and Forbidden Planet. You folks are nerds – I love it.

Eyes sharp, blades sharper!